PENGUIN BOOKS

THE MULBERRY FOREST

Dalene Matthee was born in October 1938 in Riversdale,
near the southern tip of Africa. Although she has formally
studied and taught music, her first love has always been
metaphysics, and over the years she has divided her time
between music, metaphysics, astronomy, history and writing
first children's stories, then short stories and novels. Penguin also publishes *Circles in a Forest*, her fifth book and the
first to be translated from Afrikaans, and *Fiela's Child*.

Dalene Matthee is married and has three daughters. Her
husband is a retired bank manager, and they live a very
quiet life at the sea, not far away from the forest that was
the subject of *Circles in a Forest*.

THE
MULBERRY FOREST

DALENE MATTHEE

PENGUIN BOOKS
in association with Michael Joseph

To the forest, with love

PENGUIN BOOKS

Published by the Penguin Group
27 Wrights Lane, London W8 5TZ, England
Viking Penguin, a division of Penguin Books USA Inc.
375 Hudson Street, New York, New York 10014, USA
Penguin Books Australia Ltd, Ringwood, Victoria, Australia
Penguin Books Canada Ltd, 2801 John Street, Markham, Ontario, Canada L3R 1B4
Penguin Books (NZ) Ltd, 182–190 Wairau Road, Auckland 10, New Zealand

Penguin Books Ltd, Registered Offices: Harmondsworth, Middlesex, England

First published by Tafelberg, Cape Town 1987
First published in Great Britain by Michael Joseph 1989
Published in Penguin Books 1990
1 3 5 7 9 10 8 6 4 2

Copyright © Dalene Matthee, 1987, 1989
All rights reserved

Printed in England by Clays Ltd, St Ives plc

ACKNOWLEDGEMENTS

I should like to extend my sincere thanks and recognition to the following persons and bodies, without whom *The Mulberry Forest* could not have been written.

Eddy Mangiagalli	Cassie Lamprecht
Bradford Mangiagalli	Maans McCarthy
James Sciocatti (Cuicatti)	T. C. Roux
Domenico Tomé	Luigi Lottino
Joseph Rabbolini (Robolini)	Tossie Lochner, Aulla, Italy

The Assistant Regional Director, C. F. Erasmus, and staff of the Department of Environment Affairs, Knysna

Axel Jooste of the Department of Environment Affairs, Knysna

Willie Cooper of the Department of Environment Affairs, Knysna (Deep Walls)

SA Library, Cape Town

State Archives, Cape Town

SA Astronomical Observatory, for information about the comet

The SA Consul-General in Milan, Mr Johan Schutte, for arranging an interpreter, Sabina Mastropasqua

Dr Dawie Kriel, Cultural Attaché, SA Embassy, Rome

Dr Meryl R. Foster, Public Record Office, Kew, London

The British Library, Reference Division, London

Other sources:

The original diaries of John Barrington

Katharine Newdigate, *Honey, Silk and Cider*, H. A. Balkema, Cape Town/Amsterdam, 1956

Winifred Tapson, *Timber and Tides*, Juta & Company Ltd, Cape Town, 1973

Luigi Barzini, *The Italians*, Hamish Hamilton, London, 1965

Dr F. C. Calitz, 'Die Knysna-boswerkers: Hulle taalvorm en denkvorm, met spesiale verwysing na hul bedryfsafrikaans' ('The Knysna woodcutters: Their grammatical form and habit of thought, with special reference to their practice of Afrikaans'), MA thesis, University of Stellenbosch, 1957

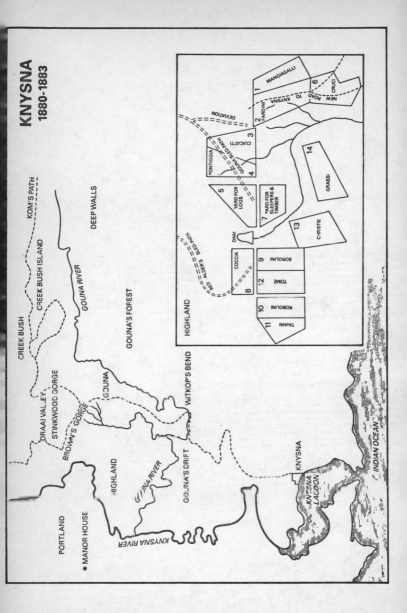

KNYSNA
1880-1883

ONE

FOR FIFTEEN YEARS, I, Silas Miggel, lived in peace on the forest's edge up at Gouna on what we called the highland. I and my daughter Miriam. On the eleventh day of June of the year 1881, just a day after my forty-fifth birthday, I went outside to fetch water from the water-butt and when I looked up, the very blood in my body went cold from shock.

From the wooded gorge to the east came a huge, heavily laden sled drawn by four oxen. It was impossible, there was no road there, not through those gorges and drifts, there was only a footpath that could hardly take a narrow sled drawn by one ox. Behind the first sled, a second one followed. Big wood-sleds, the kind used for bringing out heavy logs from the forest. I said to myself: don't be alarmed, it's an apparition. I did not hold with ghosts, but what else? From where I stood, I couldn't make out whose sleds they were and I started walking closer as if in a dream I wished would end.

Miriam had left early that morning to get provisions from the store in the village; somewhere along the way she would have met the sleds. I looked at the sun and judged the time: two and a half hours' walk to the village, half an hour at the store, three hours back – for back was nine miles of heavy climbing. No, she was not late. And she did have the gun with her. I seldom allowed her to go anywhere without the gun and I myself had taught her to shoot when she was but little more than ten.

A third sled came from the gorge.

Closer now, I saw that the one in front belonged to Jacobus Gerber, woodcutter from Deep Walls. 'Jacobus,' I said when I reached him, 'what the devil's going on this morning?'

1

'Don't ask me, Silas.' His beard was days old and his eyes bloodshot. 'Up at Witkop's Bend, we came to within an ox's hair of rolling down to the bottom of the gorge.'

'I'm astonished that you didn't go down,' I said. 'How on earth did you get up here?'

'Don't ask me. It's five days since we left the village. Most of the way we had to cut the footpath wider and in places we had to hack out a new path altogether. We're as fagged out as the oxen.'

There were bundles and trunks and lanterns and huge wooden boxes on the sled. 'Who does all this belong to?' I was afraid to ask, but I had to, and when Jacobus didn't answer me, I repeated, 'I asked you whose stuff this is!'

'I told Mr White he would come up against Silas Miggel when we got here, but he took no notice.'

Worse news than White's name he could not have given me. White was the government official in the village appointed over all foreigners: Superintendent of Immigrants in Knysna.

'Where is White?'

'Behind somewhere. And don't blame me, Silas, I took a load of wood to the village last Saturday and had just finished off-loading when someone came and said they were looking for wood-sleds to bring a large group of people to Gouna. Pound a day. I took my wagon back and fetched my sled – a windfall like this doesn't come a man's way every day. The blasted woodbuyer had cheated me dreadfully again. I had to off-load first-class wood at third-class prices. I see you're standing stiff as a tree, I told them they would come up against you here.'

The second sled was Gert Stoffel's. 'Did my Miriam pass you on the way?' I went and asked him.

'No, Uncle Silas.'

Miriam wasn't stupid, she would have taken cover in the thickets.

A fourth sled came from the gorge. On this sled a bundle of black-eyed, frightened children sat clutching and swaying. Behind the sled about twenty dust-dirty men and women came on foot. I saw one or two women cried as they walked.

'And this?' I asked Gert.

'I don't know, uncle. Some of the women have been crying since we left the village.'

The oxen made a wide turn across the clearing and stopped.

2

The men helped the children from the sled and they all came and stood staring at *me*.

'Where's the government's man that's with you?' I asked the nearest one.

'Scusi, signor?'

Maybe they're English, I said to myself and changed over from Dutch to English. But again it was 'Scusi, signor?' Not English, not Dutch. They didn't look like English people. And they continued to cluster around me, waving their hands and talking in the strangest tongue. I half wondered if they themselves knew what they were carrying on about.

'I don't know what you're saying!' I shouted at them. 'I only speak Dutch and a few mouthfuls of English.'

Two of the men stood holding a plank. On the plank, under a wet sack, was a square object and another man kept sprinkling water over it from a bucket, as if the thing needed reviving. 'What have you got under the sack?' I asked, but they didn't understand me.

It was then that I saw White coming from the thicket. With him was another stranger who looked like an Englishman.

'Mr Miggel! Mr Miggel!' White started calling out when he saw me. He waved his arms at me and carried on like one sending goodwill ahead of him.

Every time White called me *Mister* Miggel, it meant trouble.

'What's this rabble doing up here at my place?' I asked him when he got to me. 'Do you want me to drop dead with shock this morning, mister?'

'Wait! Wait!' He put up a hand as if to push me back. 'Let me first of all introduce you to Mr Christie. Mr Christie comes from London and does not speak Dutch.' Both of them stood panting like dogs.

I gave the Christie fellow a look that made him walk straight past me. 'What's he want in the forest if he belongs in London?' I asked White. 'Who are these people? What's going on?'

'Please stay calm, Miggel. They are tired and hungry and upset. According to my map we are nine miles north of Knysna, but these sly woodcutters brought us here in a most terrible roundabout way in order to make more money. It's been five days since we left the village.'

'Consider it a miracle that you made it here in five days,

mister. Consider it a miracle that you made it here at all. I can assure you there is no roundabout way here, and I would like to know where mister is actually on the way to with them.' In my heart I knew, but I still hoped.

White paced up and down. 'I have enough trouble as it is, Miggel. Please. This is Crown land. You've known it all these years, we told you and warned you. I'm bringing these people *here*, we are not going any further, and it won't help you to stand looking at me like that. You know this is Crown land.'

It was as if a hangman's rope were slung round my neck.

Crown land. Crown forest. Crown everything. Every blessed forest warder's first and last defence. Everything belonged to the Crown: blue buck, bush-buck, bush-pigs, elephants, footpaths, sled-paths, the wagon-road at Deep Walls. Every tree in the forest was the Crown's tree and before you could fell it, the Crown's licence had to be in your pocket. Before you could lift your gun to shoot a bigfoot, an elephant, Crown's permission had to be in your pocket as well, for if they caught you without it, it was off to the village with you to pay up or to be thrown in the Crown's jail. Not that everyone took notice of permission or licence. They said Josafat Stander smuggled more elephant tusks from the forest than the Crown could count and he had never asked permission from anyone for anything. The only luck on the side of the forest people was that the Crown's forest was too big for the Crown's warders to ever patrol properly; a man could always catch enough of the Crown's game for his pot, so long as he laid his snares well away from the footpaths. Warders were scared of getting lost, they rarely deviated from a footpath.

Ask the warders who the Crown is, and you'll get a different answer from each one: Queen Victoria; the government; Jackson, the magistrate in the village; Mr White; Captain Harison, Conservator of Forests who hardly ever put his feet in the forest; or the Honourable Barrington of Portland who at times went to sit in the Crown's Parliament in Cape Town, which is when I, Silas Miggel, had to go and see to everything over at Portland for him. The way I understood it, it was only God and the woodcutters that had no say in the Crown. Jeremiah Eye of Big Island once asked a warder who he then thought the woodcutters belonged to. The man said they belonged to the Crown, to whom else? Jeremiah pushed him into a bee-sting bush, telling him the woodcutters belong to no one but themselves, but afterwards Jeremiah had to sell an ox to pay damages. As long as you stayed *in* the forest, on one of the islands, in one of the clearings, where the Crown could not see you, there was very little trouble. The Crown needed wood for railways and telegraph poles and harbours and chairs and beds and tables, and the wood had to be cut and hauled from the forest and for that there had to be woodcutters.

The troublemaker was I, Silas Miggel. I had been bold enough one day to put up a house on the edge of Gouna's part of the forest in the large clearing we called the highland, and where the Crown could see me openly if it so wished. A house for Miriam and me. She had not yet reached two then. But long before she was even born, I'd already had my eye on the highland. At the time I was head cutter in my late father's team. When we were cutting down in Gouna's forest, we always drove our cattle out to the highland to graze.

To me, the highland was the best and biggest clearing of the forest: three miles from north to south, two miles from east to west. To Portland's side, on the west, lies the deep wooded gorge with the Knysna River flowing through it; to the east lies the wooded gorge through which the Gouna River flows, while its side streams have cut themselves a way right round the foot of the highland in the distance where they all come together and spill into the Knysna River. To the north lies the main forest: thick forest, rain forest, tall forest, Gouna's forest, old forest. It is no place for a timid man.

I had not been on the highland long when the first warder came protesting: 'Who gave you the right, uncle? This is Crown land! Break down this house and go and put it up on Big Island, or Creek Bush Island, or Barnard's Island or wherever.'

'To whom do those islands belong?'

'The Crown, of course.'

'In other words, I may live on the Crown's island *in* the forest, but not in the Crown's clearing here at Gouna?'

'That's right.'

'Why not?'

'Because it's land that has been put aside.'

'For whom and for what?'

.That he could not quite explain to me; he suggested that I should go and ask the government man in the village, the one appointed over Crown lands and immigrants. In those days it was another man, White came later.

I let the warders talk and carry on. Sometimes they stayed away for months. I would not be moved. Miriam needed sun and space and lots of blue sky over her. As cow elephants took their calves out into the sun when the forest got too cold and wet so I took Miriam out into the sun because it was better we should live apart from others until the day when she would be grown up and had to face whatever fate had waiting for her. She was not like other girls.

I must have been up there on the highland for at least three years when White, the new government man, had me waylaid by his clerk in the village one day and brought to his office.

'Are you the man they call Silas Miggel?' he asked when I stood before his table with Miriam.

'That's me, mister. Actually I'm Silas van Huyssteen, but I'm known as Silas Miggel and this here is my daughter, Miriam. Miriam, greet the uncle.' She gave him her hand as I had taught her and I saw that he had difficulty in taking his eyes off her again.

'She is an exceptionally beautiful child,' he admitted a little uneasily.

'Yes, she is,' I said, 'and I'm bringing her up alone because her mother's soul left this earth but an hour after she was born.' It was not something I talk about lightly, I just mentioned it in the hope of softening him up a bit. When you came from the forest, there was little mercy on your side; what you had, you had to make use of.

'I was informed that you are the man who's squatting unlawfully up at Gouna on the forest's edge. On Crown land. The warders report to me that they've been having trouble with you for years now.'

'That's right, yes.' One must never stand up against the truth. And when the other man sits vexed already, don't get vexed yourself. 'You see, mister, we forest people are very stupid,' I explained to him. 'Everyone in this village thinks this and tries to cheat us where they can – Miriam, leave the uncle's papers alone! Seeing that I am a man from the forest myself and

6

therefore not so bright, I don't understand why I may live ten paces into the forest, but not ten paces out. I'm telling you, mister, my arm is too short to catch that bird.'

'Gouna's highland is Crown land that has been set aside for immigrants. You don't need many brains to understand that, Mr Miggel,' he shot back at me nicely.

'No, I suppose not,' I said. 'If mister can just tell me what I must do to become an immigrant, I would be most grateful.' I knew very well what an immigrant was, I only wanted to show him how stupid I was.

'An immigrant is a person that comes to live here from another country. Mostly from England, or Holland or Scotland.'

'You get here and the Crown gives you a piece of land as a present?'

'No. If a person comes here as an Agricultural Immigrant, land is granted him which he must pay off yearly.'

'How much land?' The man was losing his patience, but I had to know.

'Twenty acres.'

'How does one pay?'

'You are not going to get away with your unlawful living up at Gouna, Miggel!'

'I know, mister, but I would very much like to know about the paying.'

'It's a complicated matter.'

'Give it to me simple, mister.'

'It's a kind of yearly rent at the rate of one shilling per acre. The immigrant gets an allotment of twenty acres, as I've said, and he starts paying after a year for a period of ten years.'

He rattled it off, but my head kept up with him and the sum was easy to calculate. I lowered the half-bag of mealies I had with me, and sat down on the chair that stood beside me.

'Mister,' I said, 'in other words, for ten pounds a man can get hold of twenty acres of land?' Ten pounds I did not have at the time, but my money tin wasn't completely empty either. I always said that a man who had his own land, sat with his backside on his own throne. 'Could one perhaps get hold of more than one piece of land and pay it off?'

'No. However, each immigrant has access to one hundred and eighty acres of commonage, which he can use for grazing

7

and which he can start paying off after five years under the same conditions as for the first twenty acres. And I would like to know who gave you permission to sit down.'

I got up. 'I was absent-minded for a moment, mister. This thing about the hundred and eighty acres is very good.'

'That's enough, Miggel! Your unlawful living on Crown land must come to an end immediately.'

'My grandfather was born in the forest, mister, my father was born in the forest, I was born in the forest, but I must swim to England and back again because I don't have money for a ship to get there, and only then can I get a piece of Crown land? I find this a bit perplexing, mister.'

'Be done with you, Miggel!'

He was fed up with me, but I behaved as if I didn't notice it. 'Can't you work something out for me? My forefathers all came here from Holland – Miriam, let go of your plait!' The child had a way of fidgeting with her hair when she was bored. 'Mister must please excuse me for allowing the child to stand here before you with only one plait on her head; I did not have time this morning to make two, we had to leave home before dawn. I promise, if you can help me get a piece of the highland, even if it is only the twenty acres, I promise you won't ever have to wait for my payments. I'll work like a slave. I'm not afraid of work. Ask Mr Barrington of Portland – he's a man who gives you two men's work to do in a day and that's why his workers don't last and why he always has to send for me to come and help out. Ask him.'

'I believe you, Miggel.' He sounded a bit softer. 'But there is nothing I can do for you. The Crown land does not belong to me: I am simply here to see that the terms and conditions laid down for Crown land, are executed in this district. What do you think would happen if everyone just simply went and put up houses on Crown land?'

'You need not worry about the Crown land up at Gouna. As long as I'm there, I'll shoot the first person that comes to nail two planks together on the highland. I keep my eye on things up there. It's for the child's sake I'm living there.'

'Sorry, Miggel, I cannot allow it. All I can do is to be reasonable and grant you three months in which to find another place to live. More than that I cannot do.'

'I understand.'

There was no discord between him and me when I took my leave; we parted by shaking hands like decent people. The next day the warder from Deep Walls brought White's words after me: three months, then I had to be off. I told the man to stand aside, he was treading on the sweet potato runners I was getting into the ground.

I did not move from the highland. White had me warned regularly, or warned me himself when he had the chance. And a good two years later, on a rainy afternoon up on Red Alder's sled-path, a bit of luck came my way that was to make things between me and White look like friendship afterwards. I came upon two soaking wet, totally lost Englishmen with permission in their pockets to shoot one elephant. Their trouble had started that morning when the coloured man they had hired to track for them refused to go any further, saying they didn't shoot to his liking. They decided to go ahead on their own – and within an hour they were lost.

'We did not realise the immensity of this forest, sir,' one admitted.

'It is a very dangerous place,' the other one added.

'Yes, it is,' I said.

'That's a very pretty child you have on your back, sir.'

'Yes, it is. It's my Miriam.'

It was only when I was on my way with them to the village that it came out one was White's own blood cousin and the other one his friend.

I took Miriam to my sister Hannie on Creek Bush Island the next morning, and stayed with the Englishmen for two days, tracking down the old cow in Kom's Bush for them. I helped them until she was down and the head hacked off and salted; they wanted to take it back to England with them to hang on a wall. Imagine the stench.

From then on White and the warders' protests became less frequent. Every time there were rumours of strangers getting off the ships at the village, they were given land in other parts of the district. Not on the highland. On my part I saw to it that White always got a tin of forest honey or a bag of sweet potatoes or a pumpkin or two. Not to tie him down, only to wash his hands in gratitude because he had grown so fond of Miriam through the years.

9

Early in April of the year 1881, I again took him something and asked him if there was still no chance of a piece of land up on the highland for me.

'The letter is lying right here, Miggel,' he said, and pointed to the papers lying in front of him, 'ready to be posted to Mr Laing, the Commissioner of Crown Lands in Cape Town, in which I am requesting them to send no more immigrants here. The Crown lots in the village all have owners now, and I don't want any more in the district either.'

Better news I could not have wished for. That same afternoon I started clearing a new bit of land below the house, and I also made another flower bed for Miriam's garden behind the house. She was seventeen then and forever coming back from Portland with a cutting or a seedling. Whenever someone died on one of the islands in the forest, the family knew Miriam would have flowers for the grave.

White's words, about the letter to the Commissioner in Cape Town, were hardly three months old when he turned up on the highland with the bunch of strangers. And almost had me out of my mind with shock. It was as if the branch I had been hanging on to for fifteen years had started tearing loose and there was nothing under me if I fell.

But there was something very much the matter with the creatures he arrived with. They were a sorry lot. They made no move to off-load the sleds, they just stood there, and the women kept on crying, especially the one wearing a purple coloured dress. The smaller children, who were being carried on the hip by older ones, peered around in fright.

'Who are these people?' I asked White.

'Italians.'

'From where?'

'From Italy.'

'How many are they?'

'Thirty-three. I mean, thirty-two. Actually it's still thirty-three.'

'It seems to me mister can't get them counted.'

'One is missing, one joined them on the way, and that is but a fraction of the problems I have had to deal with. I'm tired, Miggel. Mr Christie, the man I introduced you to, came with them. He speaks their language and will look after them. But I

10

can't just leave him here, I will have to stay a few days to assist him. Could you perhaps put me up for a few days?'

'No.'

'Don't try and make things any more difficult for me.' White was very despondent. 'I've got myself into a real predicament with these people. If I don't get the cooperation of everyone, things are going to go wrong. I was under the impression that the whole matter of their coming here was still under negotiation, next I was informed that they were on their way. Do you realise that I have had them in tents at the lagoon in the village for the past five weeks already?'

'It's better than here. Take them back.'

'I can't, winter is upon us, it's too damp at the water's edge.'

'Mister, you've never seen the highland after it has rained for eight days in a row. That's why I have set my house here, standing high. Take them back, I say.'

But there was some commotion flaring up among the foreigners, they started crowding around White and me and the Christie fellow like a swarm of angry bees smoked from a nest; they all gabbled at the same time, waving their hands, stamping their feet; some pointed towards the mountains, some towards the sea, the others to heaven. Christie tried talking to them in their own tongue, but they carried on right over him. White took off his hat and waved it about, but that fanned the fire rather than putting it out. And one of the young men kept pulling on my coat.

'America? America?' he asked, pointing to the ground. He hardly seemed twenty to me. Straight black hair.

'What are you saying?' I asked.

'America? America?'

I told him I didn't know what it was he wanted, he must talk to the foreman, to Christie. But he just kept on. To stand looking a man in the face while he speaks to you and have no clue what he's on about is worse than being deaf. He just kept on, 'America, America.'

'What does this man want?' I managed to ask White.

'He wants to know if this is America, he was under the impression that it was to America they were going.'

'Tell him this is not America, it's Gouna's highland.'

'I have, it's no use.'

11

It was crazy. The woman in the purple dress pushed her way through to the front and stood there crying till the tears ran down her neck. And next to me, the other creature just kept on, 'America, America.'

'Stop it, man,' I said, 'this is Gouna.'

Two of the other women came and led away the woman in the purple dress and a man, the one who seemed to be the eldest amongst them, stepped forward and spoke to Christie. Not for long; and then the Englishman pointed to me and suddenly they all turned to stare at me again.

'Wait!' I said, 'don't look at me, this has got nothing to do with me.' But that only seemed to encourage them for the swarm closed in around me. They all talked at the same time, hands waving. 'Shut up!' I shouted at them, and it was like pitching a bucket of water on a fire, here and there it still wanted to flame up, but when I gave them a second 'shut up!' they fell quiet.

'Mr Miggel,' Christie said, and I could see the man was troubled, 'first of all these people want to know where the mulberry forest is.'

'The what?' My English was not very good.

'The *mulberry forest*, Miggel,' White said, shaking his head. 'The cause of more than half the trouble is the mulberry forest. They were told in Italy that they were coming to a mulberry forest. A *moerbeibos*,' he added in Dutch.

'Are you people trying to be funny?' I asked. 'What mulberry forest? This is not an orchard, it's a natural forest planted by God himself. Stinkwood and yellowwood and candlewood and quar and white alder, red alder, saffron, white pear, wild elder, kamassi, hard pear, and so on. I can go on naming them until I've gone right through the forest and then I can start on the underbush – but never in my life have I heard of a mulberry forest. What do they want with mulberries? Do they live on mulberries?'

White just stood shaking his head and told Christie to tell them there was no mulberry forest, and that they were to stay calm. Christie wiped his face with his hand like someone about to pass out. When he spoke to them it was in their own tongue and I saw him pointing in the direction of the mountains. They seemed to calm down surprisingly quickly, turning away one after the other, and started off-loading the sleds. I found it odd.

I asked White if the foreman had not perhaps cooked up some story; how else did he get them pacified so easily?

'I don't know, Miggel,' White said, 'I'm too tired to care. Let us be thankful that they're quiet for a moment.'

But something else inside me was stirring and making me suspicious. Very suspicious. 'Mr White, why are they looking for a mulberry forest?' I asked again.

'They are silk farmers, Miggel. Silk people. They come from the north of their country and are all experts especially recruited to come here. I was under the impression that they were weavers, silk weavers, but they're not. They produce the worms that spin the cocoons, which they harvest to sell. There seems to have been a dreadful misunderstanding, however. You heard for yourself that they were under the impression that this is a mulberry forest. The whole matter has been completely mishandled.'

Italians. Silkworms. Barrington. It was like plaiting three cords together to make one cord, and relief came over me like water over a parched tongue.

'Mr White,' I said, 'it *is* a misunderstanding. Thank God. It's over to Portland they must go. These are Barrington's people, he's waiting for them. It would be best if you were to take them right back to the village, cross the river at the causeway and then take the road to Portland. I mean, over there in the distance you can see Portland, but the gorge between here and there is too deep, you'll have too much trouble getting through with the sleds. Tell them to stop off-loading, they're Barrington's people, I swear.'

'He does not want them, Miggel.'

I heard White's words and told myself I did not hear them. They were Barrington's Italians and to Portland they would go, even if I had to drag them through the gorge myself. If White was afraid to go and tell Barrington that his Italians had arrived, I would go and do it. He would not dare to deny to my face that they were his.

'Mr White,' I said, 'don't let them off-load, stop them. Give me time to get to Portland, that's all I'm asking.'

'You can try, Miggel, but I don't know.'

I ran to lock the door of my house and I put the key under the

13

stone for Miriam. I couldn't wait for her to get back, an hour's walking lay between me and Portland.

They were Barrington's Italians. The only man in the district who had dreams of that kind in his head was the Honourable Barrington of Portland. Or *Poort*land, as the forest people called it.

'*Port*land, Silas, *Port*land!' he used to remind me angrily from time to time.

'It has always been Poortland, a *poort* is a kind of pass, not a port.'

Barrington descended from noble people in England. He had the kind of mind that could think up things no one else was able to. When his hives were dry, he blamed the forest bees for being too lazy and ordered more hardworking bees from England by ship. The swarm that did not escape in Cape Town on arrival, escaped here. Hardly a ship anchored at the quay at the foot of the village without carrying a wooden box of things for Portland. If it wasn't an engine for the water sawmill from England, it was the engine's broken parts on their way back to be repaired. Or clothes for him and his wife and their seven children. There was a time when all three of his sons ran away from home, one after the other, to get away from the old man. I was glad for their mother's sake that they came back again.

Portland. Redlands. Karawater. All Barrington land. Thousands of acres and little that wasn't a failure, everything that got into his head, had to get into the ground as well. If it wasn't orange pips he planted, it was olives or grapes or cotton, or tobacco or tangerines or turnips or cork-trees or cucumbers and walnuts, and so it continued over the years. Everything had to be put into the earth in expectation of producing the miracle that would bring prosperity to Portland at last. I spoke to the old man nicely so many times, telling him to stick to his cattle and sheep and wood from the bit of forest he owned. But no. It always had to be an outlandish miracle. Like the silkworm business. Almost every year, hundreds of mulberry cuttings came by ship to be planted at Portland, only to wither and die. Only the mulberry hedge behind the house and the few trees to the west survived and with it Barrington's dream of a shed as big as a mealie field where the worms were to eat and grow fat and spin yellow cocoons.

14

'I'll start with ten ounces of eggs, Silas.' The Honourable Barrington loved to tell me about his plans for the silk-farming business as we were counting cattle up on Redlands, or struggling down in the gorge to get the water sawmill going. 'One single ounce of silkworm eggs yields about a hundred pounds of cocoons, Miggel, and from a hundred pounds of cocoons one gets about twelve pounds of raw silk.'

'To do what with, Mr Barrington?' I always asked him. 'You can't eat silkworms or cocoons.'

'It will be a most profitable business, Silas. For the first few years, I will farm only to export cocoons. To Italy. Perhaps a few to France as well. The best weavers are in Italy, the best silk farmers too. I will get Italians to come and do the work for me.'

'I think your calves have worms again. You must send Oujan to get forest grape roots to boil with milk to give them. The medicine you ordered from England last time was no good. Perhaps it only works for an English type of worm.'

I don't think he even heard me. The days he wanted to talk about the silkworms, you had to leave him be and deal with the calves some other time. One thing was sure, he knew about silkworms, he was not a stupid old man. He once told me that the thread you got from the cocoons of one ounce of eggs was long enough to go round the world five times.

'That sounds like quite a bit of thread, Honourable,' I said. 'Just think how far I've got to walk to reach the honey in Stripe Bush and back again to my house, and it sounds to me that that little thread would be far from finished yet.'

'You forest people have no conception of things outside the forest, Silas.' He reminded me of that regularly. 'I don't think you have the vaguest idea of the real extent of the earth's circumference. Perhaps you would understand better if I tell you that the thread of three cocoons are enough to stretch from your house to the village, and that's nine miles.'

'That gives a man respect for the three worms that made the thread, Honourable.'

'Farming with silk is a fine art, a very fine art. Not only is it best to feed the worms only the leaves of the white mulberry, the leaves themselves must be harvested in just the right way. For each stage of the worms, the leaves must be cut into strips of the right size, your shed must be as clean as a hospital and no hands

15

must touch the worms. They are very susceptible to disease. If your worms are sick, your eggs are sick and a good harvest of cocoons starts with the quality of your eggs. You must pay attention to what I'm saying, Silas! The day I start farming silk on a proper scale, I'm going to appoint you as full-time overseer in the shed.'

That was another of his dreams. 'You know that we forest people don't work for others,' I reminded him. 'I only come and help out here when you can't manage without me.'

'You'll change your mind, Silas. I've imported the best eggs from Italy and have already sent back cocoons twice. The first time I sent away twelve, and the report I received back was excellent. My second crop was not as good as it should have been, it was suggested that I might have handled the worms incorrectly. I have even sent some of Portland's eggs to an expert in Italy, a certain Zappa. Sir James Hudson in Florence – that's a place in Italy – acted on my behalf and wrote to me saying that Mr Zappa had reacted most favourably to the eggs.'

Barrington knew many important people.

'The mulberry cutting you gave Miriam died. She took good care of it, but it would not take.'

'I actually gave her the cutting because she kept on asking for one. Gouna's soil is not suitable for mulberries at all. Mrs Barrington asked me to tell you that there are some of Imar and Gabrielle's dresses you can buy for Miriam again. Don't forget that the money comes to me.'

'I'll have to sell some honey first.'

'I can take it off your wages.'

'Then I will stand in your debt like the woodcutters with the storekeepers in the village. No thank you.'

'You're a thick-headed man, Silas.'

'Yes, Mr Barrington.'

However, there were plenty of setbacks for Barrington's worms; sometimes he had more dead worms than live ones, but he never gave up on his dream. Every year he said: 'Silas, next year I'll start building the shed and get three or four Italian families out here to farm the silk.'

'Yes, Mr Barrington.'

Many a day it seemed that it was only the silkworms and I, Silas Miggel, that kept the old man going. On many occasions he complained of being tired, saying he would not live for much longer. 'I've been battling to make a decent living from my land for forty years, but everything is a failure. My sons are not interested, I don't know what to make of them.'

'You're driving them too hard,' I told him. Sometimes he got vexed if I came too close to the truth, at other times he seemed too tired to get vexed at all.

'I don't know if it is worth trying to carry on here any longer. Perhaps I should sell up and return to England to wait there in peace for the end.'

'What if Mr Barrington sells everything and gets there to find that peace is not there either?' I warned him. 'Peace is not a thing you can go looking for like a stray ox, Honourable.'

The old man was in a black mood that day. 'I sometimes wonder if you poor forest people aren't better off in spite of your poverty and simple-mindedness. You live from day to day, you strive only to have enough to eat.'

'You've got it all wrong,' I said. 'One does not live to eat, or to get rich or to stay poor. One only lives to become good. That's all.'

I should have kept my mouth shut. We were laying flagstones at the back door of Portland Manor that day, Barrington measuring and me bedding them in. He dropped the yardstick and looked at me with a kind of displeased astonishment on his face: '*What* did you say, Silas?'

'One only lives for a single reason, and that's to become good. One has no other tasks.'

'Who told you that?'

'Nobody, Mr Barrington. I've figured it out for myself over the years.'

'And what do you call *good*, Silas?' He seemed to be mocking me.

'Good is good. Good is not bad and bad is not good.'

'If I sit out in the sun all day, does that mean I am busy becoming good?'

'Not if you sit there because you're too lazy to work. That won't make Mr Barrington good, only worse. But I know mister is not a lazy man.'

'How good do you intend to get, Silas?'

'You're making a joke of it now.'

17

'I'm not, Silas. I'm curious to find out how your mind works.'

'I just try and get gooder and gooder as time goes by. I live over there on the highland, Miriam and me, I bother no one. If a man comes to me to borrow an ox, I give him one. If Mr Barrington sends for me, I come and work for every penny mister pays me at the end of the day. It's Mr Barrington that must decide whether it's good to pay me only three shillings a day. Everyone must become good in his own way.'

Mr Barrington was sullen for the rest of the day. The next day, he started on the silkworms again. 'I'm not getting any younger, Silas, my time is running out. The only hope I have left is the silk farming. I have written to the government for a second time, pointing out the importance of my experiments with silk here at Portland, and bringing to their attention the immense value it may have for the whole country in the future. I have again suggested that a group of selected silk farmers be recruited in Italy and that they be given free passage here. I am prepared to allocate lots of ten acres each to them for a period of three years. If all goes well, I may extend the period.'

'And what if it fails?' I asked, but he did not answer me, he just went on dreaming.

'Mr Laing, Commissioner of Crown lands as well as Immigration Agent in Cape Town, favours my proposal and has already written to Mr Burnett, Cape Emigration Agent in London, about the matter. You will see, Silas, once the Italians are here, Portland will at last prosper. My brother writes from England that Italians are also excellent servants.'

'I thought they had to come here to farm their worms.'

'Silk farming is the sort of farming that does not keep you occupied all the year round. From the hatching of the eggs to the harvesting of the cocoons takes a little more than six weeks. After that, of course, the cocoons must be packed and sent away, but all that remains to be done then is the pruning of the trees to keep them growing low and putting in new cuttings. The women can help Mrs Barrington in the house, the children – Italians always have many children – can help herding the cattle and there will be more than enough for the men to do. More wood could be cut in my forest.'

Then White turned up with his bunch of Italians on the

highland saying Barrington didn't want them? On what grounds could he deny that they were his? They *were* his.

It was past midday when I got to Portland. The large, grey, two-storey stone house towered like a church over the farm. I walked to the back door because Barrington's rule was lesser people knocked at the back. John, the eldest of his sons, opened the door.

'Good afternoon, Uncle Silas.'

'Good afternoon. I'm here to see your father.'

'Mr Barrington is busy, you will have to come some other day, uncle.'

'Go and tell your father I'm here.' The Italians were his.

John put on a swaggering manner and swung a leg over the half-door. 'As far as I know, we didn't send for you today, uncle. Mr Barrington was going to send Hal over tomorrow to fetch you. There's work to be done in the vegetable garden.'

'I'm not looking for work, I'm looking for your father.'

'I told you, Mr Barrington is busy.'

'Then I'll wait until he's finished.' I turned my back on him and went to stand around the corner of the house.

John Barrington was a wind that hardly blew enough to stir a twig – one did not get oneself ruffled by a wind like that. And he surely did not learn his manners from his mother or his father. Mr Barrington was often more bookwise than headwise, but he was a gentleman. Always. And Mrs Barrington was a lady.

'I don't think you heard me, uncle!' John had followed me and was trying to pick a quarrel. 'I said, Mr Barrington is busy.'

I made as if I didn't hear him. Just then, Mrs Barrington arrived from the direction of the chicken run, dignified and friendly as always. 'Good afternoon, Silas,' she greeted me and asked where Miriam was, why they were seeing so little of her lately. Mrs Barrington always spoke English to me and I spoke Dutch to her and we understood each other well. She said Imar and Gabrielle had hoped all Saturday that Miriam would come over to Portland to visit them.

'I stacked a fence on Saturday, Miriam had to help me.'

'Have you had some coffee yet, Silas?'

'I don't want any coffee, Mrs Barrington. I've come to talk to Mr Barrington about a very serious matter.'

'Then I will call him for you.'

19

A good woman. They say Barrington got on a ship one day, went back to England, picked her for his wife, married her and brought her back together with furniture, a piano and nine white servants. The piano was still there, but the servants had left long ago.

The times I had liked working at Portland most had been when the Honourable Barrington still used to go to Cape Town to sit in Parliament. Then Mrs Barrington and I watched over Portland and planned the work together. Every time Barrington returned, the cattle were fat, the wood and hides sold, crops planted, potatoes or onions harvested and the surplus sold. Everything was in its place. The best time of all was when John had been away too, when he went up country somewhere to dig for diamonds; instead of staying away a few months, he stayed away seven years and came back with nothing but the swagger he had acquired up there.

'Uncle Silas!' John stood at the lemon tree and started looking for trouble again. 'In future I want you to address Mr Barrington, as well as Mrs Barrington, with greater respect than you are doing.'

I let the wind go by and looked the other way. Fortunately Barrington came out shortly afterwards.

'Good afternoon, Silas.'

'Good afternoon, Mr Barrington. I've just come to tell you that your Italians have arrived and that they're over on the highland. They apparently don't know that they should have come to Portland.' Barrington pulled himself up as was his habit when he was prepared to stand firm. 'You could hire the same sleds that took them there by accident, to bring them here.'

'Ignore him, sir,' John suggested, lounging beside the lemon tree.

'It won't help to ignore this,' I said. 'They have arrived, and they must be brought here.'

'I have nothing to do with those Italians,' Barrington said bluntly. 'They have been brought to this country by the government on government conditions, not on my conditions.'

I thought my legs would give way under me. 'What do you mean?' I asked. 'The government may have let them come, but from a fire you started, yes.' That was the wrong thing to say; there were still people who insisted that it was Barrington's grass-burning years ago which had started the biggest forest fire man has ever witnessed. Even his own home had burned down. 'What does the government know about silkworms? How many times have you told me with your own mouth about writing everywhere to get Italians for Portland's silk business? How many mulberry cuttings did I plant with my own two hands so that there could be leaves for the worms when they arrived? Now they've arrived and you stand here denying it?'

'Ignore him, sir.'

'John Barrington,' I said, 'just you interrupt with your ignoring once more, and I'll ignore you where you'll feel it! I'll go to the village and swear on oath before Magistrate Jackson whose Italians these are, and then I'll come and drag them here one after the other, baggage and all.'

Barrington did not move, and when he spoke, he did not even raise his voice. 'You know, Silas, I have so often told you that the ignorance and arrogance of you forest people will always be your downfall, and here you are today, a fine example of my words.'

'Leave the words, Mr Barrington, the silkworms are over on the highland and they must be fetched.'

'I know about the Italians being there, Silas, I think I can tell you far more about them than you might suspect. Perhaps I should do just that, perhaps I should make it my Christian duty so that you can then compose yourself and hang your head in shame for coming to my door to make trouble today, a door that has always stood wide open for you and Miriam.'

'I did not come here to make trouble, I just came to say that your Italians have arrived. It's you that wants to make trouble by denying it.'

'I am well aware of their arrival. I know that they arrived in Knysna on the seventh of May on board the *Natal*. Six families from the north of Italy.'

'Six families? If there are six families, each woman has two husbands.'

'I haven't counted them personally,' Barrington defended himself hurriedly. 'I do, however, know that they went from Italy to London, and from London they went by train to Plymouth. From there they left on April the first on board the *Anglian* for Cape Town where they arrived on the evening of April the

21

twenty-sixth – and I believe a certain Mr Christie accompanies them.'

Don't ask me where Barrington got hold of all this information, he rattled it off as if it were nothing. 'The Christie man is over there with them as well, yes,' I said. 'He'll come with the Italians to Portland.'

'I'm going to lose my patience, Silas.'

'This matter is not asking for patience, Mr Barrington, it's asking for the truth.'

'I can show you a copy of a letter from Mr Burnett in London to Mr Laing in Cape Town, in which the *government* is informed that the final selection of the silk farmers had been made by him, Burnett, personally, that they are from such a good class of people that he did not even subject them to the customary medical examination in London.'

'You're not going to put me off with words today. The Italians have come, and they must be fetched here. That's all.'

'In the same letter Mr Burnett requests the *government* to see that they are properly met on arrival in Cape Town and that they are well taken care of should it be necessary for them to wait for one of the coastal steamers to take them to Knysna. My name is not mentioned anywhere in the letter. As it happened, there was no one to meet them when they arrived in Cape Town so they were immediately transferred to the *Natal* where they waited for more than a week before the ship could sail. I only heard of their arrival after they'd already been put in tents in the village. Does that sound like *my* Italians to you? What I did do was to send John to them with an offer of land here on Portland for a period of at least three years. I even sent a few cocoons for them to see and this made them very happy. They assured John that the cocoons were amongst the best they had ever seen.'

'That's a lie.' I said it straight out. 'I don't believe a word John says. How could they have told him all that if they don't even speak English or Dutch?'

'You're forgetting about the interpreter, uncle!' John said, angrily.

'Why, if the cocoons were so wonderful, did they not want to come here?'

Barrington gave the answer himself: 'Because the government is offering them Crown land. *My* suggestion of only two or three

22

families was ignored in any case; far too many were brought out and the Italians themselves decided to refuse my offer. Apart from that, Mr White has been appointed over them and not me. Now you can ask yourself again whose Italians they are.'

'The Bible says the one that starts a thing –'

'Uncle Silas!' John called out to me with a grin, his hands in his pockets. 'Be honest now and admit that you're trying to push the Italians on us because your shack and your camps and your daughter are in danger and because you know very well that your unlawful living on the highland is over now.'

Had Barrington not intervened, I would have pushed John's head right in between his legs. And then Barrington suddenly started trying to patch things up. 'Silas,' he said, 'you and I have come a long way together, Miriam is almost like another daughter to us, so why let strife come between us now?'

'If you want to get at the truth, I'll take you there. Of all those who have ever worked here on Portland, I, Silas Miggel, am the only one that has never laid down the work and walked out on you. Not once. I have always been straight with you, but because of your blooming silkworms I now see Miriam and myself out in the cold.'

'No, Silas, I have a place for you at Karawater. You can move there tomorrow.'

'To herd pigs? Do you think I've brought up my Miriam on the open highland only to have her grow wild out at Karawater now? It's a full day's walk from there to the village, to get back again means we would have to sleep in the underbush along the way somewhere. And since when is a man from the forest another man's hireling? The first day I came to help you out here on Portland, I told you: I'll put my hand out to you, but I am not your servant. My place is on the highland. And now you come and say it's the government's Italians?' I had never been so upset in all my life. 'But I'm warning you today that over there on the highland those Italians are going to die like dogs if they're not removed, and every corpse is going to be on your conscience.'

'Go tell that to the government, Silas, not to me. And I think it's time that you went home now to think about my offer of Karawater. Come back when you have composed yourself.' He turned around and walked into the house.

John stood laughing. 'Uncle Silas,' he said, 'I noticed quite a few pretty women among them. If you were to clean yourself up a bit, you could get one perhaps.'

'Go to hell, John Barrington!' I told him.

TWO

MIRIAM WAS WAITING for me when I got back. To the east, about three throws of a stone's distance from my house, stood a cluster of round white tents like a plague risen from the earth. Eleven tents. Here and there the Italians were still driving in pegs and tightening the ropes. They milled around restlessly and noisily like creatures who have found a place to lie but cannot settle, and I stood like one who had been sent out of his mind.

'I was worried about you. Mr White said you'd gone to Portland. He says they're Italians and they've come to live here. I'm sorry, Pa. I came across them in the second gorge from here this morning and I hid in the underbush until they had passed; they all had to help push the sleds up the slope, but first they had to clear a path.' She babbled on without taking a breath the way she did when she was scared. 'I don't know how they managed to get here, Pa. The road they've hacked out is something dreadful. I knew you'd get a terrible shock. Just please say something, Pa! What did Mr Barrington say?'

'He doesn't want them.' I walked past her into the house and got myself some water to drink. She followed me.

'But they *are* Mr Barrington's Italians! He ordered an Italian dictionary long ago and Imar and Gabrielle and Flos and Kate had to learn a few words from it every day so that they could speak to them when they arrived.'

'He does not want them.'

I went outside to the woodshed to tidy up a bit, but my hands would not hold on to anything securely and I had a bad headache. The day the world gives way under you, it hits you suddenly first and then it starts hitting you slowly, and that's when panic gets its grip on you. Miriam followed me to the woodshed.

'Does this mean we must move away from here now, Pa?'

'I must first get the shock out of my body before I can think properly again. In the meantime, I don't want you to worry about what's to become of us. I'll see to that. Go and make us something to eat and put the plates on the table.'

'You didn't expect it any more, did you, Pa? Strangers on the highland.'

'No.'

'Are you afraid, Pa?'

'I've never been a man that's easily scared, but I would be lying if I say I'm easy about this thing. This is something bad. We might be in big trouble and I'll have to think in every direction to get us out of it.'

'We thought we were safe.'

'Go and make us something to eat, the sun is down.'

Her loosely plaited hair hung down to the small of her back, and shone in the last light of the day as she walked away. Where was I to hide her from the eyes at the tents? It had already become a battle to keep her away from the eyes of every young woodcutter in the forest, forever coming to the highland with the excuse of looking for a stray ox, or taking a short cut somewhere, but just to come and stare at her. The problem was that Miriam was able to make them go weak at the knees without even saying a blooming word to them; it was the way she walked and held herself and looked at them. She wasn't a flirt, it was something else; a winsomeness born into her that I could not get out of her.

The night that my wife, Magriet, had struggled with the child and with death, I prayed that it would be a boy. Magriet's mother had died the night *she* was born, Magriet died the night Miriam was born. We lived on Creek Bush Island then. The day after we buried Magriet, I wrapped the child and carried her to the village to have her christened. I was afraid that something would happen to her too. The minister told me that the next Sunday was christening day and I must come back then; I told him I couldn't walk all the way with the child again, he must christen her now for me or leave it. In the end he christened her in a side room of the church, and in Kom's Bush I rechristened

26

her in one of the forest streams because he had not done it to my liking. And on my knees in the water I promised God I would see to it that the same lot that had befallen her mother and her grandmother would not befall her.

What I did not know that day was that the little creature in my hands would become the most beautiful girl. The mistake I made was to hide the truth from her too long. Over the years, when she asked about her mother, I told her everything except how she had died. I knew I had to talk to her about it before she was grown up, but I kept on putting it off. The highland was like time granted to me in which to keep her safe. Not that I was stupid; I kept her on a long rope and let it go slack when she wanted to go to the village or to Portland on a Saturday or a Sunday; I gave her enough slack so that she would trust me the day I had to tell her the truth and pull in the rope.

And then, suddenly, she was grown up, she was seventeen, but still I kept on putting it off because there are things a man does not talk about easily, things a girl needed a mother for. All I did in the meantime was to see that enough money fell into the money tin so that she would be provided for when I died. We lived on the money I made by selling honey and the wages I earned over at Portland; money for the tin I earned by selling the folding chairs I made. Now and again I still felled a little wood to sell and the money from that also went into the tin. I had about eighty pounds saved; for a man from the forest I was a rich man. And Smit, the woodbuyer in the village, said he would buy every chair my hands could deliver. Why people liked the chairs, I did not know, but he shipped them by the dozen to wherever.

To be able to make something you could sell, you needed seasoned wood; to have seasoned wood you needed time: sometimes two years, sometimes three, sometimes longer. In the beginning it was hard to leave wood to dry that could have bought coffee and sugar and meal and a bit of clothing. At first I left half of what I felled to dry, the other half I dressed and hauled out to the village to exchange for provisions at the woodbuyers' stores like all woodcutters did. The day I took the first chair to Smit, he wanted to barter that for provisions as well, but I told him then I'd rather take it back and put it in the fire and find something else to earn a little extra with. He made me stand and wait outside for an answer until the sun went down; but I stood where I stood, firm. He wanted the chairs, I wanted the money; he could not make chairs and I could not make money. In the end I agreed to three shillings a chair, the same as a day's wages at Portland. As I put the money in my pocket, I knew my Miriam would never have to eat from another's plate.

The candle was already burning on the table when Miriam called me in to eat. Things were not the same; it felt as if eleven tents were hanging over my table and the food had no taste in my mouth. We were still eating when someone knocked on the door. I thought it would be White, but when I opened the door, the woman in the purple dress stood there, her eyes swollen from crying, and when she spoke I knew she was pleading for something and her hands pleaded too. All I could make out was that it was something about a *bambina*.

'I don't know what you're saying,' I said, trying to get her to stop. 'Go talk to your foreman, with Christie. Mr Christie!'

'Don't shout so, Pa, she's not deaf.'

'What does she want?'

'I don't know, maybe she's asking for food.'

'Give her food.'

Miriam fetched bread and sweet potatoes from the table and held it out to her, but she turned away her head and would not take it. She became more and more impatient, it was as if she wanted to force the strange sounding words into our ears to make us understand.

'Go to Mr Christie, we don't know what it is you want,' I repeated.

'Maybe she wants drinking water,' Miriam suggested. 'They wouldn't know where to fetch water from, it's dark.'

'Give her water.'

It wasn't water either. When Miriam held out the mug to her, she made a gesture of hopelessness, turned around and walked away.

'Walk with her to the tents, Pa.'

'No. She came here by herself, she can get back by herself.'

'She wanted something from us, Pa, she was pleading!'

'That is what the foreman is there for, Mr White too.'

'Maybe someone is sick.'

'No one's sick, she's been carrying on like that since they arrived this morning.'

I bolted the door and went back to the table and pretended not to see the accusing look in Miriam's eyes. I was worried. Miriam was forever finding something to pity: if it wasn't a little plant, it was a bird, and for everyone she had a good word to say. One Sunday afternoon not long before, she had come back from Portland, from Imar and Gabrielle, and said that no one was ever again to say Mr Barrington was mean or unfriendly or haughty. He was a good man. One of his pigs had died that afternoon and he had said it was because nobody had loved the pig.

'You should have gone with her to the tents!'

'Miriam, a little pity in its proper place is a good thing, but hand it out with your eyes closed and one two three you land up blind. Draw the curtain, I keep getting the feeling that there are eyes looking in through my window.'

The sun was hardly up the next morning when White was at my door, a troubled man if ever I had seen one.

'Good morning, Miggel.'

'Good morning, Mr White. Come inside. Have you people found the mulberry forest yet?'

'You wouldn't feel like making fun if you were in my shoes this morning. I've come to borrow a hand-axe from you, the people must have firewood, but there is nothing to cut it with. Please lend me an axe.'

'Which day of the week is it, Mr White?' I asked.

'Sunday. Why?'

'Do you see my hand-axe on the hack-log over there?'

'Yes, I see it.'

'For almost thirty years that axe has been cutting my firewood, but it has never been lifted on a Sunday and it won't be lifted today either.'

'The Word of God says: when the calf is drowning, Miggel.'

'That's right. But there's a difference between a calf that has been pushed into the water and one that fell in. My axe does not cut on a Sunday. They can go and break wood with their hands.'

After White had stalked out of the house, Miriam burst out of her room. 'You're wrong, Pa, you should have lent him the axe!' she cried.

'My axe does not cut on a Sunday.'

'Are you going to make war against these people, Pa?'

'No. But neither am I going to shake hands with them. This is not the place for them and the sooner the government takes them away from here, the better it will be.'

I took the Bible and went outside as was my habit every Sunday. The only difference was that I didn't go and sit on the eastern side of the house, but on the western side where my eyes would not have to look at the tents. I am a man that troubles God every day; on Sundays I did all the talking for the week lying ahead and asked forgiveness for the bad patches of the one that was past. I opened at the psalms and started reading. Halfway through I realised I was reading right over the words. My mind was too tangled up with worries. Where was I to move if they forced me to? What about my vegetable patches? What about the potatoes, ready to be harrowed? What about my house? The planks were still good enough to be used again if I was forced to pull it down. Every tree from which those planks had been sawn, my own two hands had felled. Only when I was putting up the house did Martiens Botha bring his team of woodcutters to help me and at the same time he gave me another of his sermons.

'You cannot bring up the child on your own, Silas. Especially not here where there isn't a living soul in sight. Let your eyes go through the forest and take yourself a wife again. Jogebed of Frans Gerber is young and hardworking; if she does not take your fancy, there's always Annie of my brother Bart.'

Only once, the year Miriam had turned ten, did a fancy for a new wife stir in me again – for Johanna, widow of Petrus Jonker who had gone down with yellow fever one day and had never got up again. Yes, I took a fancy to Johanna. But one day, as I sat looking at her four little half-orphans, every drop of desire and fancy seeped out of me, for to share a piece of bread between two mouths was a different thing from sharing it between seven mouths. Leave it, I said to myself, bring the child up by yourself.

I tried reading another psalm. White had not told the whole truth when he said he hadn't really been expecting them. I remembered that it was in March of that same year when, one day, he had asked me if I knew of anything with which they could arrest the spread of the beetle that was destroying the trees in the village. I asked him what beetle? He said it was an Australian bug. I told him I'd never heard of the pest. He added that every mulberry tree in the village had been destroyed by it as well, and this was exceedingly bad since there was talk of a silk industry for the district, perhaps the silk farmers were even on their way already. I took no notice, my head had still been on the beetle and I told him as long as the plague stayed in the village and did not move to the forest it was all right. The week after that I'd gone to Portland and found Barrington with his head in the mulberry fence, looking for signs of the very same beetle. He said it would be a disaster for him if the silkworm people arrived and there were beetles in his mulberry. And again I hadn't taken any notice, I thought it was just the old dream.

I knew I couldn't move to Creek Bush Island: there were too many young woodcutters that would run after Miriam. To the village? But a man couldn't just pull down his house and go and put it up in the village again. Before you had the first nail in, Magistrate Jackson would have you in court and your oxen in the pound; anyway, Miriam would not be safe there either, I had seen too many eyes turn to look at her there too.

I was still sitting outside my house when Josafat Stander appeared in front of me, his gun over his shoulder. Josafat Stander heeded neither the laws of man nor God, he was a man with his own laws.

'I see you're sitting on the wrong side of the house today, uncle.'

I closed the Bible. 'Good morning, Josafat. Are you not ashamed of yourself, walking with a gun on Sunday?'

'The bigfeet won't ask which day of the week it is if they want to trample me.' He let the gun slide from his shoulder and sat down beside me.

'Miriam!' I called inside, 'bring Uncle Josafat some coffee.'

'I thought I would pay you a visit today and see what had hit uncle here. They're Italians, I hear.'

'Where did you hear?'

'In the village. Joram Barnard asked me to tell you that there's room for a house up on Big Island. He'll come down Red

31

Alder's sled-path with his wagon and get as near to the highland as he can and help you move there, uncle.'

'I'm a long way from moving yet. I'm still getting over the shock. Where have you made your shelter?'

'I haven't made a shelter for winter yet, I sleep where the sun goes down on me.'

I had long given up preaching to Josafat Stander. The forest was his home, his gun his woman. Sometimes months went by without anyone seeing him and the rumours would start that the elephants had at last trampled and killed him. Then he would just turn up. Two forest warders caught him up at Michiel's Crossing one day with an elephant tusk over his shoulder and no permission in his pocket. They started walking him to the village. Apparently they had him almost in the village when he suddenly just disappeared in front of them. Tusk and all. They knew he had swerved into the thickets and had to be an arm's length from them somewhere, but they couldn't find him. Others say they had let him get away for if there were two things a warder feared, they were an elephant and Josafat Stander.

There were many stories about Josafat Stander. Riddles. Like the time he lay wounded in the arm on Creek Bush Island with old Mieta, the medicine-woman. He never told who it was who had shot him. Some said that it was the warder at Deep Walls who had caught him with his wife. Others maintained that it was one of the constables in the village that had lain in wait for him one night and wounded him as he was carrying tusks to a ship. I always said Josafat Stander's trouble started years ago when his father got killed under his own wagon, riding out wood to the village. That same day Josafat swore he would never cut wood for a living. When his mother remarried and moved away, he stayed behind and grew wild.

'How many bigfeet did you shoot last week?'

'Only two, uncle.'

'They are still going to trample you.'

'You've all been saying that for years.'

'What do you do with the tusks?'

'That's my business. Actually I came here to tell you about a place you can move to up in Lily Bush. It's one of my winter hide-outs, but you can have it. It's not a large clearing, but there's water and it's near a sled-path.'

32

'I'm still far from moving away.'

Miriam came out of the house with two mugs of coffee. Her hair was loose and she had on the pretty dress with the little blue flowers that I had bought from Mrs Barrington for her.

'I've tidied the house and made your food.'

'Where are you going?'

'To Portland, Pa.'

It was a long time since she had been to Portland. I would have preferred to have stopped her because I was too cross with Barrington. But her going to Portland was better than her going too near the tents. 'Put your bonnet on before you go,' I told her.

'It's Sunday, Pa, I'm not on my way to hoe.'

'Put on your bonnet, Miriam! It may be June, but the sun still has enough heat in it to burn your face.'

'The bonnet flattens my hair, Pa,' she kept on answering back.

'Miriam!' Josafat said, brusquely. 'Listen to your father.' She wheeled around angrily and walked back into the house. However, when she came out again, she had the bonnet on.

I waited until she was a good way off before I asked Josafat a little more about the clearing up in Lily Bush. 'You say there aren't any other people living there?'

'No, uncle.' He cleaned out his pipe and lit it.

'I say it again, I'm still far from moving away from here, but it's good to know of a place where we would be able to be alone again – should things turn out the wrong way for me, of course.'

'Miriam's growing up and becoming headstrong like a woman, uncle, you can't keep her away from other people for the rest of her life.'

'It can't be helped. I must.'

'Why?'

Apart from his confounded ways, Josafat was a person to whom one could talk about many things; it's just that there are some things one simply couldn't talk about. 'I owe you an answer,' I said, 'and there is an answer, believe me. And thank Joram Barnard for having offered.'

'I believe they're silk farmers.'

'Yes.' A little flock of white-eyes flew past, followed by two yellow-throated warblers. I knew the flock well.

33

'I think you'll have to move, uncle.'

'No. The highland is my home.' The words came straight out.

Josafat stayed a while longer, then got up and disappeared into the forest – to where, he alone knew. I opened the Bible again and tried to find some peace for myself, but the Book would not speak to me, the words stayed dark like the words in the mouth of the woman with the purple dress.

I kept my eyes away from the tents the whole day long. When I fetched water from the tub on the corner of the house, I didn't look up, but I heard them well enough. They kept on calling out to one another; they incessantly hammered in tent pegs; if one child stopped crying, the next one started. I could not wish them away, I could not think them away.

It was almost dark by the time Miriam got home. Singing.

'Here we are, practically surrounded by strangers and you come back from Portland at this hour, singing!' I didn't want to quarrel with her, but it had been a worrying day. 'I hope you've told Mr Barrington to come and fetch his blooming silkworms away from here!'

'He knows about them, Pa.'

'What's he going to do about it?'

'I don't know, Pa.'

White was back at my door early on Monday morning.

'Things are bad, Miggel, very bad.'

'I'm glad to hear that, mister.'

'These people are becoming uncontrollable! They say they have been wronged and cheated and now they want everything from me. Christie is on their side. They carry on about the tents being too cramped with too few to house them all, and that's after I already did the impossible and found them two extra ones while they were in the village.'

'What made mister bring them here? I want to know.'

'It was a government decision, Miggel. Crown land is not suitable everywhere. The choice was between Quar and Gouna's highland, and we reckoned Gouna would be more suitable for mulberries than Quar, for our instructions are that the Italians are to establish a silk industry here.'

I pushed back the mug standing in front of me on the table, spilling the coffee. 'Mister,' I said, 'go and tell the government what Silas Miggel says: the first silkworm they rear on this highland, I'll eat skin and all and spin the cocoon myself.'

'Don't be rash, Miggel.'

'Fine then.' I was angry. 'Let's say a whole lot of mulberry cuttings drops from the sky tomorrow and they plant them and another miracle drops from the sky and they take root, on what do you and the government think they and their worms are going to live for three, four years while the trees are getting strong enough to yield a proper crop of leaves?'

'That is all part of their rebellion, Miggel. According to Christie they were under the impression that they would be supplied with food for six months after their arrival, which will give them time to plant and harvest their own crops. For the rest, every head of family and bachelor was supposed to get an ox and a plough as well as axes, spades, blankets, cooking pots, seed, and I don't know what else.'

'I'm surprised that the government didn't promise them each a pearl from the crown itself.'

'It's easy for you to talk, Miggel. I am the one that must deal with reality. According to the immigration papers that came with them, papers specially drawn up for them in their own language, each head of family and every bachelor had to have an amount of money not less than twenty pounds. Personal money. The papers had to be completed under supervision in Italy and checked in England. Christie says it was done and they did have the money, but now they suddenly know nothing about it and they don't have a penny. They say they bought food and stuff in Cape Town while they had to wait on the *Natal* to get here.'

'Stick with reality, as you call it. On what are they going to live?'

'They're demanding an allowance of a shilling per day per head as well as all the other things promised them.'

'What?' Miriam was pouring White some coffee and stirred in three spoons of sugar.

'Easy!' I cautioned her. 'The government's not going to give you and me one lump of sugar.'

'Don't be rude, Pa.'

Miriam sometimes had a way of chiding me which I did not like at all.

White stirred on, bewailing his lot. 'I had hoped their

discontent would lessen once I had them on the highland and they realised the possibilities of the place, but this morning they are more difficult than ever. I suspect Christie is helping them instead of helping me to appease them. He keeps on citing section ten of the Immigration Act which stipulates that the government *may* consider advancing small sums of money to immigrants – which they are to pay back over a period of two years, of course. He forgets about section nine which puts it very clearly that all immigrants are to provide their own food from the date of arrival. I have already made an exception for them while they were at the lagoon these past five weeks by providing rations, but I told them it would only be until they got here. Now they just keep on demanding more and more. On Saturday, when we arrived here, they refused to do anything unless their demands were met, they claim that all these things had been promised them. And last night and this morning they've come up with a totally different demand again.'

'Mister, learn one thing from me today: once a thing has been muddled, it's muddled; you never make it right by more muddling. The highland is no place for silkworms, take them away from here.'

'This is a government matter, Miggel. I am but the Superintendent of Immigrants at Knysna, all I usually do is carry out instructions. These people have been totally mis-informed but I have no proof of what they were promised.'

'They are not misinformed, mister. It's plain they've been taken for a blooming long ride. Where, in your life, have you ever heard of a mulberry forest?'

'I've written to Mr Laing in Cape Town, asking for a full and thorough investigation right away.'

'Just let me know when they start handing out the promises so that I can come and stand in line for a plough. The highland does not know what such a thing is. Every sod that I've turned here, I did by spade and sweat.'

'Don't you start making the mistake of thinking that I have bags full of government money to hand out, too, Miggel. I need authorisation for everything. To supply them with oxen and ploughs and other implements will cost over five hundred pounds. One shilling per day per head for six months, another forty-two pounds per month – if I don't count the children under three years of age, or Canovi that joined them on the way here, or the one that is missing. Should I get authorisation, which I doubt, to comply with their demands, they must still pay back everything within a period of two years; the question is: pay it back out of what? Christie says they were brought here under the impression that a silk industry had already been started here, they were to come and extend it.'

'That will be Barrington's jam jar of silkworms they've heard about, yes.'

'They were under the impression that the sheds for the worms had already been built.'

'That's the dream in Barrington's head they've heard about.'

'Now they want everything from me. I'm only the official that had to receive them at the end of a line, and I'm on the verge of a breakdown.'

'Take them to Portland.'

'That's not what they want, Miggel. They've come up with a new demand. They had a long meeting last night after which I was informed that they had unanimously decided to go back to Italy, and now they are demanding a ship.'

I wanted to jump up and down with relief, but the slow-witted White just sat there, bowed down as if by a yoke of cares. He obviously didn't see our way was clear. 'Rejoice, mister!' I said. 'This is the best thing they could have decided. I'll take my own sled and ox and help you get them back to the lagoon. My sled is only a small one, but I'll ride them out day and night. Miriam, pour Mr White some more coffee.' I couldn't understand why his head stayed down. 'Take courage,' I told him, 'we're going to get rid of them!'

'Immigration, Miggel, is a long and complicated process. A legal process. The law says that only those immigrants the government *desires* to send back will get free passage back as well. Long before that can happen, the law remains a wheel that follows its own track, a government wheel. And once a government wheel has started on its course, you don't just stop it.'

'Listen, mister, you have more than enough boulders to place in front of that wheel. Where on earth have you heard of silkworms on the highland? The government might just as well send me to plant mealies on the moon. Use those boulders, mister, use them!'

'We are doing what we can. Mr Christie and I were up early this morning, writing to various dignitaries at the Cape; we wrote to Mr Laing again, explaining everything in detail to him right from the start. At the request of the Italians, Mr Christie drew up a petition which they all came and signed this morning.'

'Why are you sitting like one overcome by darkness then, mister? If you and Mr Christie picked your boulders right and placed them well, you'll stop that wheel in its tracks before you know it. I hope you've mentioned that there is not a *single* mulberry tree on the highland.'

'We mention it in every letter.'

'What about the wild mulberry in the forest, Pa?' Miriam suddenly chipped in. God knows what made her ask it, but she did. I had kept quiet about the wild mulberry because it could only make trouble if it was heard by the wrong ears. Then my own daughter had to mention it. White sat up immediately, peering at me with the greatest suspicion.

'What wild mulberry?' he asked.

'It's Miriam speaking out of turn about a stupid underbush tree we call the wild mulberry, mister. No worm would even look at it.'

'How do you know?'

'I know. I know silkworms, I've seen them eat and spin over at Portland.'

'What does the tree look like?' He would not let go of this straw.

'Miriam!' I said. 'See what you've done now?' I turned to White: 'It's but a flimsy, limp-trunked tree in the underbush, mister. If Miriam was but an inch less of a grown-up girl, she would have had a hiding from me this morning to teach her to keep quiet when it's not her turn to speak.'

'Does it look like a real mulberry?'

'There is a similarity to the leaves, yes, but that is all. That's why it was given the name. I promise you, mister, no worms would open their mouths for it.'

'Are you sure?'

'Yes. Drink up your coffee, mister. The day's getting on and all those letters must get to the village and on the post-cart so that the boulders can start rolling in under that wheel.'

'I've actually come to ask whether you'll take the letters to that

38

village for us. I don't want to leave Mr Christie alone and there's no one else I can ask.'

Could he not have said it sooner? 'Leave that coffee and go and get the letters, I could have been halfway there already. Miriam, fetch my shoes and then keep out of my way so that I can't reach you!' She had almost wrecked everything.

Shortly before midday I handed the envelope with the letters in at the Post Office and three times told the man behind the bars to see that it got on the first post-cart to Cape Town. Government matters. Of the highest kind.

When I walked out of the village, it was not without hope. It would be best, I said to myself, if the government would send a fast ship for them; not one with sails, one with engines that did not need to wait out at sea for the wind and tide in order to get through the heads and into the lagoon and up to the quay. I knew it would not be for a week or two, but I would be patient. Fortunately I had stacked strong branch-fences round my vegetable patches through the years to keep out the bush-pigs and bush-buck and grysbuck. Until the ship came, the fences just had to keep out the Italians and their brood of dark-eyed children as well. They would not come and breathe round Silas Miggel's place.

It was only the blooming elephants you could not keep out with a fence. They just waited until your mealies were growing nicely and then, while you lay in your bed at night, they came quietly and trampled your fences flat and ate you out of every bit of crop. I must have mended my fences about six or seven times in fifteen years after they had flattened them. What else could you do? It was no good taking a shot at them. How many could you shoot out of a herd of fourteen and more, and in the dark? Not that they always waited for dark if they were up to mischief; sometimes your back was not even turned.

Like the day I was carrying pumpkins up on to the flat roof to lay them out in the sun. Ten years of Silas Miggel's life went by that day. The house was then only the one long room; I added the two bedrooms later on. I put the ladder up on the south side of the house, the side away from the forest. Miriam stood at the bottom of the ladder, passing me the pumpkins with which I then climbed up on to the roof. She was nine, but already smart enough to be very helpful. And it was her anxious 'Pa!' that stopped me halfway up the ladder, a pumpkin under each arm, to find myself looking at seven fully-grown cow elephants with three calves, not twenty yards from the house to the east. I said to myself: stay calm, stay very calm. The breeze was from the west, carrying our scent straight to them and I had to think fast. Had the wind not been against us, I could have taken the child and fled into the forest with her, climbing a tree or scrambling down into a gorge where they would not follow us. As I still stood there wavering, they slowly started coming towards the house, plucking at a tuft of grass here and a tuft there and at the fence the one in front deftly flattened herself a way through, followed easily by the others.

'Pa!'

'Get up!' I dropped the pumpkins and pulled her up by the arm. 'Lie down!' When I fell down next to her, my heart thudded against the corrugated iron under me. And then the leader cow, the one with the huge curved-in tusks came straight to the house and started rubbing her massive body on the corner as if it were a tree. But it wasn't a tree rooted to the earth with thick, strong roots, it was a house of plank anchored but a spade's depth into the ground. The longer she stood there rubbing herself, the more it felt up on the roof as if we were lying on a rickety bed. The child became so afraid, I could not calm her. All I could do was gather her skirt and bundle it up in front of her mouth and hold her head into it.

When I was younger, I once saw the remains of a man that had been killed by the elephants. For more than a year afterwards I could not skin a buck or look at raw flesh.

Up on the roof that day I learned a strange thing: I learned that life was quite different when death stood right below you. Then life is not breathing, it's something apart from your body and you're that something and you lie clinging to your body to stay inside, for you know if you let go, you are gone. And with that you cling with the child's life to the child's body. You don't pray like you do when you go on your knees at your bed, you shout to heaven.

Ten years of my life went by for the elephants took their time to eat and destroy my crops. When another got bored, she too came to rub her wrinkled bulk on the corner of the house and I had to keep the child down once more. It was November and summertime, by midday the roof was so hot that I had to put pumpkins under us. When the sun went down, the elephants went back into the forest. The only mercy they left behind was the ladder.

I hoped White had thought of mentioning the elephants in his letters. One bad-tempered bull was enough to trample all eleven tents into the earth with ease. Then one would see the Italians fly.

When I got home, the door was locked and the key under the stone. Miriam was not there. Neither had she left me a message on the table. If one of us was away from home and the other one had also to go somewhere, we had a code of messages we left on the table: the blue bowl for having gone to Portland, a tin mug for having gone to the forest to get kindling, a spoon for having gone to the village, a knife for having gone to set or visit a snare. There was nothing on the table. This was strange. I was the one who sometimes forgot to leave a message, never Miriam.

I made the fire, put on water for coffee and started washing the sweet potatoes. Before I left for the village that morning, I explicitly forbade her to go near the tents. Not that that meant she would obey me. There had been a time when Miriam suddenly became very stubborn and in the end it got so bad that I had to talk to Mrs Barrington about it. She told me to be very patient with the child and to leave her alone: girls became like that, they got better again too. Shortly afterwards she asked me to let Miriam go with her and the three eldest Barrington girls to Karawater for a week. At first I wouldn't allow it. But they talked me round, and when Miriam came back, she was much better. I think Mrs Barrington told her things I could not.

I also knew then that it was time to talk to her about her mother and her grandmother, but somehow I couldn't find the courage. How did you tell your beautiful daughter her days could be counted should she ever take a man? How did you tell a tree: don't grow? How did you tell a bird: don't fly? Every time she had a birthday, I said to myself: Silas Miggel, you must speak to her. But I failed to. In my stupidity I thought it was safe as long as I could keep her away from other people. And then? Then suddenly eleven tents stood on the highland and I got home and she was not there and the devil took my thoughts and ran with them. Before the sun goes down, I said to myself, I would go to White and Christie and tell them: the first tom-cat

Italian I caught near my daughter would be shot dead by me. And the instant the government sends word of the ship, I would start riding them back to the village and I hoped the government made the Honourable Barrington pay for the ship to teach him to keep his dreams in his head.

The coffee was made and the sweet potatoes halfway cooked when Miriam pushed open the door and walked past me to her room without a word. Sulky.

'Miriam!'

'I'm coming, Pa, I'm just taking off my shoes.'

I washed her mug and poured her some coffee. When she came back into the room, I made as if I didn't notice the angry look she gave me and I asked her where she had been.

'They are without firewood, Pa. I took the axe and wanted to go and show them where they could cut wood for themselves, but they wouldn't go into the forest. They are scared of the forest. They wanted to know if there are wolves in the forest. *Wolves*, Pa.'

'I told you to stay away from them!'

'Things aren't going well in those tents, Pa. I have never seen such a lot of frightened people. It won't help you to pretend that they're not here, they are.'

'Because of the stupidity of others, yes. I said I would help to get them back to the village when the ship comes.'

'And in the meantime?'

'In the meantime it's White and Christie and the government's concern. Not yours or mine. Drink your coffee.'

'What does Mr White or Mr Christie or the government know about the forest and the highland – let alone the Italians? And Pa just wants to turn Pa's back?'

'That's enough, Miriam.'

'It's not enough, Pa!'

She was a girl that could go and plant herself right in the middle of a road so stubborn she was. 'That's enough!' I had to tell her a second time before she would keep quiet. 'They came here on Saturday, yes? Today is Monday. Two working days have gone by without a hand having been lifted round my house to do a thing. I have not finished a single chair, no bread has been baked, not a snare laid, no hoeing done. How long do you think it will take before things start going wrong in this house as

42

well? It's no use you trying to clear up another person's mess and land in it yourself. Where one has stooled, he either picks it up or steps in it. The government stooled, the government will come and pick it up.'

'That may be so, Pa, but what I want to know is what's to become of them in the meantime.'

'Neither Mr White nor Mr Christie nor the government will worry about what becomes of us. The government doesn't even know that Silas Miggel exists. Over there on Portland Mr Barrington sits nicely in a soft chair, but does it worry him what happens here in the tents? No. But you want to know from me what's to become of them in the meantime. They can all drop dead for all I care.'

She picked up the bread bowl and the meal and started getting ready to make bread. I went outside to the woodshed.

This is going to be a great worry, I said to myself, it's going to be extremely worrying. If I knew how long it would be before the ship came for the Italians, I could take her to my sister Hannie on Creek Bush Island. But that could be leaping from one fire into the other, because Stefaans van Rooyen's eldest son, Sias, has already turned up on the highland twice, ironed and shaved as smooth as a bottle, to come and visit Miriam openly. And what about Martiens of Old Martiens, or Jacob Terblans who was supposed to court my own cousin Grieta's daughter, Susanna? Jacob may have been courting Susanna, but I've seen the way he looked at Miriam. Granted, Jacob was not from Creek Bush Island but from Deep Walls, but still. In the end, wasn't it better that she should remain at home where I could at least keep my own eye on her? I could not decide what to do for the best. And my hands were stiff from worrying when I started fastening the narrow strips of leather thongs for the seat of the chair.

Ever since I had arrived on the highland, I had been used to quiet; now it was quiet no longer. The Italians were a noisy lot; it sounded as if they kept on calling the children or each other, they went from tent to tent, talking, scolding, carrying on. How long could a man stand it?

It was almost dark when Miriam came and said the food was ready, curtly, like one still puffed up with the sulks. We ate in silence. When we were finished, she washed the plates and went to her room without saying good night. It was an old trick of hers when there was discord between us. I remained sitting at the table and waited: one of us had to give in first and say good night, for under Silas Miggel's roof no one laid down to rest in anger. She knew it. After a while I heard her blowing out the candle, but I said to myself I would not give in, she had her way far too much. When one brings up a child on one's own, especially a girl, too much spoiling sneaks in that should stay out. She did not sleep, she kept on tossing. Then she coughed, not badly, but then she coughed again and I didn't like it. She was not one that coughed, she had a strong chest. I took the candle and got up.

'Miriam?' She lay with her eyes open. 'Miriam, are you sick? Is your throat swollen?'

'No, Pa.' Her mood was better, I could hear it.

'There is conflict in this house, Miriam, we must put an end to it. Tell me what's going on in your heart.'

'Pa, are you going to stay cross with Mr Barrington for the rest of your life and never go to Portland again when he sends for you?'

Old Sarel van Rensburg, who outlived four wives, once said if a woman starts a discussion at her feet, you always know she's actually on her way to her head. Never starts at the real truth. I just had a feeling that this time Miriam had started at her feet.

'The day they load the last Italian and his bundle on to the sled, that day I will put my feet on Portland ground again. Not before then. All this is Barrington's doing.'

'He can't get along without you and you know it, now you want to punish him with it.'

'Are you on Barrington's side or on your father's side?' She turned her head away and ran her fingers across the plank wall beside her. 'I'm talking to you, Miriam.'

'You don't have a heart, Pa. Not you, not Mr White and neither Mr Christie.'

Just like old Sarel had said: starts at the feet. 'What are you talking about now? I thought I was the only one without a heart on the highland, now it seems as if there are at least two more.'

'Yours is the hardest!' she said and sat up. 'I pleaded with you that first night to walk back to the tents with the woman and find out what it was she wanted, but you wouldn't.'

44

'What are you on about now?'

'Do you know why that woman keeps on crying, Pa?'

'How am I to know?'

'They've *stolen* her child!'

'What?'

'Yes. In Cape Town.'

White had said something about one being missing, but he had never said it was a child. 'What child?'

'A little girl. She is ten and her name is Catarina.'

'How do you know that?'

'I asked Mr Christie when we went looking for wood.'

That made me cross again. 'Who went looking for wood?'

'See? You're more worried about who was with me than about the woman's child.'

'I asked you who went with you!'

'Mr Christie and three of the Italians: Pontiggia, Canovi and Coccia.'

'Lord preserve us!' The worst was that she sat there reeling off the strange-sounding names as if she had practised them. 'How far did you go into the forest?'

'We did not go into the forest, Pa, I told you they're too scared. We gathered kindling along the edge of the forest with which they won't even be able to make one decent fire. You must go and find out about the child from Mr White. I don't understand Mr Christie very well, he speaks a different kind of English from the English around here and on top of that he was cross because he had to go and help with the wood. You must go ask Mr White about the child.'

'Does the woman have a husband?'

'I think so. Her name is Petroniglia, her surname is Grassi. Will you go and find out tomorrow morning?'

'I can't go looking for the woman's child, Miriam, it's work for the police.'

'I know, just go and find out. She keeps on crying.'

'I'll go and find out.' What else could I say?

'Promise?'

'Promise.'

'Good night, Pa. Thank you.'

'Good night, Miriam.'

THREE

SHE WAS RIGHT. The woman's child was missing. White told me the whole story in desperation, for the woman carried on night and day. He, White, and Christie had gone with her and her husband, Ilario, to the police the very day they arrived in Knysna, to make the necessary statements which were sent back to Cape Town.

According to Petroniglia and her husband, another Italian, a certain Nicolo Tomasso, stole the child. They met this man in Cape Town while stopping over for the week there. Because it was so cramped on the ship, Tomasso and his wife offered to put some of them up in their house, and among those they took in were three of the Grassi's five children, one being Catarina. The Tomassos grew very fond of the child and after a few days Signor Tomasso asked Ilario to give them the child, saying he and his wife wanted to bring her up as their own. Ilario went and told Petroniglia and the next day she went to Signor Tomasso to fetch the children. Tomasso begged her to leave Catarina a while longer with them, promising to bring her to the quay on the eve of their ship sailing for Knysna. On the Tuesday night of the third of May they heard that everyone had to be on board by that evening since the ship was sailing the next morning. Ilario sent Tomasso a message, telling him to bring the child, but he didn't turn up with her. The next morning Ilario got permission to leave the ship to fetch the child. When he got to Tomasso's house, Tomasso told him the child had run away, she was no longer with them. Ilario thought she must have run to the ship and went back. She was not there. Fortunately the ship could not sail because of the fog, and Petroniglia then got permission to leave the ship to go to Tomasso. He told her the same story, but promised her he'd go and look for the child and that he would put her on the next ship to Knysna. That would be within a week or ten days' time at the most. Petroniglia believed him and made it back to the ship just in time, because the fog was lifting.

When White finished telling me the story, I told him straight out that there was something about it that didn't sound right to me. 'Aren't they making this up, mister?'

'How could they have made it up, Miggel?' White asked, indignantly. 'When they were still camping at the lagoon, the woman walked to the Police Office every day to enquire whether they had heard anything about the child yet. Constable Hall told me he just shook his head when she came in at the door so that she could turn back and go away. She was making quite a nuisance of herself. But the actual trouble started when they had to pack up and move out here. Now she can no longer go and enquire about the child; she is too scared to walk to the village alone and the others are just as scared. Mr Christie and I have assured her that the police have promised they will send any news of the child with one of the forest warders, but even this won't calm her down.'

'Why didn't you say anything about this yesterday? I went past the Police Office with the letters, I could have gone in and asked about the child.'

'She wants to go herself, Miggel.'

'And who do you think will go with her, mister? Not Silas Miggel, my work won't wait for another day.'

'I was hoping Miriam would go with her.'

'Forget it. I'm not sending Miriam with her. As it is I'm having trouble keeping her away from them.' As I said it, I knew I would have to go if only to stop Miriam from going. Because of their stupidity and lying and Miriam's soft-heartedness, I had to lift my feet and step into the muck.

'Help us out, Miggel. Please,' White said. 'Listen to them out there, they're getting more and more angry. If only I could speak to them myself and explain things to them, it would be better. I'm sure Christie stirs them up. If you leave me in the lurch today, I have no one else to turn to, and I promised the woman last night that I'd find a way of getting her to the village this morning.'

'How long will it be before the ship comes?'

'As soon as the letters reach Mr Laing. The Italians' own petition will carry a lot of weight. This situation should never have arisen and Cape Town will have to do something about it immediately. In the meantime, I need your help. I'm asking you to go to the village with the woman for me, she's driving me out of my mind!'

'Go and tell her to get ready.' What else could I do? 'Tell her that I'm just going back to my house to give Miriam certain orders, and when I get back here, she must be ready. And, mister, the government will have to buy me a new pair of shoes seeing that I'm wearing out the old ones on their blooming business.'

'I shall recommend that in my next letter.'

Miriam was a bit too pleased for my liking when she heard that I had agreed to go to the village with the woman; she seemed just a bit too relieved about something.

'You must stay away from the tents!' I said. 'Far away.'

'I will, Pa. But then you must promise me not to be nasty to Petroniglia on the way, she is not used to walking like we are. Let her rest at Gouna's Drift on the way there, and when you come back. Be kind to her, Pa.'

'There won't be time for kindnesses, I must get back to my chairs. She'll just have to move her feet.'

'Shame on you, Pa.'

'And you must start hoeing the potatoes, work the earth up nicely round the plants.'

'Yes, Pa. Promise you will let her rest at the drift first?'

'I'll let her rest if it will get you to rest from going on at me!'

'It will.'

When I got to the tents, she was ready. The others were taking leave of her as though she was going on a long journey. Strange creatures. They looked at you with distrust, daring you at the same time to deny it. The women had good dark-coloured dresses on, some with white lace collars; the children had shoes on and their clothes were clean. The men had a kind of swagger.

48

The foreman, Christie, came up to me and told me to take good care of the woman during the dangerous journey to the village. If I had had more English words at my disposal, I would have put him in his place for good, for since when did you teach a fish about water and a man of the forest about a forest? And if he thought dangerous conditions lay south of the highland, one could only wonder what he would have said about what lay to the north: about Brown's Gorge, about the Red Alder's Gorges, about Stinkwood Gorge and Draai Valley? I suppose he would have dirtied himself, had he known.

I was not gone half an hour with the woman when we were quarrelling. She in her tongue and I in mine. We quarrelled because she kept on walking like a bush-buck ewe that wanted to jump at every little creak in the underbush. When I made her walk in front of me, she walked slower and slower as if holding back from the danger that was to come from ahead until I was treading on her heels. She wanted to duck at every cobweb. If I made her walk behind me, she kept on looking round for whatever might come from behind. Before we were through the first gorge I had had enough.

'Look here, Petronella,' I said.

'*Petroniglia!*' She stopped and spat it at me, correcting her name.

'Petronella-Petroniglia, as you wish, if you walk with Silas Miggel, you walk properly! If there's danger, I'll be on the lookout for it, not you. Now come on!'

For every word of mine, she had ten of her own; they rolled from her tongue like little pebbles and her hands and eyes bounced around too. The more I told her to keep quiet, the angrier she got. Had the big lourie not saved me, I don't know where it would have ended. She was still in full flood when the lourie kok-kok-koked right above us in the tree top, shutting her up in the middle of whatever she was telling me.

'It's a bird,' I said. 'A *voël*, big lourie.' I tried English and Dutch, but it made no difference. It was not the first time I saw a stranger frightened by a lourie's call; if one didn't know it was a bird, I suppose it would give you a fright. When the second batch of kok-kok-koks fell from the tree, it looked as if she wanted to turn around and run. 'It's a bird!' I cried, trying to stop her. I put out my arms and flapped and flapped them like wings; like a blooming fool I stood there flying until she calmed down. But enough was enough, and I had had enough of her. I took out my knife and cut myself a nice stick from the underbush and made her to fall in ahead of me, and I kept her there with the stick like one did with a headstrong ox.

At Gouna's Drift I let her have a drink and rest a while. She took out a fine handkerchief and washed her face, and when she was finished, I told her to get up and hurry since it was getting late. Fortunately the river was low enough for us to tiptoe through on the stones without having to take off our shoes.

Miriam need not have worried that the Italian woman would not be able to keep up with me, she kept up well. At times scolding away, then quiet and sulking for long stretches. When we came out of the thickets to the west of the village, and she realised where she was, it was I that had to keep up with her as she raced to the Police Office.

Chief Constable Ralph was behind the counter. 'What's the stick for, uncle?' he asked. 'Don't tell me you drove her here with it!'

'Good morning, constable. She's come to find out whether you've heard anything yet about the child.'

'The interpreter isn't with you by any chance?'

'Do you see him with me?'

'I'm only asking, uncle.'

We had to speak loudly and over her to hear ourselves. 'She wants to find out about the child.'

'Can't you tell her to keep quiet for a moment, uncle?'

'I can't even say good day to her in her own language, let alone telling her to shut up. Have you heard anything?'

'Yes, uncle. The police in Cape Town found Tomasso. The child is with him and his wife, but he says these people *gave* him the child.'

'What?'

'Yes.'

'And for that I had to leave my work?' I was furious. 'Petronella!'

'*Petroniglia!*'

When I raised the stick, the constable stopped me. 'Wait, uncle!' he said and leaned over the counter to try and speak to her himself. 'Signora Grassi, Catarina in Cape Town.' He waved both arms in the direction of Cape Town. 'Bambino Cape Town. Tomasso.'

'Bambina!' she said and it seemed as though she might brighten up.

'Bambina Cape Town with Tomasso.'

'Sì sì!'

'In Cape Town.'

'Sì, sì.'

It was hopeless. 'Leave it,' I said. 'You two are going to sì sì and Cape Town till dark and get no further. I'll tell Christie to tell her.'

Then I had to battle to get her to leave the Police Office again. But I got it into her head at last that we had to go and see Christie, and for the first hour on our way back she kept up without trouble. And had I stopped a little sooner to let her rest, it may not have happened, because the next thing she just sat down in the middle of the hacked-out path, slap on her behind, and started crying like a child that could not get its way.

'Listen here, woman,' I said when she wouldn't get up, 'Silas Miggel is only flesh and bone. You gave the child to Tomasso and regretted it afterwards and now you think you can sit here kicking and crying. I promise you, I'll leave you right here. Now get up!' She would not move. Next I tried speaking to her nicely, but still she just sat there. Perhaps her feet were hurting. Perhaps she had a stitch. How was I to know? I scolded her, I threatened her, but she would not get up. I was still standing there, trying to think of what else I could do, when a branch cracked somewhere close to us.

'Bigfeet!' I said. 'Bigfeet!' I wasn't sure, but when a second branch snapped, I was somewhat alarmed. If it was a single elephant, there was no immediate danger, the wind was on our side; but if it was a herd, half of them could be to the east of us and the other half still to the west with us in the middle. I could run and climb a tree, but what about her? They would trample her dead right there on the path and afterwards I would be blamed.

A third branch snapped. '*Bigfeet*, Petroniglia! Get up!' She just sat. And for the second time that day I made a bloody fool of myself: I went down on my hands and knees in front of her, I lifted up one arm and held it in front of my face like a trunk but all she did was to cry a little more quietly.

51

There was only one thing left to do and that was to walk on and leave her there. I was hardly round the first bend when the ruse worked and I heard: 'Signor Miggel! Signor Miggel!'

Signor Miggel! Imagine. At Gouna's Drift I let her drink again and rest for a while. She wasn't looking very well. Her shoes and the hem of her skirt were dirty with dust and in places her hair had come loose from the combs holding it. She was a strange sort of woman, one from a strange collection of people. Still, quite pretty.

I gave Christie the message as soon as we arrived back at the tents, and waited until he had translated it for her. When her eyes started to flash with anger, I turned round and walked away.

Miriam was in one corner of the potato patch, hoeing, without a bonnet on her head. When I reached her, I saw that she had not even finished one row. What had she been doing the whole morning then?

'Miriam?'

'Did the woman get news of her child, Pa?' She didn't look up.

'Yes,' I said. 'Tomasso says they gave him the child.' Her cheeks were hot as if she had been running. 'Why isn't there even one row finished? Were you at the tents again?'

'No, Pa.' She carried on working with a fervour which said: leave me alone!

'Miriam, I want to know why almost nothing has been done here during more than half a day.'

'Hal's waiting up at the house for you, Pa.'

Hal? Hal was Barrington's second son and my imagination took flight to where it's never been before. Was there something between Hal and Miriam that I hadn't noticed? Commonsense told me I was barking up the wrong tree, for when could there have been anything between Miriam and him? Where? Hal had run away from home the year before like his brother John and his brother Will had done previously, he had only been back a few weeks. But still I kept on imagining the worst. Why had Miriam seemed so pleased that morning when I told her I was going to the village with the woman? Had she known Hal was coming? Where was she half the day if it wasn't at the tents or in the potato patch? The housework had been done when I left.

There was a time when I suspected Will, Barrington's third son, of having a fancy for Miriam, with the result that I had had to keep a close watch on him for quite a while. All three of Barrington's sons were good-looking and I never really trusted them. But when Miriam became reluctant to accompany me to Portland, it put me at my ease again; if she had had a fancy for one of them, she wouldn't have chosen to stay at home.

Barrington and I had words about the same thing one day. He started it: 'Your daughter is growing up, Silas, and she is very pretty.'

'I know that, Mr Barrington.'

'I have three sons, I would not like to see her get hurt.'

'The man that hurts my Miriam will be hanged from the highest tree I can find,' I promised him.

'Let us talk about this sensibly, Silas. These things do happen. I'll undertake to speak to my sons and you undertake to speak to Miriam.'

'About what shall I speak to her, Mr Barrington?' I pretended I didn't know. Barrington was pretty narrow-minded. He didn't even want his bull to graze near the house from where his wife and daughters could see it. And no one dared to speak of *stink*wood in his presence. At Portland stinkwood was *sting*wood, even if the wood still stank, and not stung, when you worked with it. 'About what must I speak to Miriam, Mr Barrington?'

'About the differences between people, Silas. My sons are from another class than Miriam. My sons and your child come from very different backgrounds.'

I almost exploded. I told him I may be poor and a nobody compared to him, but I was decent and hardworking and Miriam was the same. I would, in any case, never allow John or Hal or Will to turn an eye in her direction.

Now, on the day I had been to the village with the Italian woman, Hal was sitting on my doorstep.

'Good afternoon, Uncle Silas.'

I thought he sounded a bit guilty. 'Afternoon.' If I were to discover that there was something between him and Miriam, he would wish that he had never returned home.

'I've been waiting for hours to see you, uncle.'

'Why didn't you remove yourself when you found out I wasn't here? Why did you have to keep Miriam from her work?'

'I didn't keep Miriam from her work, uncle,' he said, indignantly. 'She had only just got here. She wouldn't even make me some coffee, she went straight to the potatoes.'

It wasn't Hal. I wanted to ask him whether she had come from the tents or from the forest, but my pride wouldn't let me. 'I suppose your father has sent you,' I said to get away from the subject of Miriam, and walked past him into the house.

'He did, uncle.'

One thing I will say about Hal: of all Barrington's children he was the only one that ever sat down at Silas Miggel's table. John and Will wouldn't come further than the door with a message and the girls never walked with Miriam further than the other side of the gorge.

'Sit down.'

'Thank you, uncle.'

I started making up the fire and tried to act normally, but I was still concerned about Miriam. 'Help yourself to a sweet potato, they're under the cloth.'

'Thank you, uncle. My father wants to know if you would please come and help with the cupboards. The dining-room's walls must be plastered as well. The house just never seems to get finished.'

'How many years is it since it burnt down?' I decided to keep Hal's chatter between Miriam and me so that I could calm down. Why hadn't she looked me in the face?

'It's ten years, uncle.'

'What's your father saying about the Italians?'

'Not much. But I know he feels guilty. He watched them through the telescope for a long time yesterday afternoon. My father isn't well, uncle. He worries about the wood and the gardens and the cattle and about Will at Karawater. You mustn't leave him now, uncle. There are no other workers at Portland at the moment; John took his horse this morning to fetch one or two back, but he couldn't find any to come.'

'John must stop behaving like that, rounding up workers on horseback as if they're cattle. Why don't you and John help your father yourselves?'

'You know my father, uncle, nothing we ever do is good enough.'

That was not quite true, but I was too worried about Miriam

to argue with Hal. And Hal was not as innocent as he tried to make out; he was the one that loved to irritate his father and had the infuriating habit of speaking softer and softer when addressing his father, letting the old man think he was becoming deaf. The big mistake Barrington made years ago was when he took John and Hal and the eldest daughter, Flos, small as they were, on a ship to England where they were put in a school. They stayed there for five years to learn to read and write. What for? My late father taught us to read and write himself. Five years is a long time for children to be away. When they got back, they were strangers. And once that happens between a father and his children, it stays that way. It was not to happen between me and Miriam. Never.

For the four younger children Barrington ordered a school-teacher from England to come to teach them at Portland itself. A certain Miss Ritchie. The children were quite grown up already: Imar was twelve, Gabrielle six and Kate surely about fourteen. Miriam was eleven. Miss Ritchie hadn't been there long when Imar and Gabrielle and even Mrs Barrington began insisting that a place should be made for Miriam in the schoolroom on the days I worked over at Portland. I had no objections, but Barrington had plenty. He said Miss Ritchie was costing him a lot of money. Not only did he have to pay her passage from England, but he had to pay her sixty pounds a year, as well as give her board and lodging. Room could be made for Miriam in the school, but it would cost me a shilling a day. Blood. But I paid it. For six months. Then Barrington stopped Miriam going to school, saying Miss Ritchie was having difficulty with the child being Dutch-speaking. That was a damned lie. The child had always played with Imar and Gabrielle in English. But what could I do? It wasn't my schoolteacher. Miriam cried for a whole week when she heard she could no longer go to school. From then on she had to play round the house until the children were released from the schoolroom. Miss Ritchie stayed for three years. One day, long after she had gone, Mrs Barrington asked me if Mr Barrington had ever told me how clever Miriam had been in school. Barrington had never said a word about it to me.

'May I tell my father that he can be expecting you tomorrow, Uncle Silas?' Hal asked.

'No. The day the ship comes for them, on that day your father can send for me again. Not before that. Your father is a learned man and of high standing with the government, tell him he must write a letter asking that the ship be sent before the month is out. When the winter rains start, the whole lot of them are going to die of cold in those tents.'

'I'll tell my father, uncle.'

Miriam didn't come near the house while Hal was there. And Hal had hardly gone when White turned up. For fifteen years Miriam and I had lived in peace on the highland, only now and then with a soul to offer a mug of coffee to. Now my house was suddenly like a port of call. Where would it all end?

White scarcely had a chair under him, when he started moaning: 'I don't know which way to turn any more, Miggel.'

'Neither do I, mister.'

'The Grassis say they did *not* give the child to Tomasso.'

'Do you think they'll admit it if they had, mister? I might be dumb, but I'm not stupid. Would you have got on to that ship, knowing your child was supposed to have run away? Never. That ship could have sailed to the other side of the sea but I wouldn't have been on it, I would have gone looking for my child. I wouldn't have waited until I was here to start crying. I'm telling you, mister, they just regretted giving her away afterwards.'

'I cannot agree with that, Miggel. This man and woman are truly shattered with grief over their child.'

'Mister, if you are going to feel sorry for every tear you see, you're going to stay sorry for the rest of your life. Chew before you swallow. And what kind of a foreman is this Christie that he didn't go looking for the child? I'm telling you, mister, they gave that child away, and now they're regretting it.'

'I never realised you could be so heartless, Miggel.'

'I'm suddenly heartless because I don't want to start wailing along with the rest of you.'

'Christie is busy writing a very firm letter to the police, informing them that the Grassis did not give the child to Tomasso. She must be taken away from him immediately and proceedings started against him.'

'I do hope this doesn't turn into just a lengthy exchange of letters, otherwise the child will never get on to a ship. Why don't you suggest that the police keep the child in Cape Town and let her parents pick her up on their way home?'

'We'll wait and see first what the response to Christie's letter is.'

'Are you by any chance waiting for a drop of my coffee as well, mister?'

'As a matter of fact, I wouldn't mind having a cup.' It was when White had the coffee that it came out that he was actually there to complain about Christie. 'If only I knew what he was saying to them, and what they are saying to him, Miggel. They're getting more and more discontented and Christie does as he pleases. He knows very well that I can't manage without him. The government employed him to accompany them here, to act as interpreter for them, and for that he was paid up to the day of their arrival here. And then what happened? When they were all off the ship and standing on the quay, he walked away, leaving me alone with them not being able to speak a word of Italian.'

'That must have been awkward, yes.' My mind was with Miriam. Things would have to be talked out. Urgently.

'That compelled me, right there and without authorisation, to extend his services by six months, offering him eight pounds a month which he turned down. He stated his price was now ten pounds a month *plus* his own twenty acres of Crown land as well as all the other benefits of immigration. He said he had already completed the documents. I had to agree to everything without authorisation, I had no choice. I immediately wrote to Mr Laing to explain the circumstances to him, and in the end this could count against me.'

'Fortunately you will not have to keep him for the full six months now, the government will not take that long with the ship.'

'No. But I cannot stay here longer than the day after tomorrow. I must get back to my office and at the same time I cannot leave Christie behind with them on his own.'

'Take them back with you, mister. Pitch their tents back at the lagoon and they will be ready at the quay when the ship arrives.'

'I have no authorisation for that yet, Miggel. They will have to stay here and you will have to assist Mr Christie.'

'I *beg* your pardon? You must be out of your mind if you think I'm going to assist *him*, mister. I told you I'll help to get them back to the village, but for the rest I want nothing to do with them. Unless . . .' I don't know where the idea came from, it just did. Like a gate swinging open in front of me. 'Unless mister pays me my price too.'

'What price?' He was careful.

'Twenty acres of Crown land. Give me twenty acres of Crown land on the same conditions as they have, and I promise you I'll help Mr Christie day and night until the ship comes.'

White put up his hand immediately. 'Wait, Miggel, you know very well that that is not possible, I can't just hand out Crown land.'

'But you could do it for Mr Christie.'

'He is looked upon as an immigrant.'

'I'll count out the money and put it down for you right now.'

White shook his head. 'I'm sorry, Miggel. This land has been set aside for immigrants. But if you agree today to keep an eye on Christie and the Italians for me until the government has decided about them, I promise to close my ears and my eyes should anyone ever again mention Silas Miggel's unlawful living up here on the highland.'

It was like a gift being placed in front of me, but a gift I dared not pick up because it could have been a trap as well. On the other hand it could be the biggest piece of luck ever to come my way. 'Are you saying, mister, that if I agree to help Mr Christie until the ship comes, then I can stay on the highland for the rest of my life?' I said it as if it were nothing; if it were a trap, I wanted him to step into it.

'That's right.'

'And what if mister drops dead tomorrow and lies there unable to say anything further?'

'I will write to Mr Laing and suggest that you be appointed Mr Christie's assistant in exchange for dwelling rights.'

'What if the ship comes and takes them away and the government says: Silas Miggel, off with you, we don't have any further need of you?'

'I will ask that dwelling rights be granted to you for the rest of your life.'

'No, not for the rest of *my* life only, for the rest of Miriam's life too. If the Crown grants me that, mister, I'll wash every Italian's feet at night and put them all to bed. Christie's feet too.'

'I'll write and ask that Miriam, as well as you, be given dwelling rights for life on the highland.'

'You're not making promises just to get me caught?'

'I give you my word.'

I took the gift with both hands and for the first time in my life I knew what it felt like to be sure about the roof over my head. I had never really known how much time there was left on the highland for me and Miriam, where my bed would stand on the day the angelings came for my soul, where Miriam would then find a home. I felt at that moment like one who had stood outside in the wind for years and then suddenly found shelter. Fine, the highland would never have Portland's water and prospects, but the highland was my home. On the highland a sweet potato struggled to shoot and a mealie to ripen. You learned never to leave a bit of elephant or ox's dung behind which you could have picked up to work into the earth. On the highland you had to earn everything the hard way, but the highland was my place.

'Very well then,' I said to White and gave him my hand. 'I'll stand in for you and help Mr Christie with the Italians.'

After White left, I called Miriam into the house and made her sit across the table from me. 'We are not going to quarrel,' I told her. 'Where there's quarrel in a house every day, the devil has moved in – and the devil will not move in with Silas Miggel. A piece of very good fortune has just come our way, but before we get to that, there are things we've got to talk about. I want to know where you were this morning.'

Miriam looked me straight in the face and didn't even try to hide the protest in her eyes. 'I went to the forest. I set four blue buck snares and five bush-buck snares.'

'*Nine* snares?'

'They're without food, Pa. And in case you want to know if any of the Italians went with me, the answer is no.'

She told me what I wanted to know, but something about her was odd, a rebelliousness I'd never seen in her before. I knew when she was sulky, or plain difficult, but this was something else. 'What's bothering you, Miriam?'

'Nothing.'

'Don't speak to me like that, girl! And don't let this table become a rock between us. I know you, something's bothering you and I want to know what it is.'

'It's not what's bothering me that's causing the trouble, it's what's bothering you. Now that eleven tents are pitched on the highland, I am being watched more than ever before, because you go around with things in your head and heart about me, and you think I don't know it. On top of that you make out as if I'm still ten years old. And I'm not!'

What was she talking about? 'What things?'

'Many things.'

'Like what?'

'Every time a man so much as looks at me, you want to grab a gun. If you could stack the highest wall of stone around this highland to keep me in and the world out, you would get up and start heaving stones right away.'

I was at a loss. Totally. The child was like a pot that was coming to the boil. 'Are you saying I'm tying you down on the highland?'

'Yes.' She said it without a blink. 'If I go to the village, I have to count every step I make, because you're at home judging how long I've stayed away by the sun. If I say ten words to anyone in the village, I am ten steps behind and it shows on your face like doom when I get home. How many times do I ask you to let us walk to Creek Bush Island on a Sunday, or the Big Island, but you don't even hear me? If Sias or Martiens come here for whatever reason, I'm sent into the garden or to fetch water even if the buckets stand full to the rim on the cupboard. The last time Jacob Terblans came to borrow a pit-saw, you wouldn't even invite him into the house because I was here. Why you still allow me to go to Portland, I don't know. Or perhaps you're blind on that particular point, never thinking of the possibility of John or Hal or Will lying in wait for me down at the river when I come back.'

I jumped up in horror. 'What did you say?'

'Sit down, Pa. It's too late to load the gun, they stopped doing it long ago. I fended for myself.'

The child was talking about things she didn't understand. Things a girl needed a mother for, not a father that was speechless with shock and anxiety. Before my very eyes she was discarding the rope I had so carefully tied her with and I didn't know how to stop her. 'There are things you don't understand, Miriam!' I said. 'Things I will talk to you about when the time is right. Now, Mr White was here, and he says if I stand in for him and help Mr Christie with the Italians, he'll write to Cape Town and get us dwelling rights on the highland for as long as we live. For you as well. All I have to do is to help Christie with them until the ship comes.'

'What will you do with me until then?' she asked in a challenging way. 'Pull a sack over my head? Lock me up until they've gone and we're alone on the highland again?'

'Miriam, you're being difficult and wilful! There are things you don't understand.'

'I'm not wilful, Pa. I'm just tired of being kept apart as if I have the plague. I don't have the plague, Pa!'

'Miriam.'

'Pa, do you know how many times I've secretly gone to Creek Bush Island while you were over at Portland? Do you know why, Pa? Just so I can talk to girls like myself, not to be kept away from others all the time.'

I was right then, I said to myself, she had her eye on one already, she was already doing things behind my back. I didn't know whether it was Sias or Martiens, but the shock suddenly gave me courage to tell her the truth at last. 'Miriam, there is a reason why I always want to grab a gun when a man looks at you, there is a reason why I sometimes wake up in a sweat in the middle of the night, and I must now put that reason on the table between us and it's not going to be easy.'

'I know why I don't have a mother, and I know why my mother didn't have a mother.'

One moment you are standing ready with the axe to cut down the tree and the next moment the tree topples over before your eyes without you having touched it. She said it as though she didn't care, she only turned her head away. I wanted to get up and walk away to the foot of the highland and stand there on the cliffs until the pain in me went away. I suddenly wished I had something to give her, a dress or combs for her hair like the Petroniglia woman had. Or a cat. Anything to comfort her, but I had nothing.

'How do you know, Miriam?' I asked, completely dejected.

'Aunt Hannie told me.'

61

That was the second shock. Hannie was a person who seldom minded her tongue. 'What did she tell you?' I had to know.

'That my great-grandfather brought a curse on us. That a man came to borrow a pack-ox from him one night when he had to get his wife to the village to a doctor. Great-grandfather refused him the ox. So the man then carried the woman and at Bokbaard's Turning he fell with her and there both she and the child died.'

'That is a confounded, stupid, bloody forest story!' I screamed at her. 'A story that was made up afterwards and gossiped about for years – and now it's in your head too! Some people say it was an ox the man came to borrow, others say it was a woman in labour that asked for shelter, and I'm telling you it's a made-up story. Since when have we forest people turned away one another?' When I got hold of Hannie, there was going to be big trouble. How was I to get it out of the child's head now? 'Miriam, you must believe me, it's a lie!'

'It doesn't matter, Pa. The truth is that my grandmother died when my mother was born, and my mother died when I was born. I've known that for a long time.' She got up and walked over to the hearth. Only when she threw a piece of wood on to the fire, sending up a burst of sparks, did she betray the bitterness in her. 'It doesn't matter, it only makes a difference. Johanna of Uncle Willem, Susanna of Aunt Grieta, Bettie of Aunt Bet, all the girls can talk and dream of who they want to go to the village with one day to marry. But not me.' She started washing the sweet potatoes and kept on and on talking as was her way when she was guilty or scared. 'Bettie says she wants to go with Martiens. Susanna with Jacob Terblans. Pa, did you know that four of the Italians were married by the magistrate in the village shortly after they arrived? Antonia Fardini married Domenico Tomé and her sister, Giuditta, married Angelo Mangiagalli.'

'Are you making the names up?'

'I'm not making them up, Pa. One must just listen very carefully, some are difficult to say and you have to try a few times before you get it right. But it's nice, it's so different.' She paused a moment before rushing on. 'Mr Christie says Giuditta is as old as I am. Seventeen. And Mr Christie's expecting trouble because of Mangiagalli because his people don't know that he came here with the silk farmers. They are very important people in Italy and Mangiagalli was supposed to have married another girl, not Giuditta. Antonia and Domenico met on the ship coming from England. You will have to come with me to the snares tomorrow morning. If there is more than one catch, I won't be able to get them home by myself. Perhaps we should take the sled. Things are going to go wrong at the tents, Pa. It's as if they keep on going round and round, not knowing where to go. And you needn't be afraid that I will marry, I will not. I'd rather live.'

The worst was that I had to sit there without a word of comfort to give her. I couldn't say to her: don't worry, perhaps you're not like your mother or your grandmother. No one has the right to give false comfort. And it was easy for her to say now that she would never marry. She didn't know what it would be like on the day that she got a certain feeling for a man. The real feeling. When that special feeling comes, you change. It's a feeling that comes and stands between your head and your body, between your feet and the earth, it makes you breathe differently, see differently. You find that earth becomes heaven.

The only drop of comfort I had was for myself, and that was that she was my child. A child of Silas Miggel would always keep her eyes wide open and tread safely. How many times had I taken her through the thickest forest just a stone's throw from a herd of elephants? Her slight little body ahead of me on the path might have been stiff with fright, but not a twig would snap under her feet to let a bigfoot know we were there. I remembered the time when I realised for sure that she had my own determination. It was the day the cloudburst trapped us in the village with the result that it was almost dark by the time we got to Gouna's Drift. I saw there was still just a chance to get across the river if I carried her on my shoulders. She was only eight and so light that the water would have swept her away if I had let her walk through herself. But I had to get her home; we were wet through to our skins, and we couldn't sleep there.

'We're going through,' I said to her. The water was surging past in front of us.

'We're going through,' she repeated.

'The water's not going to sweep us away,' I said and picked her up.

'The water's not going to sweep us away,' she repeated.

I walked forward slowly into the swirl of brown, muddy water. When we reached the middle, I knew I had misjudged my strength, the torrent was going to take us. But step by step I fought the torrent until we reached the other side. Only when I had her home and warm by the fire, did she ask: 'Were you scared, Pa?'

'Yes,' I said, 'but I didn't shake.'

'No,' she said, 'we did not shake.'

FOUR

We checked all nine snares just after dawn. Every one had been well set and in the right places as I had taught her, but not even a buck's hair was caught.

She was quiet. When we got home, I helped her make a fire outside; it was time we baked sweet potatoes under the ash for a change, one got tired of them boiled all the time. When we had the fire going, I went and worked in the woodshed. Over at the tents it was a little less noisy; here and there a piece of washing hung from a tent-rope, and some of the men stood around in groups, talking. I turned my back on them and put the bow-saw securely on the mark in the wood, and began a new chair. My task at the tents would not begin before White had gone; two masters on the same job never worked out.

The sky was clear. A marsh lourie called from down in the gorge: do do-do-do, stopped, started again. When the marsh lourie called, rain was coming, and that was good news. I had already decided that if it had not rained by the Friday, I would have to open the clay furrow in order to get some water to the potato and cabbage patches. One of the first things I would do after the Italians had gone, I stood thinking as I worked, would be to make a better wall up at the clay furrow and catch a little more water for the hot, mountain-wind days of May and June that dried out everything. The highland would never have a dam like Portland's, for there wasn't enough water to catch. Just two shallow creeks brought water to the highland: the one above my house a little to the west, and the other one to the east of where the tents were pitched; the latter was where I watered my two oxen and from where I told White to let the Italians fetch water.

I didn't want them near the clay furrow, that was my water. For my house, I caught rain-water from the roof in the butt. When the butt was empty, we carried water from the furrow, but that wasn't often because the forest rarely saw a drought. No, the highland would never have a dam like Portland's; the best rivers, the Gouna and the Knysna, ran deep down in the gorges round the highland, but I wasn't complaining; if I was given dwelling rights, I had nothing to complain about.

The wood for the chairs was nice and dry and worked well. My thoughts went back to the day I felled that very tree up in Lily Bush, deep in the forest. I was on my way back from gathering honey when I saw the tree and my head immediately started working out how many folding chairs I would get from it. I told Miriam I was going to cut it down straight away. If a forest warder came along, we were to run west and hide down in the gorge, because my woodcutter's licence had expired about two weeks before and I wasn't in the mood to think up excuses for a warder.

It was a good tree. Well planted. If I felled it to fall right, it would not be too steep to saw into the right lengths for hauling out. I explained to Miriam that by the time the wood of that tree was dry, she would be grown up. She was fourteen then, little more than a child and I didn't have to worry about her so much then.

I was hacking into the tree quite happily when I looked up and saw the man standing above me on the sled-path. I said to myself: Silas Miggel, it's too late to run. You've been caught without a licence today, and it's a new warder. But when I looked at the man again, he didn't look like a warder, he didn't even look like an ordinary person, there was something different about him. I greeted him. He greeted me back in English. I laid down my axe and walked up to him. I saw it was a man who had been walking for a long time, the bundle on his back was heavy and his hair as long as a woman's. Tied to his bundle was a thing with legs, sticking out past his head like two horns, and I asked him what it was. He said it was an easel on which he put his paper when he was drawing. I asked him what he was drawing; he said he was drawing the forest. I told him he'd need a mountain of paper to draw the forest, the forest was big. He asked me if I could tell him about the lilies. What lilies? He said

66

the little marsh full of red lilies that people said was somewhere in the forest and for which he had been searching for weeks.

'Mister,' I asked him, 'have you, in all the weeks you've been walking, come across one single lily?'

'No,' he said.

'*If* the forest hides a marsh full of lilies and *if* the forest wanted you to find it, you would have found it by now. Go home.' But the man kept on, almost pleading with me to show him the way to the lilies. 'Mister,' I said, 'there is no road leading to the lilies.' Then he asked if he could draw Miriam, but I said I wouldn't allow a graven image to be made of my daughter.

I was about halfway through sawing out the chair when White and Christie came across. I told them that if they wanted to stay, they would have to sit outside with me, I was not putting down my work. I was behind with the chairs. White sat down on a log and Christie remained standing. White said they had come over to the woodshed so that I could be present when he gave his last orders, he would speak English so that Mr Christie could follow.

He said Christie and I were to do everything in our power to keep the Italians as calm and as happy as possible under the circumstances, and until such time as the government decided whether they were to get free passage back or not, and if so, when. He said that the answers to his first letters, the ones he wrote while still in the village with the Italians, were sure to be waiting for him at his office and he would send all news out to us with one of the warders. Should it so happen that authorisation was given him to advance them a shilling per head per day, he would buy the necessary provisions every week and send them out to the highland as well. Christie wouldn't agree to that. He said he had already advanced them quite a bit of money himself and they had promised to pay him back. He thought White should pay out the allowance in cash each week. Silently, I wondered who they thought would carry the bag of shillings out to the highland every week, but I kept quiet. It would not be Silas Miggel. Then Christie started giving his orders: he told White not to forget about sending a few more tents, and blankets, and cooking pots, and water buckets and and and . . .

I just went on with my work. Trouble there would be, but I

67

decided that the best thing was to say nothing and just wait until White was out of the way.

When Miriam brought them coffee, I saw Christie's eyes going over her like a woodbuyer's over a load of good wood. I asked White, in Dutch, whether the man had a wife somewhere. White said he didn't know, the man spoke very little about himself.

'And you will have to handle him carefully, Miggel,' White warned me in Dutch. 'He is under a lot of pressure and rather short tempered.'

'Mr White, you needn't have a single care when you walk away from here tomorrow. We'll get on. Just see to it that you write to the government and inform them that I'm now standing in here for you in exchange for dwelling rights.'

'That will be the first thing I do when I get to my office.'

'How will you get to the village?'

'I have arranged with one of the warders to help me carry my things. I'm taking the letter Mr Christie wrote about the Grassi child, to take to Constable Ralph. Please try to be more sympathetic towards the Grassis, Miggel, they didn't give the child to Tomasso.'

'Mister believes as mister believes, I believe as I believe.'

'These people are confused, Miggel, be reasonable to them and look after them well.'

'Mister,' I assured him, 'as long as I am looking after them, they are safe. Perhaps you would like to count them before you go. Am I imagining it, or does the Grassi man not look very well?'

'I believe he was very sick on the ship from England.'

I practised my English a little that evening. I didn't worry much about the words in between; as long as I had the main words, Christie would more or less understand what I meant. And should there be any serious misunderstanding, Miriam could always come and help out, she was good with English.

'What's the correct word for Gouna's *platrand* – highland – in English, Miriam?' I called from the table, for she was already in bed.

'Gouna's plateau, Pa.'

'That doesn't sound right to me.'

'You asked me, I tell you, and then you disagree.'

'How does one tell a man in English and in a nice way that he does not belong here?'

'You mustn't quarrel with Mr Christie, Pa!'

'Now, am I a quarrelsome man, Miriam?'

'I wouldn't say that, but when you get difficult, you're tougher than a piece of ironwood.'

'I only get difficult when I know I'm right and somebody else comes and tells me I'm wrong.'

'As long as you don't forget that it's Mr Christie who's appointed over the Italians, and not you.'

'Since when does Christie stand above the Crown? He was employed because he can speak their language. White is the government's man and I'm standing in for White. Until the ship comes for them, you can say Silas Miggel is the Crown over them. The most difficult task I see ahead of me is to get to know this caboodle by their names.'

The next moment she was standing at the table in front of me. 'They are not a caboodle, Pa, they are *people*!'

'Well then, I've never heard of *people* with names like they've got. How I'm ever to fit the right names to the right faces I don't know, let alone getting my tongue in a twist over some of them.'

'There is the sweetest little boy with pitch-black curls amongst them, Pa. His name is Felitze Radulfini.'

'Just listen to it! Why can't they call him plain Fielies?'

'Now don't start giving them nicknames, Pa,' she said, going back to her room.

If only there was somewhere I could send her until they were gone, but where? The candle was burning unevenly, wax dripped down one side and formed a blob on the candlestick. Through the window, I saw lightning far off in the distance towards the sea; lightning out at sea meant rain within three days. That could be troublesome, I thought to myself.

I got up before dawn and visited the snares again. In the third one was a blue buck but it hardly had enough meat on it for two people. The rest of the snares were empty. When I got back to the house, Miriam said White had been there to say goodbye, and that he had now left. I was still busy skinning the buck outside the house when Christie came round the corner like he owned the place to tell me that they needed firewood at the tents. Not good morning or good day, only the order for the wood. I said to myself: Silas Miggel, don't let this man make you angry, you must be dignified. I called Miriam to come and take over skinning the buck. Then I told Christie that while I was washing my hands, he could go and collect a couple of the men. I would bring the axes and the ropes.

'The Italians, Mr Miggel,' he said with a sneer, 'won't go into the forest to cut wood.'

'Then they will have to get along without wood, Mr Christie: if you don't cut wood, you don't have wood. Law of the forest.' Miriam started laughing because I hadn't got all the English words right or in their right places. 'Just you laugh at me again,' I told her, 'and I'll appoint you to tell him what I'm saying so that he can tell them what you're saying I'm saying and then we'll see the mess.'

Christie was getting impatient. 'The people must have wood, Mr Miggel!'

'I'm sure they must. One can't live without wood. You go and fetch three of the strong ones and tell them I'll be there right away with the axes.' I wanted to add that he had better tell them to put on old clothes, but he was already on his way back to the tents, marching like a constable.

I collected three long-handled axes, the hand-axe and the ropes, put on my shoes and walked across to the tents. Some of the Italians were standing around, some were sitting around and of Christie there was no sign.

'Buon giorno, Signor Miggel.' It was Petroniglia. She sounded weary. The others repeated the words she had said and one by one they came up to me, looking at me as if I was hope turned up. But next to one of the tents one remained seated, his head on his knees and not even glancing up.

I looked them over and had no choice but to speak Dutch to them. 'I'm trying to make up my mind whether you're dead or alive,' I said. 'Whatever the case may be, you better bestir yourselves, there's rain coming and before it does, there's a lot to be done. First of all, the firewood.'

Christie must have heard me because he came flying out of a tent and almost poked his finger in my face when he got to me.

70

'Mr Miggel,' he said, 'I am at this moment writing to Mr White demanding that another person be sent here to assist me.'

'You better leave off writing letters, there's rain coming on. The wood must be cut, a cooking shelter must be made, and a hundred other things done.'

'I don't see any clouds.'

'I'm telling you, mister, before your ink is properly dry, this wind will change to the west and you will be flooded out of your tent. But what I would actually like to know from you is why these people are looking the way they do. If the government sees them like this, there will be trouble and you're supposed to be the foreman. What's the matter with the man sitting over there? Is he lame?'

'He was under the impression that this is America. Two of his cousins emigrated to America.'

Something about him *did* look familiar: short and skinny as if he was not yet fully grown. 'What's his name?' I asked Christie.

'Antonio Mazera.'

When he heard his name, the man looked up and, when he saw me, it was 'America, America' again and again. But it was no longer a question, it was a lamentation. I walked up to him and said: 'Goodness, man, are still moaning about America? Stop it and get to your feet!' He didn't look well. 'You can't just sit there to die. The government has counted you, if there's one missing, they're going to blame me. Get up!' He stood up. His eyebrows were thick and met above his nose. His eyes were black and pleading. 'Now see that you stay on your feet,' I told him.

But then Christie wasn't satisfied by this. 'Mr Miggel,' he said, '*I* am the interpreter. I want to know exactly what you've just said to that man.'

'Don't worry, Mr Christie, he didn't understand a word of what I said, only what I meant. If you can now help me tell them that there is firewood to be cut, I'd be grateful. And before they go into the forest there are things they must know if they want to get out of it again, so you mustn't skip a word of what I'm going to tell you to tell them.'

'You won't get them into the forest.'

'Mister, don't let's argue right from the start. Tell them I want three men because we're going to cut proper wood, not

71

gather kindling on the forest's edge. Tell them they need not be afraid of going into the forest when Silas Miggel is with them; I will see to it that they don't get lost or trampled by the bigfeet. Unfortunately I can't tell mister the real name for bigfeet, not even in English, because they are very clever, more so than people, they understand everything. When you use their real name, they hear you and think you're calling them and then they might suddenly arrive.' I realised from his face that he didn't know what I was talking about. 'Law of the forest, mister. I'm talking about those big animals with the big ears and the . . .' It was a waste of time. I didn't know what the English was for *slurp* – trunk – at the time and Miriam was not there to help. 'Never mind,' I said, 'get them together and tell them the wood must be cut, time's getting on.'

What he told them, I don't know, but he was finished after no more than ten words. The next moment every tongue started lashing out at me as if a snake had been thrown in among them. And Christie stood there like one whose very shadow was important.

'I warned you, Miggel.' I was suddenly no longer *mister* either. 'They say that where they come from, only robbers and fugitives go into forests, not decent people.'

'*What?*' I couldn't believe what I'd heard. I thought I would have a fit. 'You tell them from me that the only people who live in this forest are woodcutters and their kin and they're hiding from no one and robbing no one. The robbers live in the village, we call them woodbuyers. Tell them that.' I kept quiet about Josafat Stander.

Again Christie said just a few words and got a commotion for an answer. 'They say they are not woodcutters, they are respected silk farmers in the country they come from.'

'Ask them why, if they were so respected there, did they come here?'

'Because they were lured here by wonderful promises and now they've been dumped in a wilderness!' he answered himself. 'These people are angry. They have been made fools of and they have been insulted! Where they, as well as I, come from, barbarians live in tents or in plank houses.'

'Are you saying I'm a barbarian?'

'They said it, Miggel. What I would like to add is that you

72

don't have any idea of what civilisation is, and these Italians, as well as I, come from civilised countries.'

'Does firewood fall from the sky over there?'

'No. They suggest that you should cut the wood for them.'

'What?'

I couldn't decide whether to walk away or stay and fight. If a breadwinner lies sick, you pick up his axe and cut his wood, then you ride it out to the village, all without accepting a grain of his coffee or his sugar in return. But you don't pick up an axe for a healthy man, much less for a bunch of strangers.

The breeze cutting across the highland was getting colder, playing with the tents and blowing the women's skirts against their legs. They were mostly young women, only one was older. They were wrapped in shawls, and their eyes were full of distrust.

'Signor Miggel?'

A woman with a headscarf knotted under her chin and a hook nose called me by name. 'Yes?' I asked.

She said something to Christie. 'Mariarosa wants to know how big this forest is,' Christie interpreted.

'Tell her it's a fortnight's walk to the east; north to where the mountains are, south to where the sea gets in its way and to the west I don't know.'

'She wants to know when you're going to cut the wood, they need fire quickly because the children are hungry.'

I said to myself: Silas Miggel, stand calm, you're trapped and when you're trapped, you're trapped. Forget your pride and go cut them the wood, it's getting late. Go and cut the wood, haul it out, carry it out, let them sit in the blooming tents. But for this, you are going to get paid with your dwelling rights.

'Very well,' I said to Christie, 'I'll go and cut the wood. Tell them I think it's best after all. Tell them that this forest has a way of making a coward wet himself and that would just turn them into bigger fools than they are now, and you it will turn into the biggest fool of all.' Whether he understood everything I said, I don't know, I had to use quite a few Dutch words in between the English ones which was a pity.

I fetched the ox grazing at the foot of the highland, drove it to the house and yoked it to the sled. Miriam packed some bread and sweet potatoes in the knapsack.

73

'Can't I come and help you, Pa?'

'No.'

'Are you cross with me too, Pa?'

'No.'

'Why don't you give them some of our wood in the meantime?'

'Then they'll want some of my wood again tomorrow.'

I took Red Alder's sled-path into the forest, heading for the place where the storm had uprooted an old candlewood the year before. No one would be able to say that Silas Miggel had cut them green wood; and a better fire than from candlewood, one could not make. But they would pay for it. The government would pay for it. No one spat in Silas Miggel's face.

The forest was cool and damp and quiet. Up in the roof of the forest the wind stirred, making specks of sunlight dance on the ox's back. The highland was my home, but the forest was my second coat. There was no better place a man could turn to when he had to be alone; where you could find a moment's rest when a blooming bundle of strangers had come and taken away your peace. Or where you could hide from the forest warder when there was no money for a wood licence; where you could go and thrash the bitterness out of your body after the woodbuyer had cheated you again.

Jeremiah Eye once had the good fortune to score against a woodbuyer for a change. For weeks Jeremiah had been cutting and dressing stinkwood up in the forest, hauling it out through the gorges on the sleds, through the drifts, loading it on to the wagon at Deep Walls, but when he got to the village with it, the woodbuyer said he couldn't give him more than five shillings' worth of provisions on the book for the wood because the colour was too light. Jeremiah didn't off-load, he turned back hungry. But a few days later, he went back to the same woodbuyer's yard, again with a load of stinkwood. This time, however, the woodbuyer said for everyone to hear and learn from, that it was the best stinkwood that had turned up at his yard for months. He didn't realise that it was the same wood, that Jeremiah had only stained it a bit darker with skunk bush brew.

But retaliating never paid off. I just had to pick up my axe and think of the dwelling rights that I was earning. That calmed me down a little. The candlewood was about half an hour into the forest, not too far from the sled-path; I would have to drag the wood up a bit of a slope to get it to the sled, but it wasn't too steep. I would show those Italians what one man could do with an axe. Cutting wood was not silkworm minding.

I tied each bundle I finished splitting with the ropes and dragged it up to the sled until there was a green, slippery path up through the underbush. I must have taken up about six bundles when gunshot cracked to the north of me. Heavy gun. At least a quarter-pounder. A second shot followed, another and then the fourth: the death shot. Someone had brought down an elephant. It wasn't Josafat Stander; he never needed more than two shots to bring down an elephant, and it was said that he never shot a cow.

I was never attracted by elephant shooting. To cut a 150-foot high yellowwood tree, to see it slowly coming over for the fall, was a terrible thing to watch, but a pleasure too; to see an elephant go down with a ball of lead in its brains was not a pleasure. To cut firewood for a blooming bunch of silkwormers, neither. But I kept on until the sled was piled high and I had a bundle to carry on my back as well. I wanted to be out of the forest before dark and I also wanted to check the two nearest snares. There wouldn't be time to visit the snares the next day because then the silkworm-minders were going to find out that Silas Miggel was not going to do everything for them.

There was a bush-buck in each of the snares. One was still alive and I had a struggle to cut its throat, with the result that I got myself covered with blood. It was almost dark when I arrived at the tents with the wood and the buck on top. Women and children scattered out of my way.

'Have you never seen a tired man before?' I shouted at them. 'Come and unload the stuff!' Two of the men came closer. Then another two. The woman with the hook nose also. 'Step forward and do something, Maryrosa!' I said to her.

'*Mariarosa!*' she snapped back at me.

'I hope your hands are as willing as your tongue. Undo the ropes.' One of the men pointed to the buck and asked me something. When I motioned that it was for them, it was like a flock of vultures closing in. 'You better eat your fill and go to bed early because there won't be time for rest tomorrow. I'll be here at daybreak to see that things get right. Off-load the sled,

I'll come back for it later.' I unyoked the ox and took it to the creek.

When I got home, I saw there was a skinned bush-buck hanging in the woodshed – and Christie was with Miriam in the house. There was no time to think about the right words, I just let go in a mixture of Dutch and English, asking him what the devil he was doing in my house with my daughter when I was not there. 'I'm sent off to cut wood so that you can come and sit in my house!'

'Pa!'

'Just you go near my daughter again and I'll strangle you!'

'I beg you to stay calm, Mr Miggel.'

'Calm? I won't ever be calm again until you and those confounded silkworms get off the highland. What are you doing in my house when I'm not here!'

'I was waiting to discuss a certain matter with you, but seeing that you are obviously not in a state to talk to me in a civilised way, I'll leave it.' He got up and stalked out with his nose in the air.

'Shame on you, Pa!' Miriam said.

'What's that buck hanging in the woodshed?' It didn't bother me if she was ashamed of me.

'Jacob Terblans brought it. He'd heard about the Italians and thought there could be a problem over meat.'

'So he carried the buck all the way from Deep Walls? I'm not stupid, Miriam, but I think it's time Jacob decided where his heart is, with you or with Susanna.'

'He's courting Susanna, Pa. And he didn't carry the buck all the way from Deep Walls, they're cutting in Creek Bush. I take it that the bigfeet chased you, and that is why you're being so tetchy.'

'On Monday morning, I want you to take the gun and go to the village and ask White whether he's heard anything from the government yet. If he hasn't, tell him he'd better write again. Tell him that this was the first and last firewood I will cut for his blessed Italians. When it's finished, they can use tent-pegs for all I care. And you can fetch the buck inside. I've already given them two.'

At dawn I went back to the tents. It was cold and the highland was soaked in dew. The women were getting a fire going, the hems of their skirts were wet, and the children stood huddled in shawls, waiting for the fire to give off some heat. Their hair had not yet been combed and tied.

'Buon giorno, Signor Miggel.'

'Buon giorno, Signor Miggel.'

'Buon giorno, Signor Miggel.'

'Morning.'

I went on to Christie's tent and called from outside: 'You must get up, Englishman!' Not a movement or a sound. 'I said, you must get up!' Perhaps he lay frozen to death. 'Are you alive still, Mr Christie? You must get up. The tents must be moved near the slope and you must come and interpret for me.' Something stirred. 'The tents must be moved. Before the sun goes down this evening, the wind is going to change and the rain start falling.'

When at last Christie stuck out his head, it was to launch into a tirade about who was in charge and who was not. Who would give orders and who would not and how many letters would be written, some as far as London, to report me. The more he carried on, the bigger the words were that he threw at me and in the end I didn't understand half of them.

I didn't get cross, I let him talk. I had thought about many things during the previous night; what use would it be for me to get my dwelling rights if I was first driven mad by a lot of silkwormers and their foreman? What had to be done, I would do, but dog and servant I would not be to them. I stood where I would.

'It won't help you to be scratchy,' I told Christie. 'The tents must still be moved because the rain is still going to come.'

'I can't see any sign of rain, and I see no reason why the tents must be moved.'

'They're standing in a dip, man! The person that decided that they should be pitched there in the first place was not right in his head.'

'*I* gave the order.'

'I thought there was something wrong with your head.' I didn't say it in anger, I said it from my heart and added that he could go back to bed again, I would get on by myself. I would see to it that his tent was left until last, and then I'd have it moved with him and all.

When I turned round, Petroniglia was standing behind me and in her hand she held a beautiful little porcelain cup. She was no longer wearing the purple dress, but had on an older, brown dress with no lace collar. 'Caffè, Signor Miggel?' she asked. Her eyes were puffy from crying. I took the coffee, but when I took the first sip, I had to swallow fast, for never in my life had I tasted coffee as pitch-black strong as that. It could have killed an ox. And there wasn't a chance to throw away the rest since she stood looking at me as if she wanted to make sure she was poisoning me. Fortunately the cup was small and there wasn't much coffee.

Behind her another Italian had come to say good morning, or whatever it was they said: 'Buon giorno, Signor Miggel.' It was America Mazera.

'Good morning, America. Now, I want to speak to you all together. I must get on without Christie and you must help me. Get everyone here.' I waved my arms towards the tents, beckoning and beckoning, and before long he understood what I wanted and gathered them together for me.

'It's going to rain,' I told them. I snatched the rain from the sky, wiggling my fingers downwards, showing them how it was going to fall. Twice I did that, and then they said: 'Sì, sì, signor.' They weren't stupid. I showed them that the tents had to be moved. I took a spade and showed them that I first wanted the new place cleared of all grass and shrub, and again it was: 'Sì, sì, signor.'

By the time Christie was dressed and out of his tent, four men were clearing the ground and the rest were clearing their things out of the tents.

'What, if I may ask, is going on here?' Christie said pompously.

'The tents are being moved.'

'I told you the tents are to stay where they are!' He turned and spoke to the nearest Italians. The others left what they were doing and came closer. It wasn't long before I realised they were having an argument and that Christie was losing. It seemed that they agreed that the tents should be moved, and moved they were.

By mid-afternoon, we had all the tents close to the foot of the

78

slope, pitched in two neat rows, and above them a proper earth bank had been thrown to block any water running down from above. Every tent had a floor of soft bedding-bush which America and two of the other bachelors, Angelo Borolini and Paolo Coccia, and I had cut from along the edge of the forest. Borolini seemed a quiet sort of person; his eyes didn't dart about as much as the others'; he had a narrow kind of face with a nose like a hawk's. Maybe he was related to Mariarosa.

It was the Coccia chap I didn't trust. He rolled up his sleeves as high as he could get them, making sure his muscles were seen. He had far too handsome a face as well. Later, when Miriam came with the hand-axe to help, his eyes were more on her than on the bedding-bush, with the result that I had to tell her to cut further back from us. Soon after, and he was cutting back there as well.

'Leave him, Pa.'

'Hit him with the axe.'

'You're turning into a real old hen.'

'Yes, because every young rooster is suddenly after my chicken.'

'I can take care of myself, Pa.'

'You must stay well away from these rascals. They'll interfere with anything wearing a skirt, I've looked them over.'

'How many cups of coffee has Petroniglia already brought you?'

I didn't like her saying that; there are things you can make fun of, and things you don't make fun of. 'Mind your tongue, girl!' I warned her. 'The woman thinks she can come and poison me in the hope that I'll arrange for her to go to the village again. Remind me to take some medicine before I go to bed tonight, she's put my liver in danger. And the first one of us that goes to the village must get some milkwood bark to brew. I want to give them each a good measure of it since they say it's very good for heavy-heartedness. America must get a double dose.'

'His name is Antonio, Pa.'

'He answers quickly enough when I call him America.'

'Petroniglia's husband doesn't look too well, Pa.'

'I've noticed.'

'Borolini neither.'

By the time we had the bedding-bush well trodden down in

the tents, Christie was in a better mood and admitted that the tents were better against the slope. I made him write down that the corrugated iron sheets and ironwood poles used for making the wood-shelter behind the tents came from Silas Miggel's woodshed. Also the tin bath and water bucket and iron sheets for the fire-shelter. These were not to go on the ship with them.

Then Christie came and told me that the next problem would be fish. What fish? Surely the two bucks' meat couldn't be finished already? It was then I learnt that they had a religion that forbade meat on Fridays. They could eat only fish. Straight out I suggested that they get themselves another religion, for where was I to get fish from? The nearest things to fish in the forest were eels, and the eels lived down in the gorges in water-holes, but since they were too scared to go into the forest, they would have to stay without eels. I had no intention of going to catch frogs for eel-bait in any case. Christie said their meal and lard was just about finished as well, they had to have garlic and tomatoes and olive oil too. And soap? Soap? Forest holly's leaves were as good as soap, I said, but seeing that they wouldn't go into the forest, they would just have to stay dirty and that was that. I wasn't going to carry leaves from the forest for them.

There was another thing I wanted Christie to tell them, something I wanted there to be no misconception about. 'Tell them,' I said, 'that Silas Miggel is not their servant; what I'm doing, I'm doing for dwelling rights on the highland, and for nothing else.' He told them.

The last thing I helped them to do was to throw a better dam across the creek to the east of the tents, and again I called Christie to tell them that that was where they should fetch their water, *not* from the clay furrow above my house. I would not drink from the same bucket as they did.

But the strangest thing that day was the last tent we had to move to the slope. First thing that morning I noticed that they always worked rather quietly around that particular tent. At first I thought there was perhaps a child or someone still sleeping in there. But then I realised that it was the tent shared by four of the bachelors: Borolini, America, Taiani and the tall one with the blue eyes, Cuicatti. It was when they finally started bringing out their belongings that I saw the plank, raised on four stones in the middle of the tent, and on the plank was the square thing still under the wet sack that they had carried on the first day. When Borolini took off the sack, a glass box with a glass lid stood on the plank and in it were a whole pile of little muslin bags, all knotted at the necks.

'And this?' I asked Christie.

'The silkworm eggs.'

Up to that moment I thought an egg was an egg, and that Barrington knew everything there was to know about eggs, but I was mistaken. From Christie I learned that every male and female moth that had finished mating were put into a muslin bag so that the female moth could lay her eggs and subsequently die together with the male. The dead moths were taken out and pounded to a powder which was then looked at under a magnifying-thing; every bit of moth-dust was inspected to see if there was any disease. If there was, everything was burnt, bag and eggs and all. Every bag in the glass case, Christie said, was free of any ailment and were the most expensive eggs one could buy. The problem was they had to be kept cool so that they didn't start hatching before there were enough leaves on the mulberry trees to feed them.

'Mulberry trees that are where?' I asked.

'In this case,' he said, 'it's a matter of keeping them cool so that the Italians can take them back with them and at least have something to start with again.'

Borolini and Taiani carried the glass case to the slope, Cuicatti shaded it with a blanket and America kept on sprinkling water over it to keep it cool.

When Miriam and I got home that evening, I felt at ease: the rain could come but the silkwormers would not wash away; the firewood would stay dry, the fire would burn, the children would sleep better with the comfortable bedding-bush under them, and above all I knew that a large portion of my dwelling rights had been paid off.

'They're different people from us, Miriam,' I said.

'Yes, they are.'

'What are those strings of beads with the crucifixes on that the women have round their necks or in their pockets? I even saw some of the men with them.'

'It has something to do with their religion.'

81

'Funny kind of religion.'

'I think they pray with it.'

'Who is the man that kept following you around all afternoon?'

'Giovanni Pontiggia. He doesn't talk so much with his hands like the others, his eyes are different too. And please stop letting your imagination run away with you, I will not take a man.'

She made us something to eat. We were just about finished when we heard it: music. Coming from the tents. They were making music, one played a violin and one played a mandolin; one of the others sang a strange but beautiful song. When we got outside, the notes seemed to roll and roll across the highland, falling into the gorges and dying away deep in the forest.

FIVE

❧

IT STARTED RAINING shortly before dawn the next morning. At first it was a drop here and a drop there, and then it came down in torrents as it did on the highland during the winter. That was the Saturday. By the Sunday things were bad at the tents. The children kept crying, the women kept scolding or chattering, and it wasn't always possible to say which was which. Anyone that needed to leave the tent for any reason looked sorrier than the one before him did. Miriam baked ash-bread and made a big pot of soup which I took across to them. Late on Sunday afternoon a couple of the men and I went and strengthened the earth bank above the tents and placed two more corrugated iron sheets against the fire-shelter for the women were struggling to keep the fire going; their feet were wet, their faces drawn.

By evening, Miriam was getting frantic. 'If only the rain would stop, Pa!'

'It's the rain's time and the rain's place,' I said, reproving her. 'The worser it gets over at those tents, the better and the happier I shall be since the Italians will go away sooner.'

'Can't we bring some of the children into the house, Pa?'

'No.'

'Don't you have a heart, Pa?'

'How many would you fetch, how many would you leave? You're the one that always complains about the house being too small, now you want to go fetch more?'

'Petroniglia's husband is not well!'

'He arrived here like that. I'm keeping my eye on him.'

Miriam was restless. 'When do you think the ship will come for them, Pa?'

83

'Week after next. By now, the government will have realised what they've done and they should be nicely eaten by their conscience.'

The rain started clearing up on Monday. On Tuesday, everything that had been soaked was out in the sun: clothes, bedding, children. Christie was like a lion that wanted to attack, but didn't know who to start with. The Italians were not only in revolt, two of them were sick and three had almost hit Christie that morning. He wouldn't tell me the reason.

'I must go to the village urgently, Miggel.'

'Go and sit in your tent. The way is impassable. You wouldn't get through Gouna's Drift, not even if your arms were oars.'

But he wouldn't return to his tent, he kept sitting at my table and after a while he asked me about something totally different: he wanted to know if I knew anything about a certain Fox & Dunn. I told him I had never heard of them, maybe they were new forest warders. He asked if I knew anything about a railway sleeper contract concluded by the government. I knew about that, yes. The contract was for five hundred thousand yellowwood sleepers delivered at a rate of a hundred thousand per year for five years. I knew about it because Barrington himself had tendered for it months ago, dreaming high dreams about what the profits would do for Portland. I never asked him who he thought would cut and haul out the wood for him. Fortunately he didn't get the contract; he told me himself afterwards that his price per sleeper had been too high.

Fox & Dunn were not new forest warders, Christie said, they were partners in a steam sawmill and *they* had got the contract, and with the contract they got part of the highland on which to erect their mill.

'I beg your pardon?' My ears started ringing. 'What did you say?'

It was then that Christie told me the whole story: on the day I had gone to cut firewood for the Italians, a man had come to see him, a certain Mr Robinson. Robinson was the other partner of Fox & Dunn and he was furious because the Italians had also been promised land on Gouna's highland. He had assured Christie that the government would have to remove them immediately. I could have rejoiced about that if he had not added that the machinery for the mill was already on its way

84

from England, together with twenty-five men to cut the wood and work the machinery. Twenty-five foreign woodcutters? At the first heap of elephant dung they came across, they would dirty themselves and run for the village.

I said to myself, Silas Miggel, stay calm. How many sawmills had already been put up in the forest just to be closed down again? And remember how much damage had been caused each time? When they erected the one up in Grey Bush, the foreman himself told me after less than a year that he had come to the conclusion that the forest was putting a spell on the mill: the machinery kept breaking down, the workers kept staying away, not a thing was going right, not a single day was a profitable one. No one had told him that it was almost impossible to get the wood to the village from up there. The government had given the owner a map of the forest, a paper map; on the map they made a mark, pointing out to him where he could put up the mill and that was all. The foreman showed me the map. On it, the forest was all nice and flat: lines were drawn in for the rivers and creeks and sled-paths, here and there even a footpath was marked, but nothing showed the hellish gorges through which everything had to pass, nothing of what the sled-paths looked like; if you didn't know better, you could have taken them for wagon roads. Of the forest itself there was no sign, nothing, only the flat white paper. I had seen five sawmills come and go in my time. One couldn't help wondering if perhaps the forest *did* put a spell on them. Even over at Portland, Barrington kept struggling year in and year out to keep his water sawmill going in one of the gorges. I knew without a grain of doubt that no sawmill would ever succeed on the highland.

'This latest story sounds like a second mulberry forest to me,' I said. 'It might have rained recently, but do you see enough water around here for a steam sawmill, Mr Christie?'

'No. And I brought it to Mr Robinson's attention.'

'What did he say?'

'He said this is where the government had granted them land for the mill. For a period of five years.'

'If that is the truth, the government is plain mad.'

'I'm certain the matter will have to be reconsidered. I speak quite a few languages – apart from Italian, I also speak German and French and Spanish. I also happen to be a surveyor and I know about planting trees to ensure a higher rainfall.'

'We have enough trees.'

'I am also very knowledgeable about water. As a matter of fact, I am at the moment writing to Mr Laing in Cape Town to bring this to his attention.'

'The only thing you need to write to him about is that there is no water for a steam mill on this highland. Tell them they must send for an expert urgently to come and see things for himself. Give me the letter so that I can get it on the post-cart!'

As I stood ready to go to the village with Christie's letters the next morning, Jacobus Gerber's sled came from the forest gorge again and behind him came Stefaans van Rooyen's sled. The sleds were piled high with blankets and cooking pots, water buckets and axes, saws, a wooden box containing medicines, meal, sugar, coffee; all kinds of provisions plus two ploughs, a table and a chair.

'Have you started peddling now?' I asked them in dismay.

'It's for the Italians. Bart's sled is still behind somewhere, he's bringing the mulberry cuttings and the other two ploughs.'

I could hardly get air into my lungs. I felt like sitting down right there and staying down. One moment everyone stood waiting for news of a ship, the next moment news of a sled full of mulberry cuttings arrived. How was a man to stay sane? Christie walked round the sleds like a sort of inspector, most displeased because only three extra tents had been sent. When he told the Italians the stuff was theirs, hands stretched out eagerly to loosen the ropes.

I didn't say another word, I just turned away and started walking to the village and to White. I had almost reached the bottom of the first gorge before I realised that Petroniglia was following me.

The whole day had started off wrong. Miriam had got out of bed on the wrong side that morning. There was nothing she didn't get impatient about: with the water for the coffee which did not want to boil, with her hair that did not want to stay the way she wanted it to, with me because I didn't get out of the house quickly enough so that she could sweep the floor. When I asked her what the matter was, she said she was in a hurry to get to the snares; because of the rain, we hadn't been able to check them and there could have been something trapped in them for days. It didn't sound like the truth to me, but I had no basis for an argument.

At midday, I stood in front of White's table. I had left Petroniglia outside with a very clear order that should she be gone when I came out, I would simply go back without her.

White was just too friendly for my liking. 'How is everybody up on the highland, my good friend?' he asked.

'Apart from the fact that all the Italians would have been drowned had it not been for Silas Miggel, and that half of them would have been starved to death had it not been for Silas Miggel, I can only add that things are bad up there, mister. Every morning I go over to the tents to see if they have murdered Christie or if that task is still lying ahead. For the rest, I'm standing here to try and find out whether the sun is coming up or going down because I can no longer make out to which side the world is toppling over. The food and the blankets and the tents I can understand, the implements and the ploughs are bit dark, but pitch-black dark is the sled-load of wilted mulberry cuttings in wooden boxes that I met on the other side of Gouna's Drift. I want to know if you people are messing around with Silas Miggel to get him off the highland or off his mind or if you're perhaps out of your own minds?'

'Sit down, Miggel, you're upset.'

'I don't sit where I've once been asked to get up from. I'll stay on my feet until I've got the truth.'

'The truth is simple and nothing to get upset about. As a result of my *first* letters to the government, six, seven weeks ago, just after the Italians arrived here, as well as the result of Mr Christie's letters at that time about their grievances, I received authorisation to buy supplies for them to the value of five hundred pounds. This morning I also received authorisation by telegraph to give them an allowance of a shilling per head per day for a period of six months. All these advances must of course be paid back by them. Interest-free.'

'For *six* months?' I didn't know which awful piece of news to tackle first.

'Miggel, this is all the result of my *first* letters.'

'And the mulberry cuttings?'

'The government sent the cuttings on the *Paquita* last week

87

and has given orders that they must be planted on the highland.'

'But mulberry does not *grow* on the highland! Two spades down and you're into pot-clay!'

'Don't shout so, Miggel, people can hear you in the street.'

'They can hear me on the other side of the lagoon, mister! Last week I was told if I help Christie till the ship comes . . .'

He put up his hand and stopped me. 'I said until the government has decided what was to be done about them, Miggel.'

'Are you twisting words now, mister?'

'No, I'm only repeating what I said.'

'You said that you wrote to the government to say that the Italians are demanding a ship to take them back home.'

'That's right. And I did. That was the *second* batch of letters I wrote.'

'I presume you also wrote and told them that you have in the meantime appointed Silas Miggel as fool to cut their firewood and lay their snares and everything else.'

'Miggel, Miggel, Miggel!' He was trying to wheedle me but I'm not stupid. 'I have already written to Mr Laing to inform him that I have appointed you as assistant to Mr Christie, and that I want them to grant you dwelling rights in exchange for your enormously important task. Everything on the sleds is in reply to my first letters. The answer to my second letter of appeal – that they are demanding a ship to take them back – hasn't yet reached me.'

'When will the ship be here?'

'Within the next few weeks. A ship, Miggel, is not as simple as tents and axes and blankets.'

'What happens if the government doesn't send a ship for them?' I had to know.

'There is no other solution.'

'They cannot stay up there for six months.'

'I know. That's why I implore you to be patient and to stand by Mr Christie as I've asked you to do. A government matter like this is a slow-turning wheel.'

'However slow-turning, that wheel had better find itself brakes if it isn't to come here and destroy everything.'

'Just be patient, Miggel.'

'Patient? What's this other story I've heard about a steam sawmill?'

He suddenly began shuffling the papers on the table in front of him. 'That is a matter between Fox & Dunn and the government. I wrote to Mr Laing early in April, telling him that in my opinion Gouna was the best place to settle the Italians *providing* Fox & Dunn had no claim to the land. Shortly after that, I received authority to settle the Italians on the highland at Gouna which means that Fox & Dunn has no claim on land up there. Mr Robinson left for Cape Town yesterday to negotiate with the government about other land in the district.'

'It seems to me that too many people are doing the talking around here. The best thing would be if you were to write to the government and ask them to send a man with proper brains to come and see for himself the upset that has been caused by all this nonsense.'

That made him angry. 'I am quite capable of handling matters around here,' he said. 'Don't come and interfere with things you do not understand. Apply yourself to the task I've given you, and leave the rest to me. I am as convinced as you are that the Italians cannot be left up there.'

'Can I take one of the ploughs?'

'Which ploughs?'

'The ones that arrived there this morning.'

'Those ploughs belong to the government!' White reacted as though I had asked for his breeches. 'Until such time as a decision has been made about the Italians, I have no authorisation to sell you a plough.'

'I'm not talking about buying one, I'm talking about taking one in exchange for the firewood and bucks and for the bag of sweet potatoes I went and shared out amongst them yesterday.'

'I knew I couldn't have appointed a better man to assist Mr Christie than you, Miggel. Don't worry, I'll see to it that you are rewarded. Please tell Mr Christie that he must come and see me urgently. Tomorrow, if possible.'

Petroniglia was where I had told her to be. And Chief Constable Ralph was behind the counter at the Police Office.

'She's come to enquire about the child.'

89

'You sound snappy this morning, Uncle Silas.'

'Have you heard anything?'

'How did you manage to get her so quiet?'

'I asked if you've heard anything!'

'Yes, we did. Tomasso promised to put the child on a ship as soon as possible.'

'When will that be?'

'I don't know, uncle. As soon as we hear anything more, I'll send a message.'

'When will that be?'

'I told you, uncle, as soon as we hear anything.'

'I'll let Christie tell her that.'

Petroniglia was unusually quiet. She stood there, listening to every word between me and Ralph, trying to understand them herself. When we were finished, she fell in ahead of me and there she stayed until we got to Gouna's Drift without once looking round or ducking the cobwebs. I had picked her a switch and had shown her how to walk, clearing away the cobwebs from across the path when they got too troublesome. She was wearing the purple dress again. On our way to the village that morning, she had stopped dead in her tracks when we got to the drift at the sight of the brown, muddy water and it took some hard talking to get her to take off her shoes, bundle up her dress and follow me through to the other side, step by step.

When we got to the drift on the way back, she sat down without a word and started taking off her shoes. She pointed to the water and showed me she was thirsty. 'No,' I said, 'you cannot drink that, it's too muddy. Sit a while and rest first. Gouna's Rise is just ahead, and you saw yourself what a slippery mess it is when we came down this morning.' I was getting into the blooming habit of using my hands almost as much as the Italians did when I talked.

The dampness and cold of the thickly-wooded stretch we had just come through had seeped right into my clothes. The best thing was to sit there in the sun for a little while and get some warmth back in her as well as in myself. I had wanted to buy myself a coat from Barrington before the winter, but that had to wait now. Portland's wages were no longer coming in and if that were to continue, the day was not far off when I would have to put my hand in the money tin and use some of the future-money.

When that day dawned, it was downwards for Silas Miggel. I had to keep my head. I had to get more chairs finished.

'Signor Miggel?'

'Yes, Petroniglia?' It was odd sitting there with someone who could not talk to you, it's as if she were behind glass.

A flock of big louries flew from the tree tops on our side of the drift to the tree tops on the other side. I pointed to the birds, but she hardly noticed. Whenever I watched a flock of big louries fly across a clearing, it seemed to me the red-feathered wings would never get the green-feathered bodies to their destination. Once they reached a tree, it was all right for then they scrambled to where they wanted to be. When Miriam was a little girl, she kept a bundle of lourie feathers tied up in a cloth for a long time. Sometimes she laid them out on the table in the shape of a bird; or she would stick them in her hair saying I must buy her a dress with a green body and red sleeves. A new dress.

'Signor Miggel?'

'Yes, Petroniglia?' She wanted to tell me something, but stopped again and just shook her head. She sat hunched up and looked as though she hadn't a drop of courage left in her; her skirts hung between her legs and her hands lay limp over her knees. The shawl she had draped over her head and shoulders had slipped down and the sun was shining on her hair. I watched her. She had a finely-cut sort of face; when she looked at me, her eyes seemed unafraid, yet her mouth was soft and scared. A twinge of pity shot through my body for her and I had to call myself to heel immediately. I told myself that she had known exactly what she was doing when she went and gave the child away. Let her sit, let her conscience trouble her properly and let the sun warm her a little longer.

'Signor Miggel?'

'It won't help you to sit there and keep on saying Signor Miggel; take out your beads instead and pray that the government sends you people a ship to get you away from here. I'm worried about the highland. I'm worried about the rumours of that sawmill because I don't know whether Fox & Dunn will be given alternative land. The government won't send *me* a sled full of food and clothes or a penny's allowance a day. I must take care of myself. What's happening over at Portland without me, I don't know, and neither do I care; I should have dragged all of you over there on the first day and left you at his door.' I knew she didn't understand a word of what I was saying, but it made me feel better. I was never a man to show my inner feelings but perhaps I spoke then because I knew she couldn't understand what I was saying. I told her about Miriam: 'There's something the matter with my daughter, Petroniglia. She's slipping from my hands and I don't know how to stop her. It's as if her head has gone off in one direction and her body another.'

'Signor Miggel?'

'Get up, Petroniglia, we must go.'

When we got back to the highland, the three new tents were pitched with the others and there was more trouble between Christie and the Italians.

'They are getting absolutely impossible, Miggel! I can no longer carry out my task as interpreter, supervisor and administrator of supplies from the confines of one tent only. I am entitled to a second tent as an office.'

'These people will surely inflict grave damage on you,' I warned him. 'Since when can one man have two tents while there's up to four people plus their belongings in most of the other tents?' Petroniglia kept pulling at my coat. 'I suggest you do your job and tell this woman the news is that Tomasso will put the child on a ship to Knysna, they'll let us know when, and Mr White wants to see you urgently. Tomorrow.'

I went home but Miriam was not yet back.

I sat down on the doorstep and started scraping the mud from my shoes. It couldn't have taken her that long to visit the snares, not even if she visited each one twice. Where was she? Suddenly I was asking a flow of questions I could not stem. Was Miriam going somewhere, to someone? Had she been going there for longer than I suspected? Did I only discover it because I was no longer going to Portland? Was my being home trapping her now? I stepped in before my imagination ran too wild and told myself there could be many reasons for her not being home yet. She could have gone looking for a few late forest grapes for making jam. She could have been forced to take a longer way home in order to get past a herd of elephants. It often happened. The more I stood up for her, however, the less I believed myself. It's no good having a pain and denying it in the hope that it will go away; it sometimes does, but not always. I could go and look for her, but where do you start looking for someone in the forest? Especially if that person does not want herself to be found. Say I did go looking for her and found her with Sias or Martiens or with Jacob Terblans? What then? Would she let me take her by the hand and bring her home? Not Miriam. She had told me not to worry, she would never take herself a man. She didn't say she wouldn't get involved with one. Say I found her with one of the Italians?

For three years Magriet and I had a place up in Creek Bush where we met on Sundays to be alone. No matter how tired my body was from swinging an axe the whole week long, I was always alive on Sundays. There was no money to get married on, hardly enough for food and clothes. And then one Sunday Magriet said we better get married before we landed ourselves in trouble, and three months later we were wed.

If Miriam had become attached to someone, marriage would not be the result. She would have to give him up. Magriet hadn't known that she should give me up. How long could Miriam put it off? How strong was she? My imagination ran on and on. I said to myself, your Miriam is not stupid, she will tread carefully. All I could hope for was to know what to do when the time came and, indeed, still be here on that day. I would buy her a green dress with red sleeves; I would work in her garden for her and plant her all the flowers she loved; I would trim back her violets that were already growing right up to the forest. I would add another room to the house for her. I would make her a little table of stinkwood and buy her a wash-basin and ewer made of porcelain to place on it. Barrington had sent for me one day and when I got there, I had to take off my hat, go into the house and up the stairs to the room where he lay in a huge bed with a roof over it. He wasn't well. I hadn't quite known where to put my feet or direct my eyes. I hadn't desired anything of what I saw for myself, only for Miriam. And in the room was a beautiful basin and ewer made of porcelain, standing on a little table.

But a basin and ewer would not fall out of the sky, I said to myself, and neither would money. I got up and went to the woodshed as if something was driving me and started on the half-finished chair. Food could wait until later. Although matters seemed to be in confusion, I wasn't totally without hope

93

for the dwelling rights that had been promised me. And I didn't think there could be much more trouble with the Italians: the tents were against the slope, firewood was under the shelter, the government had sent food and blankets and medicine, and Tomasso had promised to put the child on a ship. All that was left for me to do was to keep an eye on them and get hold of a plough. I had never stolen so much as a splinter from anyone in my life, but I did plan to acquire one of those ploughs, for what use were four ploughs without oxen in any case? You might as well send a man a wagon without wheels.

I began to be anxious about Miriam again. Perhaps she had decided to walk over to my sister Hannie up on Creek Bush Island. Perhaps there was something between her and Sias van Rooyen. If it were Sias, it was all right, no girl would cry over him for long.

Mrs Barrington once gave me quite a talking-to about Miriam, saying I shouldn't bring up the child as roughly as I did, she was a sensitive child. But I wasn't rough on Miriam. It's just that every child in the forest, whether a boy or a girl, had to know the laws of the forest. When the fog rose up from the sea, creeping inland to lie in the forest until the world was a grey, blind place, every child had to know which way was straight ahead or straight back, or he would never find his way home again. It wasn't rough to teach a girl every footpath and sled-path. The day an elephant charged and she had to run because there wasn't a tree she could climb, she had to know which paths would lead to safety. Every eye had to be wary of the tree-snake, sunning itself on the footpath. A forest child was different from other children, but a lady like Mrs Barrington didn't understand that.

'Pa.'

I hadn't seen her coming. 'Good evening, Miriam.'

'It's not that late, Pa.' She was guilty, it showed in the way she stood there and it was on her face.

'Miriam,' I said, 'I'm not going to ask you where you've been. What had to be said, was said last week, but today I've been thinking. If one talks about the same thing every day, before long the words become meaningless; they become like nails that no longer go into the wood, no matter how hard you drive them. That is why I'm not going to ask you where you've been because

94

I don't want you to lie to me.' I saw her body relax with relief. I saw it clearly. I said to myself: now, Silas Miggel, stand still, you're doing the right thing, don't say anything more about it. But it wasn't easy. My lips did as my mind willed, while my whole being wanted to know where she'd been. With whom? She certainly wasn't innocent or she would have argued with me. She hadn't been to my sister Hannie since she would have said so. 'Go and make us something to eat,' I said. 'I haven't eaten since this morning and I assume you haven't either.'

I finished the chair and started on a new one. The breeze, blowing across the highland, left a cold, cold patch between my shoulder blades.

Early next morning Christie knocked at my door. 'I need you to guide me to the village, Miggel.'

'I was there yesterday, I'm not going there again today.'

'Then send your daughter with me.'

'No.'

'I shan't go alone. Some of the Italians and their wives also want to go to the village, but they don't want to walk alone either.'

'If you're with them, they won't be alone.'

He got cross. 'I will report that you have refused to assist me in my duty to get to the village as ordered by Mr White.'

'It's not that I'm refusing. It's that I don't understand them being too scared to go north into the forest to get firewood, but not too scared to go south through the forest and the gorges to the village.'

'There is at least a sort of road cut through to the village.'

'There are also sled-paths and footpaths to the north.'

'Mr White told me that the forest to the south has been cleared quite considerably and that there is no comparison with the dangers that lie to the north. I therefore request you to accompany me and the Italians to the village, and back again.'

'Have you finished fighting over the tent? Or is that why you're scared to go alone with them?'

'The tent is mine. Are you going to accompany us, or not?'

'I'm not going anywhere.' I was fed up with him. And it would have been the end of the incident had Miriam not come out of her room and started fending for the man.

'Can't you see that he needs help, Pa?' She spoke Dutch so he wouldn't understand. 'Don't you realise that he is as trapped as the Italians are? Have pity on them, Pa. Let me walk with them to the village. Please. There are four bigfeet cows and a calf close by in the forest, I had quite a struggle to stay downwind from them yesterday to get back home.'

'Which way were they heading?'

'I think they were on their way to the highland to get to the sun for the forest is still very wet. Don't forget, Pa, that if I'm alone here with the others and the bigfeet come, I'm in trouble. I've never used the heavy gun.'

I had actually been expecting the elephants for some time. They had quite a streak of inquisitiveness in them, especially when there were strangers in the forest that could be sniffed out.

'Where did you come across them?'

'Up on Gouna's sled-path, Pa.'

What was she doing up there? There wasn't a snare in that direction. 'There's nothing I can do to stop them; if they're on their way here, they'll come and walk over whatever they want to.' Christie was getting impatient and asked us to speak English so that he could understand what we were saying. 'We are not talking about you,' I told him.

'Don't be so pig-headed, Pa, let me go with them. Please. You said yourself that Mr White wants to see Mr Christie urgently.'

'If I give permission, it's against my will and against what my head tells me to do. These are a different sort of people, Miriam, I don't want you to get too friendly with them. I've studied them carefully: their eyes are livelier than the English's, their tongues as well.'

Christie started threatening to report me if I didn't stop speaking Dutch.

'Go ahead, man!' I said. When Miriam giggled, the tension between us was suddenly gone. That was good – but it didn't stop me worrying about her still. I had started noticing a sort of happiness about her when she swept the house, or made the food, when she wasn't aware that I was watching her. It was like a light shining from her, and it wasn't a good sign.

I told Christie that I would give permission for her to go with

96

them but that it was the only time. If they wanted to go to the village again, they could go alone.

I dragged my workbench to the eastern side of the house so that I could keep my eyes on the forest and tents while I worked. One thing I intended doing as soon as possible was to get Christie to call them together so that I could talk to them about the elephants. I couldn't be caught on the highland with a bunch of Italians on my hands if they started running in every direction when danger came. Where would I round them up again? And another thing: an ash-pit had to be dug immediately, the forest was not a rubbish dump and they had started throwing vegetable peel and other things into the squatting closet I had made them dig and screen off from the tents. I didn't want a second one made; I didn't want the highland full of shit holes by the time they left.

It was rather quiet over at the tents. About ten of the Italians had gone to the village with Miriam and Christie. Petroniglia tagged along as well so she could get news about the child.

Two of the women were listlessly sweeping near the tents with a broom made from twigs; two more were hanging out washing. The children were playing a game which involved everyone standing in a circle. But Felitze, the little boy with the black curly hair of whom Miriam took far too much notice, wouldn't stay in the circle and kept running away. Twice he came as far as my gate, but I chased him back.

As I stood there, working and keeping my eyes on everything, I saw one of the forest warders, coming towards the house, obviously looking for trouble.

'Morning, uncle.'

'Morning, warder.'

'I see you are still on the highland, uncle, as unlawfully as ever.'

'That's right, yes. But before you get too excited, I would advise you to go and find out from Mr White – the government's own man in the village, as you know – about my new position. My staying on the highland has now become a government matter.'

'How come?'

'Go and ask Mr White. And seeing that you have nothing to do, hand me the tin with the bone-glue over there.'

He passed me the tin reluctantly and then walked over to the woodshed to look at my wood. When he returned he asked to see my licence. I fetched the piece of paper from the kitchen and he stood looking at it for a long time as though he was sure to find something wrong if he looked hard enough. A warder was always a warder.

'This licence expires in a month's time.'

'I know.'

'And I notice that you're still cutting mostly stinkwood. I hope you know that you're only allowed to cut stinkwood during the months of June and July.'

'I know that too. It's the woodbuyers in the village that don't know it.'

'We have instructions from Captain Harison, Chief Conservator, to bring in all you people cutting out of season.'

'The woodbuyers don't ask whether it's time to cut or not; if they want wood to fill the ships, they want it. And Smit doesn't want the chairs if they're not made of stinkwood.'

'We're going to prosecute, uncle. I'm warning you.'

'I heard you.'

'But I'm actually here because of other trouble on the highland. Serious trouble.'

'I assure you that all the trouble that can be here is here already. You may therefore take your leave.' He was standing in my way.

'It would be to your own advantage to cooperate, uncle. It's about these Italians. They have smallpox.'

'*What?*' I almost dropped the tin of glue. 'Are you drunk or something?'

'No, uncle. The whole world is full of smallpox. In London they are dying like flies and they're expecting it to break out at the Cape any day now. The ships won't come in to anchor, they'll sail right past our harbours. Magistrate Jackson called us together to inform us; he says it's the immigrants that are bringing in the disease.'

'Aren't you telling me something you've only half-heard?'

'No, uncle.'

'Well, I'm telling you that these people don't have smallpox. They're a noisy lot and strange in their ways, they're scared of the forest and two of them had a bit of a cold, but for the rest they're healthy. The only one that is rather morose is the Grassi man, Ilario. But he arrived here like that. Mr Christie, the foreman, says he got on the ship that way.'

'It's smallpox.'

He was determined that it should be smallpox. 'If I were you, I would go and find out about this thing again before being so certain. And until then I would advise you not to start spreading rumours. The government will shortly be sending a ship to take the Italians home since they cannot stay here. But no ship will take them if they're sick.' I began to tell him about the silkworms and kept on until his mouth was hanging open and the story of the smallpox had shifted to the back of his mind. But then he started on a new topic. 'Do you happen to know in which direction Josafat Stander is shooting, uncle?'

'Is he shooting then?'

'He's smuggling ivory, uncle. In a serious way. He's never had permission to shoot bigfeet and he will never get permission; the only thing he's going to get is trouble. We have instructions to catch him and bring him in once and for all.'

'You haven't been in this forest long, have you?'

'Nine months.'

'Have you seen Josafat Stander, do you know what he looks like?'

'No. They say he's a tall man, you'll know it's him when you see him. In summer he wanders from place to place, but in winter he makes himself a shelter and that's where I am going to get him.'

'How are you going to find him? You can't think that you're the first person to try?'

'Don't worry, uncle, I've thought up a very good plan. You'll hear about it when we've got him. All I'm asking is that all you forest people cooperate and help me find out where he'll be making his shelter this winter.'

'I'll keep a lookout.'

'I'll be glad if you would, uncle. And I'd better be going now. I still want to go as far as Brown's Gorge. I believe the woodcutters are cutting quite a lot up there. You don't happen to know if there are any bigfeet on the way there, uncle?'

'Not that my two eyes have seen, but you better keep yours open.'

I waited until he was well out of the way before I went across to the tents. I found the Italians standing and sitting around like people who had gone limp from inactivity. When they saw me, however, they came to life a little.

'Buon giorno, Signor Miggel.'

'Buon giorno, Signor Miggel.'

All in a row, children as well. With a broad smile America tried it in Dutch: 'Good morning, Signor Miggel.'

'It's no longer morning, it's afternoon,' I said and pointed to the sun. I drew him a path against the sky from the east to the position of the midday sun and told him that that was for *good morning*, then I went onwards for *good afternoon*; I repeated it once and then he said:

'Good afternoon, Signor Miggel.' The others repeated the words as well.

'That's enough now,' I said and asked where Ilario Grassi was. They pointed to his tent where I found him on his narrow canvas bed, his body hardly making a bulge under the blankets. When he opened his eyes and saw me, he put out his hand as if I were help that had come to his aid. Everything in the tent was in neat piles, but it was still exceedingly cramped.

'You're not looking well,' I told him. 'We'll have to do something to get you better, but I don't have much faith in the medicine the government has sent. I'll have to think of something else. You can't just lie here and die, you've all been counted.' I was sure he didn't have smallpox because he didn't have sores on him. I decided I would have to go to Creek Bush Island and ask Mieta to come and have a look at him. I was sure he didn't have smallpox. They would take him on the ship.

When Miriam came back with the others late that afternoon, her feet were dragging with tiredness. 'I couldn't keep them together, Pa. Everyone pulled in a different direction, and Petroniglia had Mr Christie in such a state at the Police Office. She insisted on being told exactly when the child was going to be put on a ship and on which ship. She wanted Mr Christie to squeeze the information out of Constable Ralph, she wouldn't accept that he didn't know.'

'I hope that doesn't mean that she'll want to go to the quay every day from now on. What was it White wanted to see Christie about so urgently?'

'I don't know. But Mr Christie was with Mr White for a long time and came out with a lot of stuff: rolled-up papers and things. I must say, he was in a much better mood than when he went in.'

'I think Mieta will have to come and tend to Ilario.'

'You will have to fetch her then, I've got the baking to do tomorrow.'

Strange. I thought she would have jumped at the opportunity of going to Creek Bush Island.

And I didn't get to Creek Bush Island the next day either for just as it was getting light, the devil got loose at the tents. From the screaming that went up, it sounded as if at least half of them were being murdered. Miriam was out of bed in a flash, all of a dither in her nightdress.

'What's happening, Pa? What's going on?'

'Bigfeet. Pass me the gun.'

'How do you know, Pa?'

'What else?'

'Are you going to shoot at them, Pa?'

'Only if I have to. Put something on and blow out the candle.'

I was still busy ramming down the gunpowder when fists started hammering on my door. 'Signor Miggell! Aiuto! Elefanti! Elefanti!'

When I opened the door, there was a circle of faces outside. Those not yet there were on their way from the tents, lugging their children by the arm or clutching them to their hips. 'Keep your bloody mouths shut!' I shouted. 'Don't call them by their names! They might know your language too and come and trample my house to the ground!' Most of them were still in their nightclothes or wrapped in blankets and shawls, some carried bundles as though in panic they had grabbed whatever was nearest to save. The women cried, the children cried, they all stood shivering from cold or shock, and closest to my door were Petroniglia and Mariarosa, Borolini and Coccia. Everyone babbled at the same time, hands waving, eyes flashing, the ones at the back pushing the ones in front, the ones in front trying to push me out of the way and get into the house.

'Where's Christie?' I shouted. Half pointed in the direction of the tents, the others to the far end of the highland. 'Miriam!' I shouted over my shoulder, 'slam the door behind me when I'm out and bolt it!'

'Let the children in, Pa! They're getting cold!'

'No!'

'Please, Pa, let the children in!'

I couldn't keep them back any more; they were pushing forward harder and Miriam wouldn't help me. When they started squeezing past the only thing left for me to do was to force a way out for myself. When I got clear I saw four cows and a calf plucking at the grass about five hundred yards below the tents, apparently unaware of the havoc they were causing.

The wind was from the south. I got past to the tents safely and found the tracks coming from the forest immediately above. They must have come out shortly before dawn, making their inspection thoroughly and quietly as only a bigfoot could do when he wanted to. In the process, it was as if they had deliberately chosen the most awkward places between the tents to drop their enormous balls of dung for the fleeing Italians had stepped right into it everywhere.

Christie was in his tent, a complete disgrace: a grown-up man cowering on a ridiculous canvas bed, nightshirt between his legs like a woman's skirts, nightcap on his head and a length of plank for a weapon. I told him to get up and make himself decent so that he could come and help me to get the damned Italians out of my house.

The only other person I found was Ilario. I simply picked him up, blankets and all, and carried him to my woodshed where I propped him up in a corner. Christie made it to the woodshed with the speed of a horse. Nothing I did or said would move him or a single Italian back to the tents.

It was a long day. The elephants were in no hurry. At times, they just stood in the sun, swaying, as if rocking themselves to sleep. Then again they would slowly graze towards my two oxen way down on the highland, or they would just play with the calf.

Those Italians who hadn't managed to get shelter in my home sat like baboons on the wood in my shed. Inside the house, the women sat counting their beads with shaking hands, even some men outside in the shed sat fingering the beads and kissing the little crucifixes or making the sign of a cross over their chests. The children seemed paralysed with fear; most of them were inside, sitting under the table with wildly starting eyes. It was only Fielies that couldn't decide where he wanted to be: one moment he was in the shed with the men, the next with the women in the house. Each time he came out, I had to call Miriam to fetch him back.

'His name isn't Fielies, Pa! His name is Felitze.'

So long as I stayed between the house and the shed with the gun, the Italians were quiet, but as soon as I turned my back, they became restless. Especially Christie. Miriam made fires both inside and out in order to cook enough ash-bread and sweet potatoes for everyone.

'The government will have to pay me back for a bag of meal and a bag of sweet potatoes,' I told Christie. 'I cannot afford to feed thirty mouths or more like this.'

'I will make a note of it, Mr Miggel.' I was suddenly *mister* again. 'Just please keep your eyes and your gun on those wild beasts down there!'

'They're not wild beasts,' I told him, 'they're bigfeet. When you talk about them, you must do so with respect because in this forest they go first and you go second. If they decide to come on to the highland to sun themselves, you must stand aside. And before there's any more trouble, I'm going to teach you and these blooming silkwormers the law of the forest when it comes to bigfeet.'

'What law?'

'Not a government law, that I can assure you. The only law the government has over them is to hand out permission for them to be shot. You must tell these Italians that when a bigfoot gets a whiff of your scent and doesn't like it, he'll trample you so flat that you wouldn't recognise yourself even if you were alive to look. And don't forget, they don't like the smell of *foreigners*,' I added on purpose. 'The best thing is to stay downwind from them so that they can't pick up your scent. But when the day comes that there's no time to get below the wind, you had better have all your wits about you if you don't want a bigfoot tusk through your back.'

'Pa, stop scaring the man like that!' Miriam called from the house.

I pretended I hadn't heard her. 'If you have to climb a tree, you must know which tree to climb – but the right tree won't

103

necessarily be near at hand. You can climb a white alder or a stinkwood, but they don't grow every five paces in this forest. When a bigfoot chases you and you need time to find the right tree, throw down your coat or your shirt and run; a bigfoot will first trample the scent from your clothes before giving chase again and by that time you had better be up a tree.'

'What will happen if those creatures down there decide to turn this way and charge this house?'

'Then I can let the government know that there is no longer any need for the ship. You're gone already.'

'Pa!'

'You're a cruel man, Miggel. Why don't you fire a few shots in their direction and drive them back into the forest?'

'I'd rather shoot you than wound a bigfoot on the highland today.'

Christie was suddenly most offended. 'Mr White warned me about you,' he cried. 'John Barrington warned me about you, and the forest warders too. I will see to it that your conduct is brought to the attention of the highest authorities.'

'I wonder whom the Italians would vouch for if they had to, for you or for me.'

'Definitely for you, Miggel,' he said with a jeer. 'They like a good entertainer who can sometimes help them forget their troubles.'

I didn't quite know what he meant.

When the sun went down, the cows went back into the forest, and it was pitch dark by the time I got the last of the Italians back to the tents. America seemed to think he could move in under my table for good.

The next morning, the Saturday, Miriam offered to fetch Mieta, and I took a bucket and a spade and collected up the elephant dung for my garden. By the time Miriam returned with Mieta, I had it worked into the earth, as well as thonging the seats of two chairs.

I had an awful struggle getting Mieta into Ilario's tent because the blooming children started screaming the moment they saw her, and the women wouldn't let her get near him either.

'They're scared because the woman's skin is so black,' Christie said.

'What? Tell them Mieta might have a black skin, but she's a good person and the best to see to Ilario. She's like a doctor.'

It still took a lot of talking to get them to stand aside so that Mieta could get into the tent. And a lot of talking at Ilario's bedside because four mouths had to be used to question and interpret: Mieta to me, me to Christie, Christie to Ilario and back down the line again.

'He's got the big standstill,' Mieta declared at last. 'Everything appears to have come to a halt: his stomach, his liver, his heart, his blood, everything. I'm going to mix him three brews which you and Miriam must give him every day at sunrise and sunset. For a week. Tell them it will cost five shillings and if they don't have the money, I will take the shawl the man's wife has round her shoulders. I like it.'

'Your price has gone up,' I said.

'It's not ordinary medicine this man needs. What he needs takes me a long time to find and pick.'

In my youth, I had often seen old Mieta walk into the forest with her candle on a wind-still night to go and pick her herbs. What you pick at night, she said, was stronger than what you picked during the day. When the woodcutters didn't have money to pay her, she took meal and coffee and sugar instead, but she never left before she was paid. Petroniglia borrowed the money from Christie to pay her.

As we walked away from the tents, Mieta and I, she asked me to stop because she wanted to have a talk with me before we got to the house.

'Talk about what?' I asked her.

'About your Miriam, Silas Miggel.'

'What about Miriam?'

'The young men get a strange look in their eyes when they speak of her. They're plucking up courage to come to the highland and I want to know what you are going to do about it? Remember, I was with my mother when she had to close Miriam's grandmother's eyes, and I was the one that closed her mother's eyes. Don't let me have to come and close her eyes as well.'

A shudder went through me. 'You mustn't talk like that, woman!' I said. 'Miriam knows all about it, she knows everything. She won't take a husband.'

105

Mieta snorted. 'It's not just the one curse on her, Silas Miggel. The second curse she carries is a face like an angel's and a body to go with it. I'm warning you, she's pretty and she's ripe. Have you noticed some of the eyes at the tents? They look right through her clothes.'

'Be done with you!' I could have strangled her. 'Miriam isn't stupid, she knows what she's doing! She knows where it's safe to tread.'

'There's that thing of nature, Silas Miggel, that drives all commonsense from one's body. If anything should happen to Miriam, get her to me so that I can give her medicine. But you must bring her to me quickly.'

'I don't know what you're talking about, you old witch!'

'You lie, Silas Miggel, you know.'

I went back to my work in the shed while she went into the house to see Miriam. I didn't like what she had said.

On the Monday, when the sun came out behind the forest, Ilario was sitting outside his tent in better health.

SIX

ON THE SAME DAY, Christie started surveying the highland.

Rope, string, planks, poles, all kinds of strange implements and four Italians to help him: Coccia, America, Borolini and Lucinetti, the last was the one with the fairer hair and the scar across the one cheek. On the ground, held flat by stones at each corner, lay a huge map.

'What the devil are you doing?' I asked him, hardly able to breathe from the shock.

'Implementing the law.'

'What law?'

'Immigration law.'

'You're not speaking to a child!' I said to him. 'You're speaking to Silas Miggel and he's not a leaf that was blown here yesterday. I want to know what's going on and I want it in plain words.'

Christie was unravelling a ball of string with Coccia and answered me grudgingly. 'The law requires us to take formal possession of the land allocated to us.'

'I thought you were waiting for a ship.'

'Please see that the mulberry cuttings are watered, get Cruci to help you.'

'They can perish where they are for all I care. I said, I thought you people were waiting for a ship!'

'That's right, we are waiting for a ship. The Italians asked me again last night to write to the authorities about the matter. In the meantime the allotments are being surveyed and allocated so that Fox & Dunn will not be able to say that we didn't take proper possession of the land.'

'In other words,' I said, 'it's like a man that puts on his coat to leave but then sits down to keep his chair warm. What for? If he doesn't want the chair, what the devil does it matter if anyone takes it?'

'Careful, Miggel, your choice might lie between the Italians and a sawmill.'

'Don't try to push me between two fires, Englishman, this highland is no place for either!'

Christie bent over the map on the ground, measuring and making marks on it as if he were already doing it for real. The map was covered with lines and squares and letters that I couldn't decipher. 'What's it say?' I asked him, tapping him on the shoulder.

He jumped up. 'How dare you push me!' he said.

'I want to know what's written on that map!'

' "Plan of Italians' allotments at Gouna's Forest",' he chanted.

'What else?' My whole body was sweating.

'Can't you read yourself?'

'I only read Dutch. Read! What are those lines up there looking like snakes?'

' "Slip path from Red Alder River".'

'*What?*' They had Red Alder's sled-path drawn in on the map. 'Then that other one up there will be Gouna Ridge's sled-path, I suppose,' I said, pointing.

'That's right.'

'And I take it that those squares are your so-called allotments.'

'Yes. Allotments of approximately twenty acres each.'

The more I understood of the map, the more appalled I was. 'What about the sled-paths going right through those top allotments?' I grabbed at the first thing that didn't look right to me.

'Gouna Ridge's slip path – as it is called on the map – will be diverted to the east where it says "deviation" there.'

'Tear up your map and throw it away. It's another mulberry forest. The man who drew this map can never have hauled wood out from this forest if he thinks that path can be diverted to where he's marked it.'

'The survey was made by the Government Surveyor, Mr Twaites.'

'When was he here? I never saw him.'

'He was definitely here.'

I suppose he could have been there on a day when I was over at Portland, but where had Miriam been then? 'What's this line coming up here from the bottom?'

' "New Road to Knysna".'

A new road to Knysna? If it were night, I might have thought I was dreaming, but it was broad daylight. 'What's written on those two squares up there in the middle?'

'On the top one it says "Yard for Logs" and the one below, "Yard for Sleepers and Timber".'

Yard for logs. Yard for sleepers and timber. Fox & Dunn. The person who had drawn this map knew about the Italians *and* the sawmill. White had said that he had written to the government and told them that if the sawmill had no claim to the highland, he suggested the Italians got the land instead. Something somewhere was too dark for my liking.

'How can one put a sawmill between silkworm allotments?' I asked Christie.

'Mr White has already written to Mr Laing, the Commissioner of Crown Lands in Cape Town, about it.'

There was something I feared to ask but which I could put off no longer. 'Show me on the map where my house is. Point it out to me exactly.'

He put his finger on the narrow strip between the *Yard for Logs* and the *Yard for Sleepers and Timber* and a cold shiver ran over me: the man who had drawn the map knew of the Italians and the sawmill *and* of Silas Miggel. I was neatly squeezed in between the two sawmill yards like a louse between body and bed. Bastards, I said to myself, now you're messing about with Silas Miggel.

That was the Monday. For the whole of Tuesday, Christie marched up and down the highland, taking measurements and driving in pegs. Towards the end of the afternoon, he came and nagged at me until I went and helped him survey the four allotments that lay right in the forest among the trees and underbush because the Italians wouldn't go in there for anything. And all the time I held his blessed poles and strings, I felt like a man helping to knot a rope round his own neck.

'Who are you going to give these upper lots to if they're too scared to put a foot in the forest?'

109

'Fortunately only three are immigrant allotments, the fourth one is the yard for logs. And the lots won't just be handed out to the Italians; they will draw lots for them. According to the Immigration Act, only those prepared to pay cash for an allotment have the right to choose, and I'm afraid none of them has money for that.'

'Sell me two, I'll count out the money for you right away.'

'You're not an immigrant.'

'Sell me one.'

'Don't be daft, Miggel.'

'When will the lots be drawn?'

'On Friday.'

'What about my dwelling rights?'

'Mr White has written to Mr Laing about it. I don't think there will be any objection to your staying where you are,' he said as if *he* had say about where I could stay or not.

'I suggest that you move the yard for logs and the yard for sleepers and timber down to the foot of the highland,' I said.

'Things will be done according to law and map, Miggel. If you aren't satisfied, you may appeal to the authorities. I take it that you've noticed the firewood is rather low and that you will see to it that more is cut.'

I had to keep a hold on myself; the man had a different attitude since he started surveying the highland. It was as if his shoes had grown taller beneath his feet, and they seemed to grow still higher when I came near him. I suppose it was because the Italians were now taking less and less notice of him.

On the Wednesday morning, I went and cut the wood because no one was going to have the pleasure of saying that Silas Miggel did not keep his part of the deal. Dwelling rights had been promised me, dwelling rights was what I wanted – but not between two sawmill yards. I had done a lot of thinking during the night: commonsense told me they could divide the highland between sawmill and silkworms as much as they liked, but not one of them would survive there. Never. Only Silas Miggel would.

And I took them more than just the firewood that day. I went and caught thirteen eels as well. Big ones. When I got to the tents with the slippery things I thought my hands would be kissed. Angelo Mangiagalli, one of the four who had got married

110

shortly after their arrival, took me by the arm and led me into his tent. He took a dark green bottle from a trunk, his wife, Giuditta, handed him a beautiful little glass and when he poured out the wine, it was as if he said goodbye to every drop. The more I told him that I wasn't one for wine, the more he apparently thought I was thanking him. Fortunately he only half filled the glass and topped it up with water. I didn't exactly like the taste, but it was better than the coffee Petroniglia had ready for me when I went outside again.

On the Thursday, Miriam and five of the women went to the village to get provisions from the store, taking an ox and the sled. They had to get the weekly shillings from White before they could buy anything for the Italians. Mercifully I had six chairs to send Smit, and once more was spared from taking money from the tin for my own provisions. There was no doubt that I was feeling the loss of Portland's wages more and more.

And as if Barrington knew it, John arrived on the highland on horseback that morning. He didn't get down, but stayed in the saddle on the other side of the hedge where I was busy hoeing.

'Uncle Silas,' he called out to me, 'how long are you going to keep up this grudge?'

'Until the day the menace that your father is the cause of has left this highland,' I said and carried on working.

'We've heard that they're now demanding a ship to take them back to Italy.'

'Yes.'

The horse wouldn't keep still under him. 'It appears that Christie has started surveying nonetheless.'

'Yes.'

'The water is running strongly down in Genakloof. Mr Barrington has sent me to tell you that the mill is working well; you must come and help with the wood. Mr Barrington is prepared to put up your wages to five shillings a day, uncle.'

Five shillings a day! It was good money and it was tempting. And it wouldn't be the first time that Barrington had tried to buy a man to get him back. 'Tell your father that is good news. Tell him the sooner he writes to the government and hurries them on with the ship, the sooner I'll be there.'

'Don't be a fool, uncle. You could earn a lot while you're waiting for that to happen. Where's Miriam?'

'It's got nothing to do with you where she is.'

'Says who?' He sat up there on the horse, a broad smile on his face as if he knew something no one else did.

'John Barrington,' I warned him, 'just you come near my daughter and I'll shoot you so dead, you'll never laugh again. Be off with you.'

'Five shillings a day as from tomorrow.'

'Go!'

Later that afternoon, as I was on my way to the tents to give Ilario some medicine, Miriam came across the highland with the sled and the women; when I heard them laughing like a lot of silly girls I got cross. When they came closer, I saw a long bamboo ladder lying on top of the bags on the sled. I remembered that old Sarel van der Merwe always used to say: if you want to go down properly, give a woman your money and send her to the store. The moment the group stopped, I flew at them.

'What's all this laughing and what's this blooming ladder for?'

'It's the loft ladder from Mr White's office, Pa. They nagged and nagged at him to let them have it and in the end he sold it to them for seven shillings. He says it's the government's ladder and that he had no authority to sell it, but they wouldn't give him any peace.'

'Why do they want it?'

'I don't know, Pa.'

'And what was all the laughing about?' I noticed Petroniglia coming up way behind the others, feet dragging.

'They're laughing from shock more than anything else, Pa. Just before we came out of the gorge, we came upon a pack of baboons. Half the women jumped right on to the sled and made such a racket that the baboons took flight.'

'Off-load the stuff and then go and give Ilario his medicine.' I was not in the mood for frivolity.

'Would you please take Petroniglia to Mr Christie? Tell him that Constable Ralph says Tomasso should have put the child on the *Natal* last week but when he got her to the ship, it turned out that there wasn't any more room left for passengers.'

I took Petroniglia to Christie and told him it was time he wrote to Cape Town telling them to put the child on the post-cart so that the matter could be resolved and the child rejoin her mother. I was getting fed up with it.

When Miriam returned from the tents, her mind was not on what she was doing. She made the fire, but forgot to put on the water for coffee; she put on the water for the sweet potatoes, but left the sweet potatoes on the table. She went outside to fetch water but was away so long that I went out and found her standing behind the house with the bucket still empty. When I asked her what the matter was, she didn't answer me. Which meant there was something worrying her all right. When we sat down to eat, she asked if anyone had been there during the day.

'Were you expecting someone?' I asked.

'A warder or somebody might have been here. Am I not allowed to ask?' She was being difficult.

Why I don't know but I kept quiet about John Barrington. And Miriam remained restless and agitated. It was when we were about to go to bed that she suddenly lashed out at me: 'Ever since Tuesday you've been sitting and staring ahead but seeing nothing!'

'I see many things.'

'You've hardly spoken to me, Pa!'

'I have nothing to say.'

'That's not true. You're worried stiff because the best of the highland is being handed out to the Italians tomorrow and I want to know what's going on in your mind. I want to know why Mr Christie says he thinks you're getting ready to move away and why I don't know anything about it.'

'Christie's guessing. He's just looking for an excuse to make conversation with you.'

'I want to know what you're brooding about. I want to know because I've got a right to know what's going to happen to us.'

'Use your head, Miriam,' I said. 'There is nothing a silkworm can eat on this highland, there is no water here for a steam sawmill. What's to become of us depends on our patience because we're waiting for the government to come to its senses. The meagrest hope I have is that I will be granted one of the allotments tomorrow and get dwelling rights on it. But whether I get one or not, I'm not moving anywhere else because I have now earned my dwelling rights here.'

'How many allotments are there?'

'Except for the two allocated to the sawmill, I counted twelve.'

'How many of the Italians are entitled to lots?'

'According to my calculations, ten of them should get land. Or so-called land, if one can believe Christie that all this is just a formality. I don't think all the bachelors will get lots. Canovi joined them on the way here and only filled in his papers at Knysna. Luigi Lucinetti and Borolini and Taiani and America were odd-jobbers where they came from, leaf shredders and shed cleaners. According to Christie they came here just as odd-jobbers.'

'You're beginning to know their names, Pa.'

'It seems best to stick to their surnames because half of them seem to have the same first name. If it's not Pietro, it's Domenico or Jo-soapy.'

'Not Jo-soapy, Pa, *Giuseppe*!'

'There are some that sound almost exactly the same as another – Robolini and Borolini. Or have I got it wrong?'

'No. Robolini is Giuseppe Robolini and his wife is Vittoria. Robolini is taller and much older than Borolini. Borolini isn't married.'

'The way I see it, the only real silk farmers among them are Fardini, the eldest whose hair is turning grey, then Robolini and Ilario Grassi and Pietro Cruci, husband of Mariarosa, and also that one with the blue eyes, what's his name again?'

'Cuicatti.'

'Cuicatti. I reckon Tomé and Mangiagalli and Coccia will also get land. Perhaps Giovanni Pontiggia. Add that up, and you have ten with two over which gives me a slight chance. Christie gets one too, of course.'

Miriam got up to make us some fresh coffee. 'Have you noticed that Cuicatti is courting that lively little Fardini girl, Luigia?'

'What? She's but a blooming child!' I said. I knew nothing about it.

'She's thirteen.'

'Why doesn't her father boot him away from her? I'll get Christie to talk to him.'

'Don't be silly, Pa. Her father's name is not Silas Miggel.'

'That's right. And how many times have I told you not to be so friendly with the bachelors?'

114

'Do you want me to go around with a long face all day, Pa? These are good people, Pa, and I'll miss them when they go away.'

'Then I better pray harder for that day to dawn on us soon.'

'Do you realise how cold it is in those tents, Pa? Don't you feel just a little sorry for them?'

'No. It's the government that must feel sorry for them since winter and the real cold is still to come.'

'I wish you could hear how many Dutch words they already know. Especially the women. The day the bigfeet drove them all in here, I taught them a few of the ordinary, everyday words just to pass the time; then on our way to the village this morning, Giuditta and Mariarosa and Anna Fardini wanted to know the names of some of the trees.'

'Don't bother. There's no need for them to learn Dutch.'

'Did you know that it's mostly the Fardini family that plays the music?'

'How many Fardinis are there? It seems to be at least a hundred.'

'It's the father and mother and six children, three boys and three girls. Antonia and Giuditta are the two that got married shortly after they arrived. Pietro Fardini, the father, plays the violin and Antonia plays the mandolin. The others sing. Mr Christie says Petroniglia Grassi is the best singer of them all, but she hasn't sung since they stole her child.'

'I'm far from sure that the child was stolen.'

'Don't say that, Pa.'

We didn't go to bed. Miriam fetched the sewing basket and started on the darning. 'Light another candle, you'll get cross-eyed,' I said, but in the end I got up to do it.

'Pa, did you know that they have a hidden child with them?'

My thoughts were miles away at that moment, and I was sure I hadn't heard her properly. 'What did you say?'

'A hidden child. Mr Christie says he's not on their papers. It's an extra one they brought and hid till they got here. He and Mr White only discovered about it at Knysna.'

'What are you talking about? What child?'

'Felitze, Pa. His own surname is Radulfini and Robolini says he is the child's uncle. His parents are waiting in Italy to come out here too; Robolini was to send them the money as soon as the first cocoon harvest was in, and in the meantime they've brought Felitze with them. He's so sweet, Pa, I've told Mr Christie that I'm going to keep him.'

'You leave him alone.' I didn't like this.

I got up and walked outside. The stars of the Scorpion were clear in the sky; the bright one in the head was yellow like a lantern's flame. I could hear Portland's dog barking in the distance; when one could hear Portland's dog as far as the highland, there was bad weather on the way. Don't think of the day ahead, I said to myself; let them hand out every bit of the highland, let them carry on, Silas Miggel was not stupid. Fine, I had always known that I lived on Crown land, a man does not hide the truth from himself. Over the years, I had even thought that if White were to place a family or two of British immigrants down at the foot of the highland, it wouldn't necessarily have meant that I would have had to leave the highland: I would still have been able to keep Miriam apart at the top end. I always got on well with the English. But I hadn't thought White would turn up with a bunch of Italians. What if the government didn't send them a ship? What then? A tree once fell on me in Lily Bush.

Miriam joined me outside.

'It's cold, Pa.'

'It is.' There was only one tent in which a candle still burned, the Grassis' tent. 'Did you give Ilario his medicine?'

'I did. Pa?'

'Yes, Miriam?'

'How old are you?'

'I'm in my forty-sixth year. Why?'

'I'm just asking. How old is Mr Barrington?'

'About seventy, I suppose.'

'How old do you think Mr Christie is?'

'How would I know?' Why did she want to know how old Christie was? Had she taken a liking to him?

'How old do you think Giovanni Pontiggia is, Pa?'

'Miriam, what's this all about? How should I know how old he is? It's got nothing to do with me, and nothing to do with you. All I know is that I don't trust that Pontiggia, he has a sly look.'

'How old is Aunt Hannie?'

'Three years older than I am.'

'How old is Josafat Stander?'

'Well into his thirties.'

'And Jacob Terblans?'

'Are you going to work all through the forest now? What is it you want to know?'

'Are you scared of tomorrow, Pa?'

'No.'

SEVEN

THE DRAWING OF the lots took place in front of Christie's office tent. The map was rolled out on the ground again and held down with stones but the wind kept tugging at the corners, tearing the paper. First Christie read out a long account in Italian but nobody seemed to listen to it. Miriam stood with the women, I stood near the map. When Christie finished, he fanned out strips of paper like wing-feathers in his hand and Fardini went forward to make the first draw.

'Numero due!' Christie called out.

'What does that mean?' I asked. I had to know.

'Allotment number two,' he answered brusquely and bent down to draw a line through one of the squares on the east of the map. The *New Road to Knysna* cut right through the middle of lot number two.

Ilario Grassi, still in better health, drew the next wing-feather and got allotment number fourteen, a good piece of land lying crosswise on the highland. Robolini drew allotment number ten, on the west. Cuicatti drew number three and the moment he saw that it was lying in the forest among the trees, he threw down the slip of paper and walked away. Immediately afterwards Coccia drew number eight which also lay inside the forest and did the same. Tomé drew number twelve; Mangiagalli number one and then Pontiggia drew the one next to Cuicatti in the forest, number four, and shrugged. Cruci drew the one below Fardini and the *New Road to Knysna* ran through his lot as well.

There were three allotments left. Three good ones. Especially number thirteen. The silk farmers had theirs, only the four odd-jobbers still stood around, waiting. Twice Christie dropped his pencil; each time he bent down to pick it up, his face was a little redder when he came up. His nerves were in a bad way. Every time he had to mark off an allotment on the map which lay near my feet, he did it hurriedly as though flinching away from me. Before the last ones were drawn, he blew his nose and then wiped and wiped and wiped, and in the end it was Borolini and Taiani he called up to him. Borolini drew number nine, Taiani number eleven. Number thirteen, the best one, Christie put in his own pocket.

I said to myself: Silas Miggel, bite back your tongue, don't let a sound escape from you. *Bite.* I walked right over the map and kept on walking until I got to the house, I walked past the house and into the forest. When I got to Red Alder's sled-path, I turned north in the direction of Brown's Gorge for I had to keep on walking until the fury inside me died down, even if I had to walk until the mountains stopped me. To stand and watch the world beneath your feet being handed out to strangers was no easy thing. I felt like going back to the house, tearing it down, and moving Godknowswhere to hell.

I once had a strange experience with a leopard in Kom's Bush. I didn't tell a soul about it afterwards, I don't think anyone would have believed me. It was shortly after I got married. I was coming through the forest from Deep Walls where I had been to pay my woodcutter's licence when suddenly a fully grown leopard crouched before me in the sled-path. Every day of your life, you walked the forest with ears and eyes ready for the elephants. You hardly ever thought about the leopards; they were either somewhere up in the trees or when you did see one in the underbush, it was just a streak and it was gone. Therefore a man got quite a fright when one of them suddenly appeared before you in a path, especially when you're without a gun. And the leopard stood. And I stood. I looked him right between his yellow eyes, I didn't move. I sent a message right into his head, saying: leopard, don't you dare attack me. He sent me a message back: I'm still deciding. I sent him another one: if you pounce on me, I'll put my fist down your throat and rip out your guts. Never, he said back, *I've* got the claws, *I've* got the teeth.

It could have been an hour, it could have been longer. My eyes burned like fire, but I did not blink. I stood where I stood. The leopard did too. Suddenly a little spotted warbler flew

119

down into a bush growing between us at the side of the path and started scolding noisily like they always do; what he told the leopard, I don't know, but the leopard turned around and walked away.

Always, thereafter, I lifted my hat when I saw a spotted warbler.

No, I wouldn't move away from the highland. I would hold my ground. I would stand where I had always stood. The allotments had been handed out, but that would not stop the winter rains from falling eight days in a row if they wanted to. It would not stop the cold. It would not stop the frost. At the most, the Italians would last out another month in the tents.

And the sawmill? I asked myself. What about the sawmill? With water that's where? I answered myself, and turned round at the place where the lightning had split the kalander years ago. No, I wouldn't run away. The first thing I had to do was to find time to cut more stinkwood before July was over. Perhaps I could cut a little extra and sell it green for the money tin.

If it weren't for Smit who insisted that all the chairs be made from stinkwood, I would seldom have put an axe to a stinkwood tree. Why, I couldn't really say, it was just a feeling I always had inside me about that wood. Cut it, saw it, and it stinks like a red-billed hoopoe does, but all the time you work it there is a sadness about the wood, as though every chair you put down on its legs wants to walk back to the forest to sprout again like the old trees did when they died. The old people always said that every second tree in the forest was a yellowwood and every eleventh tree a stinkwood. There were large tracts of forest where this was no longer true, stinkwood was being felled heavily because its price was better than all the other wood. In Gouna's forest, above the highland, however, there was still plenty of stinkwood trees since very little felling had been done up there.

I was walking home and thinking about the wood when Miriam suddenly came running up to me, shouting: 'Pa, come quickly! They're going to murder Mr Christie!'

'Catch your breath, girl,' I said, 'what's this all about?'

'They are going to kill Mr Christie, Pa!'

'Let them kill him and get it over with,' I said. But she took hold of my arm and started pulling me.

'Please, Pa, something has happened, I can't make out what it is. They're going to kill him!'

I suddenly realised that Miriam wouldn't carry on like that for nothing and started running.

They had pulled up every peg around Christie's house-tent and the canvas lay heaped on him and his belongings. I couldn't make out where the tent-pole was. Every time he wormed himself to the edge of the mess in an effort to get out, one of the Italians was there to tread down the canvas in his face. The ones not helping to keep him under were cheering.

'Signor Miggel! Signor Miggel!' Anna Fardini, eldest of the women, called out when she saw me coming. 'Aiuto! Aiuto!' Help, help.

'What the devil's going on here?' I asked. Cuicatti was the leader and with him was Tomé and Taiani. 'Are you blooming mad?' I shouted at them.

Christie must have heard me for he started calling out to me: 'Mr Miggel! Help me, I'm being suffocated!'

'Get away!' I shouted at Tomé and stepped in front of him to pull Christie halfway out. His shirt and hair were drenched in sweat, his face was as grey as death. 'What's going on here?' I asked him, letting him lie there to get air. He didn't answer me and I turned to the Italians: 'Aren't you supposed to be blooming adults?' I asked the gathering. Had they been children, I might have understood their behaviour.

'Water, Miggel, give me water.'

'I won't give you a drop, or let you get up before I'm told what's going on. There was nothing wrong when I left here, so let's hear it!' Behind me the Italians stepped back a little as if they knew they had to give me a chance to get the truth from Christie. 'Answer me, Englishman!'

'Get me to your house first and protect me, Miggel.'

'I won't do anything before I know what's happened.'

It appeared that some of the silkworm eggs had hatched. Pontiggia had discovered this shortly after the lots had been drawn and the news had swept through the tents like fire. The worms had to have food and the Italians were demanding that Christie should provide it. That was the first half of the story: to get the other half out of him, I had to lift the canvas three times

121

and threaten to smother him myself. Every time I did so, the wretched Italians stood clapping their hands to cheer me on. But I got it out of him in the end: the matter of the mulberry forest had never been resolved. The day they had arrived on the highland, angry and rebellious because the promised mulberry forest was not there, Christie had told them it was behind the mountains – and now they wanted to pack up and move there with the worms.

I felt like lifting my foot and putting it on Christie's neck and keeping it there. I had had more than enough. 'Get up!' I said to Christie and pulled him to his feet. 'Tell them to start packing and strike the tents. I'll go and get wagons and sleds to take you over the mountain because I've had enough of this shit!' I seldom spoke a dirty word, but there comes a time when one can no longer hold one's tongue.

'Please, Miggel, you don't understand the problems I have had to deal with. I was the one that had to calm them down that day, no matter how. It was my honest intention to inform them of the truth later on; it's just that the eggs are not supposed to have started hatching so soon. I was hoping the government would come to a decision long before it happened. You will have to stand by me now. We must tell them the mulberry forest has been felled. Or destroyed by fire.'

'If you think I'm going to help you make up lies, you don't know Silas Miggel yet.'

'But you've got to help me!' He suddenly pleaded like a man without pride. 'Italians are dangerous people, one will look you in the face while another one stabs you in the back. They have knives, you must fetch your gun!'

'You're talking like an old woman, man!' I said. 'Get a hold on yourself. This is the day they're going to hear the last of that blessed mulberry forest and they're going to hear it from *you*. You are going to tell them that you lied to them that day.'

'I can't do that. It wasn't me that started the thing about the mulberry forest; they were told about it in Italy. You must speak to them, Miggel, I'll interpret for you. Tell them I was as misled as they were. Please, Miggel, you've got to do this for me!'

The Italians stood around like a smouldering fire, just waiting to flare up. I knew it was no use talking to Christie any further. 'Call them together,' I said.

When I turned round, Miriam stood there with the little no-man's brat, Felitze, on her hip as if it were hers. 'Put down that child and go home!' I said to her. 'Can't you see I've got enough trouble as it is!'

Getting that mulberry forest out of their heads was like trying to climb a mountain blindfolded on another man's back for how did you speak with a tongue that was not yours? How did you stop a fire from flaring up if you could not reach it yourself? I knew Christie was adding strings of words to what I said because he had to make excuses for himself. When he finally got it out that there was no mulberry forest, not this side of the mountains, not behind the mountains, not anywhere, the Italians crossed themselves and Cruci's wife, Mariarosa, took hold of her hair and started wailing as though in agony. One of the bachelors made a sign with two fingers at Christie which could just as well have been a way of cursing him. Some of them stamped up and down as though they wanted to make holes in the earth with their feet. Anna Fardini came and stood before Christie, legs apart, hands on hips, and the words she spat at him were like venom. Only Petroniglia stood looking on as if she couldn't care whether the worms lived or died.

'Robolini says if they could just save half the worms, it would help, Mr Miggel. They are very expensive eggs. Fardini wants to know if Mr Barrington might perhaps have leaves for them?'

'It's winter time, the trees aren't even budding yet. And apart from that, he has only a few trees and it's too far to fetch leaves from Portland in any case. Tell them that.'

Again I realised that he was telling them far more than I had spoken. At this time he kept on and on until it seemed as though something were beginning to capture their interest: cautiously at first, but then more so and this made me suspicious. 'Mr Christie,' I said, 'what are you telling them?'

'I told them that there are no leaves at Portland, but that Mr White had told me about a wild mulberry in the forest. You, apparently, told him about it.'

I couldn't believe it. Before one fire was put out, he saw fit to start another. 'Englishman,' I said, 'get out of my way before I kick you back in under that tent! You don't know what you're talking about!'

'The worms must be fed, Miggel.' One moment he cowered

123

in fear, the next he was back in charge and his old important self again. 'This could be their salvation, Miggel; the wild mulberry is a chance that cannot be ignored. How far are the trees into the forest?'

'No worm would eat those leaves, stupid!'

'That, Miggel, is for the silk farmers to establish, not you.'

'Mr Christie is right, Pa.' Miriam was suddenly back in the front row with the Italians, the child still on her hip. 'They must decide for themselves what to do.'

I thought I would have a fit. 'Don't you come and interfere, girl! This whole blooming thing is your doing – and I told you to put that blooming child down!'

'Don't shout so, Pa.'

It was a hopeless mess and I, Silas Miggel, was in deep – with no way out. They wanted the wild mulberry but the wild mulberry wouldn't walk out of the forest and shake off its leaves over the worms. I was the one that would have to go and pick the leaves and bring them out to them. Christie stood talking to them, eagerly, but I knew they didn't trust him for their eyes were like stones. They discussed things amongst themselves, they talked it over with Christie, again amongst themselves, then again with Christie until Christie turned to me at last, saying:

'They want you to take them to the wild trees.'

'I beg your pardon? They don't want to go into the forest to cut firewood for themselves, but they'll go in there to look for worm food?'

'Please, Mr Miggel, don't start making trouble again. I've just managed to calm them down.'

If Miriam hadn't cried out when I lifted my arm, I would have knocked him dead, for suddenly *I* was the one that had made the trouble.

Four of the Italians made ready to go into the forest with me: Fardini, Robolini, Cuicatti and Mangiagalli. Robolini stood with a bucket half filled with water; Cuicatti and Mangiagalli carried the ladder.

'Why the ladder?' I asked.

'It's so they can get into the trees should the bigfeet charge them,' Christie said. 'They say they won't go into the forest without the ladder.'

It was a long ladder. Along a sled-path, one might somehow have been able to manage it, but I knew it would be a struggle along a footpath from beginning to end. I didn't say a word, I just took the footpath into the forest. What the bucket with the water was for, I didn't ask. Maybe it was to throw at the bigfeet, I said to myself.

And a struggle it was right from the start: not only with the ladder which forever wanted to go in a straight line when the footpath swerved, but with everything. It wasn't the first time that I had seen people frightened of the forest, but I'd never seen people *that* scared and jittery. If I hadn't kept on talking and driving them on, they would have spent more time standing still to listen and stare into the thickets than they would have walked. Robolini had apparently decided to keep a watch out for the danger that might fall on them from above because his eyes were continually up in the trees so his feet kept tripping over the roots crossing the path. Before we had got halfway, the two with the ladder were sweating heavily: if they didn't have the damn thing on its head, they had it on its side, and round the bends it was backwards and forwards as if it were a giant saw.

'You're going to get yourselves in such a tangle that you'll never get straight again!'

'Sì, sì, signor.' Everything was *sì sì signor.*

It took me almost an hour to get them to Stinkwood Gorge where I knew the wild mulberries grew plentifully in the underbush. When I pulled down the first branch for them, I suddenly had four different beings with me: experts. Men that knew all they had to know. Their eyes were different, their bodies, their hands. They were no longer a bunch of distraught tent-dwellers. Forgotten was the ladder which they had stood up against the nearest tree in case of bigfeet; forgotten was the danger they had been expecting the whole time.

First of all, they just looked at the leaves very carefully. They seemed to like what they saw. Then Fardini took a leaf, tore it from the twig with care, looked at the sap bleeding from the stalk and felt it between his fingers. The others did the same – but they were no longer smiling.

'Non latte,' Cuicatti said to me and shook his head. 'Non latte,' he said again.

'I don't know what you're saying.'

Mangiagalli went down on his haunches and acted as though he were milking a cow. 'Latte, latte,' he said.

There was no milk in the leaves.

'I told you this is not a mulberry as you know it. It's a wild tree.'

They each picked a leaf again, crumpled it, put it in their mouths and chewed with eyes fixed to the forest floor. It was difficult to tell whether the taste was to their liking or not. They spat out the gobs, washed their hands in the bucket, threw away the water, and then picked enough leaves to half-fill the bucket which they then covered with Mangiagalli's coat.

Going back was a little quicker because they were in a hurry and were more handy with the ladder. At the tents, the others received the bucket as if there were gold in it. Fardini shrugged his shoulders and shook his head as if to say they should not expect too much. Then America carefully washed his hands and cleaned his knife, tied a cloth over his nose and mouth and went and sat in the shade and cut the leaves into thin strips.

I followed Fardini to the tent where a muslin cloth had been stretched between four sticks and Cruci, also with cloth over his nose and mouth, was busy lifting the tiny grey-black worms from a bag and on to the cloth with a fine little brush. Making a guess, I would say there were about a hundred worms.

Fardini and Robolini, cloths over the nose and mouth, bent with Cruci over the worm-cradle, talking in a whisper. When America brought the shredded leaves and put them over the worms, it became so quiet all around that you could hear the oriole whistle deep in the forest. In my heart I knew the worms would not take the leaves, but I was still paralysed by one thought: say they opened their mouths and ate, and grew fat to spin cocoons? What then?

America kneeled at the cradle as if in prayer. Robolini, Fardini and Cruci stood motionless, looking and looking. Waiting and waiting. In the end it was Fardini that took the cloth from his face and shook his head. The worms would not eat.

Thank God, was all I could say.

When I got back to the house, the knife was lying on the table which meant that Miriam had gone to set the snares. I was glad. All I wanted was a mug of coffee and a moment of quiet to rest

126

my weary self. It was cold in the house. I made a fire in order to boil some water and warm the house a little. How the Italians kept warm in the tents, I didn't know. All I knew was that without a roof over your head, a blanket was a thin thing. White said the Italians were to be kept calm, but how did you keep people calm when they lay freezing? Why didn't the government put them in houses in the village whilst finding them a ship? I wished I could have talked to them myself, to the Italians, to find out what was going on in their heads. Interpreting was a stupid business. I had known the worms wouldn't take the leaves. I was glad when they didn't, but it was odd to see a man like Fardini staring up into the sky afterwards as if that were the only place where deliverance could still come from. It was just as odd to see the simple-hearted America dig a hole to bury the worms, and when it was done, to see him draw a cross in the dust over the spot with his finger.

The day I gave White my word that I would assist Christie in exchange for my dwelling rights, I hadn't quite known what I was letting myself in for. To take on responsibility for thirty-two foreign souls was no easy thing. I was forever afraid that something would happen to them and that White and the government would come blaming *me* for it. I knew Christie wouldn't stand up for me, he would only fend for himself. What would happen if the children became sick from living in the tents? Mieta could not cure everything, she couldn't perform miracles even if there were people in the forest who believed she could. Perhaps I worried too much because deep down I couldn't yet believe that dwelling rights would really be given to me. And Petroniglia was getting thinner and thinner. No matter if the child had been given away or stolen, her child was what she wanted. If Cape Town hadn't been so far away, I think I would have gone there on foot to fetch the blooming child to put an end to the whole matter. There were days when I got the feeling that some of the bachelors were sniffing the wind and making up their minds in which direction to bolt. What if they got it into their heads just to go off so that when the ship came and White counted the rest, he'd find some missing? What if he then said they couldn't be taken on as they weren't all there? I decided that the solution would be to go and count them at night: together with Fardini's two grown-up sons, Alberto and

127

Giuseppe, there were ten bachelors; six married men; six married women; two young girls – I still had to speak to Fardini about Luigia; seven children plus Felitze, another nuisance and burden. However, if Christie wanted to take his things and go, I wouldn't stop him.

It was almost dark when Miriam came back from the forest, sweet-talking and cajoling me because she knew she was in trouble.

'You're looking tired, Pa. Have you had some coffee yet?'

'I don't want coffee now, it's almost time to eat.'

'I think there's going to be frost tonight, Pa.'

'Yes.'

'I set three snares and I met Uncle Joram and his team up on Gouna's sled-path. He says no one dare cut up in Creek Bush at the moment, there's a wounded bigfoot bull tearing the world apart up there. Apparently, a man from Cape Town shot the bull. Uncle Joram says the bull had Uncle Anro up in a tree for a whole day. Uncle Anro says the bull looks bad, the lead went in at his ribs and came out on its flank.'

'They better find Josafat Stander to shoot the animal then.'

'Maybe he'll recover.'

'Maybe.'

'What if the bull comes this way?'

'He won't get through the gorges if he's in that much pain.'

She put her apron over the water bucket instead of putting it on. She put the plates on the table and then tried wiping the table. She took the bread from the cupboard, but put it back again.

'Miriam, you're not with it. What's the matter with you?'

'Nothing, Pa. I found Pontiggia at the clay furrow.'

'What's he doing at the clay furrow? They have their own place to get water from.'

She became impatient. 'Please listen to what I want to say, Pa! He sat with a piece of the yellow clay in his hands, kneading and kneading. He didn't notice me until I was almost at his feet.'

'What were you doing at his feet? Why didn't you come straight home?'

'Please, Pa! Pontiggia looked desperately unhappy. When he saw me he got up and threw the clay very hard into the water and

128

just walked away. The Italians aren't just angry any more, Pa, I think they've started to panic, or maybe it's hatred I can see in their eyes. What's to become of them, Pa?'

'Mr White himself said there's only one solution and that's a ship.'

'Do you remember the bigfoot you once made me from the furrow's clay, Pa?' she asked, going off on to quite another tangent again.

'I remember.' It was when she had chicken pox and I was at my wit's end to keep her in the house. When I had the bigfoot finished, she still wasn't satisfied because it had no tusks. In the end I had to shoot a bush-pig to get the teeth and meat at the same time.

'Pa?'

'What is it, Miriam?' I could sense she had something on her mind.

'You didn't get one of the lots then, did you?'

'No. I said the hope was a faint one.'

'And now?'

'Now nothing. I will wait. The rain and the cold will drive them away from here in the end. What else is bothering you?'

She stared at the table for long before she answered me. 'I wish I could talk to you.'

'Talk about what? Since when can't you talk to me?'

'There are things one cannot talk to you about.'

'Things like what?'

She looked down at her hands and played with her fingers, then she suddenly asked me a very strange thing: 'Pa, have you ever made up a woman for yourself since Ma died?'

'What?'

'Have you ever made up a woman for yourself?'

I sat there dumbstruck. Where did she get hold of things like that? 'What are you talking about, Miriam?'

'A woman, Pa. Someone you make up. With a body, someone you can talk to, that talks to you, someone that walks with you, someone that's good to you and who you can be good to. You make up that person to be the way you would like a real person to be. It's your secret-woman or secret-man.'

'It's those blooming newspapers Christie brings you to read

when he's finished with them that puts all these things into your head!'

She just kept on. 'All I wanted to tell you was that sometimes you meet someone and suddenly you realise that that is what your secret-person is like, that is how you wanted his face to be and then you no longer have a secret-person, but someone real. And then it makes you very happy.'

I realised what she was saying. I wanted to jump up, grab the gun and go shoot Pontiggia, for who else? 'Miriam, if you get mixed up with one of these Italians, there will be murder!'

'It's not Pontiggia, Pa.'

How did she know I was thinking of Pontiggia? In other words, there *was* someone, she had more or less admitted it. All my intentions of staying calm, of doing the right thing, flew from me. I wanted to take hold of the table and turn it over, plates and all. There were many bachelors at the tents apart from Pontiggia; which one was I to start with?

'Miriam, there's enough trouble on the highland, don't you start any more. Who are you mixed up with?'

'Please, Pa.'

'You know what will happen to you if you don't look after yourself!'

'Pa, listen to me!' she said and started crying. 'The other day, when you said you weren't going to ask me where I had been because you didn't want me to lie to you, I was so relieved because I didn't want to lie to you. Since then, I'd begun to hope that if I talked to you openly, in a nice way, you'd understand and stop watching me all the time as if I were a criminal. I'm not, Pa, and I'm not stupid. Trust me. *Please.*'

'Who have you got yourself mixed up with?'

'You said once that if anyone should ever ask me where the lilies grow, I must turn around and walk away for it's the forest's secret. If anyone goes there, he'll be treading on the forest's heart.'

When I lay on my bed that night, a burden like a mountain lay on top of me. At midnight I still hadn't closed an eye when there was a sudden knock at the door. If it's serious illness at the tents, I said to myself, I'll have to go to the village for help. I wouldn't dare go north in the dark to Creek Bush Island to get Mieta, not with a wounded elephant up there. If it was Christie, looking for shelter, he could go and lie down in the woodshed.

But no one was ill at the tents. It was Josafat Stander. His hair was long, his face unshaved, he wore a buckskin cloak over his clothes against the cold which hung almost to his feet and was tied round the waist with a rope. Gun across his back, knapsack over the shoulder and exhausted to death. Only the reflection of the candle in his eyes betrayed the devil in him.

'If it was daytime now,' I said as I held open the door, 'the Italians would say they were proved right, only robbers and dangerous things keep to forests. Come inside and sit down. Where have you come from at this time of night?'

'Good evening, Uncle Silas.' Miriam stood in the middle door, pale with fright.

'Go and put on your shoes and get something warm round you,' I told her and gave Josafat some water to drink. 'What brings you to my house at this time of the night?' I asked him.

'Food. I've still got to reach Lily Bush, but you must first give me something to eat, uncle. I'll shoot you a couple of buck for the tents later.'

'Put some wood on the fire, Miriam, see that Uncle Josafat gets something to eat.' It was only when he sat down at the table that I noticed how bad he really looked. 'Are you in trouble, Josafat?'

'From a certain point of view I'm always in trouble, uncle. But three days ago a stranger turned up at my place, dragging one leg, breeches torn, leg all wrapped up in bandages and oozing blood. He said a leopard had mauled him and asked if I could help him get to the village since he was weak and had lost a lot of blood. I bent over him and smelt *buck's* blood, not human blood. I didn't say anything about that. I just reassured him, saying I would help him get to the village. Then, when I crept up on him from behind to get a rope round him, there was suddenly nothing wrong with the leg. He fought like an ox and I realised I had captured a warder. I secured his hands but left his legs free and then I set out with him straightaway. I took him through Millwood and up into Skuins Bush, there I turned east and kept all along Dwars Mountain's foothills till we were in Kees's Bush and from there to the other side of Buffalo's Neck and Yzer

131

Neck. By that time, two days had passed and he could hardly speak. I made him walk another day and then tonight, just after dark, I propped him up against a hedge in the main street of the village.'

'No wonder you're done for, you could have killed both of you.'

'He won't be back in the forest for some time.'

'He came here, asking about you.'

'He was everywhere asking for me.'

Miriam put bread and mealies and sweet potatoes on a plate for him but he seemed almost too tired to chew.

'Josafat,' I said, 'I realise you're just about to fall from that chair, but I'm in grave trouble on the highland. *All* kinds of trouble,' I added so Miriam could hear.

'They should take these people away from here, uncle, very cold weather's on the way.'

'I agree with you. But my question is, *when* are they going to take them away. The stupid Englishman that's been appointed their foreman has used up endless pots of ink writing to Cape Town about matters; from the village, Mr White keeps on writing letter after letter but one seldom hears of an answer. In the meantime, troubles lie heaped at my door. And I can't even tell you about certain other troubles I have.' I looked straight at Miriam when I said that because I wanted her to know I meant her.

'Perhaps you should move away from here, uncle.'

'Never! I'm not moving. This is my home. I have another plan: you're a man that has contact with ships, so you must find me a ship that will take them as far as Cape Town.'

'Pa!'

'Stay out of this, Miriam. The water's boiling, make the coffee.'

'You have no right to do this, Pa!'

'Miriam!'

'No ship will carry them for free, uncle.'

'I'm not stupid, I know that. If I give you my gun and shot, and you shoot me a couple of bigfeet for the tusks, I'm sure a captain will take them to Cape Town for that?'

'Pa, you're out of your mind if you think you'll get away with it!'

132

'I'll hang a label round each one's neck with the government's address on it,' I said. I swore I would. Miriam continued to protest but Josafat thought it might be possible and promised to find out if a ship would take them in exchange for some ivory. I liked the idea. Something told me it could work.

I asked Josafat to stay until dawn, but he declined; once a man has grown wild, he stays wild. It was only Josafat Stander who would have dared to go out into the wilderness in the middle of the night. I took the candle and walked with him to the start of the footpath so that at least I knew he had found it. Then I made a round of the tents and all was quiet. If I could get them as far as Cape Town, to the government's door, I had no doubt they would be put on the fastest ship back to their country.

On the Monday morning, Christie gave the order for the mulberry cuttings to be planted. I told him that I was convinced his brains had been fitted back to front.

'It's the government's orders and must be carried out, Miggel.'

'Then the government's brains are facing the same direction as yours,' I said. 'Why can't they come to a decision about these people? Why don't they send someone to come and see what's going on here? Why don't they let me show them how near to the surface the clay lies and then they can ask themselves how the devil a mulberry can take root in it. What's keeping them from coming to a decision?'

'Decisions like these are never easy, Miggel. And I wouldn't be satisfied with just any decision about the Italians either.'

The man's air of importance made me want to spit. 'They want a ship to take them home, they're not interested in what satisfies you,' I said. 'Just as a mulberry won't take root here, they won't either.'

But he was determined that the mulberries should be planted. Down at the foot of the highland where, according to him, their common land was – what he called their commonage. I didn't ask him how he reckoned they would get water down there should one take root. He was the expert. I went and skinned two buck for the tents and then I started on a chair.

Late in the afternoon on the Tuesday, the Italians planted the last of the cuttings with reluctant hands. But every row was straight and neat. One thing I had come to notice: when they did something, they did it well. They carried water down there until dark to get the cuttings thoroughly soaked.

'Not from my furrow, you don't!' I had to keep watching and warning them.

On the Thursday, so help me, White had twelve skeletons, called oxen, driven to the highland for the ploughs and on that very first night they ate every single mulberry cutting to the ground. On Friday, two oxen were missing and Christie started them ploughing. By the evening, the first plough had broken. On Saturday, the second plough broke and two more oxen were missing.

'Why do they struggle so much, Pa?'

'Because Christie doesn't want to listen to me. Let them struggle.'

On a bitterly cold Monday the third plough broke and another ox was missing.

'You must go and look for the oxen, Miggel,' Christie came and told me.

'And where do you suggest I start looking for them, mister?' I asked. By that time, things were bad between him and me.

'I don't care where you start looking. Those oxen are government property and must be found.'

'There are enough oxen left with which to break the last of the ploughs. After that I suggest you slaughter one for the Italians so that they can eat properly for a change. I can't keep on supplying them with meat any more.'

I was like a blooming bird with thirty-three mouths in the nest to feed, plus Christie as well. The colder the winter got, the hungrier they seemed to be. The weekly shillings hardly covered the provisions from the store: onions seven shillings a bag; meal two pounds a bag; eggs two shillings and two pennies a dozen *if* you could get any; butter and lard, potatoes at ten shillings a bag; milk by the pail from Stewart's stable halfway to the village so the children could have milk. Tobacco, warm stockings, extra blankets, a better bed for Ilario, shoes for America and Coccia, clothes for some of the children, sugar and coffee. They were never satisfied with the coffee, it was never strong enough for their taste. Garlic; tomatoes we could no longer get; olive oil by the can – I don't know if they drank it.

134

Fardini kept a record of the money, Christie wasn't allowed near it. On Thursdays, fish or eels had to be caught for Fridays. I caught the eels myself since it was too much of a bother to try and get them down to the waterholes, because they wouldn't go without the ladder. Towards the end of June, I made two fishing lines and took Lucinetti and Taiani west of the village where the Knysna River flows into the lagoon, and taught them to dig for bloodworms and catch fish. I made a gin trap for America and taught him to listen where the francolins whistled at dusk before going to roost, and in the mornings to set the gin there on the forest's edge and mind it all day long. Sometimes he caught a few, sometimes he caught nothing, but every feather helped. Every sweet potato the woodcutters sent, every buck Josafat Stander shot.

Less than a week after he had turned up at my house that night, he was back to tell me that he had found a captain prepared to take the Italians to Cape Town for four elephant tusks. I thought Miriam would have a fit. And when I went and told Christie that I had found them a place on a ship as far as Cape Town, I thought he would eat me, clothes and all. The next day he hurried to the village to report me to White, and White sent *two* warders and a constable to tell me that if I wanted to land in the biggest trouble on earth, I should go ahead and take the law into my own hands. The government would decide about them. Not me.

'When?'

'It's a matter of patience.'

They tied me up with legal knots so that I couldn't move. Every time Christie came back from the village and I asked him if there was any news yet, the answer was the same: 'No.'

July came. Sometimes I managed to catch a bush-pig in a snare and this made the women happy for they made a kind of sausage from the meat, and melted down the fat. Anna Fardini always sent Miriam and me some sausage as well and it was very tasty. Christie said they were old hands at making sausage. But the funny little flat cakes with stuff inside which they made just about every day tasted so awful that no human being should have been able to eat it. But they did. And with a piece of dough, they could do things I had never seen anyone do in my life. They pulled it and stretched it and twisted it until it looked like a pile of thinly cut thongs, and then they boiled it in water. A bag of meal didn't last long at the tents.

Food, food, food. Firewood by the load. Just after the second lot of heavy rains, I said to Christie that I would continue no longer; I wanted three men to help cut and haul out the wood. Christie took no notice. Instead, he came twice to warn me that the firewood was getting low, asking me what was I going to do about it. I said nothing. On the Thursday they made their fire with the last of the twigs and hardly managed to heat the water for their coffee. I was busy boiling up bones to make glue and I took no notice. Christie came about the wood, Robolini came about the wood with the ten words he had learned, Mariarosa came about the wood, Fardini came about the wood. I took no notice but I said to Miriam that I had better sleep in the woodshed that night for not a single piece of my wood would be taken. In the end she was in tears, offering to go and help me cut the wood.

'Sit still, girl,' I said.

At midday Christie turned up with America and Taiani and Coccia and the ladder. They had offered to come and help me cut the wood, but should anything happen to any one of them, Christie warned me, I wouldn't see an end to the trouble that I would get into. I didn't say a word, I just fetched the ox and yoked it to the sled and told the three of them to follow me, it was getting late.

I took Gouna Ridge's sled-path to get to a fallen quar that I knew would be dry enough for firewood. Not far into the forest, we came on toadstools which were clustered along the path on the damp forest floor like they did every year at that time. Suddenly the three Italians cheered up as though a miracle had shot up there. Before I could stop them, they started picking. The more I told them it was devil's bread, that they must not touch them, the more they picked. They even took off their coats to carry them in. It had taken old Karel Swart three days to die on Barnard's Island after eating toadstools. By the third day, two men had had to hold him down so that he did not fall off the bed as he raged in agony. They say it's a terrible death. And the blooming Italians kept on picking.

After we'd brought out the wood, I went and told Christie about old Karel, but Christie was sour and busy writing letters, he hardly looked up. I told him they had picked toadstools, he must go and talk to them! He replied that they had grown up with toadstools, I must leave them to it. So I left them. And as I walked home, I said to myself: well, let them die then and get it over with.

I thought it best not to tell Miriam about the impending disaster. We ate. We went to bed. But as I lay there in the dark, I started wrestling with my conscience like old Karel had wrestled with death itself. I could have taken the toadstools away from them. I could have *made* Christie warn them. In the end, I must have got up a dozen times during that night to go to the tents and listen whether they were still sleeping or whether they had already started the battle. Every time a child cried, I stood waiting until it was quiet again. There were moments when I imagined them lying buried at the foot of the highland, and felt peace return to the world around me again. I knew it was a sin to think things like that, but I couldn't help myself – and, on top of it, I hoped that they had given Christie some to eat as well.

However, they were all still there the next morning. The whole blooming lot of them.

It was bitterly cold. Christie came back from the village once again without hope or news of the ship. I said to myself: Silas Miggel, you've got to hold out, somehow things must come to a head. Every third or fourth day, I saw to it that fresh bedding-bush was cut for the floors of the tents. For days on end, the snares stayed empty but I didn't worry about that too much since I knew they had slaughtered an ox. I had found the hide. And when Willem of Elias van Rooyen came to borrow a whetstone from me, he said he had seen John Barrington buying an ox from two strangers just outside the village, he reckoned they looked like two of the Italians.

I had no idea what was happening over at Portland. There was many a day when I wanted to kick my pride aside and go back to work there for a day or two a week because I needed the wages more and more. But I could not bring myself to go. There were not enough days in the week and I had to keep an eye on Miriam.

One morning shortly before the end of July, however, Hal again arrived on the highland. It was a Monday. He said his mother had sent him, not his father. She wanted to know if I

137

would not please come and help out, Mr Barrington was not at all well and everything was at a standstill.

'Where's John?' I asked him.

'He's gone to George with a load of wood, uncle. Prices are believed to be better there.'

'Tell your mother that the ship still hasn't come to fetch the Italians yet, we're all still waiting. I can't get away from the highland until that happens.'

'My father is sick, uncle. Very sick. We had to get the doctor from the village twice last week.'

Suddenly, I found it very strange that Miriam hadn't said a word about Barrington being so sick when she had got home from Portland the day before. Almost every Sunday she dressed herself up nicely and went to spend the day with Imar and Gabrielle. I had no choice: I asked Hal straight out whether Miriam had been to Portland the day before. I had to know. He said she hadn't been there for months.

Years before, a very serious thing once happened to me up in Lily Bush. Miriam was still small, not yet five. When I was felling, I always tethered her up with a long rope so that she had enough slack to play without getting in the way of a falling tree. But on this particular day, I had been persuaded by her stubbornness and had left her loose. When the tree had started to fall, I had seen her coming through the underbush on the other side, and all I remembered afterwards was that I had started shouting and running. Whether the tree had knocked me to the ground, or whether I had stumbled, I don't know; when I got my senses back, I was lying with my face on the ground between the ferns and the tree was lying across my legs. It was not a very big tree, but it was an ironwood and as heavy as a mountain, for ironwood is ironwood. When Jan Helgard ended up under the yellowwood that time, we dug him out before he had time to have a proper fright, but there were six of us to do the digging. When I lay there under the ironwood, all I had to help me was a tiny child who was screaming her breath away. It was no use calling for help, there wasn't a soul for miles around to hear me. And the child was too small to send to the nearest island to fetch help, all she could do was drag the axe to within my reach and fetch water from the stream to pour over my head

138

when I was about to pass out. I dug myself out with the axe-head. It took hours. Afterwards I was so bruised and hurt that I had to crawl all the way home on my hands and knees, the child on my back. Fortunately not a single bone in my legs was broken.

When Hal told me that Miriam hadn't been to Portland for months, it felt like the day the ironwood fell on me. I was so horrified, I couldn't think straight. Miriam wasn't at home when Hal told me since she had gone to the village with Petroniglia to enquire about the child. Perhaps that was for the best because it gave me time to calm down and think of a way I could get out from under the tree. And I must have been given help from Above that day, for when she got home, I didn't say anything. Not a word. I knew what I had to do.

When it was Sunday again, I let her get dressed and go off as usual. Spying was the work of a warder and warders didn't have work to do, they were spies. But that day I lowered myself and became a spy because I had to. I had to relieve the anxiety and doubt about my own daughter. Things could not go on like that any longer.

She went straight into the gorge along Portland's footpath. At the river, her footprints turned north and shortly after that, just before the marshy stretch, I thought I would collapse for, hanging over a bush, was her dress and under it her shoes. I had to crouch down to give myself time to recover from the most terrible feeling that had come over me. Was my daughter a harlot? I didn't want to ask the question, but I had to. I didn't want to follow her any further; at that moment, I wished that darkness would cover her up because I feared the light too much. I wanted to keep my beautiful, hardworking, cheerful Miriam whole and turn away from the Miriam I didn't know or understand.

But I did not turn back. I went on to where I found her. With Pontiggia. She was wearing one of her old dresses and was sitting on a boulder by the water while he was moulding a huge lump of clay with his hands. She sat there staring away into the sky as though seeing something so beautiful that it made her glow all over – and it was a Miriam I did not know.

When she had told me that it wasn't Pontiggia, I had believed

139

her. I believed her because I had brought her up never to lie. And because she had told me it wasn't Pontiggia, I didn't take too much notice when he sometimes hung around her. As a matter of fact, I had started distrusting Taiani more than him. The day Miriam and two of the Fardini girls went to watch Pontiggia clip and trim the wild elder up at the clay furrow until it was shaped like a bird, I didn't call her back to the house, I let her sit there with them for almost half a day. About a week after that, I walked up to the furrow one afternoon and came across the graven image of a woman standing two feet high, rising from the clay and still wet, so recently had she been formed. Naked. There was even a navel in the rounded belly. The nipples. The bones under the flesh of the hips. Everything. Not even I, Silas Miggel, a man who had been married for two years, had ever looked upon a woman that naked. She stood with her hands behind her back, her head down as though looking deep into the water, and I stood rooted there as if my own body had become clay. I wanted to step forward to push her over, but something stopped me. All I did was to pick a few sprigs from a nearby bush with which I covered her shame. I knew it was Pontiggia's work. That night we had a shower of rain and mercifully melted her down, but I told Miriam to stay away from Pontiggia.

If I had found her with Sias van Rooyen down at the river that Sunday, or with Martiens, or with John or Hal, I could have driven them off to where they belonged, but where did I drive Pontiggia? I couldn't even lash at him with my tongue. I stood there in the underbush, not twenty yards away from them, and the ironwood lay across my heart. There was no digging out. I could go home and fetch the gun and come back and shoot but something warned me that it would be Miriam I would wound, not him.

I turned around without a twig snapping beneath my feet and went home. I was as far down as a man could get, but my mind was clear. I knew what I had to do. I should have done it the first day the Italians arrived on the highland. I went and fetched the sled from behind the woodshed and dragged it right up to the door. Then I waited.

Shortly after midday, Pontiggia came past on his way to the tents. I did not return his wave. Miriam came back hours later, best dress over the old one, shoes nicely back on her feet. It was only when she saw the sled that she stopped in her tracks.

'Why's the sled standing at the door?' she asked.

'I'm waiting for midnight, I'm waiting for the Sabbath day to pass.'

'Pa?'

'Then you start packing. At daybreak I will yoke the ox and I'll take you to Creek Bush Island to stay with your Aunt Hannie until the ship comes.'

Her whole body seemed to stiffen. 'Has something happened, Pa?'

'Don't ask me if something has happened. At midnight you pack your things and as soon as it's light I'm taking you to Creek Bush.'

'I'm not going.' It was like a tree that said: cut me, but I won't fall.

'Miriam, you're going to Creek Bush Island.' I was the axe and she the tree; I would cut until she fell, for like her mother she would not die. I would put the deepest forest gorges between her and Pontiggia.

'I'm staying here, Pa. I'm not going anywhere.'

'Is this the day then that you are going to defy me?'

'Yes, Pa. I'm staying on the highland, I'm staying here with you. I cannot go away from you.' She wanted to soften me up.

'You can come back when the Italians have gone.'

'What has happened here, Pa? When I left this morning, you were fine, now you're behaving like someone who is out of his mind.'

'Perhaps you should tell me where you have been all day.' I asked it as innocently as I could. But she must have felt the wind change, for her eyes were suddenly alert. 'Have you been to Portland, Miriam?'

At first she remained silent, watching me closely. Then she said: 'No, Pa.'

'Did you go to Portland last week?'

'No, Pa.'

The worst of it was that she didn't appear guilty or frightened. It was as if she had decided on the truth because it was the only tree she could find shelter behind.

'When were you last at Portland?'

141

'I can't remember.'

'Is there something between you and Pontiggia?' I could no longer stop myself.

'Not the way you think.'

'What am I thinking?'

'I don't know. I only know it's not the way you think it is.'

'Go and pack your things.'

'You can't drive me away from the highland.' She stood her ground. The tree would not fall. She walked past me into the house and to her room; it was as though she had turned her back on me.

EIGHT

ON THE TWENTY-NINTH of August, on a Monday, a warder brought the news that the child had been put on a ship in Cape Town the day before. She was on her way. The name of the ship was the *Natal* and it would anchor first at Mossel Bay, reaching Knysna on the Wednesday morning.

'What is the date today?' I asked the warder. I knew quite well what it was, but I just wanted him actually to say it.

'The twenty-ninth of August, uncle.'

'Right. Can you remember when the Italians arrived here on the highland?'

'No, uncle.'

'On the eleventh day of June. When I counted the days yesterday, it was seventy-nine days ago. Eighty today.'

'There's nothing I can do about it, uncle. Just don't stop watching for any signs of smallpox amongst them, Magistrate Jackson is very concerned about the smallpox.'

I threw a piece of wood I had in my hand at the wretch, and had I hit him, he would have been dead. Eighty days' tension and frustration was in my body, and the man seemed most cross that I had thrown the wood at him.

'You could have hit me, uncle!'

'Get out of my sight.'

'You're looking for trouble, uncle. I'm going to report you.'

'I told you to get out of my sight.' I had to pick up a second piece of wood before he understood.

So Catarina Grassi was on her way. Eighty days of rumours and false promises were at an end. One day they told us that the child had been taken away from Tomasso and put in the care of two English ladies until the next ship sailed to Knysna. Then we

143

heard that the child was back with Tomasso again because the English ladies couldn't speak Italian. Next thing was the child didn't have money for her fare and so White had to write to the government to ask that she be sent on free passage because her parents and the others had been sent on free passage all the way to Knysna. Then came the news that the child had again been taken away from Tomasso and this time put under the care of two immigrant ladies on their way to Knysna. And so it went on, week after week, until I began to wonder if the child even existed.

In the meantime, Petroniglia got as thin as a plank. And Catarina was not her only sorrow either; Monica, her eldest child, a mere fourteen years old and the one that was supposed to help her with the other three children, had started running after one of the bachelors, Canovi. Canovi was a stranger that had joined them somewhere along the route from Italy. A man from nowhere. I told Christie there was no future in it and he must talk to them, but he refused. And then every two weeks or so I had to fetch Mieta to come and get Ilario on his feet again.

When the warder came to say that Catarina was at last on her way, I, Silas Miggel, received the news alone because Christie was in Cape Town. But at least there was hope that, at last, things had begun to move. The day he left, I told him the first thing he was to do when he got to Cape Town was to see that the child was put on a ship. The actual reason for his going to Cape Town, however, was to see the government face to face and ask them what had happened to the ship that all the Italians were waiting for in misery at the tents. If it hadn't been for the sun that warmed and dried them during the day, they would have moulded together with the canvas during those winter months. Every morning the women stooped a little more when they came out of the tents to make the fire to get the children warm. There were times when the rain kept them in their tents for five, six days running. How they stayed alive through that winter, I don't know. Things couldn't keep on like that. Letters upon letters were written, and nothing happened. I began to wonder if the government existed.

I didn't go over to the tents with the news of Catarina's coming. I sat down and began to finish the last of the six chairs I was working on. Before dark the money had to be in my hand.

Of the eighty pounds that had been in the tin the day the Italians arrived, only twenty were left. Silas Miggel was on his way to ruin. Again and again I had to put my hand in the money tin in order to buy provisions from the store, for the wood licence, shoes for Miriam, loans to Christie because not a penny of the ten pounds a month he had been hired for had been paid out to him yet. Letters upon letters were written, but nothing happened. Just like the ship. Every time he went and complained to White, he was told that the matter was being investigated, it was a case of time and patience. Just like the ship.

I no longer asked what had become of my dwelling rights. Dwelling rights I had assumed because I had more than earned them. What worried me most was what would happen the day the last penny went from the money tin.

Eighty days of waiting. And now Christie was in Cape Town. The ten pounds he had needed in order to get there, he had borrowed from me. But when the news about Catarina arrived, I thought that if this is what he accomplished in one week, I would concede the ten pounds willingly for surely he could accomplish the rest as well.

'Things cannot go on like this, Miggel,' he had said to me on a Friday in the middle of August. He had been to the village, and once again there had been no post for him. Not a word about the child, not a sign of his money, not a word about the ship. He hadn't been able to see White who was away at Kruis River seeing to the British immigrants there. White never came to Gouna's highland to see the Italians. I had endlessly asked him to come and see what was going on, I had pleaded with him. I had asked him a dozen times to write to the Cape requesting that they send somebody to come, but no. 'There now remains only one thing I can do, Miggel,' Christie told me that afternoon, 'and that is to go to Cape Town personally to plead my case.'

'Not *your* case, the Italians' case,' I had to correct him. I always had to correct him.

'That is what I meant.'

'At last you are showing some sense. If I were you, I would have been in Cape Town long ago.' Miriam came in from the cabbage patch and hung her bonnet behind the door. 'Make Mr Christie some coffee,' I told her.

145

'Are you friends again for a change?' she asked in Dutch, putting the water on to boil.

'No. But it seems as if his head has started to work at last. Make him some nice strong coffee.'

'The Italians have given you a taste for strong coffee, haven't they?'

I didn't reply to that.

Christie sat there as if he didn't have the will to lift a hand any more, his clothes were no longer neat and ironed like they had been when he came first to the highland; all his energy had disappeared.

'I can't handle them any more, Miggel, they're perpetually angry and rebellious.'

'At least they played their music again last night,' I reminded him.

'Yes. And afterwards they surrounded my tent, demanding day and date from me when the ship was coming to take them back. They insulted me, saying I have no friends in high places to do me favours, saying that is why I too am sitting in a tent in the wilderness like a barbarian. On the other hand, while we're waiting for a decision about them White expects me to see that the terms under which they were recruited are honoured. The government expects that an attempt at least should be made to start a silk industry here.'

'Why do you stand for all this? Why are you still here?' This was something I had wanted to ask him for some time.

'I'm not the kind of person that leaves a task half done. I have my pride and responsibility. Also, the government owes me money, and there is the land that has been allocated to me. Should the Italians get their free passage back and I am sent to accompany them again, I would most certainly consider returning here to make use of my land.'

'Forget it, you'll never survive here. Did you write and tell the government that the last of the eggs had also hatched, and that they were buried as well?'

'I did. But what good did it do? My health is deteriorating, Miggel. It's inhuman to expect me to live in a tent through all this cold and rain.'

Miriam swung round from where she was standing. 'What about the Italians? What about the children?' she asked him.

'Italians are tough people. If you could see the tunnels which they have dug through the mountains in their country, you'd know what I mean. Countries like America have imported thousands of Italians to build them their railways simply because they are so hardened from digging tunnels.'

'This lot in the tents here don't look like tunnel diggers to me,' I said.

'That's correct, they are silk farmers, but they still come from a tough people.'

'A tent is a tent, mister, it doesn't matter over whose head it's pitched. I think it's a good idea that you've decided to go to Cape Town, maybe it will help to get them away from here. Go on the post-cart, they say that it only takes thirty-six hours to reach Cape Town.'

'I haven't received any salary yet. I haven't a penny to my name.'

'But you always manage to find a penny from somewhere for a blooming newspaper when you go to the village. I've also asked you I don't know how many times not to give them to Miriam when you're finished with them, she just fills her head with all kinds of rubbish.'

'Don't be silly, Pa.'

'I'm not being silly. One can scarcely believe what a man says with his mouth these days, let alone what he writes down on paper. In future, you must put them in the fire,' I said to Christie. 'Or better still, don't buy them.'

'Be reasonable, Miggel. At the moment newspapers are my only link with civilisation. You people have no idea how backward you are in this colony – and I don't just mean this confounded forest.'

'Let the forest alone and see that you get to Cape Town. Go and find out on which days the post-cart runs.'

'I prefer to travel by ship.'

'Then get on a ship, but whichever way you go, go soon. See that you get to the government and tell them that mulberry trees won't grow here, tell them that the Italians want to go home, tell them that Catarina must get to her mother. Tell them, too, that Silas Miggel says he has had enough of everyone's stupidity. You go and tell them that, don't leave out a word.'

'I am quite used to negotiating, Miggel.' He was suddenly his

147

old important self again. 'I won't come back until I have had a chance to fully state my case, nor before I've received absolute satisfaction.'

'Not *your* case, the *whole* case! From the beginning to where it is now.'

'That is what I meant.'

'Miriam, fill Mr Christie's mug and stir in a lot of sugar, he's going to need plenty of strength.'

'*And* money to get to the Cape with,' she said teasingly, and in Dutch.

Although I worried about Miriam constantly, things between her and me were fine so long as I didn't meddle with what went on inside her. The Sunday after I had found her with Pontiggia down by the river, she got dressed quite unconcernedly and came to where I was sitting outside with the Bible to say goodbye.

'I've made your food.'

'Where are you going?'

'You can come with me if you want to, I'm going to Portland. I'm not lying to you, I've never really lied to you. It was you who *assumed* I was going to Portland every Sunday.'

'Where did you go then?'

'To the lilies.'

'Don't give me riddles for answers, Miriam.'

'I must go now, Pa.'

She did go to Portland that day. When she came back, she had a pitcher of milk that Mrs Barrington had sent over for the Italians, and a message from Barrington saying that I needn't come back to Portland again, they were getting on splendidly without me. I knew that wasn't true.

Where Miriam disappeared to at other times, I didn't know. Sometimes Pontiggia was at the tents when I went to see, sometimes he wasn't.

On the day that Christie set off with his case in his hand to walk to the village and get on the ship, I could not watch him go without a feeling of apprehension. Christie was Christie, but without an interpreter it would be extremely awkward if things really went wrong. I foresaw no problems so long as nothing untoward happened. The children already knew many Dutch

148

words that Miriam had taught them in the so-called school she kept for them under the kalander tree behind the house. I told her again and again to stop bothering but she wouldn't listen and the children now liked their lessons. In the end I put my foot down, and stipulated that there should be 'school' no more than three times a week and on condition that the children didn't come near my fences or into my house. Or went into the forest, for they were now in danger of losing their respect for it. I had no intention of searching for lost brats. In fact, the 'school' helped to keep them busy and out from under everybody's feet. There was plenty to do for the women: every second day, they carried all their belongings out of the tents, aired them, and carried them back in again. For the rest of the time, they were forever preparing food and doing the washing.

Christie left on the Friday. On the Monday, the first problem cropped up. Robolini, myself and four of the others were cutting branches for stacking a fence around a vegetable patch on Fardini's allotment. We had to plant some kind of crop on some of the allotments; on Robolini's we had already fenced a little patch and his mealies were standing finger-high. We couldn't make too many gardens, however, because on the highland every mealie or pumpkin or whatever had to have a fence around it if you didn't want the bucks and bush-pigs eating everything that was planted. Apart from that, you had to plant according to the water available: if the rains stayed away, what water there was had to be shared among the vegetable patches – and my patches had first right to the water. I made that clear to them. I didn't get a shilling a day from the government like they did. And every sod that was turned needed manure as well. Fortunately, they learned quickly never go to the village without a sack and a spade; the main street was long, and every horse or ox that went up or down meant a good bit of dung.

Cuicatti and Taiani had exchanged lots so that Cuicatti could have one out in the open where crops could be planted, instead of one that ran into the forest. Taiani said he didn't mind where his so-called allotment was, if the ship didn't turn up before Christmas, he was leaving anyway. I told Christie to tell him that as long as Silas Miggel was on the highland, not a single Italian would leave before the others, the full number would get on the ship. I had noticed right from the start that Taiani's hands

149

stayed in his pockets and his eyes fixed in the direction of the village; I was surprised that he had agreed to help with the cutting of the firewood.

We were just about finished with the branches for Fardini's fence when Anna Fardini came across to us. From the way she talked and waved her hands, I made out immediately that something was wrong. Fardini's youngest son, Pietro, the eight-year-old who Miriam said was so clever at school, came and interpreted with the words he knew. It transpired that Petroniglia had gone to the village early that morning to enquire about the child, but had not yet returned. She was never usually that late. I hadn't seen her at the tents all day, I had assumed that Ilario was on his back again and that she was with him. Time after time I had made Christie forbid her, in my presence, to go to the village alone, but she would not listen; if she wanted to go, she went. If there was news, one of the constables wrote it down on a piece of paper which she brought to Christie.

'Signor Miggel will look for her?' Pietro asked. The others stood waiting for the answer.

'Yes,' I said, 'Signor Miggel will go and find her and bring her home by the scruff of her neck. I wonder what would happen to you lot if Signor Miggel was not here.'

I was angry. The sun was low down in the west and my body cried out for rest after a whole day of cutting and dragging and stacking the branches. I was in no mood to start out for the village at that time of the day. And not one of the Italians came forward and offered to go; they reckoned the sun was far too low. It was always the same at the end of the day: when the forest grew black with shadows, not one of them dared go far from a tent. They would never get used to the forest. Except for America and Taiani and Coccia, the three who helped me to cut the firewood – on condition that the ladder came with us every day – not one of them ever ventured so much as a foot into the forest.

I went and put on my coat and set out to find Petroniglia. Christie had told me one day that the Italians had felled most of their forests hundreds of years ago. They did not like places such as forests, they liked places of stone. Everything in their country was of stone. Churches, everything. Not small churches like the church in Knysna that was built of stone too, their churches were as big as palaces, Christie said. Covered with graven images. Hundreds of churches, thousands of graven images. Everything made of noble stone. Shining stone. Houses, everything. Streets too. Maybe Christie made it up, or maybe it was true. There were days I wished I could ask Fardini myself; he was not only the eldest amongst them, he had a lot of sense in his head as well.

I asked Christie about Pontiggia one day, and I learned then that Pontiggia was not a silk farmer, but a weaver. A journeyman weaver, Christie called him – a travelling weaver. It made me think of someone who couldn't keep still in one place. According to Christie, a journeyman weaver walked from town to town and wherever he found a vacancy at a loom, he stayed and weaved for a few weeks or months and then moved on again. Apparently he had been quite a well-known weaver around a place called Firenze. He came out with the silk farmers because he thought he would, in time, be able to start a small spinning mill. His brother owned a loom and was to have followed as soon as the cocoon crops started producing. Petroniglia would have worked for him too. She was what they called a throwster: the person who soaked the cocoons in water until the threads came loose and then twisted four or five or more of the threads together to form a single strand with which they could weave.

I found Petroniglia coming up the steep hill on the highland side of Gouna's Drift: step by step, her body leaning into the climb. She didn't see me since she didn't look up. I waited until she was a few yards from me before I spoke.

'Petroniglia!' I said and stopped in front of her. Her hair looked as if it hadn't been combed for at least a week, her shoes were dirty and her shawl was tied round her waist. 'Petroniglia, this is the last time that I come out looking for you.' Whether I myself was too tired for scolding, I couldn't say, I only knew that my words suddenly had no weight to them. She just stood there as though she couldn't care whether she was scolded or not. How did one fight with such a woman? 'This has got to stop,' I said nicely, not scolding. 'If Christie doesn't succeed in getting the child here, you will have to accept that Tomasso is not going to give up the child. You will have to wait until you all return to Cape Town again on your way back, and then you will be able to fetch her yourself. But till then, you must look after Ilario and your other children. And after yourself. It's no good my seeing to it that you get the liver and best of the meat when we share out a buck because you don't put on any weight. See how thin you are.'

'Signor Miggel?' She took the piece of paper from her pocket on which the constable had written the usual message and held it out to me.

'I can't read English, Petroniglia,' I said. 'Miriam will have to read it and Pietro will have to interpret.' I noticed that there was quite a lot written on the paper, more than usual.

And Miriam had to light a candle to read it by because it was dark by the time we got back to the highland. It said that Mr Alfred Brown of Knysna was in Cape Town and had agreed to escort the child to Knysna. The necessary arrangements had already been made. As soon as Mr Brown's business affairs were settled, the child would be put on a ship with him.

Pietro interpreted, the others rejoiced. When Petroniglia started crying, Miriam joined in too. I told her to go slow on the tears because the next news would most probably be that the child had run away again. But it was the Monday after that that the warder came to say the child had been put on the ship the day before. I carried on with my work and in a little while Miriam came up from the mealie plot.

'What did the warder want, Pa?'

'Catarina was dispatched yesterday. The ship will first anchor at Mossel Bay and will be here on Wednesday.'

She threw her hands in the air, and then flew at me. 'And you just sit there as if it's nothing, Pa? You haven't even taken the trouble to go and tell Petroniglia?'

'No, because I'll believe it when the child stands before my own two eyes.'

'We must tell her, Pa! I'll fetch Pietro to interpret.'

'You stay where you are, nobody's going to tell her.'

'We *must* tell her! It's her right to know.'

'Miriam, your brain is beginning to work like Christie's and White's. If I go and tell Petroniglia, she'll be on her way to the village right away in case the ship has jumped its way here. Then tomorrow she'll go again and at the end of the day it's me that must go looking for her again. As soon as I'm finished here, I'm taking the chairs to Smit. Then I'll go to White myself and find out if the warder has given us the correct story. If it is, I'll fetch the child on Wednesday and bring her to her mother. I know what Mr Brown looks like. The iron pot that lies behind the house under the bush, the one the robins nested in, I bought that from his shop. And it only took a year to burn through!'

When I looked up, Fardini's youngest daughter, Luigia, was standing at the gate.

'Morning, Signor Miggel!'

'What do you want?'

'Don't be so rude to the child, Pa.'

'Now she's suddenly a child again? When she runs after Cuicatti and I say she's too young, you tell me to stay out of it.'

'Signor Miggel!' she called. 'No meal.'

'Didn't Miriam teach you to say "please"?'

'Signor Miggel, please, no meal.'

'I'll buy some meal for your mother from the store.'

Whenever they saw me bringing the sled round from the back and making ready to go to the village, the children were sent one after the other to tell me what they needed. Then, suddenly, none of them seemed to own feet which could take them to the village to buy provisions and carry them back to the highland. A bag of meal on a man's shoulder up Plat Bush's hill was enough to make his knees give way; up Gouna's hill, it was enough to break his back.

The next one that arrived, was Roberto, Robolini's eldest child. Quite a pretty child. 'Signor Miggel, nothing meal, nothing sugar, nothing lard, nothing please thank you, Signor Miggel.'

'Have you come reciting?'

'He can't hear what you're saying, Pa, his ears are plugged with notsung leaves which you said weren't to come out before tomorrow.'

'Keep them in until the day after.' The child was forever having earache.

One thing I would say for the Italians, they kept their children clean. Every day, except when it rained, the ropes between the tents were full of washing. Strange people. You knew them by the bark like you knew an upright yellowwood or a kalander yellowwood, or a candlewood, but deep down you didn't know them at all. Everything had to be in neat rows: inside the tents, outside the tents; every mealie-grain went into the earth with precision, every vegetable patch was square to an inch. Christie once said that the main reason why they feared the forest so was because it was so dense and disorderly and intertwining. I asked him if they thought God had had time to plant mile upon mile of trees in rows, or trim the underbush to look like fences. Noisy people, too. They were forever calling out to one another, singing, whistling, anything so long as it was noisy.

The next person to come to the gate with his order was America: 'Good morning, Signor Miggel!' It was time his hair was cut, his clothes were wearing thin too.

'Good morning, America. How are you?'

'Well, Signor Miggel. No sleep, very cold. Onions and meal everything finished, Signor Miggel.'

'I'll get it. Go and tell Fardini to get the money ready.' America looked blank. 'The money. Soldi! Soldi!' I said, and when he walked away, Miriam was laughing at me.

'If the government doesn't hurry up, Pa, you're going to speak Italian one of these days.'

'I'm more worried that they'll all be speaking Dutch by the time the ship comes.'

'Can't we tell Petroniglia about Catarina, Pa?' she pleaded.

'No. Go and fetch the money from Fardini and get all the orders together, otherwise the children will keep on coming to the gate. I'm now going to fetch the ox.'

I off-loaded the chairs at Smit's yard and then had to wait an hour before I got my money. At White's office it was almost another hour before he could put down his work to see me. And the first thing he wanted to know was where Christie was.

'Why ask me? You know he's in Cape Town.'

'I didn't give him permission to leave his post.'

'He told me you knew he was going to Cape Town.'

'That doesn't mean that I had given him permission to do so. The Grassi child was put on board the *Natal* yesterday and will be here early on Wednesday morning.'

'That's why I'm here, to find out if this is at last the truth, or just another rumour.'

'She will be here on Wednesday morning and has to be met.

154

I'll go to the quay and collect her from Mr Brown, but I can't then take her all the way to Gouna.'

'I've noticed that you never come out to Gouna any more, and that's why you have no idea of what's going on up there. It doesn't seem to help my telling you to write and ask the government to send someone, either.'

White became angry. 'All I hear coming from the highland are demands and complaints, complaints and demands. My patience is running out, Miggel!'

'Mine too, mister. But at least it's a relief to know that Mr Christie succeeded in getting the child on a ship. It gives one hope for the rest.'

'It was *my* representations which got the child on the ship, not Mr Christie.'

'Then you'd better keep on representing because things aren't going to get better up there, it's going to get worse. You people must take the Italians away from there.'

'Miggel, I think you should come with me to Kruis River one day, to the British immigrants that received land up there and see what people are capable of doing when they have the will. They are also having a hard time, this is also a foreign country to them, and they didn't get ploughs and oxen, they're not getting an allowance every week. They went out and started cutting wood and selling it; quite a few even found employment in the village.'

'Mister,' I said, 'I'm not here today to stand up for the Italians, but perhaps you're forgetting that the English immigrants weren't lured to come here and farm their silkworms, they weren't promised a mulberry forest. Maybe they're not as scared of the forest as the Italians are. And how do you think the Italians can go out and find work if they can't even yes and no properly? It's easy for you to talk but it's me that's got to look after the mess up there while everybody's waiting for the government's wheel to start braking. I sometimes get the feeling that that wheel isn't going to stop before the whole blooming wagon tumbles down the cliffs.'

'I've told you many a time not to interfere with matters you have no grasp of, Miggel. Right at the beginning I warned you that Immigration is an intricate legal process. I admit that the attempt to start a silk industry up at Gouna has failed, but that

155

doesn't repeal the Immigration Act. Correct procedures still have to be followed and that takes time.'

'Mister can say that again. It took *eighty* days to get Catarina Grassi on a ship from Cape Town which is two days' sailing from here. But if I were now to go and tell Captain Harison in his office next door, this very minute, that Martiens Botha is busy hauling out wood without the warder's seal – the mark of permission – on it, the Law would be in the forest before dark.'

'Where's Martiens hauling the wood out from?'

'He's not hauling out wood, I just used him as an example to show you that there are fast laws and slow laws, and that I have difficulty understanding many of them. While you people are writing letters, my life is going downhill. Because of you people I've lost my wages over at Portland; I haven't had time to collect any honey, and I've only had time to cut two stinkwood trees for myself. I'm about to see the bottom of my money tin because every penny I get for the chairs has to be spent on provisions. Incidentally, how far did you get with my dwelling rights? Is it on paper yet? I'm just asking, I've taken dwelling rights in any case. I've more than earned it, mister.'

'Miggel, don't start behaving like Mr Christie.'

'What do you mean?'

'He tries to dictate to us how things should be done in this colony, at the same time claiming one right after the other for himself. It will not be tolerated.'

'I notice you're dodging the question of my dwelling rights, but never mind. What time is the ship expected tomorrow?'

'Early.'

'What you village people call early is quarterday to us in the forest.'

'Just see that you're on the quay to receive the child.'

'I'll be there, mister.'

I was there long before him. A thin fog was lying over the lagoon, making the world grey and still. An unending march of little waves kept lapping and breaking against the stone quay, a seagull sat nearby as if too cold to spread its wings and fly off.

There was no sign of a ship yet. It must have been the fog that kept it from finding its way in from the sea and through the heads to get up the lagoon. The tide was right. There was no

wind, but the *Natal* didn't need wind, it had no sails, only a
smokestack. I couldn't count the times that I had gone to fetch
things for Barrington from a ship, and had then had to wait the
whole day for the wind and tide to change if it was a ship with
sails. They say John Benn, the pilot down at the heads, would
have stopped a fish from coming in through the heads if the
wind and the tide were not to his liking. The danger lay on the
two reefs every boat and ship had to cross to get into the lagoon.

Things started stirring on the quay; more and more people
arrived from the village to peer into the fog, trying to see the
ship. There were quite a few miles between the quay and the
heads. Barrington once mentioned that a new quay was going to
be built, one made of wood. It would be a good thing, too, since
the old one wasn't big enough any more. Stack upon stack of
wood cluttered the place, waiting to be loaded on the ships.
Stacks of beautiful wood. Stinkwood, yellowwood, white pear,
red alder, white alder. Blood-and-sweat from the forest. Neatly
dressed wood, otherwise the woodbuyer gave you little more
than nothing for it. Flooring-boards, beams, railway sleepers,
telegraph poles. Here and there a stinkwood log still in its bark.
Wood. Wood. Wood.

The fog started lifting and the sun peered through.

'Morning, Miggel, I'm glad to see that you're here.' It was
White.

'Yes, I'm here. Good morning, Mr White.'

'Constable Hall has just come back from the heads on
horseback, he says the pilot boat has gone out to take Mr Benn
to the *Natal*. They should be here any minute now.'

'I'm watching closely.'

'I will go on board, get the child from Mr Brown and bring
her to you.'

'I'll be waiting.'

Before I left home, I had told Miriam to get the wild parsley
bush-brew ready to give Ilario for the shock when I arrived there
with the child. For Petroniglia as well. That's *if* the child was on
the ship. Miriam kept on at me to tell Petroniglia, or to take
Fardini with me to the village so he could talk to the child in her
own language. I said no. I wanted to see Catarina Grassi get off
that ship with my own two eyes before I believed it. *If* she was on
the ship, I said to myself, there was hope that the day wasn't too

157

far off when I would be standing with them all on the quay. I would give them a nice bag of sweet potatoes to take with them, plus enough dried meat. Fortunately most of them already had mattresses which they had brought with them when they came; in the lowest class, where they berthed, everyone had to provide his own mattress, Christie said, or sleep on the bare boards. I would see to it that all the mattresses were freshly stuffed with bedding-bush when the time came, and when I had them all on the ship, then surely I would have to take a mouthful of the parsley-brew myself.

Not that I thought all my worries would go on the ship with them. The road ahead for Miriam and me would not be an easy one, that I knew. But at least it was a road I had always known would lie ahead for us. I couldn't expect to refill the money tin at once, that would take a lot of hard work, but rather that than thirty-two souls to care for. Thirty-three if I counted the child. Thirty-four if I reckoned Christie in. Thirty-five, thirty-six, counting Miriam and myself. It was no easy task for one man.

The people on the quay began to stir, voices were raised, hands started waving. From out of the haze, dark and slowly, the ship took shape. Deep within its body the engines thumped evenly, the smoke from its stack was greyish-white and thick, similar to the smoke from a fire made with green wood. Closer, like a vast creature set on its own course; clearer and clearer out of the last haziness, slower and slower until the engines suddenly stopped and it drifted by itself across the remaining distance to its berth at the quay. Ropes flew through the air, hands caught them deftly down below and secured them round the bollards.

On the ship itself, it was strangely quiet, there was hardly anyone on deck. They usually hung like finches over the railings to wave. Where were all the people everybody had been waiting for? Next to me, an Englishwoman cupped her hands round her mouth and called up to the deck: 'George? George?' George didn't answer. A seaman came to the railings and looked down. 'Have you got Cape Town passengers on board?' she called up to him. The man just shrugged. I moved along with everyone else to where the gangplank would be lowered. White was in the front row and next to him I recognised Brown's wife and my hopes rose: she wouldn't have been there if her husband was not on the ship. Not that that meant the child was on the ship. Chief Constable Ralph was in the front row as well, and when the plank was lowered, it was only he, White and two other men that got permission to go on board. All the others had to wait on the quay.

White and Ralph didn't stay on the ship long before they came down again. The people thronged around them, asking where the passengers were. Ralph spoke to those clustered in front and White pushed through to me and by his face I knew something was wrong, and I felt anger mounting in me.

'Sorry, Miggel,' White said, hurriedly, 'all the Knysna passengers were taken on board the *Teuton* yesterday morning, not on the *Natal* the day before yesterday as we had been told.'

'No shit, mister!' I said, I couldn't help myself. 'I set out from my house before dawn to be here in time and now you tell me this? You told me that the news of the child being on this ship had come by telegraph. Has the telegraph wire learned to lie like all of you people now?'

I saw him getting cross. 'Listen here, Miggel, I'm not in charge of Shipping!'

'Where's the child?'

'She should have been on this ship. The captain said they waited until Sunday morning for the *Teuton* to arrive from England because she had more passengers for Knysna on board. When the ship didn't arrive, it was decided to divert all the Knysna passengers that were to board in Cape Town on to the *Teuton* which is, in any case, passing here on its way to Port Elizabeth. The *Teuton* arrived in Cape Town on Sunday evening and departed again on Monday morning.'

'Where's Catarina?'

'On the *Teuton*.'

'Where's Mr Brown?'

'Also on the *Teuton*, she's in his care.'

'How long have I got to stand and wait here for the *Teuton* to arrive?'

'The *Teuton* cannot call at this port, Miggel, it's too big a ship to enter through the heads. She's sailing past to Port Elizabeth where all the Knysna passengers will disembark. The *Natal* is also on its way to Port Elizabeth, she will take them on board when she gets there and drop them off when she comes back here on her way to Cape Town again.'

I had to listen carefully to keep up with it all. 'In other words,' I said, 'it's just as if I leave the highland with a load of wood for the village, but I keep going until I reach Deep Walls where I off-load the wood, put it on another wagon, and come back along the same track to arrive at last at the village.'

'I've warned you many times not to try and reason about things you have no knowledge of! Shipping is not felling trees. The *Natal* will be back here a week from today and if Mr Christie is not back by then, you will see to it that you're here to receive the child.'

Shortly after midday I got back home. 'You see now why I would not tell Petroniglia?' I said to Miriam.

'Yes, Pa.'

'You see now that I am not always wrong as you like to make out?'

'Yes, Pa.'

She hadn't been to the forest for a long time. 'Pour me some coffee, I've got to go and see how far they are with stacking the fence. We've got to cut some more branches but if I don't stand with them on the forest's edge to keep a watch-out, they won't cut a single twig.'

'You know very well they don't like to work so close to the forest when they're alone,' she said and then added, 'Hal was here.'

'This is the third time he's been here when I'm not home. Does he keep a watch on my place to see when I turn my back?'

'He says Mr Barrington wants to see you urgently. It's not about work, Hal says his father isn't at all well.'

Strange, the wish to go to Portland had started growing in me for some time now. Every time I tried to kick it away from me, it just crept up on me again. Was it an omen? I asked myself. Were the angelings on their way perhaps to fetch Barrington to the hereafter? Were they perhaps on their way to fetch *me*? The very thought made me break out in a sweat. What was to become of Miriam if anything happened to me? What would she live on?

'I'll make arrangements to go Portland tomorrow.'

'Will you really, Pa?'

'Yes.'

160

'I'm glad. I know it worries Mr Barrington that you're cross with him. It worries Mrs Barrington too.'

'Why should it bother Barrington that I'm cross with him?'

'It bothers you too.'

'It does not bother me. I didn't keep silkworms, nor did I order Italians.'

Still, there comes a day and a time when a man must put straight what's gone askew, even if it is a bitter pill to swallow. Man is mortal. I decided to go to Portland the next day and offer Barrington my hand, even though I felt like dragging every Italian with me and lining them up at his door.

'Coccia and Pietro Cruci had a very serious argument while you were gone. It almost ended with a fist fight.'

'What about?'

'I couldn't make it out. Mariarosa parted them.'

I had begun to notice that all the sitting around and waiting was beginning to make trouble in all sorts of ways. I should have made them dig and plant and stack fences sooner than I had. Anna Fardini and Petroniglia had been at each other because of some small problem with the children; Canovi and Borolini had had a fight about a bag of meal that Borolini had dropped just outside the village. At one point Taiani had taken his belongings from his tent and gone and made himself a shelter at the foot of the highland; the very same night, it got so cold that the world lay covered with a stiff white blanket of frost the next morning and he just had to move back into the tent with the other three again. It was too crowded in the tents, I said. Sit so close to one another's breath all day and before long it hisses and bites.

We continued cutting branches and dragging them out to Fardini's allotment until dusk. I managed to make them understand that I would be going to Portland the next morning, and that they were to go on stacking until I got back.

When I got home, Miriam was cooking a francolin which she had got from America, and she had sweet potatoes under the ashes. The house was scrubbed clean and everything was in its place. There was no sign of moodiness about her, but I still felt strangely gloomy. Was something driving me to Portland so I could say goodbye to Barrington? Or was it so he could say goodbye to me? I told my imagination to slow down; for fifteen years my feet had walked the footpath to Portland, and there was

161

nothing sinister now that was taking me back. In our own kind of way there was friendship between the Honourable Barrington and me, even though he was high and I was low.

And Miriam must have sensed something for she wanted to know what was worrying me.

'Everything, I suppose.'

'Catarina will be on the ship on Wednesday, Pa, you'll see.'

'I'm not worrying about the child. I'm worrying about what's to become of you should anything happen to me.'

She was immediately on the alert. 'Why did you say that, Pa?'

'I don't know, it's just a feeling that's come over me.'

'What feeling?'

'About what's to become of you should anything happen to me.'

'Don't talk like that, Pa. You're the one that always says, what you say is what you get.'

'What will you live on?'

'I can plant, I can set a good snare, I can cut my own firewood, I can shoot.'

'You cannot live without money, there are things that must be bought, clothes, other things. What will happen to you if I'm not there to watch out for the pitfalls? You don't ever see wrong in anything. And why are Pontiggia's footprints outside my door?'

'Pa watches closely.'

'You can't play round a bee-sting bush and not expect to get stung by it.'

'I'm not stupid, Pa. I know how long and how close I can play to it.'

'Miriam!'

'It's the truth, Pa. I may start a fire but I'm not allowed to get too close to its warmth no matter how cold I am.' She said it shamelessly, and didn't even try to hide how bitter she was. I got up to put a new candle in the candlestick.

'Promise me you won't take Pontiggia should anything happen to me.'

'I won't take anyone, Pa. You needn't be afraid of that.'

'Is it Pontiggia?'

'Don't start again, Pa.'

Or was it Hal after all, I asked myself.

162

NINE

AT DAWN THE next morning, Fardini came and called me from the house. I didn't quite make out what he was trying to tell me, but I knew there was something wrong at the tents and he wanted me to come quickly. Quietly, so that the others would not know.

It was elephant tracks. Everywhere between the tents. Fresh tracks. Fresh dung. It was the work of one elephant: Old Foot. The head bull of the forest. King elephant. You never came across his tracks without every hair on your body standing up.

The tracks came out from the forest right behind the tents and went back into the forest at the same place, as if he had just come to make a thorough inspection.

'Fetch me the heavy gun, Miriam,' I said. She had followed us and was standing with those women who had already come out of their tents.

'It's Old Foot, Pa, you stay away from him! What was he doing here?'

'Go and fetch the gun. I must find out which way he has gone.' An elephant as cunning as Old Foot was never to be trusted.

I stayed with his tracks for almost an hour, ready to climb or flee with every step I gave, because I would only have fired a shot at him if there was no other way to save myself. Josafat Stander himself had said there was only one bull in the forest against which he would never lift his gun, and that was Old Foot. You don't shoot a king, he said, and Josafat Stander was a man that had little respect for anything. The closest to the highland I had come across Old Foot's tracks before was up in

163

Lily Bush. Never closer. Why did he now suddenly want to be on the highland? A single bull elephant has different things in his head than one in a herd. Old Foot had been going alone for years.

I turned back deep in Kom's Bush, but I still wasn't happy. Portland would have to wait another day. I couldn't leave Miriam alone on the highland with that elephant in the vicinity. Never.

I didn't get to Portland the next day either; it rained and Petroniglia kept on threatening to go to the village for news of the child. News of the child at that stage was the last thing I wanted her to get, with the result that I had to stay home to keep an eye on her.

'Tell her the child will be here on Wednesday, Pa. Tell her it's only five more days,' Miriam started pestering me again.

'No. She'll be agitating for five days if I tell her.'

We brewed bedding-bush for cough medicine instead. Half the children went around barking like dogs, and I couldn't fetch medicine from Mieta every time, each drop was costing money.

The next morning, the Saturday, I left at dawn to visit the snares and got two nice buck to skin for the Italians. It was more than two weeks since Josafat Stander had last shot something for them. Every crumb I got from somewhere helped.

When I got home with the buck the warder was sitting most comfortably at my table with a mug of coffee and a sweet potato.

'Well,' I said, 'now Silas Miggel can say a spy sat at his table and drank from his mug.' I was cross.

'Good morning, uncle.'

'You must have slept in the forest last night to be sitting in my house at this time of the day.'

'No, uncle. I left the village at daybreak, Mr White has sent me to fetch you.'

'Fetch me for what?'

'He says you must come to the village immediately.'

'You go and tell him that I'm about to skin two bucks and after that I'm going to Portland.'

He suddenly became anxious. 'You can't go to Portland today, uncle! Mr White told me to see to it that you set out for the village immediately.'

'What for?'

'I have no authority to inform you about anything. My orders are to bring the message and see that you get there. It's urgent.'

'I think you better go and see what it's about, Pa,' Miriam said.

I had my mouth open already to say I wasn't going anywhere except to Portland, when the thought suddenly struck me: it might be news of the ship! Why else would he want to see me so urgently? Catarina was on the *Teuton* and the *Teuton* was on its way to Port Elizabeth. What else could it be for? Steady, I told myself, you're wishing into the wind now, but I was suddenly in a hurry to get to the village.

'Drink up so that we can go,' I said to the warder. 'And stop staring at my daughter like that!'

'Pa!'

'Fetch my shoes, Miriam. If White has called me to the village this morning for no good reason, there will be trouble. And you keep the gun with you and your eyes on the tents.' I couldn't relax about Old Foot yet. 'See that they cut more branches and stay with them with the gun, that's the only way you'll keep them at it.'

By the time I crossed Gouna's Drift, the warder had fallen so far behind that I couldn't see him any more. I had no intention of waiting for him since I was certainly not going to enter the village accompanied by a warder like a convict. I had insisted that he should leave the house with me just to get him away from Miriam. That's all.

It was September, but the air was still cold. Barrington once told me that the trees in the forests of England, where he came from, shed all their leaves in winter, not like here where the forest stood green all year round. And yet, it always seemed to me as if the whole forest, birds and all, dozed off every year from around May to September and only came fully awake again when the red-chested cuckoo started calling. That was the sign that one could start planting again as well. If White had sent for me because the ship was on its way to collect the Italians, they would have to leave the fences and the planting. No further dung would be wasted then. The moment they're gone, I thought, I would start work over at Portland three days a week and keep the other days for the chairs and the honey. One thing was sure, I would have a fine crop, because the Italians couldn't take their vegetable patches with them.

When I got to the village, small groups of people stood gathered everywhere in the Main Street: in front of the Post Office, in front of Magistrate Jackson's office, in front of White's office. All had grim faces and most of them were standing with newspapers while others read over their shoulders. I just walked past, knowing there was something in those papers that had got a penny from everyone's pocket to buy it. Had Christie been back, I would have had to buy one too and carry it out to the highland only to be told that I had crumpled it on the way. I told him straight out one day that I had never seen him with a Bible, but regularly with a newspaper that he read from front to back. He told me he had to know what was going on in the world. What for? I told him one had nothing to do with what went on in the world, one's task was to know what went on in one's own back yard. Did the world perhaps know what went on on the highland? Not even the government knew, for had they known they would have sent the ship long ago.

There was definitely something in the paper, there was one lying open on White's table too when I got there.

'You've sent for me, mister. I was on my way to Portland.'

'Good morning, Miggel.' He was as grave as the people in the street. 'I'm glad you've come, my friend, our village is in shock and mourning.'

His words rattled me. Perhaps Magistrate Jackson had died – but then the village wouldn't have been in mourning. 'Has something happened?' I asked.

'Haven't you heard the news yet?'

'How could I have heard? I came straight here. I told Constable Hall outside that I had been sent for.'

'The *Teuton*, Miggel, the ship on which Catarina Grassi was, has foundered.'

'Foundered?' The ship had foundered. Sunk. I heard it, but my brain did not take it in.

'Yes. The ship didn't leave on Monday as was reported at first, but on Tuesday, the thirtieth of August, at ten o'clock in the morning. From Cape Town. According to the first reports, she struck a rock off Quin Point the same evening at about half past seven; Quin Point is sixty miles out from Cape Town. More

166

than two hundred people were lost, which includes forty-four immigrants on their way to Knysna from England. There were also four Knysna passengers that boarded in Cape Town, and one of them was our beloved and much honoured Mr Alfred Brown.'

'Where's the child?' I realised I was shaking my head. 'Where's Catarina?'

'I'm afraid she's not among the handful of survivors. The first the world heard of the tragedy was on Wednesday afternoon when an open lifeboat reached Simon's Bay at half past two, carrying fourteen of the rescued. Shortly afterwards another boat turned up, carrying thirteen people. Two ships were immediately sent out to search for survivors, but found only wreckage. On Thursday morning, the day before yesterday another lifeboat reached Cape Town, carrying nine more survivors. That's all.'

'Where's the child?'

'Sit down, Miggel, you've gone quite pale.'

'Where's the child, I asked you.' I did not sit down.

'I don't think you have grasped what I've said. Only one Knysna passenger has survived the disaster, a certain William Barrett, one of the immigrants on his way here.'

'Who says the child was ever on the ship?' My head would still not take in the news.

'She was. It was confirmed by telegraph this morning and her name is here in the paper as well. Alfred Brown was in the prime of his life, Miggel, a man left fatherless at an early age, taking upon him the care of his mother and brothers. There was not a day when he didn't pull his weight in this village in some way, he built up his business with extreme competence and was a committed Christian who faithfully served his church. Now he is suddenly no longer with us. His poor widow and three young children are left behind. The whole community is mourning his tragic death.'

It was just then that the devil got into me. 'But not one of you will feel for Silas Miggel who has to go back to the highland with the news that the child has arrived in heaven instead of at the quay! You sit there bemoaning Mr Brown as if he's the only one that's been counted. Who says the child isn't on one of the boats that carried survivors?'

167

'The names of the survivors have already been issued. Only one woman survived, a certain Lizzie Ross.'

'Mister, I stand here paralysed by what you've told me, but – Tuesday, Wednesday, Thursday, Friday, and today is Saturday and the news only reached the highland this morning? How am I supposed to understand that?'

'There were problems with the telegraph wire and uncertainty about the Knysna passengers because originally they had been due to transfer to the *Natal*. We had to get confirmation first.'

'Who says the child isn't still with Tomasso?'

'Her name is on the list of the drowned. She was on the ship.'

'How do you think I'm going to be able to tell that to Petroniglia, mister?'

'I am deeply sorry. The fact that Mr Christie is not here to take the task upon himself as their interpreter, will be reported to Mr Laing in Cape Town immediately.'

'What good will that do? Will it wash up the child and make her breathe again? Who says there aren't any more boats out at sea in which she could be?'

'There aren't any, Miggel. The boats that went out to search have already returned, certain there are no more survivors.'

I could not accept it. 'Let me have that paper, I will get Miriam to read it,' I said to him, but he seemed reluctant to let go of the thing. 'It's easy for you to sit there behind the table, giving out the news, it's me that must take it to Petroniglia.'

The news of the tragedy only sank in as I was leaving the village on my way back to the highland: the ship had sunk and Catarina Grassi was lying somewhere on the bottom of the sea, drowned. Given away or stolen, it no longer mattered, the child was gone. Lost. Drowned. And I was the one that had to go and tell them. I met the warder just outside the village.

'I see you're on your way back already, uncle.'

'Yes.'

'I understand there was an Italian on the ship that was wrecked.'

'Yes.'

'You must just continue watching them for any signs of smallpox, the danger is on the increase.'

'Go to hell.'

At the top of Platbos's hill, I pulled up a parsley bush, roots

168

and all, and carried it back with me. We would need a lot of brew to give them all for the shock. Could the ship not have looked where it was going? How the devil was I to tell them? It had started with a blooming jam-jar of silkworms, where would it end?

In my ignorance and distress I had asked Christie one day what a ship's ticket to Italy would cost because I thought perhaps one could make a plan if the government didn't. He said it was twelve pounds to London if you went third class. Make it fifteen to Italy, I said, and worked it out roughly: four hundred pounds if they took the children on at half price. Seven pounds ten less now that Catarina was no longer, for I had taken her into account as well. Not that it would make any difference, there wasn't that kind of money on the highland. The only hope left was that Christie would come back with news of a ship.

Miriam was cutting up the buck meat when I got home. I said nothing at first, I just told her to wash her hands and come read me the paper.

'Why, Pa? Why did Mr White send for you?' She was immediately suspicious.

'Come and look through the paper for me and you'll find out.'

'Find out what?'

'About a ship that has sunk.'

We sat down at the table and she found it on the second page: 'It says here, "*An Awful Shipwreck. Total Loss of the Teuton*".' She sat up in alarm. 'Isn't that the ship Catarina is on, Pa?'

'Now you know why I was called to the village. She went down with the ship.' When Miriam started crying, I told her to stop. 'Your eyes must remain dry so that you can read to me what they say about the child. I must then take the news to her mother.'

'This can't be true, Pa.'

'It is. Read, we must know about the child.'

'How are you going to tell Petroniglia, Pa?'

'I don't know yet. *Read*.'

She found the reading difficult. At the beginning was a long account with words we hardly understood: it was about how big the ship had been, that it would have taken one thousand eight hundred horses to pull it through the water and that it had another name before. Then it said the ship had struck a sand bank; White had said it was a rock. Then we read that one of the survivors had said that the ship's doctor had told them it was a stone that had got into the ship's propeller. How could a stone get into a propeller? Then it said that only twenty-seven people had reached the shore safely. White had said first fourteen, then thirteen, and then nine more. That was thirty-six. Miriam thought perhaps they had written the report before the last nine had turned up. It could have been so.

'Read what it says about the child. Where was she when the ship went down? What happened to her?' I had to know about the child.

'There is nothing about her so far, Pa. Maybe she was not even on the ship.'

'White says she was. Read on.'

Next came a long list with the names of all the people that had gone on board in England, and right at the end of the list they had the names of the four Knysna passengers that had got on in Cape Town: Miss C. Grassi, Mr Krom, Mr Brown, Mr Rindeman.

'What else?'

The rest repeated what the people who had got away in the lifeboats had said. It told about how young Lizzie Ross, who had lost her father, her mother and her little sister, had thrashed around in the water, repeatedly calling out: 'Save me! Save me!' At that point Miriam started crying again and again I told her to stop. I had to know about the child. But there was nothing more, only her name on the passenger list.

'What now, Pa?'

'Where's Petroniglia?' I could no longer put it off.

'I saw her go past to the clay furrow with her washing. I'll go and fetch Pietro so that we can help you to tell her.'

'No, I'll tell her by myself. You must go and tell Fardini, and he must tell Ilario. Take the parsley-brew that's left, then come back and make some more. They're going to need a lot.'

Petroniglia, barefoot, was squatting at the furrow, her sleeves pushed up high and a piece of washing foaming between her hands. I had endlessly forbidden them to go to the clay furrow but every time I turned my back, they were there.

'Petroniglia?'

'Signor Miggel!' Her face brightened when she saw it was me.

170

I walked up to her, but the words suddenly stuck in my throat. How was I to tell her?

'Petroniglia,' I said, 'I've come to you with bad news. Very bad news.' She must have sensed something from my voice or from my face for the piece of washing slipped from her hands and fell into the water.

She rose slowly. 'Ilario?' she said. 'Ilario, Signor Miggel?'

'No. Not Ilario. Catarina. She's gone. Drowned.' It was not easy to stand there and act death; the only way I could think of was to let my head drop to one side and let my tongue hang out. But she knew immediately. I could tell. She stood stock-still, straight, with her feet in the wet clay, just like that figure Pontiggia had made. The only difference was that she had a dress on over her nakedness. When I saw that she was going to faint, I took her by the arm and tried to pull her from the clay. 'You must stay on your feet, Petroniglia,' I said. 'You must get to Ilario.' It would have been best to have picked her up and carried her to her tent, but I couldn't. When a man has not touched a woman for seventeen years, something in him becomes shy. 'Stand up straight, Petroniglia!' If she fell, it would be in the wet clay and her dress would become a mess. I just had to hold on to her by her arm. 'Bring your feet forward, Petroniglia, we must go to the tents.' She didn't move, her eyes had the strangest look in them, as if she were crying without tears.

'Signor Miggel?'

'The child was on a ship and the ship sunk, but Fardini will tell you that, I don't know how to. I only know that I am very sorry for you, for if anything should happen to my Miriam, I would go out of my mind. Bring your feet forward, Petroniglia.'

Just at that moment, a woman from the tents uttered a scream that chilled my very blood, and kept on screaming as if overcome by madness. I felt a shudder go through Petroniglia's body. 'Walk, Petroniglia!' When she wouldn't move, I held her round the shoulders and started pushing her ahead of me, faster and faster, and still the screaming wouldn't stop. Anna Fardini and her daughter, Giuditta, rushed up to us and took Petroniglia from me, motioning me with anxious hands to go to the tents quickly.

The news lay on every face. The screaming came from Cruci's tent. Mariarosa, I said to myself and ran straight to

171

where the buckets of drinking water stood under the shelter and grabbed the fullest one. I had noticed for some time that Mariarosa appeared to be giving up; I had spoken to Christie about it and he had said it was because she yearned so to go home.

She sat in the middle of the tent, swaying backwards and forwards; every time she went backwards, she drew in her breath and when she came forward, she screamed like someone who didn't know what was happening. Around her stood her husband and Mangiagalli, and Tomé and his wife Antonia, and nothing they did made her stop. It was only when I threw the water all over her that she gasped herself to silence.

Lucinetti and Borolini were in the tent with Ilario. Every time they pulled the blankets from his face, he pulled them up over his head again, and lay there like a corpse. When the women came in with Petroniglia, he turned on his side with his face in the pillow and started crying.

I found Miriam behind the furthest tent. Her hair had come loose and her eyes were red from crying. Fardini and his son, Pietro, and Cuicatti and Pontiggia were with her.

'They understand that Catarina is dead, Pa, but they don't understand when I try to tell them how it happened.' She was quite despondent.

I picked up a stick and made a mark in the dust at their feet, saying: 'Cape Town.'

'Sì, sì, signor.'

From the mark I drew a line with waves to show that it was the sea, then I made the second mark: 'Knysna.'

'Sì, sì, signor.'

Then I drew a ship as best I could, under the sea and standing on its head with people falling out and some lying at the bottom and I said: 'Catarina.'

They crossed themselves.

That was Saturday. Sunday was a black day at the tents. On the Monday Christie came back. Without news or promise of a ship. He had hardly seen the government because, he said, it took planning and time to get to see the top people. And he hadn't had enough time. When he had heard of the *Teuton* and that Catarina had been on the ship, he had hurried back to convey the news to the parents and to stand by them in their bereavement.

'Don't talk shit, man!'

'Pa!'

'You've hurried back with old news, stupid Englishman!'

'Pa, you're talking half in Dutch!'

'I'm too cross to think in English. Ask him if he's Irish, maybe he's Irish. Barrington always says a dim-witted Englishman is but a finger's length better than a dim-witted Irishman.'

'I'm not going to ask him that, Pa.'

I asked him what the use was of all the expense and trouble he had gone to if he hadn't told the government the truth. 'How could you have come back with empty hands?'

'I did my best, Miggel.'

'Did you get your money out of them so that you can give me back mine?'

'The matter is being investigated.'

'Shit, man, shit!'

'Pa, don't swear like that!'

'I won't swallow their investigations any longer. What have you found out about the child? Her mother wants to know whether she had been sleeping when the ship went down, whether perhaps she had jumped off, or if there was somebody to look after her.'

'Don't be so unreasonable, Miggel. You expect me to perform miracles, the Grassis expect me to know what happened to their child out at sea on a sinking ship. I'm only human! As for the other matter, I can give you the assurance that I have seen the Italian Consul Mr W. C. Wright. He's promised to take this whole matter to Parliament.'

'I don't rely on promises or assurances any longer, Mr Christie,' I told him straight out. 'Not from you, not from White, not from the government. That time when I said I could get them on a ship to Cape Town, you people said I wanted to take the law in my own hands; had I done it, the child would not have been lying at the bottom of the sea now. That's why I want to know from you now if it would be against the law for me to put down the full amount of money for their tickets home.'

'Where will you find the money?'

'I'll get it. I'm asking whether it would be against the law.'

173

'No.'

I knew then what I had to do, I had to get to Portland.

The dogs barked at me as I approached the house, but when they saw it was me they crouched down and rubbed themselves against my legs. Mrs Barrington was glad to see me, the girls too. Hal was at the stables, Will at Karawater, John had gone to the village. I had to take off my hat, wipe my feet and go in the back door because Barrington wasn't well and confined to the house. He sat in the drawing room in a huge soft chair with a blanket over his legs.

'Honourable.'

'Silas.'

We greeted each other warily. It seemed as if there were fewer teeth in his mouth and his skin was yellow and transparent. Strange, I thought to myself, almost like a silkworm's before it starts spinning.

'You don't look well,' I said and found a place to stand inside the door. 'I'll fetch Mieta to come and administer to you.'

'Thank you, Silas, but it won't be necessary. Dr Gorman is taking care of me.'

'As you wish.' We said nothing for a while. He smoothed the blanket over his knees and I stood fumbling with my hat until I felt I had to speak again. 'One of the Italians' children was drowned.'

'I believe she was on the *Teuton*. The wreckage and cargo that has been washed up will be sold at a public sale on Saturday. It's a pity I can't send John to Cape Town at the moment, I believe there are quite a few oars and lifeboats and lanterns and masts and so forth to be sold. I would have been interested in a compass.'

He deliberately avoided talking about the child. I knew. 'You must pay attention to me today because I've come to discuss a very important matter.'

'I am glad that you've come, Silas. Between Portland and the highland lies not only the very deep Knysna River gorge, but also a gorge of differences and culture. I feel myself responsible for you and Miriam in so many ways, and therefore it is my duty to inform you of certain changes that are going to take place that will concern you directly.'

174

What he actually said was that he had missed me and that he still hoped I would move to Karawater. Or he had a new scheme on his mind. 'I thought you should know that I came across fresh leopard tracks down in the gorge by the water when I came through a while ago. And I'm glad to hear that you're in a responsible mood today because the Italians must be sent home from where they were lured under the false pretences, and there is only one way home for them.'

'Silas.' It was a warning. 'The time has come for you to look after yourself. The Italians are the responsibility of the government. You must think of Miriam, of her future, because your time on the highland is over. I sent for you many times in order to talk to you about this, warn you, but you wouldn't come.'

'Mr Barrington, if you want to frighten me today, you will have at least to make a ghost come through that wall. I don't take fright any more. I undertook to stand by Mr Christie and keep an eye on the Italians in return for which I get dwelling rights to the end of Miriam's days. Things have, however, changed so much that it takes more than an eye to keep them going. Christie, the foreman, only writes letters; all the rest has climbed on to *my* back. Things are bad at the tents. The child's father won't eat, they have to force food into him with a spoon. The mother doesn't speak to anyone, she just sits outside the tent, praying with her beads. I've already had to go and get the eldest daughter, Monica, out of Canovi's tent goodness knows how many times.'

'You must move away from there as soon as you can, Silas. Come to Portland, or to Karawater. The forest is going to be closed very soon and for ever, and then it will be sold in lots to private owners. The woodcutter's time in the forest is over, and so is yours, Silas.'

Had a ghost come through the wall behind Barrington at that very moment, I couldn't have been more shocked. Take away the forest from a woodcutter and his people, and you may as well take the shell off a tortoise and put it out in the blazing sun. If Barrington had not been such a gentleman and fierce on manners, I would have sat down right there on one of his chairs.

'What are you saying, Mr Barrington? The forest belongs to the Crown, and the Crown is the Crown.'

175

'The government, Silas, has totally failed in what we call the Conservation of Crown Forests.'

'Mr Barrington,' I said, 'don't let us try and fell two trees with one axe today. Let us hack in at my tree first, and afterwards at the one you now want to drag in here.'

He paid no attention to what I was saying, he simply continued. 'You must listen carefully to what I'm about to say to you, Silas. The present system of conservation that's followed is ridiculous. You people buy a licence for thirty shillings and fell as much as you like on it until it expires. Then you either cut illegally for a time, or buy a new licence if you have the money.'

'The woodbuyers advance us the money on the book most of the time.'

'That as well, yes. The so-called method of conservation applied is that you may only fell certain kinds of wood in certain months of the year. You may, however, *haul* out the wood whenever you wish. It so happens that I know no forest warder who would know the difference once a log has been hauled through the mud for a couple of miles. He assumes the wood has been cut in season, and puts his seal on it so that you can deliver it to the buyers. That, Silas, is the ridiculous system I'm talking about.'

'Mr Barrington,' I said, in an effort to get in a word, 'what you're saying is more or less true, but if you want to see something really ridiculous, come with me to the highland where more than thirty souls are sitting through this cold and wet winter in too few tents. And nobody comes out to have a look at what's going on. Christie went to Cape Town, but he might just as well have stayed where he was. There's no help coming from anywhere. And that is why I'm standing before you today with my hat in my hand.'

He just carried on chopping at his tree. 'The present system in fact contributes to the destruction of the Crown forests, and the forests have become nothing but a burden on this colony. Do you realise how much the forest is costing this country each year? How much do you think Captain Harison's salary amounts to every year? Plus the salary of the Superintendent of Forests, de Regné, plus the salaries of the warders; housing, office rentals; plus contributions to the Divisional Council for the maintenance of the roads worn out by your wagons and sleds –'

'Excuse me interrupting, Mr Barrington, but nothing is done about the roads. Where there are no bigfoot paths to use, we make our own. The wagon-road at Deep Walls is a disgrace.'

'It doesn't matter what they do or don't do about the roads, the contributions must still be made. I've asked you how much you think this forest costs the country each year.'

'I can't give you an answer to that, but I do know what it will cost to get the Italians back to their country.'

'It's costing this country five thousand nine hundred pounds a year if you add the interest on investments that could have been made.'

'Five thousand nine hundred pounds,' I repeated in astonishment. It was a sack full of money, more than my head could count at that moment.

'Yes,' Barrington said, 'and even then I've worked it out very conservatively. The correct amount will be much higher.'

'It will cost just over four hundred pounds to buy them all a ticket home.'

'The income from wood licences amounts to approximately one thousand three hundred pounds. Deduct that from the expenses, and the loss amounts to four thousand six hundred pounds.'

'Four hundred pounds, Honourable.'

'Tell me, Silas, what difference would it make if Captain Harison and Superintendent de Regné and all the forest warders were to disappear tomorrow?'

'It would be a happy day. The latest thing the warders have on their brains is smallpox which the Italians are supposed to have brought here.'

'You did not answer my question.'

'We are cutting two different trees, Honourable!' I said, but he took no notice.

'Let's assume they disappear and you people are allowed to cut without licence, would you cut and haul out more wood, or less wood?'

'A man cuts as much as his wagon can take, not more, not less, and I know you want to trap me.'

'Exactly. Whether there are warders or not, the forest is being felled indiscriminately and the whole country is paying for the

177

loss. We cannot even claim as dividend that we are receiving the conservation of our forests in return.'

There was only one thing left to do, and that was to hack at his blooming tree for a while and get it over with. 'Mr Barrington,' I said, putting my hat on the floor, 'this matter of conservation has been dragged into the forest and pushed down our throats for a long time now, but the whole business makes no sense to me. If I want to spare a loaf of bread, I wrap it in a cloth and put it away. I don't eat it; I don't take a slice here today, and a crust there tomorrow. I don't come and say I need bread for railway sleepers, for telegraph poles, for a hundred other things. Then it's not a case of sparing the bread but seeing how long the bread can last. Now Mr Barrington tells me they are going to cut the bread up in lots and sell it? Will the buyers be buying to cut or to conserve?' Barrington started fidgeting under the blanket. 'I want to know if they're going to cut or conserve, Mr Barrington.'

'Both. Under the present system felling takes place in any case. It is inevitable that this forest will be felled eventually, the world needs wood every day, and we are sitting with miles upon miles of noble wood, of the best and most beautiful in the world. I'm not saying that it will be felled during your or my lifetime, not even in our children's, but somewhere its end is waiting. In the meantime the colony stands to benefit by its being sold. Suppose – and this is the proposal that has already been put to the government – suppose the forest is divided and sold into lots of five hundred or a thousand morgen each, it could mean at least a hundred thousand pounds for the treasury.'

'It will cost just four hundred pounds to get them back to Italy.'

'Calculated at six per cent interest per year, it will give the country a timeless income of six thousand pounds annually.'

'Four hundred pounds, Honourable. Not only will it get them home, but it will also buy you a clean conscience, and a clean conscience is not something that comes up for sale every day.'

That made him angry. 'Forget about the Italians and think of yourself, Silas! Concentrate on letting the implications of what I've just told you filter through to you!'

'I must first get the Italians off the highland before I can start thinking about what would happen to us forest people, should the forest be sold from under us.'

'The woodcutters' misery can't get worse than it is, even with their debts at the woodbuyers' stores in the village. But their free living in the forest will come to an end. For those willing to take on responsibility, there'll be regular employment with the new owners.'

I stood where I stood. 'That means we forest people will be more inferior than we are already. In all the years that I have known you, you've had a thing against the woodcutters. It's because you don't understand why they wouldn't come and cut in Portland's forest for you. We cut for ourselves, we belong to ourselves. And apart from that, the woodcutters remember Gert Zeelie that you had thrown into jail because he had cut down a tree in Portland's forest. The people are scared of you.'

'Anyone that steals wood from my part of the forest deserves the punishment he gets.'

'Jail is a downfall for us forest people from which we never get up again.'

'Your time in the forest is over, Silas.'

'The forest is big, Mr Barrington, very big. You people can have it cut up and sold, but don't come and ask me how you are going to get us out of there.'

'Hunger will force you all out. The woodbuyers will be made by law to buy only from the legal wagons. Wood will no longer be exchanged for provisions at the stores in the village.'

Birds called outside. Behind me, I heard one of the women in the house climbing the stairs to the top of the house, and Barrington looked tired. 'How much time is left before the forest lots are sold?' I asked him.

'It will be sold according to demand. As the demand increases, the government will reduce the warders and other officials until the colony is finally rid of the burden.'

'How long is that if you count it in years?'

'It's difficult to say at this stage. At the moment representations are being made to the government from all sides of the district.'

'Then we are in no immediate danger,' I said. 'The government doesn't listen to representations. The government is a wheel that just rolls on and on without ever seeming to

179

brake.' Something told me to keep talking, it was my turn with the axe. 'And I didn't come here to reproach you about the silkwormers, reproaches resolve nothing, I'm only asking you to pay their tickets home. That's all. Give them the money, and your eyes will close on the final day with a clean conscience.' He sat stock-still in the chair. 'There's no sign of the ship that is supposed to come and fetch them. Christie has drawn up goodness knows how many petitions for them already, but nothing happens. In the meantime I have to see to everything, and my money's running out by the day. If you give them the money, I will first see to it that they get to the quay, and then I'll come straight here and work three days a week for you. Christie can buy his own ticket home as far as I care.'

The old man just kept sitting there stiff and still. Koos Muller sat like that one day too, with his back against a tree when we were cutting kalander in Kom's Bush; we were under the impression that he was still with us, then we suddenly realised that he was sitting there stone dead. The angelings had come and fetched him away from right under our noses.

'Mr Barrington?' I called, cautiously. 'Are you still here?'

'The Italians, Silas, preferred the government's proposals to mine. I am negotiating to have my own Italians come out and establish a silk industry here at Portland.'

'Take the ones sitting in the tents over on the highland, Mr Barrington!' I cried. 'Bring them here. I swear you'll find no better men to work with the worms!'

'I don't want them.'

He did not want them.

TEN

SEPTEMBER'S DAYS WENT by and summer tried to arrive on the highland: one day of sunshine, one day of cold or rain, next a bit of everything. Red alder, wild elder and camphor bush, all those that flowered during winter, were finished. By October the forest was lush with new growth and the fragrance of flowers and leaves mingled with the smell of the forest that rose from its damp floor. The old people believed it was the moss that smelled. False olive and forest chestnut started to bloom, wild grapes were budding and climbing everywhere; in the underbush, forest bramble, cross-berry, turkey-berry and numnum flowered in violet, pink and white. Up at the clay furrow, a wild pomegranate and a wild hollyhock intertwined, and the rock martins carried away beakfuls of clay.

On the fifth day of October, Miriam was eighteen. When she was small, I always walked to the village with her on her birthday and bought her a penny's worth of sweets and a lot of joy. When she got bigger, I used to buy her a dress from Portland's girls well in advance, but this year I had nothing to give her.

'God willing, I will make up for it next year,' I told her.

'Please don't feel bad, Pa, I understand.'

She got up early that morning, made the fire, swept the house, and made the beds. I was outside sorting the sweet potato runners that I wanted to plant when she called me to come and have my coffee. When I got inside, I knew she was on her way: she had on her best dress and her hair was neatly combed and plaited.

'Pa . . .' She came and faced me and when she spoke, it was clear that she had had every word ready. 'Pa, you always say there is but one day in the year that is one's own and that is your birthday. Today is my birthday, I'm going to the forest, and I'm not going to be back before dark.'

She had not been to the forest for weeks. In my heart I had come to hope that whatever there had been was over. But it obviously wasn't. Her hand shook lightly when she poured my coffee; her whole body, her face, her eyes, said: don't stop me, I must go.

But I still tried. 'Miriam,' I said, 'I told Mr Christie yesterday that it is your birthday today, that I didn't want to see a single Italian child near my house today. Him neither. I thought we could perhaps walk to Creek Bush Island to your aunt Hannie.'

'Didn't Pa say that the sweet potato runners must be planted today?'

'It can wait till tomorrow, I'll lay them in the furrow in the shade. We can go to the village. Or to Portland so you can visit Imar and Gabrielle. However, I wouldn't want to go close to the house.'

'Where I'm going, I'm going alone, Pa. I'll take the gun.'

'Why?' Every time she wanted to go to the forest, she became secretive. 'Why, Miriam?'

'Don't start again, Pa, this is my day and I want to walk on my own.'

'Just tell me who you are going to meet then! Why must this thing stay closed between you and me? Is it because it's someone from the tents?' If it wasn't Pontiggia that kept running after her, it was Taiani or Lucinetti. There were even days when it seemed to me that Christie went weak at the knees when she came near him. 'Why may I not know, Miriam?'

'Why does the forest hide its lilies?'

'Don't start your riddles again!'

'Don't ask me then, Pa. Especially not today.' She was getting impatient. 'And don't try to follow me again either, Pa. I'll know if you do.'

I was powerless. 'How can I just let you go? You yourself heard Jeremiah Eye telling me yesterday that Josafat Stander has been trampled by the bigfeet.'

'It's the third time I know of that Josafat Stander is supposed to have been trampled, and every time he has turned up whole and alive again.'

182

'Well, the bigfeet trampled *somebody* up in Kom's Bush. Jeremiah says the person's coat and knapsack with food were ripped to pieces; trees are uprooted, underbush torn.'

'I'll take the gun.'

'The whip would be as much use if there really is a troublesome bull up there.'

'It's getting late, Pa.'

The worst thing was that I had nothing left to say to her that would stop her. I couldn't understand it. I ruled thirty-two impossible Italians, but I could not rule my own daughter. Since when did a parent allow a child to defy him? Whatever it was that called her to the forest was stronger than my word and my wishes; had I taken a rope and tied her up, I was sure she would somehow have got free before my very eyes and still have walked off. Whoever she went to meet, she hid like a peach hides its stone. Why? Twice I had tried to follow her and both times she knew; after all, I myself was the person who had taught her never to walk in the forest without being alert. Her ear was too fine for me.

I waited until she had been gone for a good while before I went and made a round of the tents. Lucinetti and Taiani were there, but not Pontiggia. Christie said he had gone to the village with Borolini and Tomé. And Christie was sulking, as he did more and more often.

I went and started planting the runners, at the same time keeping an eye on the children playing hide-and-seek. If I didn't watch them, they would be swinging on my gate, clambering over my fences, playing up at the clay furrow or even in my woodshed.

I had about four rows planted when I saw the two men coming across the highland. I knew it wasn't any of the Italians. One seemed to be wearing a sort of long garment and I thought perhaps it was the priest again. On the day Christie had come back from Cape Town, he had told me that the Italians wanted a priest so I should arrange to fetch one. I told him there were two priests in the village: one preaching in Dutch in the Dutch Church and the other at the English Church. Christie said they weren't the right kind of priests, it had to be one from the Catholic Church. Which was where? At George, he said, he had made enquiries. He expected me to go to George on foot to fetch the man. I told him they could stay without a priest then, I

183

wasn't walking to George. It's two days' hard walking across sandhills and marshes and one river after another.

But Christie kept on about the priest. I told him to write a letter. The post-cart ran three times a week between Knysna and George; a priest could travel on it from George and I would fetch him from the village. He wrote. And for the first time a letter from the highland got an answer and a speedy one at that. Before a week was out, the priest sent word that he would come on the Tuesday, arriving by post-cart that afternoon at three o'clock. As promised, I went to the village to fetch him. When he got off, he was wearing a long black dress, almost like a woman's, and on his head he had a black hat. Young. A soft sort of face with rosy cheeks. He told me he didn't speak Dutch, but he understood it; he spoke English and Italian and his name was Taramasso. I asked him if he was related to Tomasso who had stolen the child, but from the way he looked at me, I knew he knew nothing. And he didn't seem to know about anything – not about the silkworms, not about the mulberry forest, he only knew about the child that had drowned. I told him the rest until his mouth hung open.

'Priest-man,' I said when we had Gouna's uphill behind us, 'I hope you have a clean dress in that trunk.' The climb had exhausted him and the hem of his skirt was covered with dust.

'How far is it still?' he asked.

'A little less than halfway.'

And when we arrived, I had no idea a priest could have caused so much joy. They stood waiting for him in their best clothes and fell down on their knees, kissing his hand one after the other. America wept unashamedly with the women. It was only Petroniglia that knelt before him without a sign of tears. Like a graven image. Ilario had the youngest of their children, Antonio, in his arms when he knelt, and tears ran down his face as well. Pontiggia sat a little way off, quite unconcerned, carving at a piece of wood and not even looking up at the priest.

'Heathen!' I went and said to him. 'You that should have been in the front row, sits at the back, yes?'

The service was a long affair; I had hoped to have done a little work with them later that afternoon, but I had to give up that hope. I didn't understand a thing about the service. Cuicatti and Borolini had knocked together a sort of table over which the

184

priest threw a cloth and placed the Communion vessels on top, together with a book and a crucifix. He then put on another black dress and when I thought the service was about to begin, they brought a chair and put it a little way away from the tents and there he sat for more than an hour while they went up to him one after the other, talking in whispers.

'Now what's going on?' I asked Christie. I had wanted them at least to repair one of the fences before dark. Christie said they first had to confess their sins before the priest could hold the service for Catarina and give them Communion. I went up to Pontiggia and told him to go and confess his sins before I went and did it for him, but he took no notice.

The two that walked across the highland now were coming my way, not towards the tents. It was not the priest. It was a stranger, and the man with him was Paulus, Mieta's eldest daughter's husband.

'Good afternoon, Master Silas.'

'Good afternoon, Paulus. Afternoon,' I greeted the stranger. He lifted his hat. 'Every time a stranger comes here, it means trouble,' I told him.

'He doesn't speak Dutch, Master Silas,' Paulus said. 'We walked all the way from the village in silence. He arrived by ship from Cape Town yesterday and slept over at Horn's Hotel. The people at the hotel asked me to bring him here. This is where he wants to be.'

'Tell him he's come to the wrong place.'

'I don't speak his language.'

'And what were you doing at the hotel?'

'Looking for work, Master Silas, things are bad.'

'Aren't you cutting in Klaas Ox's team?'

'There have been too many in the team lately, too many mouths between which everything had to be shared. Johannes Meyer and Piet Barnard and myself had to leave. I don't have children and they don't have wives. There's no work in the village, Master Silas, everyone's looking for it. Johannes says we will have to start cutting for ourselves, that's all. The problem is that we only have one axe. The woodbuyer says he'll give us axes on the book, but first we must bring out wood so that he can see how we work.'

185

'I'll lend you an axe. Don't get into debt before you've even started.'

'We hear the forest is being sold. Is that true, Master Silas?'

'I've also heard the rumour.'

'What's to become of us then?'

'It's a government matter. Let us hope that nothing will come of it. What does this man want?' The man just stood there.

'I don't know. They told me he's looking for the woman whose child was drowned when the ship sunk. He was on the ship too, but he didn't drown.'

It was just as if a miracle stood before me. 'Mister,' I said in his own tongue, 'this man says you were on the ship?'

'Yes, my name is William Barrett, I'm looking for the parents of Catarina Grassi.' The man looked destitute; his clothes were too big for his body, his eyes seemed dead.

'They are at the tents, mister, I'll take you to them.'

'Is there an interpreter?'

'Yes.'

I told Paulus to take an axe from the woodshed and to look after it well. I was in a hurry to get to the tents with the man. Not a day passed that Petroniglia didn't keep on at Christie to write and find out what had happened to Catarina that night. She was not satisfied with being told that the child had been drowned and nothing more. Christie said there was nowhere he could write, but she persisted. She wanted to know.

But instead of being glad about the man I took across to the tents, the stupid Christie started carrying on about how impossible his task as interpreter and guardian had become. He told the man that he had still not received a penny of his salary; that the Grassis expected *him* to know what had happened to the child that night; he told the man how he had hastened back from Cape Town to stand by them; how he had given advice in Cape Town about trees being planted to ensure a higher rainfall which would rid the place of the foulness that encouraged smallpox, but no one would take heed because the wrong people had been elected to Parliament.

I thought I would explode. 'Can't you see the man has no interest in what you're saying? Give him a chair, let him sit down and go and tell Petroniglia that someone has come that knows

186

about the child. She said she wouldn't rest before she knew the full story.'

Christie got cross and reminded me that I had said it was Miriam's birthday and that I would be staying at home for the day. I told him I was there to hear what the man had to say; *my* two feet had walked to the village time after time to find out about the child, and I alone had had to carry the final news to the highland. 'I'm staying right here until I've heard what he has to say.'

They all came, not only Petroniglia and Ilario. At first, the Barrett man just looked at his feet, but when he got started, it was as though he was back on the ship and Christie had to interpret fast to keep up with him.

'The child got on the ship with Mr Brown that afternoon: Mr Brown first class, she third class. The ship was due to sail the next morning. Mr Brown had asked me and my wife, also travelling third class, please to look after the child for him. She couldn't speak English, only Italian. Her parents were silk farmers at Gouna, north of Knysna. The child had a trunk and a blanket with her, and the next morning my wife said the child had slept sitting up the whole night, she had never lain down. She didn't have a mattress. We couldn't talk to her as she didn't understand us. Early the next morning the child tried to get off the ship, but a seaman had seen her and brought her back below. When the food arrived, my wife dished up for the child as well and at ten o'clock the ship sailed. Later, when my wife couldn't find the child, she sent me to look for her. I found her on the deck and I saw how frightened she was. I stayed with her and managed to find out that her name was Catarina Grassi. She tried to tell me something about a certain Nicolo Tomasso and kept pointing to the land.

'Later in the day the child seemed better and my wife saw to it that she had something to eat again at midday. In the afternoon, she started taking notice of our baby and played with her. Towards the evening, I went on deck with another immigrant from England, Joseph Allen, because Allen liked to play his concertina on deck at dusk. After a while, we noticed that the child was standing with us and she seemed to enjoy the music. It was just after seven in the evening, the sea was calm and the moon was shining brightly. You could see land clearly and I

187

wondered to myself why the ship was sailing so close to the shore. After a while I went back down below because I had promised three of the other men I would play cards with them. Catarina stayed on deck with Allen who promised to look after her.

'We had just dealt the second hand when the ship suddenly rolled heavily and, at the same time, I heard a noise like a lot of grinding machinery. One of my companions jumped up saying the ship was scraping over a rock. People started running up to the deck. One of the officers came past, saying it was nothing, the ship had touched bottom but it was free again. I returned below to tell my wife it was nothing, and my wife sent me to look for Catarina. At first, I couldn't find her among all the people on deck, then I saw her going from one person to the next, asking them something, but no one understood her. I took her by the hand to go with her back to my wife but she pulled herself free. I couldn't go after her because I had been ordered to the pumps to help pump out the water.

'All this time the ship had been turning away from the land until her bows were pointing to the west again, from where we had come. Rumours circulated that the Captain said we should be able to reach Simon's Bay quite easily which was why we had turned round. Some of the men at the pumps were not happy about this; they wanted the ship to be stopped so that the lifeboats could be lowered and the people taken off the ship.'

'Dov'era Catarina?' Petroniglia asked, impatiently. She wanted to know where Catarina had been. She stood right in front of Barrett and her face was strained.

'I saw Catarina several times amongst the people on the deck,' Barrett said. 'More and more women and children came up from below and they all had to stay together on the poop-deck. We all remained very calm. The ship's doctor, Dr Rose-Innes, stayed with the people on the poop-deck the whole time and spoke to them kindly, telling them there was no danger; should the ship sink, the lifeboats would get us safely to shore. Around a quarter past eight, my first shift at the pumps ended and I fetched my wife and child from below and brought them up on deck.'

Fardini interrupted Barrett and asked Christie to ask him if the people had lifebelts on. Barrett said no one had lifebelts on, there were no lifebelts on the ship except in the lifeboats. By half past eight, there had been six feet of water here and there down below and the men had been ordered to help throw cargo overboard. Others had helped to get the lifeboats ready in case they were needed.

'Dov'era Catarina?'

'She was with my wife on the poop-deck and behaving very well. The pumps couldn't cope with the water, the lifeboats were lowered as far as the railings, but no one tried to get into them, everyone was calm. Most of the men stayed with their families on the poop, and Dr Rose-Innes never left us. Then Catarina indicated that she wanted to go back below to fetch her blanket. I took her by the hand and went with her. When we were about halfway down the last stairway, however, we were unable to go any further, the water was too deep and there were trunks and other belongings floating in the passages. When Catarina saw this, she started to cry; I myself was alarmed. I picked her up and carried her back to the deck. I asked an officer why the Captain did not stop the ship so that the people could be put in the lifeboats. The officer said it was dangerous to transfer people in the dark, even though it was a moonlit night. It was safer on the ship, he said. By half past nine, the ship's head was very low in the water, she was taking on water fast. The men were ordered to stop throwing cargo overboard and one of the officers started sending up rockets.'

'Dov'era Catarina?' Petroniglia was getting more impatient and she seemed greatly agitated.

'Catarina was still with my wife and child on the poop-deck. All the passengers were on the poop-deck. The doctor ordered everyone to sit down; if the ship could not reach Simon's Bay, everyone would get in the lifeboats if we stayed calm, he said. We were not to start pushing or stampeding. There was enough room in the boats for all of us. And no one was to try and save any possessions; only what we had on our bodies could go into the boats. Many of the people then put on more clothes over the ones they had on and stuffed as many things as possible into their pockets. Most of the men gave the money they had on them to the women to hide on their persons because if the ship did not reach Simon's Bay, the women and children would be saved first. The officers came and checked the people to see that they hadn't made any bundles secretly. Only one woman had a bundle under her shawl. When the officer ordered her to open it, it was her little baby she had wrapped up so tight.'

I thought to myself the child could have smothered. Barrett carried on:

'Shortly after ten o'clock that night, we heard that the ship wouldn't steer any more. The ship was then stopped, the engines stopped and the steam blown off gradually. No one attempted to get into the lifeboats, and the doctor continued to talk to us very calmly all the time. It was only when the order was given that the first women and children were to move forward to boat number three on the starboard side that some started crying because it was time for some of us to say farewell to our wives and children.'

Barrett suddenly stopped talking and it became very quiet. All one could hear was the red-chested cuckoo up at the clay furrow that kept calling, and the wind tugging at the tents.

'The man's not feeling well,' I said to Christie. 'Send someone to fetch him some water to drink. For Petroniglia and Ilario too. See how they look.' Christie sent Giuditta to fetch the water and I told him to ask the man why the blooming captain had not stopped the ship sooner. Christie said that it had been reported in the newspapers: the captain had to try and save the ship because the company who owned the ship would have lost a lot of money if it were to sink. Giuditta came back with the water and when Barrett felt better, he went on again.

'Some thirty women and children went down the gangplank and got into the first boat without any trouble. Catarina clambered into the boat with my wife and child; Allen's wife and children were with them and Catarina carried one of the Allens' children. Catarina cried a little. By that time, the captain himself had joined the people on the deck and he was extremely cross that the boats were not brought round to the gangplank faster. Allen asked why the gangplank on the other side of the ship were not lowered as well so that people could be taken into the boats on both sides. Nobody answered him and the boats continued coming round from the port to the starboard side. Allen and I were together when the second batch of women started moving forward to the gangplank to get into a boat. The boat which held our own women and children and Catarina was still down at the stern of the ship and we leaned over to try and see them. There was, however, a sudden rumbling of water and steam, then a gust of air and the ship ploughed her bows into the water. Allen and I tried to run over to the other side, but the deck was suddenly at a very steep angle with the result that we slipped and fell. I got hold of a rope and crawled to the rail. Allen was behind me. The ship had water up to its funnel now, its stern rearing up out of the water. Allen and I then jumped into the sea. The ship must have gone down at that moment, because I was pulled down and down and when I came up, there was nothing. I swam around and finally a lifeboat, with the ship's carpenter in it, picked me up. I asked where the boat with the women and children was; someone told me they had been pulled down with the ship because, at the time, they had still been fastened to the ship by a rope. We rowed around until midnight and picked up a few more people from the sea, but after that there were no more survivors. Of the estimated two hundred and forty people, thirty-six survived and I am one of them.'

Petroniglia stood there without a tear. At first I thought it was because of the shock, but then I saw the bitterness in her. Someone had brought Ilario a stool to sit on; he cracked his knuckles one after the other, staring at the ground. The sun had gone down. The red-chested cuckoo was silent and the frogs had started croaking here and there. When a branch snapped in the forest nearby, I said in my heart: may it be the wind and not an elephant. Not then. He would have walked right over Petroniglia without her even looking up.

When I got home, Miriam stood at the tub on the corner of the house. Her hair was loose and her dress soiled, but she was glowing with a gladness that came from deep down inside her.

ELEVEN

THE DAYS OF October went by slowly. Every night the stars edged a little closer to their positions for Christmas. The nights were short, the days long. A man's hands could do a lot in a day: finish more chairs, set more snares, do more digging, plant more, hoe more, cut more branches and stack more fences around the Italians' vegetable patches, cut more firewood, catch more eels. Only the money in the tin didn't increase.

There were days when I looked at those tents and wanted to tear the world apart until I got my hands on the government. If only they would send someone to come and *see* the state things were reaching. The tents looked as if they wanted to fall over and just lie down and die; the Italians' clothes were limp and faded. The women dragged their feet and the lace collars round their necks were no longer white, but yellow. Everything was falling apart – only a glimmer in their eyes told me they weren't yet prepared to give in. But giving in they were. And what made me hold out was the knowledge that everything had to come to an end sometime, a wheel could roll so far but no further when something got in its way.

Early in October, Christie spent days writing a letter as thick as a book, telling me it was to a very important man in England. A titled man: the Earl of Kimberley. 'See that I am not disturbed, Miggel, keep the Italians occupied and away from my tents. This is one of the most important documents I have ever compiled; I am now turning to Lord Kimberley, Secretary of State for the Colonies. The recruitment and selection of the silk farmers was done according to *his* instructions and I happen to know that he took a personal interest in their coming here.

192

White did write to him once, but not in as much detail as I am doing now.'

'Tell him that Silas Miggel of the highland says that, for a titled man, he is addle-pated if he thought silkworms and Italians could survive here.'

It took him a week to finish the letter, and then I had to take it to the village and pay the one-and-six stamp money as well because Christie was still without a penny. But at least the letter meant hope again.

Mieta came to see Ilario twice and I noticed that she trusted Miriam more and more with her secrets of what to pick and how to brew and how to mix. I was pleased about this because every child we could doctor ourselves, saved money. Petroniglia started combing her hair again although she was not out of mourning yet and still very quiet. Sometimes, when I was working on the chairs, she would come and sit with me in the woodshed, staring out in front of her.

'Petroniglia,' I scolded, 'don't just stare at one spot like that, you must take notice of what's going on around you. And if I have to fetch that Monica of yours from Canovi's tent again, I'll take a hobble and tie her up.'

Portland was quiet. Hal came to the highland one day, saying his mother had sent him to ask if I would please come and help out, Mr Barrington was finished. 'But not too finished,' I said, 'to try and get the forest sold from under us.' Hal said his father no longer had the will to fight for things like that; John had taken over the matter of the forest and had already written to the newspapers to get more support. This was bad news but I didn't say so, I just told him to tell John that it was time he took off his fancy coat and did some work and felt what it was like to sweat.

There were days when Christie refused to come out of his tent to interpret, it was as a protest because he still hadn't been paid his salary and then I had to manage on my own or call on Fardini's Pietro to help me speak to the Italians. Mostly I got along on my own because they had come to understand quite a lot of what I said.

One afternoon, almost at the end of October, Miriam came home from the village and I immediately knew that something was wrong. Everything had been all right that morning when she and a few of the women and America had left for the village to

193

buy provisions. All I had said was that the practice of using my sled and ox for carting their meal and sugar and stuff back to the highland had to come to an end. In future, they could carry it.

Miriam seemed most agitated when they arrived back. It was as if she couldn't decide whether she wanted to sit or stand; she kept on talking and drifting from one thing to the other as was her habit when she was frightened or guilty. I just watched her and didn't stop her. Then she asked if I had seen the lace collars the women pinned to their dresses.

'What about them?'

'Anna Fardini and Mariarosa can make lace themselves, Pa. With their hands. And Vittoria Robolini has promised to teach me to make really nice food. She kept picking leaves on the way to the village, smelling them, tasting them. She says she wants leaves to add to the food.'

'You stay out of their cooking pots. I'm not a goat, I'm not eating leaves.'

'They don't want to eat the leaves, Pa, they just want to give their food more flavour. I showed her what the hard pear's leaves look like and that they smell like almonds, the white ironwood's like lemon, and stinkwood's like cinnamon. They were very excited about the wild pepper. And one of these days they are going to speak Dutch so well, we'll be able to understand everything they say. They're clever. America posted a letter to his people again, Borolini's people also. If only they would get replies. Giuditta says Mangiagalli's people are rich, and they'll send him money for their fares back. And please don't be angry, Pa, there's a penny short on the money because William asked me to buy him a newspaper.'

'William?' I didn't know any William.

'Mr Christie, Pa.'

'Since when is his name William?'

'He asked me to call him by his name, his name is William.'

'His name can be porcupine but you won't be calling him that! Start calling him William and next he'll have his arm around you. I take it that you didn't buy the paper.'

'None of the Italians would lend him a penny, Pa. As soon as his money comes, he'll pay you back everything he owes. The crowned eagle caught a rock rabbit at Witkop's Bend.'

'Miriam,' I said, 'that's enough now of talking in circles,

stepping here and touching there. You're not to go to the forest tomorrow. There are at least twenty bigfeet about half a mile into the forest. We had to turn back when we went out to cut for firewood.'

'I don't want to go to the forest tomorrow, Pa.'

It was only then that I saw her hands were shaking.

'Miriam,' I said, 'did something happen that you're hiding from me?'

'I think you'd better go to the village tomorrow, Pa.' As she spoke, she started crying and I didn't like it.

'Why?'

'When I went to fetch the Italians' shillings from Mr White, just as I've done so many times these past months, there was another man in his chair and he wouldn't give me the money. He wanted to know where the interpreter was, where Mr Christie was. I told him Mr White always trusted me with the money, that Fardini kept book of everything that was bought, that I didn't take a penny of it. I pointed out the Italians to him, standing across the street with the sled, but he hardly looked at them. If John Barrington had not turned up just then, and told him he knew me, I don't think he would have given me the money. When he did, he kept making faces to show his displeasure.'

A slight chill went through me. 'Where's White?' I asked.

'I don't know, Pa. I was too scared to ask. Perhaps he's gone to England to visit his people like he did last time.'

'That clerk of his, Dreyer, took his place then. Where was Dreyer?'

'He was there, but he didn't look up once. You'll have to go and find out.'

'Yes, I'm afraid I'll have to.'

But the next morning I had to get the last of the potatoes planted first; it was the last day of the waxing moon, and I couldn't leave it. Just the week before I had told White to see that the Italians got some seed potatoes to plant as well; the price of potatoes was high and they couldn't keep on buying and buying. Now, according to Miriam, White was not there. The news kept gnawing at me as I planted the potatoes.

I had just about finished the first row when I saw Christie flying down from the tents towards me, his coat flapping like wings at his side. Something must have driven him from the tent because he was on one of his protests again and hadn't spoken to anyone for days.

'Miggel!' he called me from afar.

'What is it?' Every time Christie came hurrying towards me, I felt like hurrying in the opposite direction. With fourteen collapsing tents full of Italians, you could never tell from which side the next crisis would hit you. All of them knew there was only one way to run when something was wrong and that was to Silas Miggel. Ilario was better, but not halfway to what a man should be. Robolini's child, Giuseppe, was down with a fever and Miriam had twice sent me to dig white ironwood roots to give him.

'Miggel!' Christie was out of breath when he got to me, newspaper in his hand. 'I've come to read you something!' he panted.

'If you've come to read to me that the so-called Consul for Italy in Cape Town had succeeded in getting them a ship from the government, you may proceed. I won't be interested in any of the other pages.'

'Wait, Miggel, wait, new light has been cast on the *Teuton* disaster!'

'New light from where? The light's gone out, man, nothing can make that ship come up and float again.'

Christie was in quite a turmoil. 'I have here a report which appeared in *The Globe* in Canada. I lived in Canada once, it's a respected newspaper.'

'What does it say?' Surely they couldn't have found the child after all this time, the thought flashed through my mind.

Christie took hold of the paper with both hands and started reading as if it were an urgent message he had to give me: ' "News was received from Cape Town, South Africa, about the total loss of the steamer, *Teuton*, off Quinn Point, ninety miles east of the Cape of Good Hope." '

'Sixty miles east of the Cape, I was told.'

' "The ship suddenly struck a rock heavily and remained fast for some time." '

'Mr Barrett said the ship went on sailing, turning back at the same time. Are you sure this is about the same ship?'

'Yes, *listen*: "She was badly shattered, but still apparently not irremediable. A scene of panic and horror ensued. The passengers, many below, mothers looking after their offspring, jumped up in consternation. They strove to reach the deck, while those on deck rushed for the boats. In vain the Captain and officers kept them back from crowding one on top of each other. Some were crushed out of all shape and had to be put out of their misery; little children were torn from their parents' arms as terrified men tore past in the endeavour to be first in reaching the boats." '

'Mr Christie,' I said, 'either you are making this up, or that blooming paper made it up!'

'Every word of it is written down here, Miggel, I'm not making it up.' He shook the paper straight and went on: ' "Meanwhile the ship had floated off the rock and the crew recalled to order. Her mighty engines forged ahead and she began to put back to port when suddenly the cry was raised that she was sinking fast. There was time to lower three boats, one so terribly overloaded that she foundered alongside with all on board, the sharks picking off all that rose to the surface, and crimsoning the waves around with their blood." '

That was too much for *my* blood. 'Englishman,' I said, 'you're reading proper shit now!'

'*The Globe* is a reputable paper, Miggel, I'm reading this as it is here, word for word!'

'You've never had a paper by that name before. It's always been the *Cape Times* or an *Argus* we've had to buy you. Where did you get this one from?'

'This is a *Cape Argus*, they've taken the report directly from *The Globe*.'

'Then they've taken over a lot of blooming lies. Mr Barrett came here specially to tell us with his own words what happened. Since when in the dark can you see the water go red with blood as the sharks kept eating the people, even if the moon was shining? Only a bloody fool could have written that for other bloody fools to swallow.'

'Don't be too hasty, Miggel, wait until I've finished. "The other two lifeboats arrived at Simon's Bay after a tedious and perilous voyage. Most survivors were crew, only four passengers were in the boats. The behaviour of the crew was of the most selfish and brutal . . ." '

'Wait. According to Mr Barrett and according to the newspaper I got from Mr White that day, more than four passengers survived.'

' "The motto of the crew was, every man for himself. Weak women were being dashed on one side, or overboard, without any compassion on the part of the ruffianly seamen. The captain and officers endeavoured to restore order, but in vain . . . the captain was either thrown or fell overboard. The passengers in one of the lifeboats wanted to pull towards him, but the crew refused. The survivors that reached Simon's Bay were more like shadows than human beings; more than one was lost on the way from exposure and fatigue." '

'That's another bloody lie. Mr Barrett said they started rowing at midnight, later on they put up a sail and shortly after midday, the next day, they reached shore. He didn't say a word about hardships and people dying on the way.'

'We only have Mr Barrett's word for it, Miggel. I suggest that the Grassis be told of this report, too. They must be given the chance to decide for themselves what they want to believe.'

'Look here, Mr Christie,' I warned him, 'I looked Mr Barrett in the face that day, he didn't lie to us. I know.'

'The Grassis still have the right to hear both sides of the story and to decide for themselves.'

I was angry enough to kill him. 'If you dare go and repeat one single word at the tents about what you've read in that devil's bible, I'll hang you so deep in the forest that not even the vultures will find you!' I tore the newspaper from his hands and trampled it into the earth at his feet. 'And that,' I said, 'was the last newspaper to come making up blooming stories on this highland.'

'That was *my* property you've just destroyed!' he shouted. 'I demand respect from you for my property, my person, my position, and you will apologise to me for your conduct! I am sick and tired of your barbarism and belittling tactics!'

He had to jump clear fast for my spade missed the tip of his shoe by less than an inch.

And White wasn't there. A stranger sat behind the table, a Mr Walker, he said his name was. He was the new Superintendent of Immigrants at Knysna. Mr White had left. The first thing he wanted to know from me was where the interpreter was.

'In his tent on the highland, sulking over his newspaper. I am Silas Miggel, the person that takes care of everything up there on the highland.'

'Mr Miggel!' he cried and stood up to give me his hand. Had I not been a cautious man, I would have thought he was delighted to see me.

'I've just come to enquire about the ship,' I said.

'Ship?'

'Yes, the ship the Italians have been waiting for for months now. It's almost Christmas.'

Walker sat down again, picked up a pen nib, and started fiddling with it quite casually, then said: 'Land was allocated to them on which to establish a silk industry. Why are they not doing so, Mr Miggel?'

'Because the mulberry forest they were promised does not exist! Because the eggs hatched and the worms all died!' I let him have the truth, word by word.

'They were supplied with mulberry cuttings by the government, free of charge.' He was as calm as a rock. I had a feeling he was not only playing with the nib, but with me too.

'Where's Mr White?'

'Mr White has returned to Cape Town. He was a most lenient man, wasn't he, Mr Miggel?'

'I don't know what you mean by that, neither do I know why you're sitting there like someone laughing inside; this is no laughing matter, things are bad up there on the highland.'

'I can assure you that I have no desire to laugh. The tents are needed for other immigrants and must be handed back at the end of December. At this office, clean and neatly folded.'

'I beg your pardon?' I had to lean forward for support against the table. 'Where are they to live after that? Out in the open?'

'The Agricultural Lands Act, of 1879, under which they came out here and took possession of the land, requires them to build themselves huts or shelters within a reasonable period of time in order that the tents may be handed back. After that, and within two years of their lease, they are to erect upon the land leased a dwelling house worth not less than twenty pounds sterling. They've been here now for almost six months, which is surely a

199

reasonable period of time? I therefore assume that they have already built themselves shelters or huts?'

I was utterly dismayed by his words. 'They don't want huts or dwelling houses, mister, they want a ship to take them home. Didn't Mr White tell you that, mister?'

'Mr White was far too lenient.'

'Has mister been appointed especially to make me go out of my mind?' I asked him. 'If you people take away those tents, you're out of *your* blooming minds!'

'Should they want further use of the tents, they may write to this office and I will submit the request to Mr Merriman in Cape Town.'

'What Mr Merriman? It's a Mr Laing that everything is submitted to – and nothing comes back in return.'

'Mr Laing has been appointed to another position. Mr John X. Merriman is the new Commissioner of Crown Lands and Public Works. I shall submit any letter to him. The weekly advance of one shilling per head per day will be paid out until November the sixth. After that, it will cease.'

He did not raise his voice, nor did he stop fiddling with the nib. Perhaps he was playing the fool with me. 'On what day and date are you planning to have their heads cut off?' I asked, but he didn't flinch.

'Until November the sixth.'

'How the hell can they buy provisions after that?'

'They arrived here on May the sixth; on November the sixth it will be six months. I take it that they're about to harvest a second crop? What's more, they are surrounded by one of the best forests in the country and have doubtless acquired woodcutters' licences by this time, cutting and selling wood to supplement their income?'

'Mister, you're delirious and you don't know it. They're not market gardeners, they're not woodcutters, they're silk farmers. They are so scared of the forest, it is with the greatest of difficulty that I get three of them in there to help me cut the firewood. As for the crops you mentioned, there are none for there isn't enough water and manure to make each of them a patch of fertile earth. For every mealie or pumpkin or whatever, you have to cut branches and stack a fence as well and now you're airily suggesting they can do without the shillings!'

200

'The Agricultural Immigrants Act of 1879, clause 21, requires all immigrants to support themselves after arrival. That applies to the Italians as well. Special expositions of the Act were drawn up for them in Italian, clearly stating that they must be self-sufficient whilst planting the cuttings and building their houses.'

I had to walk to the door and back again to the table to get myself under control. 'Mister,' I said, 'mulberry doesn't grow on the highland; a spade's depth and you're into pot-clay! Do you understand Dutch, mister? This whole blooming silkworm business has been an old man's dream and a bungle from the start. A hundred and ten letters have already been written to the government to say that the Italians are asking to be sent back to their country.' I spoke deliberately slowly. 'Do you get it, mister? They don't want to plant crops, they don't want to put up houses, they want to go home.'

'Who says they want to go home?'

I was dumbstruck for a moment. 'Are you trying to be funny now, mister?'

'No. Answer my question: *who* says they want to go home? Did they tell you so personally?'

It was a trap, but there was no time to walk round it. 'They don't speak Dutch. They said so to Mr White, they said so to Mr Christie. About a dozen petitions have gone off to Cape Town already, all signed by them, saying they want to go back.'

'Do they speak English?'

'No, only Italian.'

'How could they have told Mr White that they want to go back then?'

'Mister, if you think you're trying to trap me, you won't even catch the wind. Have you ever sat in a tent through a wet and cold winter? Is there bedding-bush on the floor of your house to keep it dry under your children? And now you want to know *who* says they want to go home? Why don't you go and ask them yourself if you think I'm lying?'

'I don't say you're lying. I'm simply asking who it is that says they want to be sent home? The interpreter? Let us assume – remember I'm saying *assume* – let us assume the interpreter is not conveying their words, or their wishes, quite correctly.'

I didn't know whether he was telling me or asking me that.

'Mister,' I said, 'you're trying to turn one thing into another thing. We forest people have a saying: don't try to make a red alder a white alder for you're going to have a long struggle. You people must find a ship to take them home, or you're going to have a long struggle ahead with them.'

'They have not been promised a ship.'

He was like a blooming blowfly against a window pane, buzzing and buzzing and getting nowhere. I couldn't understand how a learned man in a starched shirt and decent coat, sitting in a high chair, could pretend not to grasp such a simple matter.

'Mister,' I said, trying again, 'I know they were not promised a ship, they're *asking* for a ship. Do you understand that, mister?'

'I think it's you that doesn't understand, Mr Miggel.'

'How do you suggest they get along without the tents and the shillings?' I was starting to sound like a blowfly myself.

'They must get along like all the other immigrants are getting along. The British immigrants in this district didn't get a penny in advance, they didn't get implements or oxen, and their tents were handed back long before the first six months were up. I take it that the Italians are fully aware that they must pay back all advances within two years.'

'Out of what, mister, out of what?'

'About that we'll have to see. I would suggest that you don't worry about it. They are, of course, fully aware that the first payments on their land must be made in June of next year. That's in a little more than six months' time from now.'

'Mister, without the shillings they would hardly have food to eat, and you sit there talking of paying this and paying that. What happens if they can't pay?'

'Don't worry about that, Miggel.'

'I'm asking: *what then?*' I had to know.

'The law gives them six months' exemption; if they still haven't paid by then, the land is put up for sale by public auction to cover their debts.'

That was the first I had heard about that part of the law. I liked it. My mind was suddenly very clear but racing until I found it hard to remain standing there, pretending what he had said meant nothing to me. 'You're saying, if they don't pay by June, the allotments are auctioned by December of next year?'

'Yes.'

'How are they going to survive on air until then?'

'Don't you worry about that. Italians are crafty schemers; long before it comes to that, they'll think up something. You'll see.'

'Can anyone buy at the auction?'

'Yes, provided he has the money to put down.'

'What if the government does send them a ship, what happens to the allotments then?'

'According to the law, it will then be auctioned.'

Silas Miggel, I said to myself, keep your feet still, just stand as if nothing has happened, but one of those lots is as good as yours. 'Mister,' I said, 'this whole thing could be cleared up so quickly if only the government would send someone out to the highland to see what's happening there, but the nearest to the government that ever comes are the warders. And warders are only warders.'

'*I*, Mr Miggel, happen to be the Agent, or Superintendent, of Immigrants in this district, I am a government official. One of the first tasks I shall do is to go to Gouna in person to determine the actual facts.'

'When?' I could not believe it.

'Tomorrow, to tell you the truth.'

'Hallelujah, mister.'

At last. After all the months of imploring them to send someone, a government official was prepared to go to the trouble of getting to the highland himself. I didn't take to Walker much, but I could not have wished for more for the Italians at that moment, and for once I had a bit of decent news to carry back to the highland, even though it was not yet of a ship.

'Englishman,' I went and told Christie at his tent, 'you better get yourself out from under the blankets and get your speech ready. Mr White has left us, there's another man in his place and he'll be here tomorrow to carry out an inspection. If he finds things to his liking, the shillings will be cut off as from early in November, the tents will go at the end of December.' When he opened the tent fly, he stood staring at me, dazed. 'Close your mouth and get your ink, write down everything that we must say to him. Don't leave out a thing. Get the Italians together, tell them to prepare themselves. When that man goes away from here tomorrow, there must be no doubts in his mind. Take notice, Mr Christie, there's a government official on his way here at last!'

'A Mr Walker, you say?'

'Yes. He's coming here himself.'

When I turned round, Lucinetti and Cuicatti stood a little way off, Lucinetti drew a finger across his throat to show me what they planned to do to Christie; I immediately knew there had been trouble between them again. I said they could cut his throat, but not while they were still on the highland.

As I walked across to my house, a sparrowhawk and his mate soared high above the highland, round and round, whistling every so often. I would have taken off and joined them had my arms been wings, so enormous was the relief that had come over me. I had told White straight out one day that he was afraid to come to the highland because he was afraid he would step in his own muck. Higher and higher the sparrowhawks soared against the sky. There was eight pounds and a few shillings in my money tin; that wouldn't buy twenty acres of land, but there was more than a year left to the auction and, no matter how, I would have the money. I knew I would. I had two hands that could work, a body that was strong, and, for the first time in months, a light heart. The old people always said: as long as you still had a coffee bean to roast, things were good; bad only comes on the day you have to roast bladder-nuts for coffee. I was still a long way from bladder-nut coffee.

America came running up from the foot of the highland without the gin or so much as a feather in his hands. 'Signor Miggel! Signor Miggel' he called. 'Serpente, serpente!' He was so overwrought by the time he reached me that I had to take him to Christie to find out what had happened: seemingly a tree snake had come out from the thicket and slithered into the bush in which he was hiding to pull the trap. I told Christie to tell him that a tree snake is a timid creature and that it would rather flee than bite, but America just shook his head, saying, 'Not go again, Signor Miggel, not go again.' Just like a stubborn child.

I told Miriam that evening I wanted her to go and set a few snares early the next morning, but that she was not to tarry. When Walker arrived, she had to be there to tell him about the children that were forever going around with snotty noses, about Cruci's child with the wheezy chest, about Mariarosa's screaming fits, about Ilario who was on his feet one week, and in bed the next. Every word would count. I kept on telling her how important the inspection was, but I had a feeling that she wasn't really listening to me. Two Sundays in a row she had come back from the forest dragging her feet and without her usual cheerfulness. I asked her straight out whether the person she had gone to meet had not turned up. She said I was climbing the wrong tree. And I could get no more out of her.

Walker arrived early, together with Dreyer, the clerk. On horseback. Christie once asked me why I didn't buy myself a horse, and I told him only fools and strangers dared go into the forest with a horse. The first thing a horse does when he smells an elephant is to throw off his rider.

Christie took them straight to his office-tent and I positioned myself just outside the fly, pretending not to see that he wanted me away from there. He started first with his salary that hadn't been paid to him yet and straightaway Walker assured him that it would be at his office within a week, and Christie should come and fetch it. At that, I put my head into the tent and reminded him of the fourteen pounds he owed me. He pretended not to hear me, ignoring me. He then went on about the enormous amount of correspondence he had to handle, and for which he wasn't receiving any extra compensation. I asked him what the use of all the correspondence was since nobody answered him. He had not heard a word from the so-called earl either. He got cross and told me to go and do my work, there was hardly any meat at the tents. I didn't move, I stood where I would. When Walker asked who the spokesman for the Italians was, Christie said it was Robolini, which I said was a lie, it was always Fardini. In the end Walker sent me to fetch them both. When I had them there, I told Christie to let them sit down, not to make them stand like two accused, stooping to fit in under the canvas. But Christie took no notice, he left them standing. Walker asked them how long they'd been on the highland, how their general health was, how many acres of land they had already cultivated, how many children there were, how old the children were. He asked. Christie interpreted. They answered. And neither

Christie nor Walker appeared to notice that the two Italians were standing there getting angrier by the minute. Only I noticed it because I had long learned to watch their faces and bodies to know what they had on their minds. I knew they didn't trust the questioning. In addition, Walker was a man that didn't look at whoever he was speaking to while they were the kind of people that looked you close in the face when you spoke to them. I told myself not to interfere, to stand aside, because the actual inspection was still lying ahead.

And not one single tent did Walker miss. At each one he shook hands, questioned, tickled the children under the chin, squeezed the women's arms – although whether to comfort them or just to touch them, I don't know. All I knew was that the Italians were suddenly very withdrawn; they watched him with wary eyes as if to make sure that he wasn't stealing anything. I called Christie to one side and told him to tell them that the man was there for their salvation, they must speak out, make a noise, get a little rebellious! But the stupid Christie took no notice, he just kept running after Walker as if the man was there for *his* salvation. When Walker was finished at the tents, he went to inspect the allotments and I saw that things were not to his liking there.

'I told you there is not enough water or manure to go round for them all. I encourage them do a bit of digging and planting because they can't sit around idle until the ship comes.'

He made a face, but said nothing. When he was finished at the allotments, he went over to my place and started inspecting *my* vegetable patches. I told him he had no business there but he took no notice, Christie and Dreyer following him like two blooming puppy dogs. Halfway round I noticed him saying something to Christie, and Christie turning back to the tents. When he was finished at my vegetable patches he went and walked round my house, even sticking his nose into my woodshed. And as if that wasn't enough, he walked round my house a second time and then in at my door without so much as an invitation. He sat down at my table where Miriam had just started kneading the bread. Dreyer followed. I said to myself, Silas Miggel, restrain yourself, let him look under your bed if it will help to rid the highland of the Italians.

'Having such a pretty daughter, Miggel, must cause you quite

206

a few problems with all those men at the tents,' he said, chuckling as he sat down. I didn't answer him. I pulled up a chair for myself and asked him whether he was satisfied with what he had seen at the tents.

'I find it inexplicable that Mr White never came back here again after delivering the Italians.'

'Inexplicable is the word, mister,' I agreed. 'If you don't mind, I would like to know what you have decided now.'

'They will most definitely have to get permission to keep the tents for longer. If necessary, of course.'

Don't become too hopeful, I warned myself, be careful. 'Do you now believe that they themselves have asked to be sent back home, mister?'

'Undoubtedly.'

'Why, then, are you displeased about the allotments not having been properly tilled?'

He took up the spoon, lying on the table, and started playing with it. 'Like I've told you already, Miggel, Italians are schemers. I've been to their country twice; it's a beautiful place, but the people are very poor. Especially in the south.'

'These are from the north.'

'They know enough hardship up there, too. Don't you worry about them.'

'The trouble is, mister, that there are children in those tents, children forever sniffing and coughing. You should have been here when the winter was at its worst, the pigs and horses over at Portland were better sheltered. Miriam, Micta and myself had to nurse most of them through fever colds. It's a rain forest this, mister. At the moment it may not look like it, for the sun is shining and it hasn't rained for some time, but when it rains, it rains. We had to cut bedding-bush by the load, not to mention the firewood and the meat and all the other stuff.'

'I can only thank you for what you've done for these silk farmers, Miggel. It could not have been an easy task.'

'It's not. If the government doesn't do something about them, and do it quickly, I'll be a goner and they'll be goners too.'

'I agree with you.'

I was taking courage. I knew that only a fool took courage too easily, but somehow I had a feeling that there was hope. 'Miriam,' I said, 'leave the bread and make Mr Walker and Mr

207

Dreyer some coffee.' As long as he was agreeing with me, I had to hang on. 'There's no sense in us not talking straight today, mister, these Italians must be sent home and that's that.'

'How long does it take to put up a house like this one of yours, Miggel?'

'Putting it up is nothing, mister, it's the cutting and hauling out of the wood, the sawing of the planks and letting the wood get dry, that's the thing.' I didn't let on that he had started a line of questioning that I was going to have to use all my skill to head off because no houses were going to be put up on the highland for Italians. 'Mister,' I said, carefully feeling my way round every word, 'what's the use of talking about houses? Houses that would be put up where? You said yourself they're getting nothing for free, the first payments must be made on the allotments in about six months' time. They don't have money, and who will build a house for himself on another man's property?' I was a bit too close to my own situation. 'You said yourself, if they don't pay by June, the allotments would be sold in December.'

'Actually, in the March following. I didn't inform you quite correctly; they get three months' extension to which six months' grace is added. If they haven't paid by then, the allotments are sold.' The spoon in his hand tapped more insistently on the table. 'I will allow them the use of the tents for a further six months. In the meantime, I want to ask you not to help them too much any more. Don't set snares for them, don't cut their firewood, let them do it themselves.'

'I beg your pardon, mister?' I suddenly no longer trusted him. Miriam neither; she put the jug she had in her hand very hard down on the table, and stood glaring at Walker without a word. 'Mister,' I said, 'what I undertook to do, I'm doing in exchange for dwelling rights. Mr White wrote to Cape Town about it, and until such time as the Italians are taken away from here, I will keep my word so that no one will afterwards be able to say that I didn't keep my word and therefore forfeited my rights.'

'I just don't want you to spoil them any longer, Miggel.'

It was not me who answered him, but Miriam. 'When you no longer want a dog,' she said coldly, 'you can stop feeding it in the hope that it will go away and you will be rid of it.'

He hit back calmly, and without looking up: 'A dog doesn't

run away that easily; stop feeding him, and he might learn to find his own food and shelter.'

'The Italians are *scared* of the forest!' she cried.

'One only fears the unknown until one gets used to it, my dear young lady. Sometimes it's good to be forced to get to know the unknown. We English say: you must sometimes be cruel in order to be kind.'

I interrupted them. 'Listen here, mister, when I find a buck in one of my snares and it's still alive, I take a knife and cut its throat; I don't stand aside, waiting for it to struggle until it dies of exhaustion and then say I'm being cruel because I'm kind. If you're not born in this forest, it doesn't accept you. These Italians are a different kind of people, they may breathe through their noses, but they're different. You people can't take away their shillings until you send them back to where they came from – and if you break my spoon, you must buy me another one.'

'I know what I'm doing, Miggel.'

It wasn't clear whether he meant that about the spoon or the Italians. I told Miriam to leave the coffee, they weren't getting any coffee in my house. He got up and left, Dreyer following.

'And now, Pa?'

'Now nothing.' I fetched a spade and went up to the furrow to dig open the earth bank and release a little water to the sweet potato patch. Cuicatti and Borolini were stacking a fence; Mangiagalli and Cruci sat in the shade, sharing out the sweet potato runners I had given them; Mariarosa and Giuditta were doing their washing and some of the children played around them.

'Good afternoon, Signor Miggel!'

'Good afternoon, Signor Miggel!'

'How many times do I have to tell you not to come and do your washing at the clay furrow?'

'Other furrow no good.'

Petroniglia stood a little way off; she greeted me with her eyes, telling me that she still hurt inside about Catarina. Strange, I always knew what she meant.

TWELVE

THREE DAYS LATER I started working at Portland as if I had never been away. Barrington was still in bed when I got there, John had gone to the village, Hal was at the stables, Will at Karawater. Mrs Barrington and Flos and I went through the work that had to be done, and decided that it would be best if I started in the garden and vegetable patches: the weeds had taken over so badly that it was difficult to tell where one stopped and another started.

The government could starve the Italians in an effort to get rid of them, but they wouldn't starve Silas Miggel off the highland. The day the allotments were to be auctioned, I had to have money. I wouldn't rejoice too early, I decided, but neither was I prepared to cry when the chance came for me to get hold of a piece of the highland and I was caught with an empty money tin. I would work night and day if I had to, but money I would have.

'But what's to become of the Italians, Pa?' Miriam wailed, beside herself with worry when I announced that I was going back to Portland. 'Or have you decided to let Mr Walker have his way, and not help them any more?'

'This has nothing to do with what Walker wants, but I know what I want. You set the snares, and I'll fetch the catch and skin it. On the days that I am not working over at Portland, America, Coccia, Taiani and I will cut the firewood.'

'How many days each week will you be at Portland?'

'Three. That gives me fifteen shillings a week. On the days that I'm here, I'll make chairs and cut a little extra wood to sell as well. Every penny will count. If I can buy one of these lots, you are taken care of and I will never again have to be at the mercy of others for dwelling rights. And if America doesn't take the gin tomorrow and get a few feathers in it, I'll make him forget the snake by using the short whip on him.'

'Leave him, Pa. I'll show Lucinetti how to catch the francolins.'

'No, you stay away from Lucinetti. It's America's work to mind the gin. I'll catch the eels on Thursdays if it's necessary.'

'Pa, you'll never get it all done on your own.'

'I've got to.'

I must have been weeding and digging for a good two hours when Imar and Gabrielle appeared from the house, carrying a chair which they placed under the lemon tree. Barrington followed them, walking by himself but wasted and aged.

'Silas.'

'Honourable.'

It was as if I had never been away. I looked away while he shuffled to the chair, you don't watch a man whose body is finished, but still had all his old pride in the bearing of his head and in the look in his eye.

'As you will notice,' he said when he was in the chair, 'I tried to keep the vegetable garden going.'

'I noticed, Honourable.' Down in the one corner, there were signs that someone had made an effort to hoe. 'The moon is right so we can plant.'

'Yes. I've got very good seed potatoes which I ordered from England.'

'We'll get them in the earth, Mr Barrington.'

I worked. He sat. When I worked too far away from him, he made me start a new section closer to him. 'We must talk, Silas.'

'We must talk, Mr Barrington.'

'I don't know how much time I have left.'

'The best would be for you to give your orders and get it over with.' I did not want to tell him straight out that I didn't think he had much time left.

'It is my wish that Georgina should return to England, taking the girls with her. Some of my land will have to be sold to cover the costs and ensure them of an income.'

It was the first time he had ever called Mrs Barrington by her

211

name in front of me. 'As it is Mr Barrington's wish,' I said.

'I want you to stay on here until they leave.'

'I cannot work under John.'

'My sons have disappointed me deeply, Silas, but they are very dear to me. I don't even wish to talk about Will, I had expected the most of him and now he is the one who grieves me most. He hardly ever comes home from Karawater.'

'The other two grieved you too, Mr Barrington. But a child is a child, you forgive him everything. I'm just telling you that I will not work under John.'

'I want to be buried with honour, Silas. I've told my sons what I'm telling you today. My remains must be taken to the grave on my own wagon, drawn by twelve black oxen. You are to get the oxen together, and be the driver of the wagon for me.'

'Where do you expect me to get twelve black oxen from?'

'You must find them for me,' he said. 'There are four at Redlands, at Belvidere you ought to get at least three, Mr Stewart has two and there are three at Lancewood as well. That's twelve already.'

'How would you suggest I yoke twelve oxen that are not used to pulling together, and keep them in order? I'll have more trouble than I can handle.'

'I expect you to see that the oxen behave themselves.'

'I don't know. If we were talking about a wagonload of wood, it would be a different matter, but it's Honourable I'm going to have on the wagon.' What did it matter whether you were taken away by twelve black oxen or twelve whatever colour? Your soul wasn't on the wagon, your soul's gone with the angelings. But if he wanted it that way, I would do it that way.

As the shade moved round the tree, I moved him with it, chair and all, and was concerned how little weight there was left in him. If he made it to Christmas, I thought, it would be a miracle. And it was when I shifted him for the third time that he started talking to me on a subject I had almost forgotten.

'Silas,' he said, 'years ago you told me something that I gave a lot of thought to later on.'

'What was it I told you?' I'd told him many things, few he ever took notice of.

'You said that man has only one reason for being on earth, and that is to become good. At the time, I didn't realise that you, in your simple way, might have come across a very great truth. Today I have no doubt that that should be our greatest task on earth. When you reach the end of your days, and you look back, it's only the good that has not been in vain, and the only regret one has is that the good is so little and that . . .'

'Mr Barrington,' I stopped him, 'the day I said that, I didn't know what I was talking about. Had I known that you still had it in your head, I would have been here sooner to put it right. I've pushed you in the wrong direction.' He looked at me with a frown, as if most displeased. 'I'm sorry, Honourable, but one is not sent to this earth to become good, but to learn not to lie. That's all. That's the whole and simple truth I've unravelled since those Italians arrived on the highland.'

Barrington turned himself sideways in the chair, obviously vexed, and didn't speak to me for almost an hour. In the end he said: 'I have never held with the habit of lying. If some of the oxen seem too thin to you, find others in their place. It must be twelve splendid oxen and I want you yourself to be neat and tidy and dressed in black as well. Now, help me to the house and then get on with your work. Everything has fallen behind.' As if it were my fault. As if the Italians didn't exist.

I worked late and then went to the back door to take my leave. Gabrielle brought me my day's wages, saying Mr Barrington was back in bed. When the money lay in my hand, I saw it was only three shillings. I was standing there looking at it, deciding whether to give it back and go home or what, when Flos came down the stairs with two more shillings and put them in my hand, saying Mr Barrington had forgotten for the moment that he had sent John to tell me that he was now paying five shillings a day.

By the time I got home, it was dark and everything was in chaos because a marsh lourie had flown into the house, lured by the candle, and in its distress had knocked over many things. The rest Miriam had turned over in her efforts to catch the blooming bird. I took my hat, trapped it near the water bucket in the corner and threw it out of the door. When I turned round, Miriam was standing there, stiff with fright.

'Pa, Aunt Hannie says that if the marsh lourie flies in the dark, it brings bad news.'

'Your Aunt Hannie has never learned to keep her mouth shut.

213

Walker brought the news, not the lourie.' I picked up a chair and started helping her to set the house to rights again.

'Mr Christie went to the village to get his money but Mr Walker says it hasn't come yet.'

I took the five shillings from my pocket and put it in the tin and with it a feeling of relief came over me: the government won't starve me.

On Mondays, Tuesdays and Wednesdays I worked at Portland; Thursdays, Fridays and Saturdays on the highland. It was a hard time. I was so tired on Sundays, I fell asleep with the Bible on my lap, but every shilling that dropped into the tin was like a sod from one of the allotments; every penny I had to take out again for provisions, a lump of earth less.

At the tents things were much the same: noisy, rebellious, trouble between themselves, trouble with Christie, shittings, fever colds. The worst days were those when it seemed as if a total hopelessness descended on them and they were quiet and didn't play music when the sun went down. Those were the days when the women quarrelled more easily; when Cuicatti and Tomé almost came to blows about a missing tent-peg; when Fardini kept walking backwards and forwards across the highland as if he wanted to thrash a way out for them all with his feet. Christie wrote one letter after the other to the government about his salary and about the Italians' allowance that had to be extended. It wasn't long before he ran out of paper and ink and came to borrow five pounds from me.

I flew at him. 'You already owe me fourteen which I don't know if I'll ever see again! It's almost the end of October, if they haven't paid you by now, they have no intention of ever paying you but you still see fit to come and borrow more from me?'

'They are legally obliged to pay me.'

'Forget about the legality of the matter, take the blessed Italians and walk them to Cape Town while they can still use their feet, put them on the government's doorstep and leave them there. Do it before Walker stops the shillings, because if he does, there's going to be trouble, I'm telling you.'

'They wouldn't dare stop the allowance, Miggel, it's only a threat. The government won't do it, not after all my representations. And I don't expect you to lend me five pounds without

214

security, so I'm prepared to pledge my allotment to you until such time as my money comes.'

'You know very well that you cannot pledge your lot to me, it's not yours to pledge, it's the Crown's.' I would have emptied my money tin for him if it hadn't been so. However, something else sprang to mind. 'Mr Christie,' I said, 'I'll make you another offer. A good one. I'll write off whatever you owe me as well as give you a full ten pounds in return for the twenty acres that's been allocated to you. You will pay for it, but you will let them write the title deed in my name.' It was like luring an eel from under the rock with a piece of frog meat, you couldn't let your shadow move lest you frightened it away. Christie was tempted to bite, I could see. 'Ten pounds.'

He shook his head regretfully. 'The law prohibits an immigrant to dispose of his land before the expiration of five years, not even if it has been paid for already.'

The eel had no teeth, it could not bite even if it wanted to. 'What a pity,' I said, 'you could have had ten pounds now.'

'But there are many ways to get round the law, Miggel. I can appoint you my representative, I could bequeath my land to you. We could find a way.'

'Leave it. The day I buy myself a piece of this highland, I will buy it for the title-deed and nothing less. In the meantime I have dwelling rights in any case.'

'I wouldn't be so sure of that if I were you.'

There was no need for him to tell me that, I knew. In the end I gave him three pounds with Miriam as witness. I told him to call the Italians together and tell them of the possibility that the shillings might only be paid out until the sixth of November, but he refused. He said he was convinced that the government would not carry out the threat. It was only me that couldn't find enough faith to believe it; I had a feeling that from somewhere a wheel was rolling and it was rolling downhill, gathering speed. I said to myself: Silas Miggel, when the moment comes, just see that you jump fast and well clear of it.

On the days I stayed on the highland, I worked as hard as on the days I went to Portland. I never got America to work the gin again, not even the whip scared him. 'Not go again, Signor Miggel, not go again.' Then Canovi came and offered to take America's place, so one Thursday I set aside my work and went and showed him how I wanted him to set it and guard it. When I had him settled in the underbush, I went back to the woodshed and didn't give him another thought. At least, not before he came back later that afternoon with a francolin in one hand and Monica Grassi in the other. A mere blooming child. Fourteen years old. Right under my eyes, she had sneaked past to him on the forest's edge. I threw down my saw and fetched her mother right there from the tent and called Christie to come and interpret. I told him to tell her that there was enough trouble on the highland and enough on its way, she was to keep her eye on her daughter and keep her away from Canovi. Canovi was a rogue.

She didn't let Christie answer for her, she answered me herself: 'Signor Miggel has Miriam,' she said, 'Petroniglia has Monica.'

I didn't quite know whether to get cross or not, I wasn't sure that she knew what she had said. She had nothing to do with Miriam, I was the one to worry about Miriam. Or not worry about Miriam. For a strange thing had happened around this time.

I told Barrington one afternoon that I wanted to go home a little early, the weather was working up for rain and before it did, I wanted to build the weir to the east of the tents a little higher. Every extra bucket of water we could catch would help. Also, I wanted more so that I could get them away from the clay furrow. By the time I got to the highland, however, the sky was clear, the rain had passed us by again. And Miriam wasn't at home. It was too late to go back to Portland so I took the hatchet and went into the forest to collect a few bundles of kindling.

I hadn't gone far when I came across Miriam on Red Alder's sled-path, walking with her arms folded and her eyes at her feet like one deep in thought. When she looked up and saw me, she was immediately alarmed and suspicious and I had to put her at ease, telling her there was nothing wrong, that I had just got home earlier because of the weather. On that we parted: she on her way home, me on my way to collect the kindling.

Not ten minutes later, however, I came across Jacob Terblans, sitting on a fallen tree with his head hanging down like one deep in thought, I found his presence very strange. The Terblanses lived at Deep Walls and Deep Walls was a bit far for

216

one of them to be sitting on Red Alder's sled-path at that time of day. In any case, the Terblanses seldom came to Gouna's part of the forest. Good people. Of Nols Terblanses seven sons, Jacob was in the middle and the one that could beat those on either side of him when it came to working with wood. For years Jacob had been courting Susanna, daughter of my own blood cousin, Grieta, up at Big Island. Grieta liked to brag about Jacob, she often began spreading a rumour that the wedding was not far off. She had reason to be proud of her daughter marrying Jacob. He was a young man that had already built himself a wagon in his spare time, cutting and dressing the wood all by himself. Good people, the Terblanses. His grandmother on his mother's side was so fat that when she sat on a wagon there was room for nothing else and the village people had given her the name of 'forest fairy'.

When I asked Jacob why he was sitting there like that, he said he was resting, he had walked through to our side of the forest to see how much white pear there was to cut. On their side, the best white pear had been felled already and apparently the woodbuyers wanted white pear; the furniture makers in Cape Town were all of a sudden asking for white pear. I asked him if they had heard or seen anything of Josafat Stander recently. Not a sound nor a sign, he said, the man passed into eternity without a funeral, like a heathen. We walked together to where he had to turn off for Kom's Bush, and I sent greetings to Grieta and the people of her house with him.

At table that night, I told Miriam that I had seen Jacob, and I said I wondered when he and Susanna were going to get married. Abruptly she pushed back her plate, saying that things between Jacob and Susanna had been off for some time. And at that moment a silence fell over the table that was no ordinary silence. I said to myself: Silas Miggel, hold your tongue, you're either treading on the lilies or very near to them. I said nothing more on the subject and I didn't ask her how she knew, I just started talking about the dough-cakes Petroniglia had brought across when I got home – I couldn't get them down my throat, Miriam had to eat them.

But when I went to bed that night, I was very sad because I knew Miriam was lying in her room, crying. I could hear her. I didn't get up, I knew it was a cry she had to cry alone. I brought

together all the bits I knew and had no doubt that she and Jacob
had been together in the forest that afternoon. The fact that it
was Jacob comforted me more than I expected. If there was one
man I could have given my daughter to, it was Jacob Terblans.
Jacob would have taken good care of her, he would have freed
me from the fear I always had that something could happen to
me before I had provided enough for her to live on. Yes, of all
the young men in the forest, I would have given her to Jacob if I
could.

It was easy for Petroniglia to talk. What did she know? Miriam
wasn't Monica, and Jacob wasn't Canovi.

Over at Portland things slowly started to get better. It was only
Barrington that didn't get any better. We hired two extra helpers
and I told him to keep John away from them, that I would see to
it that they worked properly and earned their wages. I was
actually trying to tell him to stop dragging himself from the
house every day to see that everyone was doing enough for what
he paid them at night.

It was that same afternoon that John came back from the
village on horseback like a lord, reining in to interfere where we
were busy getting a field ready to sow rye. I asked him why he
didn't take his horse to go and find someone to help his mother
in the kitchen. It was not proper for a lady like her to stand over
a fire all day long to cook and toil for everyone. The trouble in
Portland's kitchen had always been that Barrington himself
couldn't keep his nose out of the women's work; he forever
sniffed around the kitchen and at the end of the day, every
copper pot that had been used had to shine to his satisfaction
before it could be stacked away. I told John to go to Mary,
daughter of Koos Matroos, and ask her to come back to
Portland; she and Mrs Barrington had got on well when she had
worked there before. I told him to tell Mary that his father didn't
concern himself with the kitchen any more, that he was finished.
John just gave a sneering grin from his horse, however, and
suggested that I send Miriam over in the mornings to help Mrs
Barrington in the kitchen. Wages would be one pound and ten
shillings a month, the best in the whole district. I answered him
quite calmly, I would not allow myself to be vexed by the wind,
especially not a wind with a whiff of wine in it. I told him that it

218

wasn't that I considered my Miriam too good for Portland's kitchen, it was just that I didn't want her to work where vipers lay in wait for her down at the river when she had to pass through the gorge in the afternoon. And typically, like the guilty, he started picking up and throwing mud, saying that if it hadn't been for Portland, Miriam would never have crawled from the forest to learn a few manners. The day she found herself in a rotten shack on one of the islands, raising a woodcutter's brats, she would wish she was in Portland's kitchen scrubbing floors.

The following day, John was over at the tents to ask if any of the Italians' wives or daughters were interested in doing housework over at Portland. Wages were a pound a month. Mariarosa threw a cooking pot at him.

Barrington never asked me about the Italians and neither did he like me to talk about them. However, Mrs Barrington asked me one day how things were over at the tents. 'Bad, missus,' I said, 'and it seems as if there's worse to come. The only consolation I have is that the day must come when the government *has* to send them home. Not all of them will make it to that day, however, a few will stay behind in their graves for sure.' I said this in the hope that she would tell Barrington and that somehow he would still find it in his heart to do something to help to get them home. When I was ready to go home myself that afternoon, she gave me a pail of milk to take back to them.

Shortly after this, I asked Barrington straight out how far they had got with the selling of the forests. I had to know. He said the representations had not been successful because the people from the village and outlying district had not cooperated as fully as had been expected, there was too much division. A consequence of this was that Captain Harison had insulted him by reminding him, by letter, that he, Barrington, was as subject to the laws of conservation as everyone else, that he wouldn't be allowed to cut in Portland's part of the forest as he wished.

'I, Silas,' he said, 'a responsible person and a British subject, was addressed like a common woodcutter.'

'That wasn't nice of him, Honourable,' I said.

When November came, the cold weather returned as if it had never gone. For almost a week the highland lay frozen every morning. But only cold, still not a drop of rain. I brought the

219

water down to my vegetable patches, allowing a little to run past to the Italians' few beds. Twice in a row, Taiani and Lucinetti returned from the lagoon without fish or scale, forcing me to go and catch eels with the sun already almost down. Every night when I came back from Portland, Miriam was ready to tell me what had happened at the tents while I was gone.

'Cruci's child keeps on getting chest colds, Pa, she could hardly breathe today.'

'Give her honey and bedding-bush tea.'

'Can't we let Felitze sleep with us until the cold weather is gone, Pa?'

'No. Bring him here and soon I'll have a housefly on my hands.'

'Angelo Borolini has been sitting in his tent for two days now without even lifting his head, Pa. They say he's pining for a girl he left behind in Italy. He was supposed to have sent her money from the first cocoon crop so that she could follow him here.'

'Give him parsley-bush brew.'

'Mariarosa started screaming again this afternoon.'

'I think we must give her milkwood-bark brew for a change.'

That same week, two of the older children went down with chicken pox. I told Christie and Miriam to keep the news from the warders for if they heard about it, they would turn it into smallpox and nothing else. Every night I said to myself: Silas Miggel, hold out. The more I thought about it, the more convinced I became that the government was playing a stupid game to see if the Italians could get along on the highland if they were forced to. The question was: how far would they go with the game? How long? I no longer tried to understand what they had planned to do about Christie; every time he went to enquire about his money, Walker told him he was expecting it any day, it was just that that day never arrived.

'They want to get rid of me, Miggel,' he told me. 'They've discovered that I will not support their colonial stupidity, nor be frightened by their threats.'

'What threats?'

'That I will be relieved of my post if I do not stop interfering with matters that are handled by others. The truth is that I refuse to stop badgering them about my money and about the

220

Italians and that is making matters very uncomfortable for them. They know I won't give up before justice has been done.'

I kept quiet about the warder who had turned up at my house the week before, with such a friendly manner that I was cautious the moment I saw him. First he inspected my wood and my woodcutter's licence, then he came smoking his pipe to where I was skinning a buck, and said he understood I was doing such a great deal for the Italians. What was the interpreter doing then? I told him the interpreter interpreted and wrote letters to see if a ship might not fall from the sky and take the Italians home.

'Don't you think they can do without an interpreter by now, uncle? I understand they are speaking quite a bit of Dutch. I understand Miriam runs a sort of school for the children.'

'I don't know where you learn all these things, warder, but when you get back there again, ask them how the Italians are to get along without the shillings if the government doesn't relent. Find that out and then come and tell me so that I too will be able to understand.'

But he just wanted to talk about Christie: 'Do you think they could get along without an interpreter, uncle?'

'No, and neither without the shillings. Go and tell that to the person who has sent you here.'

The sixth of November was a Sunday. On the Monday, Christie, Fardini and a few of the others left for the village to collect their money and buy provisions for the week. When I came back from Portland that night, I asked Christie if he had told them that it might have been the last of the government money. No, he said, he was confident that his representations would succeed. He also expected to hear from the earl in due course because he had written to him again.

The week went by. On the Sunday night, the one before the Monday the fourteenth, the Italians made music and Miriam and I went over to the tents to listen. By now, she knew most of the songs so well that she could sing along with them. I let her sing. Petroniglia also sang. Beautifully. She was not over Catarina's death yet, and I still saw to it that the best of the meat went to the Grassis' tent. Sometimes, when I came back from Portland at dusk, she would be standing waiting for me at the end of the footpath coming from the gorge, to thank me. She was different from the other women, not so noisy. There were days that I wished I could tell her about the lilies, just to try and comfort her, but I couldn't speak her language. And she didn't understand enough of mine.

For as long as I can remember the story of the lilies was part of forest life: the story of a little marsh full of scarlet lilies hidden somewhere in the forest, but no one could tell you where. In later years, a part of Gouna's forest even got the name of Lily Bush.

'I know every bit of the forest,' my late father used to say, 'but there are no lilies in it. The lilies are up in the mountains.'

I was a young man still when I had to take shelter at Mieta's house during a heavy shower of rain one day; we talked about this and that to pass the time and so it was that I asked her if she believed the story about the lilies. She didn't answer me straight out, she answered me with a riddle:

'One person believes without his eyes having seen, the other believes only what his eyes have seen. If you must see, you will see.'

It's a myth, I said to myself when I walked away from there. Like the story of the yellowwood tree beside the Homtini River near the place where the elephants always rolled in the mud. It was surely the most beautiful yellowwood in the whole forest, and no one would take an axe to it while the story about it remained alive. Many years ago, the old people said, four woodcutters from Kom's Bush set out to fell the tree. It took them a full day's walk to get there, and when they did, they built themselves a shelter, had something to eat, and lay down to sleep so they could start cutting at dawn. During the night, however, they were woken by a glow and leaped up, thinking a forest fire had broken out. When they got outside their shelter, they saw it was the tree that was on fire – but it did not burn with flames, it glowed like a cinder from its roots right up to its crown. At first they thought it must have been struck by lightning, but it was a cloudless night. Neither did they feel a fire's heat. They stood there in fear and awe, watching the unearthly sight, then the glow slowly started fading from the tree before their very eyes until only the moonlight lay in its branches again. The tree was bewitched. And so the forest got itself another story, like the one about the lilies.

222

Years after the day I had asked Mieta about the lilies, I took a short cut through the forest to get to the honey-cliffs way up along the Knysna River. Miriam, then about twelve, was with me and I was doing what I had always told her was a dangerous thing to do: taking a short cut. To take a short cut through the forest was to look for trouble. Before you knew where you were, you were walking in circles. Lost. But, strangely enough, I had a feeling that we were on a path, not a footpath, however, nor a sled-path. I grew more and more uneasy and took the child by the hand. Elephants sometimes had a way of making themselves a secret path for reasons unknown. Should you land on one of them by accident, you had better know your step.

It was February and hot down in the forest. Every now and again a bit of rain fell, making the forest floor steam until it seemed as if we were walking through a haze of smoke. We came to a valley densely grown over with ferns, mostly tree ferns of which the old leaves made a crackling sound as we pushed our bodies through it. I didn't like it; it was a sound an elephant would hear a mile away. To turn back would have made little difference, it was best to go on.

Not long after that, I began to hear the sound of rushing water and worked out that it could only be Red Alder River so we were still going in the right direction. When we reached the river, I saw that we were still on the elephants' path as well since we had come out exactly where they must have forded the river hundreds of times through the years. There were no fresh tracks, and no fresh dung so I decided to go through. The path was so cleverly made that one had to think with an elephant's mind to stay on it. After about another hour, I said to Miriam that we would have to start turning westwards, aiming for the Knysna River if we wanted to get to the honey. Hardly had I spoken when I noticed that the path also started swerving to the west. There was no way I could get out, it was thick forest, old forest, the sun only filtered through here and there.

'Are we lost, Pa?'

'No.'

I remember that we passed a yellowwood with an ironwood on either side of it: all three equal in thickness and evenly spaced like three sentries standing there in the forest. But it seemed as if the world ahead of us was getting lighter. As if there were an opening somewhere in the forest roof. Not fifty yards further on, the forest suddenly stopped in its tracks on all sides – and I stopped in mine and the child in hers. In front of us lay a marsh covered with lilies as red as blood. Had it been in the middle of the night, I would have thought I were dreaming. Hundreds upon hundreds of lilies shimmering in the sunlight. It was so beautiful that it made me sad. It was not a big marsh, about a hundred and thirty paces long and seventy across. I stood there with my feet in the mud on the edge of the marsh and it felt as though I had walked right through the forest and into its heart. A feeling of awe welled up in me as I had never known before, and the same sensation of awe seemed to be all around me. When I looked up, I saw a single lourie fly across the marsh like a guardian, and the feathers of his wings were as red as the lilies below him. Not a kok, not a sound, not a movement in the thickets, as if everything was holding its breath to see if I would step forward into the lilies, or turn back. I could not move for I, Silas Miggel, sinner from the highland, had come upon the lilies. I had seen.

I didn't go on to the honey-cliffs, I took the child by the hand and turned back. When we were a good distance from the marsh, we sat down to eat and for the first time I could speak again.

'That, Miriam,' I said, 'was the forest's heart and the forest's secret. You are never to tell anyone about it, you are never to pick a single lily, you are never to step into the marsh because you'll be stepping right into the forest's heart.'

On the Monday, the fourteenth of November, I went to work at Portland as usual and Christie and Fardini went to the village to get the shillings. They came back empty-handed. By the time I got home, late that afternoon, the worst of their anger was over, only the feeling of utter despondency hung about the tents.

I had never seen them like that before. I think it was the first time that they were really scared. Especially the women.

'Mr Christie is drawing up a new petition,' Miriam said in tears, 'they are all going to sign it. America says he's going to sign his grandfather's name as well: his grandfather is dead already, but he would have signed. They want the priest, Pa, and Giuditta fainted. Mariarosa didn't scream, she just took hold of

224

her hair and pulled and pulled, and Aunt Grieta's Klaas was here, he came to say that there's a wedding on up at Big Island on Saturday, Jacob and Susanna are getting married.'

All this in the same breath. Everything mixed up together. 'Did you say Jacob and Susanna are getting married?' I couldn't believe it. I didn't understand it.

'Yes, on Saturday. Things are bad at the tents, Pa, you must go and talk to them. Pontiggia is sitting up at the clay furrow, he keeps on throwing lumps of clay into the water. Petroniglia doesn't cry, she's just standing behind the fire-shelter.'

'You say Jacob and Susanna are getting married?'

'Yes.' And it didn't seem to bother her.

The money didn't run out immediately at the tents. Fardini must have put some aside over the previous months because until the beginning of December they still managed to buy provisions. Less and less of course, until only one man was needed to carry them from the village to the highland, but still it was something. Especially the meal. Miriam set extra snares, I skinned and shared out the meat.

Three days a week I worked at Portland, three on the highland. All the time I repeatedly said to myself: Silas Miggel, you've got to hold out. The wheel had come and rolled right over the Italians, but it would be back. All I asked was a little time before it did. At Portland, Barrington seldom left the house any more, in my heart I asked him to hold on just a little longer so that I could be sure of my wages. I would not work under John.

On top of everything, I was becoming increasingly anxious about Miriam. Every morning she got up with a sadness in her and at night she took it back to bed with her. The day before Jacob and Susanna's wedding, she nagged me until I agreed to go to Big Island with her to the wedding. Throughout the day, there wasn't a sign of resentment or discontent. If anyone looked discontent, it was Jacob; he stood arm in arm with Susanna, but his eyes kept following Miriam. And Miriam seemed cheerful but not totally so; it was as though the cheerfulness didn't reach her eyes. The day after the wedding, the Sunday, she went into the forest for the whole day and when she came back, she walked like a bird dragging both its wings. I couldn't understand it.

225

'Miriam,' I said, 'fight against that which you cannot change, and you will fight yourself into ruin.'

'I'm not fighting against what I cannot change, Pa!' she burst out. 'I'm fighting against that which I cannot understand!'

'What is it you don't understand?'

'Pa says God sees everything and knows everything. If that is true, why doesn't God send the Italians a ship to take them home? What's to become of them?'

I got up, poured her some coffee and stirred in a good measure of sugar. 'You're starting at your feet again, Miriam. Where it is you're heading, I don't know. I only know the answer to what's wrong at your feet. If I spill all this coffee on the floor, I don't just go and sit on the chair, moaning and wailing to God to come and clean it up for me; I ask you to do it for me, or I do it myself. Barrington poured the coffee, the government spilled it, and now no one wants to bend down to clean up the mess – and you come blaming God. That is half of what you don't understand. I assume that you'll deny the other half, but I'm telling you that you don't understand why Jacob married Susanna if it's you he had his heart set on.'

'That's not true, Pa. I'm not against him marrying Susanna, he couldn't have married me anyway.'

'Something tells me you're a long way from your head still.'

'What's to become of the Italians, Pa?'

'I don't know. I only know that when a government's wheel starts rolling, it rolls and it doesn't stop to see who's in its way. But it's not going to roll over Silas Miggel, and neither is it going to roll over you. We are going to keep out of its way and the first thing to be done, is to see that there is enough money in the tin to buy one of the allotments at the end of next year.'

'What about the Italians, Pa?'

'When that wheel returns, Miriam, it will roll a few of them flat, I want you to know that.'

'Doesn't it worry you? What if the wheel runs over Petroniglia?'

Why did she pick out Petroniglia? I didn't like it. 'No one can tell who it's going to run over. All we can hope is that when it comes back, there will be something to destroy it and that they will then be sent home at last.'

'I wish I was as hard-hearted as you are.'

226

I didn't answer that. And what was really on her mind, she didn't tell me. On the Wednesday I took my whole day's wages and bought her a dress and a petticoat of Imar's from Mrs Barrington. When she tried it on that night, it was bundles too wide for her, I hadn't really noticed how thin she had become.

Summer settled over the highland at last: during the day the sun baked the tents as hot as ovens and the Italians no longer played music in the evenings. Fardini shared the meal between the tents; I shared the water between the vegetable patches and scolded the children for every drop they wasted. And still the rains stayed away. When December entered its second week, a fog came out of the sea, rolling inland to come and lie over the forest until one could hardly see ten paces ahead. I knotted some rope together and tied the smallest of the children to the tent-poles. As I was tying Cruci's Maria to the pole, Christie put his head round the fly, saying: 'Shame, Miggel, you're a cruel man.'

'Cruel?' I said. 'Cruel is when a child wanders away in a fog like this and you walk through the forest for days, calling his name, like we did when Elias van Rooyen's boy got lost and was never found again. A child cannot tell which way he's going when the fog comes and blinds the world. A grown-up hardly can, so go and sit in your tent.'

On the third day, the fog was so thick that one could scoop it up with a bucket. From a certain distance, there was little difference between the colour of the tents and the fog and the Italians became dark shapes walking to and fro like wary ghosts. I couldn't get down to the waterholes to catch eels, Lucinetti and Taiani couldn't get to the lagoon to catch fish, Canovi didn't know where to set the gin because the francolins didn't whistle and betray where they went to roost at night. All we managed to get in the snares was a little blue buck and a bush-pig and it took some careful sharing-out to get a piece into every pot.

On the Saturday, Fardini's son, Pietro, came running to the house, saying his sister Luigia was missing. His father asked if I would please help to find her, and his mother was crying. The first thing I did was to go and see whether Cuicatti was in his tent. He wasn't. Just as I had thought. And I found them right down at the foot of the highland in the fog, and I drove them back

227

to the tents. Had they not stopped me, I would have tied her to a tent pole as well. A mere blooming child. Thirteen years old.

When Sunday dawned, the fog was as thick if not thicker. When I got up, I could feel my body was glad that it was a day of rest. There were days, I swear, when I did the work not of two men but of three. I got up and cleaned out the hearth, making as little noise as possible because I wanted Miriam to sleep on. When I got outside to empty the ash-pan, a shiver shot through my body and I froze in my tracks – in the air, I had caught a whiff and I knew it was of elephant dung. My father always told us that if you smell bigfeet in thick fog, there's nothing you can do except dig a hole right where you are, get into it and cover yourself up.

I stood there and all I could hear was my heart beating in my ears and the tip-tip-tip of the fog dripping from the roof into the water-butt. I didn't know if it was one elephant or a herd, I didn't know where it or they were. I put the ash-pan down quietly so I could go and see if they were between the house and tents. I had to know. When I got to my gate, there was no gate, it was trampled flat and so was the fence on both sides of it. My mind warned me to stay where I was, but I just couldn't. I started walking slowly along the fence and as far as I went, the damage became apparent: they had gone straight through my sweet potato patch, through the cabbages, through the pumpkins and down into the mealies where they had eaten, pulled up, scattered, and trampled until there was nothing left of my whole crop. They went out through the bottom fence and the tracks disappeared into the fog towards the foot of the highland. Further than that, I dared not go.

You can stand up against many things, against every forest warder or Italian and his tent, against Walker and Christie and the whole government, but never against an elephant. You stand dejected and trampled flat, and you know you're up against a mountain that's too high for you. I also knew there would be no rest for me on that Sabbath day.

I went back to the house, loaded the heavy gun and went across to the Italians to tell them that there were elephants and started a watch between the house and the tents. The elephants were somewhere on the highland in the fog; on three sides they were hemmed in by gorges, if they wanted to get back into the

228

forest to the north, they would come up between the house and the tents, or past on either side.

I don't think the Italians had ever been so quiet in their lives as on that day. Whether they had plugged the children's mouths with rags, I don't know, but not a whisper came from the tents. Every time I patrolled past, I just saw eyes, wild with fear, following me. When I was on my second round, I found Petroniglia and Vittoria Robolini at the fire-shelter and Petroniglia managed to tell me that Ilario was ill, could I not send for Mieta? I fetched Christie to come and tell her that Ilario would have to hold out, I could not send Miriam up into Creek Bush in weather like this.

Towards afternoon, the fog started lifting and when it was clear enough to see as far as the foot of the highland, only the oxen were there. When the elephants had gone past, I could not tell. I found their tracks to the west of the house where they had passed by quietly.

Miriam took the last of the parsley-bush brew and shared it out amongst the women and children. As I sat down at the table and opened the Bible, Christie and Fardini came to my door.

'May we come in, Miggel?' Christie asked. He no longer shaved every day and his clothes looked as though he slept in them.

'Yes,' I said, 'but you mustn't stay long, I'm tired.'

When they sat down, Fardini started cracking his knuckles. 'Very bad, Signor Miggel, very bad. Meal finished, money finished. Everything.'

'We're facing a crisis, Miggel,' Christie added. 'There is no food at the tents.'

I closed the Bible and pushed it to one side. 'Why are you coming to tell me this? Why don't you go and tell Walker?'

'Bad, Signor Miggel, very bad.'

'There is no meat,' Christie said, 'there is no firewood, things are in an awful state, Miggel!' He banged my table with his fist.

'The firewood will last until Thursday, I've had a look. The reason for there being no meat is because there was nothing in the snares. If there's nothing in the snares, there's nothing in the snares. I can't go rounding up a buck for them, I'm not a dog. The man that sometimes used to shoot me a little extra has been killed by the bigfeet.'

229

'We've come to ask you to lend us a few pounds,' said Christie.

I could have kicked the chair from under him. 'Have you come here to borrow money from me on the Sabbath day?' I asked. 'Do you take me for a heathen?'

'No. But tomorrow is Monday, by the time we get up, you've already left for Portland. You could give the money to Miriam in the morning, I'll sign the necessary voucher for it and see to it that you are paid back the moment the allowance is resumed.'

'Resumed from where?'

'From the government, of course. They won't just sit back and let these people die of hunger, Miggel.'

'You're mistaken, Mr Christie,' I said, 'I think that's exactly what the government has in mind: first the worms, then the Italians, then you.'

He grew pale under his stubble. 'You have no feelings, Miggel. No conscience. You are sitting there with the Bible in front of you, but you forget that it's written there that what you do unto others, will be done unto yourself.'

'Don't you come telling me what's in the Bible. I told you weeks ago to start walking them to Cape Town to leave them on the government's doorstep, and now you want to come and leave them on mine? Tomorrow morning, before dawn, I'll go and see if there's something in the snares. On Thursday, I'll see that the firewood gets cut; if Lucinetti and Taiani get no fish, I'll go and catch them a couple of eels and on Friday I'll see to it that fresh bedding-bush gets put in the tents. I'll fetch Mieta to come and see to Ilario, I'll do whatever I have to do, but money I will not give you, and don't you come asking me again either.'

'Just five pounds, Miggel.'

'No.'

I held out until the day before Christmas. Then I took the ox and the sled and five pounds from the tin and set out for the village to buy meal and sugar, coffee and lard, and when I had it loaded, I pulled up at Walker's office and knocked the hell out of his door.

'Five pounds,' I said when I stood before him, 'five pounds the government owes me and I want it now. And then I want to tell you that they're starving to death up there on the highland.'

'Stay calm, Mr Miggel,' he said almost cheerfully. 'Take heart, maybe the outcome is nearer than you think.' He sat down behind his table, stretched out his legs, and picked up a nib.

'What outcome?' I wanted to catch hold of his words like grabbing hold of support when your feet want to give way under you. 'What outcome, mister?'

'Outcome for everyone.'

'There's only one outcome for them, and that's a ship to take them back.'

'Any one of them is free to go back, no one will stand in their way.'

'Mercy on us, mister! Where are they supposed to get the money from?'

'I repeat, Miggel, the outcome may be nearer than you think, but you don't believe me.'

'What outcome?'

'Be patient.'

'Where's Christie's money?'

'He'll get his money.'

'When?'

'Shortly. How long do you think they'll continue to need an interpreter?'

'God Almighty!' I shouted. 'It's Christmas! They don't need an interpreter, they can't skin Christie and cook him! The children must have milk. And the women must have meal, they eat differently from us, they eat dough which they boil in water. They've been without coffee for weeks now, I went into the forest and fetched them bladder-nuts to roast as coffee, but they can't get it down their throats. Things are goddamn wretched up there, mister! The children are full of sores, Miriam and I apply snake-leaf, but they kept pulling it off.'

'Sores?' He was suddenly alert. 'What kind of sores?'

'Sores.'

'It's not smallpox perhaps?'

'It's not smallpox, it's hunger-sores!'

'You better make sure that it's not smallpox.'

It was hopeless. If I had not stayed in control of myself, I might have got scared.

The next day was Sunday and Christmas Day. Christie and Robolini left early the morning to fetch the priest in the village;

231

he had sent word that he would arrive the day before and spend the night in the village. By the time they came back with him, the others had erected a thing like a throne under the sagewood tree a little way to the east of the tents. Then there was the graven image of a woman, Pontiggia's work, the same height as the one he had made up at the furrow, only this time she wore a long robe to cover her nakedness. Over her was an arch made from branches and the whole arch was decorated with flowers from Miriam's plumbago bush and between the flowers at least a dozen yellowish-white ostrich plumes had also been stuck in.

'And this?' I asked Pietro.

'Mother of Gesù, Signor Miggel.'

'Where did they get the feathers from?'

'Antonio bring feathers, Signor Miggel.' Antonio was America.

When the priest arrived, they first had to tell him all their sins again before he could hold the service round the feather-throne. I told the priest they hadn't sinned much since he had last been there, and I suggested he got Walker to tell him his sins when he went back to the village. He wouldn't let them off, however, they had to dig up sins and confess. I turned away and walked into the forest, it was too long an affair for me, but Miriam stayed.

THIRTEEN

ON THE MONDAY after Christmas, I went over to Portland as usual and when I came back that evening at dusk, four strange tents stood pitched just below the clay furrow. I said to myself: Silas Miggel, don't be alarmed, if it's another lot of silkwormers, your first task will be to drive them away from there because they are standing right in the path of the water I have to get to my flattened vegetable patches. With every step I made to reach the house, I said to myself: keep calm, keep calm.

Miriam sat at the table, her hands in her lap, her shoulders hunched and the fire lay cold.

'Miriam?'

'Pa.'

When she looked up, I saw her eyes were heavy from crying. 'What's going on here?'

'Don't be alarmed, Pa.'

'Whose tents are those?'

'Don't be alarmed, Pa.'

'How can you say I'm not to be alarmed? Whose tents are those? Why are you sitting here like this? Why haven't you made the fire? Why is there no food?'

'It's the sawmill people, Pa. The people who are going to turn the clay furrow into a dam. Mr Christie walked the priest back to the village and he saw a second team on the slope this side of the drift, making a road for the wagons that will bring the machinery here. He says they are very cross to have been put to work on a road. They told him they aren't road makers, they have come from England to erect the machinery and cut the wood. Our time on the highland is up, Pa.'

233

The day the Italians appeared from the gorge, a kind of slow shock went through me. When I heard that it was the sawmill people, I got a shock like a hot coal falling on to bare flesh. I rushed outside because I needed air. My first thought was to speak to Christie, but my feet took me straight to the sawmill tents where I found ten strangers sitting happily round a fire. When I stood in front of them, one got to his feet, a tall man with a strong face, and when we stood opposite each other, our eyes were on the same level.

'Are you bloody mad?' I asked him. 'Can't you see this is no place for a blooming sawmill? Do you understand Dutch?'

'I do.'

'I've asked you if you people are bloody mad!'

'No.'

'Over there stand fourteen tents full of government mistakes, then you come and pitch four more and want me to believe you're right in the head?'

He didn't answer me, he put out his hand as if to greet me. 'Dunn is the name,' he said. 'Brother of Dunn of Fox & Dunn. I take it that you are Silas Miggel whom Mr Walker has told me about.'

'Forget about Walker. I want to know who told you that this is a place for a sawmill!'

'Mr White, the previous Superintendent of Immigrants, was very well aware of the fact that the land up here had been allocated to us. He was told to put the Italians somewhere else. Won't you sit down?'

'Sit down? Your head must be perched in the wrong place if you think I'm here to sit down. I might fall over, yes. I'm Silas Miggel of the highland, mister, I know every bit of soil and every drop of water on this land and it is as useless a place for a sawmill as it was for the Italians' silkworms. The last I heard of you people was when you went to Cape Town to get other land from the government. Why didn't you take it?'

'Because we were assured that this is the best place for the mill; we will be able to cut all the wood we need within a mile or two from here. I believe very little has been felled in this part of the forest.'

My whole body was riddled with shivers. 'Mister,' I said, and I said it slowly, 'there is no water here for a sawmill.'

'That's why we will be building a dam, to back up enough water.'

I could not get anywhere with him. He stood looking at me as if *he* were the one who knew everything about the highland, and I was the one the hawk had just dropped there.

He patted me on the shoulder as if we were friends of long standing, and said: 'I think the two of us are going to need one another, Miggel. I've heard from quite a few people that you know this part of the forest better than anyone else: the footpaths, the sled-paths, the wood itself and everything that goes with it. We are going to employ you right away and the wages we are prepared to pay will be better than the best you can get in this district. We want to employ as many of the Italians as possible and make them the leading team, cutting the wood and hauling it out to the yards. You will be appointed foreman over them. The government is most anxious that the mill should start operating, and so are we. As you most probably know, the contract was concluded in February, almost a year ago, but due to problems with the shipping of the machinery from England, much time has been lost. To make matters worse, the ship ran into a storm on its way here, with the result that we suffered damage running into hundreds of pounds and had to order new parts from England. At the moment we're waiting for Mr Robinson, who will be in charge of erecting the mill, but his ship had to turn back to Plymouth as well because of storm damage.'

It suddenly struck me that 'the outcome' of which Walker had been so sure was none other than the sawmill. He knew the mill was on its way. He knew if he starved the Italians at the right time and for long enough they would fall in and work. He had known it all. The government had known. They had it all worked out nicely.

'Mr Dunn,' I said to the man facing me, 'up here on the highland, more than storm damage is going to hit you.'

I don't think he heard me, he just went on as if it were a pleasure for him to inform me of everything, as if taking me into his confidence. 'The most urgent matter at the moment is the road, Miggel. According to the government, Thomas Bain should have been here months ago to survey and build the new road to Knysna, but up to now nothing has been done. Which means we must get the existing sled-path into a condition that will allow the wagons to get the machinery up here. Italians are known to be very good road builders.'

'These ones aren't road builders, they're silk farmers, their hands are soft.'

'I'm sure they'll be glad of the work. I believe they are suffering badly because of the failure of the silk industry. They can choose between starting work on the road, or taking up the axes right away. The moment the mill is ready, we'll need wood. Lots of wood. We'll start with the sawing of planks for our workers' houses. I understand the Italians must hand back their tents within a couple of months; if they become employed by us, they will be housed first. In the meantime, I must also get together a smaller team of cutters to start cutting firewood for the boiler; the wood must have time to dry out.'

I picked up the only stone I could find to throw at him. 'Mister,' I said, 'you people can't just come here and start cutting as it pleases you, you must get licences, you must get permission to fell!'

'It is a government contract, Miggel. We have permission to cut without licence. I want to send in at least four teams of cutters, of course. So if you know of people in the forest interested to cut for us, they should apply to me.'

'Forest people cut for themselves, not for others.'

'For the Italians, the wages are six shillings a day and for the one appointed over them as foreman, eight shillings a day.'

'I'll go and tell the interpreter, he's their foreman.'

'We don't have work for the interpreter,' Dunn said rather bluntly. 'We want to appoint you foreman over them and we want you all to start work as soon as possible. The open shed, under which the mill will be erected, must be put up, we'll need poles for supports and they must be cut right away. We must also erect a woodshed in the village. They will start building a new jetty soon, the present one won't be able to cope with the enormous amount of railway sleepers we shall deliver.' He patted me on the shoulder again. 'The mill, Miggel, is a godsend to you all, don't kick against it too long.'

I didn't put my head on a pillow that night. Miriam and I remained sitting at the table.

'Our time on the highland is up, Pa.'

'No. I will not let myself be pushed off the highland by the government's wheel. Until the allotments are put up for sale, I grant myself dwelling rights and that's that.'

'Dwelling rights between two sawmill yards? Is that what you want?'

'I'll move the house. But they won't move me off the highland. I'm telling you, they've had this whole thing planned, and they included Silas Miggel in their plans because they know if they want the Italians, they must have me too.'

'Are you going to fall in with them, Pa?'

'Has the wheel, I wonder, hit me harder than I'd realised? Has it perhaps pushed me in with them already?' It was not a pleasant question to ask, but I had to ask it.

'We must move to the village, Pa. The Italians too, they can go and find work there.'

The child was on the run, she was no longer thinking because there was no work in the village. Not long before, Koos Oosthuys, from up in Stripe Bush, had laid down his axe in despair and had gone looking for work in the village. He had been able to choose between two jobs: street-keeper, or night-bucket carrier. He chose the streets and the broom, but shortly afterwards a new law was passed in the village: any dog seen in the streets without a licence was to be caught by the street-keeper, taken to the outskirts of the village, and poisoned. At first Koos would not agree to do this, but they said he had to, it was a law. The sooner he made an example of a dog, the sooner the people would see to it that they bought licences for their dogs. Koos caught the first dog and poisoned it, but swore afterwards that he'd never do it again. He said he'd prefer to carry night-buckets. No sooner had he started carrying the buckets when a new law was passed in the village, saying the price per bucket for each household was no longer four pennies but six pennies. Then everybody bought bigger buckets so that they could shit more for the new price. Koos took his hat and went and picked up his axe.

No, it was no good running to the village. The longer we sat into the night, the clearer my mind became. The government's wheel might have knocked me over, but my eyes were still open, and I could still see which way I had to crawl to get back on my

237

feet. Suppose, I said to myself, suppose they make the dam and catch enough water to keep the boiler filled, and suppose the mill started operating, it could mean that I had to hold out against the mill for five years at the most. Five years and five hundred thousand sleepers. It was like a gorge whose bottom you could not see. But suppose the Italians agreed to work at six shillings a day, it would mean that they could raise their own fare and I was sure that wouldn't take five years to do. I told Miriam to fetch pencil and paper and help me work out the sum.

'Does this mean you are going to work for them, Pa?'

'The Italians are trapped, Miriam. I can't see how they can avoid working at the mill. And if they start at the mill, so must I. Walker said the outcome was near, maybe he was more right than he himself realised. If you think about this calmly, you perhaps end up with a possibility of deliverance from more than one problem. Give me the pencil.'

'Pa, don't do this to yourself.'

'How many choices do I have, Miriam? Think.'

There were fifteen that could cut if I left out Ilario: Fardini and his two sons, Alberto and Giuseppe; Robolini, Cruci, Tomé, Mangiagalli, Canovi, Borolini, Cuicatti, Coccia, Taiani, Lucinetti, Pontiggia and America Mazera. It took me a while to do the sum, but I did it. It would take them eighty-nine days to earn the ship money for all of them. That was without Catarina's fare. Eighty-nine days. Stretch it, I said to myself, to a full year because one had to take into consideration the continuing need for provisions and the unforeseen problems like no wages for days when it rained, for Sundays, for days off sick – but the sum still said they could be on a ship within a year. It meant I had to work at the mill during that time as well, but at eight shillings a day, I could save for two of the allotments plus a plough and have something over as well.

I wasn't stupid, I knew that to work things out in advance like this was like digging pitfalls; you had to think and think again. Stretch it to two years, I said to myself. What are two years in a lifetime? The first pitfall I saw was the Grassis' fare. Who said the others would earn it for them? What about the bachelors who had only themselves to pay for? The married men had wives and children that had to get on the ship as well. I decided the best thing would be to hand that problem over to Fardini so long

238

as one thing was understood very clearly from the start: they all had to leave together. Not one by one.

At daybreak, I knew that I would have to work with the sawmill. There was no other way back to the highland that I could see. Whenever we used to haul out heavy wood ourselves from places the oxen could not get to, my father always drove us on, warning us to keep our eyes on the ground, not to look up and measure the distance we still had to go. The chasm that lay ahead of me might be a full five years wide. I knew, if I dared to look up, I would stagger. But there was one consolation I had without any doubt, which was that only Miriam and I would make it to the other side. Somewhere on the way, the Italians would turn off and somewhere the sawmill would fall to pieces.

When the sun came up, I started out for Portland. Not to go and work, but to go and say that I would no longer be able to help out. It was not easy. When I said goodbye to Barrington that morning, I knew it was for the last time. He had made it to Christmas, but he wouldn't see another one on this earth.

'Twelve black oxen, Silas.'

'Twelve black oxen it shall be, Honourable.'

The next day I took Dunn across to the tents so that he could speak to Christie and the Italians himself. It was best that he said what had to be said, not me. Within half an hour trouble was brewing in front of Christie's tent. I kept well away. Christie wanted the Italians to agree that he should make further representations to the government; Dunn wanted them to agree to start working at six shillings a day. While they argued, I thought about the future: the gin for the francolins would have to be handled by the women; the fish and the eels as well, although I wasn't quite sure about that yet. The only representations left for Christie to make were for the Grassis, somehow Walker and the government would have to make provision for their ship money. I had already told Dunn that there were fifteen men that could start work, but that they would only work until they had enough money to take them home. And the day they stopped working, Silas Miggel stopped working too. Dunn said he accepted this so long as they didn't get the money together too soon. I told him that the first planks produced by

239

the mill had to go to the Italians, they had to get out of the tents. He said the first planks would be theirs.

It was a long meeting. The women cried and waved their arms about, the children cried and became fractious, the men stamped around like trapped creatures unable to escape. Christie talked until two spots of foam formed in the corners of his mouth. Dunn talked until he was sweating. In the end, five voted to start work on the road: Pontiggia, America, Taiani, Lucinetti and Coccia. Ten voted for the axes on condition that I would take the gun every day, and they the ladder.

That was the Tuesday. On the Wednesday, the five that had chosen to help at the road, started work. Dunn wanted the others to start cutting the same day but I told him it was not possible before the Thursday. The only ones that knew something about handling an axe had gone to the road and just about the last food had been given to them. Fox & Dunn would have to advance the others a little money for food, no man could swing an axe on an empty stomach. They would need at least two bags of meal as well as coffee, sugar and lard. I said that Miriam and the women could fetch the provisions with the ox and sled. Dunn handed over the money. For the rest of the day I showed the ten that had to work with me the difference between the various axes, the difference between a pit-saw and a two-handed saw. I showed them how I wanted the axes sharpened: first with the flat file, then on the whetstone, every axe in a team of mine would have a clean and decent cut. Not a single 'sì, sì, signor' did I get out of them, but I persevered. Late that afternoon, I showed Luigia Fardini and Monica Grassi how to set the gin and catch the francolins; if they were old enough to run after Cuicatti and Canovi, they were old enough to mind the trap. I still could not decide about the fish and the eels. I didn't want to send Miriam to the water-holes on her own, and I didn't want to send the women past the road workers to the lagoon. They'd just have to eat dough cakes on Fridays, I decided.

'I still think you are making a mistake, Pa! We must move to the village with them.'

'What's the difference between them dying here, or dying there?'

'Pa!'

'Here at least they've now got a chance. They're not stupid,

Miriam, they know very well that this is the only way they are ever going to get home. Fardini has already asked Christie to find out exactly how much the ship money would be.'

'It looks as if little Maria Cruci has the measles, Pa.'

'Go and tie a cloth round her head to keep her eyes closed, tell them to keep the other children away from her.'

'Mariarosa has been sitting all huddled up since yesterday, Pa, I don't know what to do with her any more.'

'Give her a spade and tell her to dig, it's from doing nothing.'

As the sun went down, the five that had been working on the road came staggering across the highland, covered in dust. America came and showed me his hands. 'Sore, Signor Miggel, sore.'

'Don't worry, you have six shillings in your pocket and tomorrow you'll have twelve.'

On the Thursday, the others had to start work. When I got to the tents, they stood ready with the axes and the ladder and never in my life had I seen so much utter loathing on people's faces. And Ilario Grassi stood with them.

'You stay here,' I said to him. The axe over his shoulder was weighing him down on that side.

'Go with, Signor Miggel.'

'You're out of breath already, you can't come with us.'

'Go with, Signor Miggel.'

Robolini came forward. 'We help him, we all cut wood, Signor Miggel.'

I suddenly realised that they had planned this; they themselves had also looked ahead and worked things out. 'Right,' I said, 'he goes with.'

When I walked into the forest with them that morning, my own feet felt as heavy as rocks. Behind me my crops lay parched as did the Italians'. It still hadn't rained and the clay furrow was no longer a furrow; below it, a wall of yellow clay was rising into a dam. Where the water was to come from, I didn't ask. Away in the distance to the west, lay Portland; a stillness was over the place as if it had already buried its master. My own house lay desolate behind me; where and when I would have to move it, I didn't yet know. One thing I did know, however, was that I would stack a fence around it so high that no one would be able

241

to see in through my windows. No one would peep at my daughter. I had told Dunn that the first of his dam diggers that came near her, I would shoot so flat, he'd never get up again. I told Miriam as well.

'Don't start all that again, Pa, it's over.'

'What is over?'

'The make-believe man that came alive for a while.'

'Don't talk in the dark.'

'I am in the dark, Pa. Everything is in the dark. You say that you can hold out against the sawmill even if it takes the full five years, but what about the Italians?'

'They will just have to hold out at six shillings a day.'

'That's not what I'm talking about, Pa. How are they going to hold out against the forest? They agreed to go and cut only because they're trapped, but that doesn't make them less frightened of the forest. Do you realise how humiliating it is for them to take up axes? It's cruel to try and make woodcutters of them.'

'Cruel? What's more cruel: to let them die of hunger, or to let them cut wood?'

'You must be good to them, show them some mercy.'

'Who shows me mercy?' No one.

I took Red Alder's sled-path into the forest with them. Every time I looked round, it seemed as if a kind of hatred was growing in them, but the only one I felt sorry for was Fardini. He was older than me and, according to Christie, a man much respected from where he had come, a man to whom others had looked up and now he himself had to stoop to cut wood. It was as if Barrington had to begin cutting wood.

Yellowwood, Dunn had said, yellowwood and nothing else. There were two kinds of yellowwood: kalander and upright, and that was what they wanted. Only fully-grown trees were to be felled and before we hauled out the wood, it had to be sawn into seven-foot sleeper lengths.

'Next week I'll send in a second team to cut, the week after that, a third team and as soon as the road is finished, a fourth team. In the meantime you can tell the forest woodcutters they'll soon find out what their pride is costing them.'

'They won't ever pick up an axe for you.'

* * *

242

If ever I witnessed a farcical spectacle in the forest, it was that morning. We were about a mile into the thickets when we came across the first elephant dung, so freshly dropped that it was still steaming. 'Shoot, Signor Miggel, shoot!' the cries went up around me. Borolini pulled the ladder one way, Cuicatti pulled it the other, each one going for a different tree. I heard branches tearing to the west of us, and I knew we were safe since the breeze was from the south.

'Leave the blessed ladder,' I said to them, 'the bigfeet are going in the other direction!' But the tussle over the ladder continued because they didn't hear me. Then Cuicatti won control and the next minute half of them were hanging from a quar like a swarm of finches and the rest were dragging the ladder to a white alder. Only Fardini and Ilario remained standing on the sled-path. All I could do was what I did with Petroniglia that day, I left them right there and walked on. I hadn't gone fifty yards, and I heard them scrambling and falling from the trees to catch up with me again and from then on the only cry was: 'Torniamo indietro, Signor Miggel! Torniamo indietro!' They wanted to turn back.

'It's too late to turn back. Come on!'

The place I had planned beforehand for them to begin cutting was Draai Valley: thick forest, good wood, west of a sled-path, not too steep for the hauling out and close to a creek and a clearing where a fire could be made in safety. It was no use cutting here, there and everywhere when you had to cut a lot, better to choose a section and stay in it. It's better for the hauling out as well.

'Torniamo indietro!'

'Come on!'

Ilario kept up better than I thought he would. Fardini and Robolini looked after him and Mangiagalli carried his axe. He wouldn't be able to cut, that I realised, but I would find him something else to do. One always needed help at the shelter and I planned to build proper shelter as soon as possible. You had to have a shelter under which to sit when it rained, to keep your food out of the sun, to leave a coat or a knapsack. And you always needed someone at the shelter to mind the fire and boil water for coffee, things like that. It would also be somewhere that Ilario could lie down in when he had to.

There was another reason for me choosing the spot up in Draai Valley. Dunn said he planned to have at least four cutting teams. Strangers. I knew they would be too scared to cut as far away as Draai Valley, and that was what I wanted. With my team and axes, I would see to it that no one came further north, for the lilies were to the north of us and one never knew when someone might wander where he didn't belong.

The first thing I made the Italians do was to make a clearing for the fire. 'Not one spark will fly from a fire belonging to Silas Miggel which might start a fire in the forest,' I told them. 'I want every twig and dry leaf cleared away, I want to see the bare earth.' While they were clearing, I made a rough shelter from branches, set between an ironwood and a hard pear; for the proper shelter I would bring a few corrugated iron sheets. I then went and cut two forked sticks and a cross piece, on this we would hang the tins of water over the fire; and all the time I pretended not to notice their anguish, their ever-shifting eyes. When we had the fire going, I let them eat something and rest for a while and then I took them to where I started marking out the first five trees for them. I left Ilario at the shelter, telling him to watch the fire.

'Two men to a tree,' I said, and as I spoke, so did my hands. 'But only one man cuts the notch that will decide which way the tree is going to fall, and that man is *me*. Every tree will fall where I decide it is to. It's no good cutting one tree and destroying three, four others with it when it falls. I cut the notches, you follow them: one in front and one at the back.' When I went over it a second time, I got a reluctant 'Sì, sì, signor' from them. I blazed every tree at the front and at the back and put them two to a tree to start cutting. The sixth tree I blazed for myself. We were an uneven number which meant I had to cut on my own.

What a performance! I never thought they could be that clumsy. I hardly got cutting with my own axe because I had to keep going from tree to tree, urging them on. 'Keep your feet still! Stay in one place! It's not a silkworm's head you're cutting off now, it's wood! Swing those axes higher! Hit in deeper!'

'Woodcut no good, Signor Miggel.'

'Hack in!'

After every ten or so swings, they stopped to spit on their hands and shake their heads as if to say they were not going to make it. Then again they would stop to listen in case something was about to pounce on them from the thickets. If I moved away but one step too far from the gun for their liking, they became even more restless. The ladder stood propped up and ready against a candlewood all the time.

'Cut! I'll keep a lookout for danger.'

'Tired, Signor Miggel.'

'Tired my foot, cut! Tell yourselves you're going home. Every hack is a step closer to the ship. Swing higher! See how the shadows are lengthening already and you've hardly earned a shilling yet. Dunn said he wants a report from me every night about how much we have cut during the day.'

'Tired, Signor Miggel.'

'Keep your eyes on your axe, Cuicatti! I'll keep a lookout to see from which side the bigfoot's going to come and trample you flat.'

Sweat broke out under their shirts and streamed down their faces. The number of blows between each rest became fewer and fewer.

Every time I went to see how Ilario was doing, he was sitting a little closer to the fire, although the sun was still blazing down on the clearing. 'Tomorrow, I shall show you how to bake sweet potatoes in the ashes without drying them out. I'm going to show you how to make coffee in the tins. If your body holds out, I'll teach you how to set snares in the afternoons and visit them in the mornings; the rest of us will collect any catch and carry it home. Dunn can't pay you for doing nothing.'

Somehow we would have to find the time to cut firewood as well, the women couldn't do it. They could split and stack it away, but we had to do the felling.

When the first flock of louries came in to roost, I stopped the axes. Only two trees were down and they were the ones where I had helped most with the cutting. My spirits were low. Very low. If it had not been for the wages that had to get them off the highland, I would have gone straight to Dunn to say to him: a baboon is a baboon, an Italian an Italian, and you will never make either a woodcutter. Never.

When we got back to the tents, there was little difference between my men and the five that came from the road. They were all equally done for. At the house, two bags of sweet potatoes stood outside the door. Martiens Botha had sent the one and Jeremiah Eye the other, Miriam said.

'We can do with it.'

'Mr Christie went to the village and got his money.'

'What?'

'Yes. Every penny of it.'

'In other words, the government had that planned as well? They waited until the Italians were safely working in the forest, and then paid him. At least now he'll be able to pay me back.'

'Monica and Luigia got six francolins. And Mr Dunn came asking for drinking water. He wants to see you.'

I sensed that Miriam was talking round something again. 'Dunn must stay away from my house when I'm not here. He can get himself water from the furrow.'

'The water is muddy from the work on the dam, Pa.'

'Then he can climb down to the river and fetch water from there like we will have to soon if it doesn't rain. Or he can go and get water on the other side of the tents.'

'The creek on that side is almost dry, Pa. The Italians catch very little at the moment. And Constable Clark was here.'

'Constable Clark? Who's he?'

'He says he's new in the village.'

'What did he want?' I didn't like constables round my place.

'He came looking for America, Pa. He's got to appear in court on Tuesday morning, the third of January, in connection with an ostrich.'

'What?'

'It's about an ostrich, Pa.'

Ostrich. Christmas. The feathers in the arch around the graven image. But it was only America that would not fit in. 'What has America got to do with the ostrich?'

'I don't know, Pa. I think you better go find out from Mr Christie.'

I did. And Christie was sitting in his tent like a magistrate himself. America and Taiani, Coccia and Borolini stood in front of him and they were all speaking at the same time, waving their hands in the air.

'What's this I hear about an ostrich?' I asked from behind, motioning to them to keep quiet at the same time. 'What was a constable doing on the highland about an ostrich?'

246

'That, *Mr* Miggel,' Christie said from on high, 'is but another example of the shameless thuggery of this colonial government and its officials. Antonio Mazera, an innocent man, is accused of malicious destruction of property in order to make of him, and myself, and all the other Italians, a public example. That's what it is.'

'I want to know about the ostrich,' I said.

It was a long-winded story. Christie started with the 'Poor Italians' who had never seen an ostrich before. 'All they know about these birds, Miggel, is that they ran wild in Africa. Two days before Christmas, Antonio, Taiani, Coccia and Borolini were on their way to the village when they observed, as they imagined, a wild ostrich sitting on the opposite slope of one of the gorges. Antonio, the one you call America, immediately risked his life by climbing down the near side of the dangerous gorge and up the other to reach the bird in an effort to save it. It was clear that the poor ostrich had slid down and could not get back to the top of the hill again. When, however, Antonio grabbed at the ostrich to help it, it rose to its feet and attacked him so viciously that he was forced to defend himself by means of a stick, with the result that the bird became frightened and started running down the slope at a terrific speed. Then it stumbled over some rocks and fell down the cliffs, finally killing itself in the brook at the bottom. Taiani, Coccia and Borolini, who stood watching everything from the road, could bear witness to it all. They immediately scrambled down to see if they could do anything for the bird. It was, however, already dead. They plucked the feathers, most of which they sold to Smit at his store in the village, and kept a few for themselves as a reminder of the very sad event.'

'Mr Christie,' I said, 'I sometimes wonder if you English believe everything you hear out of ignorance or innocence.'

'Antonio has *three* witnesses to stand by his word,' he said, angrily.

'He can have a hundred but I'm telling you that they are lying. I know an ostrich and I'll tell you what happened. I don't dispute that they were on their way to the village, neither do I dispute that they saw the ostrich at Stewart's place near the slope, he does keep a couple of tame ostriches there. But all the rest I dispute. I'm telling you, they decided to chase the ostrich for fun and in the hope of getting hold of a few of its feathers. America may well have picked up a stick to defend himself because he's the least brave of them all. Obviously they didn't know that an ostrich is a stupid creature. If you frighten it, it starts running without ever looking down again to see where its feet are going. Its head sits too high on its neck, it just runs. Downhill or uphill, it runs. This time it was downhill and the rocks on the slope were in the way. The ostrich wouldn't have stopped, he would have fallen to his death over the cliff. Their good fortune was not just a few feathers, but a whole bird's feathers. Misfortune only caught up with them afterwards and now America has to appear before Magistrate Jackson because he was the one with the stick. To appear before Magistrate Jackson can be worse than falling down a cliff, mister.'

'I don't agree with any of that, Miggel,' Christie said brusquely. '*I* will take up Antonio's case and see that justice is done. You people who don't know any better may tremble before Maximilian Jackson, but I do not. As an honest Britisher I will not hesitate to stand up for truth and justice.'

'Mr Christie,' I said, trying to warn him in a nice way, 'if there is one man you must stand clear of, it's Jackson the magistrate. I myself don't know him, but everyone that has ever appeared before him says it's no laughing matter. When he hits, he hits hard. I know of a man, his name is Esau Esau, who got one month's hard labour for a sixpence he had stolen, and Jan Alie got twelve months and twenty-five strokes with the cat for stealing a couple of chickens. If you end up in jail, he orders that you be put in a dark cell for two days a week so that you can think about your sins. On the very first day that he arrived in the village, he called the constables together and told them to bring everybody in, no matter who, who was heard swearing in the streets – and you want to go to him with a blooming made-up story about an ostrich? America can't afford to get into trouble now, he has got to work, every day means six shillings in his pocket. As it is, he will lose six shillings on Tuesday and so will the other three. If I may give you some advice, take him there and let him speak the truth and plead for mercy, or take him to Stewart first. Perhaps the man will withdraw the case if you tell him that America chased the bird in ignorance and that he is truly sorry for what he has done. Speak nicely to the man.'

'Why must Antonio plead guilty if he is not guilty? I don't understand you, Miggel. Here are three people he can call upon to testify his innocence, and you suggest he should plead guilty.'

'Yes. And I believe you've got your money so you owe me seventeen pounds.'

'We can talk about that later. I have a court case on hand.'

As I turned to go, America took hold of my arm. 'Signor Miggel go with?' he asked. 'Signor Miggel will say of lo struzzo?'

'Lo struzzo?'

'The ostrich,' Christie said.

'No, I'm not going anywhere. I'll be working on Tuesday so that the others can do so too. Go and tell the magistrate you chased the ostrich, tell him you're sorry.'

'Signor Miggel go with?'

'No.'

On the second day, a little more wood fell in the forest than on the first day. But my ears and my eyes had to be everywhere all the time: on the axes, on the fire, on the sweet potatoes, on Ilario, everywhere. When a man dropped out, I took his axe from him and cut in his place until he got his breath back. Fardini was the one that found it the hardest to keep up.

On the Saturday, I took four off the axes and put them on the two-handed saws to start sawing the wood into the right lengths for hauling out. Dunn said the sawmill oxen were on their way and when they came, we had to start bringing out the first wood.

It was just after midday when one of the warders turned up. 'Uncle,' he said, 'the head man appointed over this forest, the Comte de Vaselot de Regné, has heard that the tree-felling for the sawmill has started and he's sent me to see that you people cut in sections. I'm afraid you will not be allowed to cut just as you wish, uncle.'

'You go and tell him that he need not send instructions to Silas Miggel. If he wants to know about cutting wood, he can come up here and I'll teach him.'

'Uncle, you're now talking about the man sitting in the highest position over this forest. You must show respect for his word.'

'He can sit so high that his head touches the clouds, he's still a pumpkin. If he wasn't, he wouldn't have given his permission

249

for a sawmill on the highland – and don't you come telling me whose word I should respect or not.'

'You're looking for trouble, uncle.'

'No, trouble comes looking for me. Go and tell him I've been cutting in a section from the start. I know what I'm doing.'

The next day was Sunday and New Year's Day. It was quiet at the tents, the men were exhausted. Miriam and I walked to Creek Bush Island as was our custom every year on New Year's Day, but nothing would cheer her up. Not even Small Martiens or Sias who tried to cajole her out of her mood.

On Monday I was back in the forest with the full team and the first thing I did was to show Ilario how to find a place along the creek where buck and bush-pigs came to drink water and how to set a decent snare with a thong. The first two I set myself, the third one he did on his own and didn't do too bad.

At halfday, when we were gathered at the shelter to eat and rest, Fardini said: 'Signor Miggel, Antonio scared of tomorrow, not go to jail please.'

'We'll have to wait and see. If Christie does what I've told him to, Antonio will get off.'

'Christie no good.'

'We'll see.'

Mind you, I wasn't altogether easy in my mind about the whole thing. If it had been Pontiggia who had the possibility of a jail sentence hanging over him, I wouldn't have let it worry me. But somehow I felt sorry for America, there was no harm in him, they had just wanted a few feathers off the ostrich.

I stopped work a little earlier on the Tuesday. When we came out of the forest, America was sitting next to his tent, his head hanging almost down between his knees.

'And so?' I asked when we got up to him. 'At least I see you're still with us.'

'Jackson no good, Signor Miggel.'

I went on to Christie's tent where I found him sitting at his table, writing furiously. 'I suppose that is now Jackson the magistrate being reported,' I said.

'That's correct.'

'What happened?'

'Jackson is a threat to any court of justice and nobody seems to be doing anything about it.'

'That's not true; Mr Barrington once told me that the people of the village once reported him, but it made no difference. What happened?'

'You should ask instead how I was insulted! The Italians were not only insulted, they were warned that they would be turned off the land like felons unless they are very careful of what they do. No notice was taken of reason nor of witnesses; court procedures, as I know them, hardly exist in his court; the accused was not tried, but simply accused. The case will not, however, be left as it is.'

'What was the sentence?'

'The fact that I took up the case saved him from imprisonment. He had to pay the value of the bird which was six pounds.'

'Where did he get six pounds from?'

'I advanced him the money against his wages. He will repay me weekly.'

'He can call himself lucky that it was only six pounds, ostriches are expensive things these days.'

'The case will not be left there.'

'Mr Christie, there are trees one can climb, and trees one can't climb, not even with a ladder. Leave Jackson and his court where they are. And don't forget the money you owe me.'

A little more than two weeks after that, America and Lucinetti, Pontiggia, Canovi and Taiani took their belongings and left the highland. Not Christie nor Dunn nor I could stop them. The *Natal* was in the harbour, and they had enough money to get themselves to Port Elizabeth where they planned to find work until they had earned enough to get back to Italy. They were done with the wilderness, they said. They were done with picks and shovels and making roads for others, they were done with axes for other people's wood.

They came to say goodbye to me early one Tuesday morning and brought Pietro Fardini with them to interpret where necessary.

'You're making a big mistake,' I told them. 'Six shillings a day is good money. Who says you're going to get better in Port Elizabeth? You don't even know where the place is.' It wasn't so much that I wanted to stop them, I just wanted to warn them.

251

'Finish with forest, Signor Miggel. Finish with foreman at road,' Lucinetti said. 'Finito!'

'Finito!' the others said after him.

'You will have to find a place to stay, and then pay to stay there. Here you are at least staying for nothing.'

'Finish with tents. Finito.'

Miriam gave them bread and coffee which they ate. When they got up to take their leave, America waited until last to say goodbye. 'I write Signor Miggel, I write Signor Miggel letter,' he said.

'All right, you write me a letter. I'll get Christie to read it.'

'Christie no good. He take my blanket, my mattress, he take my knife for lo struzzo.'

'That will teach you to stay away from ostriches.'

Miriam and I walked with them as far as the tents. When they were ready to leave, Miriam stood crying with the women as if it were her own family going away. And Monica Grassi clung to Canovi shamelessly until the last moment. According to Miriam, he said he would fetch her and take her back to Italy with him as soon as he had the money. I'd just like to see that happen, I said. When it was Pontiggia's turn to say goodbye to Miriam, I watched them closely. Fortunately she held herself away from him in a seemly manner, but then they stood looking at each other as if saying things no one else could hear. It took a few hard clearings of my throat to get them apart.

'The day you leave,' I said to those remaining, 'it won't be on foot. I'll get the biggest sleds to cart you to the village, I promise. But that day will never arrive if we continue to stand around like this. Get the axes!' I had a new man in the team, Coccia. He had decided to take Canovi's place instead of going back to work on the road. Fortunately he knew how to handle an axe for I had taught him to cut for firewood.

The fact that the first five Italians had gone was not the only good thing to enjoy when we walked into the forest that morning. The night before, Dunn had come to tell me that they had decided to move the *Yard for Logs* and the *Yard for Sleepers and Timber*, as well as the whole mill, about five hundred yards further west, nearer to the dam, so my house could stay where it was. It was like a rock moving out of my way. When a man's house has stood in the same place for sixteen years, it stands deep and you stand with it; to move it was not like moving a chicken-house. All I had to do now was to stack a higher fence round my house and therefore round Miriam. Where I was going to find the time to do it, I didn't know. All I could think of was to stack it at night, by lantern.

Miriam still had a sadness about her that I couldn't quite fathom. I even saw her being downright rude a couple of times to some of the dam diggers and bachelors at the tents when they kept pestering her. It was comforting for me – but it was untypical of Miriam. On Sundays, she usually went to Portland, returning with the Barrington news in the afternoons: they had planted pumpkins between the apple trees; Barrington was planning a cellar in which to make cider as soon as he was well again; John had gone to Cape Town to await the schooner *Hettie* which was carrying a large load of wood from Portland's part of the forest which he was going to sell in Cape Town.

'I hope they see him again,' I said.

Dunn was most displeased about the five Italians who had gone off. Every hand was important, he said, and the road had to be finished urgently. When I asked him where the other teams of cutters were that were supposed to have started work already, he said they were on their way. And the oxen? They were also on their way. Everything was on the way.

'And the water?' I asked. 'Where is the water for the dam coming from?'

'It must rain sometime. As long as the dam is full by the time we are ready to start sawing, there'll be no problem.'

'In the meantime, there are no crops on the highland,' I said. 'The few buckets of water Miriam and I carry to my vegetables every morning before dawn is not enough. Over there, the few patches the Italians have planted stand withered because we can no longer take water from the furrow. Your blooming dam wall is cutting us off.'

'You are all earning enough to buy food with.'

'The Italians are not working for food, they're working for their fares home!' I reminded him.

'As long as they don't manage to get it together too soon, Miggel. And I wanted to ask you about the Grassi man, he doesn't seem strong enough to me to swing an axe. Do you think it's necessary for him to go with you every day and be paid for it?'

'Leave him alone. I see to it that he works.'

The very next night Dunn was at my door again. I thought that he'd come to talk about work again, but it was about something quite different. 'There's a dance in the village on Saturday night, Miggel,' he said. 'I would like to ask your daughter to go with me if she has a decent dress to wear.'

Just like that. And before I could get up to throw him out, chair and all, Miriam had come from her room, and I saw she was very angry. But when she spoke, it was in his own tongue, like a lady and straight to the face.

'Mr Dunn,' she said, 'if you want to go dancing with me, you ask me first and then my father. Had you asked me first, the answer would have been no and I would have saved you the bother of asking my father. And should there be a next time you want to ask me, first decide if you want to go dancing with me, or with my dress.'

My mouth fell open. His too. This was a side of my daughter that I had never seen before. I suddenly realised that any man who fell for her would go through hell to get her out of his blood again – and I couldn't help wondering how it was going with Jacob and Susanna.

Dunn shook his head and tried to laugh. 'Well,' he said, 'I've heard that your father is difficult, but they didn't warn me about you.'

She did not respond to that, she just walked out of the door. Later, when I looked for her, she was but a shadow in the moonlight, far down at the foot of the highland.

FOURTEEN

HALFWAY THROUGH FEBRUARY, the fence was up round my house: strong and high and with a stout gate on the eastern side. I had cut the branches and stacked it at night by the glow of the lantern. My woodshed was enclosed, half of Miriam's flower garden was enclosed, as was a little vegetable patch on the south side. I felt I was well dug in for whatever lay ahead.

And just in time too, for when the month reached its end, the road was finished and the wagons began arriving. Six wagons: three belonged to Fox & Dunn, and three were woodcutters' wagons, hired with drivers, oxen and all. They carted stuff on to the highland for days. First the tents for the workers, most of which, mercifully, were pitched down at the bottom of the highland. Then they started bringing components for the sawmill: pieces of machinery, three wagons to get the boiler up there, wooden boxes with large letters painted on them, implements, sheets of iron, trunks, bundles. The oxen ended each day with bleeding shoulders having dragged their hellish loads from the village. Worst off were Fox & Dunn's oxen; at least, woodcutters knew how far to load a wagon without killing their oxen.

Miriam started getting scared. 'When will it stop, Pa?'

'God knows.' It was like the plagues one reads of in the Bible descending upon the highland. Every day I said to myself: Silas Miggel, keep your eyes in front of your feet, don't look up to see how far away the other side is. I really got alarmed the day the oxen came. One hundred and twenty-one of them I counted in despair, and went and asked Dunn if he was bloody mad. Where were they to graze? Where were they to drink water? A hundred and twenty-one oxen.

At the Italians' tents, life became unbearable. The bit of catchwater to the east of the tents became the oxen's watering-place and within a week the place was covered with dung and the ground churned up. The women had to carry drinking water from the gorge. Every day Christie waved the Immigration Act under Dunn's nose but was ignored. The whole world lay strewn with sawmill parts. The only hope I had was that Robinson, the man responsible for putting up the mill, wouldn't manage it.

Three teams of cutters arrived together with the forest warders who showed them where to fell and what to fell. Every morning I saw to it that I was first to go into the forest with my team and last to come out at night. No axe would cut further north than mine.

On the first Sunday in March, I woke up in the morning and heard the marsh lourie calling. That very night, it started raining. The next morning, when I was getting ready to go out to work, I thought Miriam would have a fit.

'Where are you going, Pa? You can't take them out to cut in weather like this!'

'I've never heard of rain melting people, it's soft rain, just the weather for hauling out wood.'

'They'll get ill!'

'Don't suggest such things, Miriam. Nothing's going to happen to them; all they're going to do is learn how to haul out wood and, at the same time, earn a day's wages.'

In damp conditions we could haul out the wood bare, without sleds. If you haul out bare in dry weather and the logs sink down into the black forest earth, it is a battle to get them out again; the oxen get sore from heaving against the strain and in the end it takes you twice the time to get the wood out.

I went to the tents and tugged the full team, except Ilario, out from under their blankets, and rounded up twelve of the best sawmill oxen. Not one of the other teams was preparing to go out to work, only mine. At halfday, when we came out with the first load and unhooked them at the new yard for logs, Dunn praised us as if it were at least a hundred elephant tusks we had brought out.

'Well done, Miggel, well done!' He must have said it a dozen times, ensuring that all who came up from the sawmill tents should hear. 'You and your men are setting a fine example today!' I took no notice. Neither did the Italians. It was another of those days when they were like dogs that have been beaten again and again, they didn't even bother to growl any more.

We continued to bring out wood until the Wednesday. When we started cutting again, things seemed to improve. There were times when I even got them to put a little heart into the cutting: 'Swing those axes, people! Say to yourselves the wages are good, you're going home. Milano! Firenze! Venezia!' By that time I knew most of the names of the places they came from. Sometimes I made a game of it, letting them give each hack a name, keeping the axes in rhythm at the same time.

'Milano!' Mangiagalli's place.

'Treviso!' Borolini called. 'Bergamo!' he always added when it was his turn again; it was where his girl came from, the one that was to have followed him.

'Como!' That was a place anyone could call out because that was where most of their cocoons used to be sent to the spinning mills.

'Milano!' Cruci's place as well.

'Gouna!' I joined in sometimes.

'Bergamo!'

'Firenze!' That was the place they called out most. It was Fardini's home town, Cuicatti's, Robolini's and Coccia's.

'Ilario, where does Ilario come from?'

'Milano!'

True woodcutters one would. never turn them into, but they were not stupid either. And then the day arrived when I could let them cut the notches themselves, and every tree was felled to land exactly where I would have let it.

'Venezia!' Tomé's home.

'Gouna!' My home.

'Roma!' That was not anyone's home, but one they liked calling out all the same.

As we were cutting like this one day, calling out the names from where we were cutting, I looked up into the face of the warder from Deep Walls. He stood there quite dumbstruck and frowning.

257

'Warder,' I shouted, 'this tree's going to get you when it falls. Stand clear!'

He did it so in a hurry and then asked: 'Is the foreman at the tents, uncle?'

'Which foreman? There are so many foremen on the highland nowadays.'

'The interpreter, uncle. I have an urgent message for him.'

'What message?'

'Mr McNaughton, the Assistant Commissioner of Crown Lands from Cape Town, will come to Gouna tomorrow to hear the Italians' complaints.'

I slowly put my axe down. 'What did you say?'

'He's visiting all the immigrants in the district and will be at Gouna tomorrow. Apparently most complaints emanate from there, that's why he's coming to see things for himself. I was on my way with the message yesterday but a herd of bigfeet cut me off.'

'What did you say his name was?'

'McNaughton, uncle.'

'He'd better be here before dawn or late afternoon if he wants to see them; they can't sit around waiting for him and lose wages.'

'Uncle, you must stop causing trouble. Look what's happened to Pieter Kapp.'

I didn't know what had happened to Pieter Kapp. Since I hardly ever got to the village any more, I knew very little of what was going on. Pieter Kapp was a woodcutter, he had been living at Krans Bush for years. 'What about Pieter Kapp?'

'He also built a house for himself at Krans Bush on Crown land. Just like you, uncle. Now he's in big trouble. He's got to be off by the end of the month and he's not allowed to take a single plank of his house with him. Immigrants on their way from England are due to take over the land.'

I didn't like it. I did not like it at all. But Pieter Kapp is not Silas Miggel, I told myself. Things are different for him, he was not appointed to look after a bunch of Italians. Still, when I lifted my axe to start cutting again, I felt choked by the news. Before the sun sets, I said to myself, I would make Christie give me the money he owed me and which I had asked him for a dozen times already. There were twenty-three pounds and three

258

shillings in my money tin. Together with the seventeen he owed me, I had forty pounds and three shillings. I had to be ready for the day the allotments were put up for sale. They wouldn't make a second Pieter Kapp of me. As true as God, they would not.

I went straight to Christie when we got back to the highland that afternoon. The first thing I noticed was that his hair had been cut, he had on a new pair of shoes, and he was strutting about the tents, giving orders everywhere.

'What's going on?' I asked him.

'Mr McNaughton, the Assistant Commissioner of Crown Lands, will be here tomorrow and it appears that I am the only person who realises the importance of his visit!' The man was in a dither. 'If only I can get these people to understand what the consequences of his visit could mean to them!'

'I don't think they trust any consequences any more.'

'Mr McNaughton is the *Assistant Commissioner of Crown Lands*, Miggel!' he shouted at me. 'Do you realise what it took to get him here?'

'It took some time, for sure.'

'*I* was the one that suggested during the meeting we had that we demand an enquiry at the highest level. I was the one that said we were no longer satisfied with enquiries at local level, and now that the result is on its way, those women look at me without the slightest sign of interest.'

'What meeting?'

'The immigrants' meeting held in the village in February.'

'Why don't I know anything about that meeting?'

'Because you're not an immigrant!'

'Why weren't the Italians there?'

'Because they don't speak English. All the other immigrants in the district are English speaking; I represented myself, as well as the Italians. I have already told Dunn that they will not be going to work tomorrow. There is, of course, a very definite possibility that they won't be going back to work for him at all; Mr McNaughton might not approve of it. Other land may be allocated to them, land suited to mulberries and a silk industry.'

'Are you now bloody well harping back to the worms lying buried under the earth?' I couldn't believe it. And he hadn't finished.

'I shall report that Dunn has unlawfully allowed most of the sawmill tents to be pitched on land put aside for our commonage, that he refuses to prohibit his people from walking across the Italians' allotments, and that he refuses to remove those sawmill parts which are lying on Tomé and Robolini's lots.'

'You must stop interfering with Dunn's workers, they're going to hurt you. But that's not important now, the important thing is that you sit down and start thinking, Mr Christie. I feel nothing for you, I feel very little for the Italians and even less for the sawmill, but at this moment the work is the only way out I can see for them. At least they can buy food and get their ship money together. If Mr McNaughton has a better suggestion to make, fine, but he must lay it all out for everyone to see, and you are going to lay down the money you owe me, right away, now.'

He looked at me as if I had slapped him. 'I am getting ready for Mr McNaughton's most important visit, and you come talking about money? You can come back the day after tomorrow, and then we can settle the matter.'

'*Now!*'

'Don't be over-hasty, Miggel, I know you want one of the allotments, and a better one than mine you will not get. I assure you that we will find a legal way for you to buy it from me.'

'At what price?' I would not rejoice too soon, but I had to know.

'We can talk about the price later.'

'I want to know now.'

'I cannot sell it for less than five hundred pounds.'

'*What?*' I thought it was a slip of the tongue, but he nodded and I realised he was serious. 'Has your mind disintegrated?' I asked him. 'With five hundred pounds, I could buy the whole world from here to the village and still have money over. Barrington paid forty-five pounds for the whole of Karawater's thousand acres and you want five hundred for twenty acres of pot-clay on the highland?'

'There's talk of gold.'

'Gold my arse, man! Those rumours have been circulating for years now, there are people out looking for it as well and finding nothing but a few crumbs. Mr Dunn says he knows about gold; if they find as much as a bucketful in this forest, it's a lot. And you come and put a price on your piece of land as if it's littered with gold? I think you must get yourself to the village so that Dr Gorman can take a look at your head!'

'I may consider four hundred and fifty pounds.'

'Consider? I'd consider knocking your skull in.'

'Are you threatening me?'

I had a feeling that he wanted to get away from the subject. 'Give me my money, I'm tired.'

'I will let you have it the day after tomorrow.'

I was fed up with him. I was standing with the hatchet in my hand since I still had to go and cut some kindling. When I lifted it above my head, he leapt to where his trunk stood and I did not lower it until the last pound lay in my hand.

'Your day will come, Miggel,' he said, white-faced. 'Your day will come, and I'll see to it that it does.'

He was still hurling threats after me long after I left him. The last I heard was him forbidding me to go near the tents while McNaughton was there. *He* represented the Italians, he yelled, not me.

Nobody forbids Silas Miggel to go anywhere on the highland, I said to myself.

McNaughton arrived shortly after midday, he and Dreyer, Walker's clerk. As he got off his horse, I knew he was in pain, he lowered himself with difficulty to the ground. Lumbago. This is bad, I said to myself, a man in pain has little patience, and he was going to need patience. What the Italians had been up to since early that morning, I could not quite make out.

Years before, when Miriam went to school over at Portland, Miss Ritchie sometimes let them have a concert; that meant they had to dress up differently, speak differently, walk differently, and the grown-ups clapped hands. Mrs Barrington called me into the schoolroom one day to watch them. It was a foolish business. Miriam was dressed in rags and called Cinderella. I told Miss Ritchie straight out that I didn't like it at all.

The only thing I could think of, the day McNaughton came, was that the Italians were getting ready to give him a concert – or to drive Christie out of his mind. Christie came out of his tent that morning dressed like the gentleman he was, carrying himself like one too. He even swept in front of his tents. The

Italians did exactly the opposite: the men wore their coats inside out, the women didn't comb their hair nor the children's. They slackened the tent-ropes until the canvas hung all silly and limp, and not a single piece of washing was to be seen hanging out to dry. Here and there an empty water bucket stood with a few pieces of firewood. Best of all were the two broken ploughs they dragged across from the forest's edge. On one, they draped the two smallest francolins from the previous day's catch: legs tied together, heads hanging down. It looked like certain famine.

In the end, Christie sent for me. 'Talk to them, Miggel! You must help me. Mr McNaughton will be here any moment and not only is my reputation at stake, but their own as well. It is of the utmost importance that we make a good impression on him!'

'I'm afraid my head is working like an Italian's today,' I admitted. 'I think it's better to try and impress upon him how bad things are, not how good.'

'Mr McNaughton is very well informed about conditions here, months of representations did that. The least I'm asking is that he will be received with respect and decency, but all I'm getting are blank stares and shrugging shoulders. Look at the mess between the tents. See the state they're in! What kind of impression will Mr McNaughton get from all this? He'll think these are the kind of standards I allow under my supervision. Talk to them, Miggel!'

When the two men came riding across the highland, the last touches of the concert were added: the children sat down on the bare earth near the tents and started drawing pictures in the dust; some of them threw little stones into the air, catching them as they came down. Vittoria Robolini and Antonia Tomé each took a broom and started sweeping listlessly while Fardini and Cruci and Cuicatti sat down with heads bent low over their axes, sharpening the blades with flat files. We usually sharpened at night. Ilario they had sitting on his haunches with one of the women's shawls around his shoulders despite the searing heat.

Even Miriam stopped in amazement when she came to give some medicine to Cruci's child. 'What on earth is going on, Pa?'

'I think they're putting on a concert for Mr McNaughton.'

Whose concert it was in the end, the Italians' or Christie's, is difficult to say, for the blooming stupid Christie didn't notice that the man dismounted painfully, he just launched into a long welcoming speech I thought would never finish; it was as if he wanted to hide the spectacle behind him under every grand word he knew. In the same breath, he started naming every injustice done to him and the Italians, and just as he started about the poor reception they had got at the Cape, Mariarosa and Petroniglia came out from behind the tents, their knees almost giving way under two buckets of water they carried hanging from a pole across their shoulders. Their timing to arrive with the slopping buckets at that moment was superb, and to me that was the best of the concert. They set down the buckets at McNaughton's feet and as Mariarosa unbent, she let go at him with her tongue. I would have loved to have known what she said. Christie didn't interpret, he only kept on waving to them to go away, apologising all the time to McNaughton. He should have left them. McNaughton didn't know it was a concert; in fact, unless you watched closely, you would never have guessed it. And while I stood there, I had the feeling that they were watching him to see if he was falling for it. It was Christie with his incessant running around that spoiled it all. In the end, he himself started McNaughton on the old story about how much more the Italians had got than other immigrants, and what he planned to report to the government. Talk, talk, talk. Why had so little been done to cultivate the land granted to them? he asked. Why were there no signs of a decent attempt to start a silk industry? The only conclusion he could come to, he said, was that they were wilful and a burden on the colony. I told Christie to tell him about the drought and the silkworms that died, about the sawmill oxen that were trampling everything underfoot, but Christie stood mute; he didn't interpret, he just stood there. And maybe it was as well that he kept silent, because if he had interpreted, the concert could have turned into a consternation. I went home before the end in any case.

The week after that, the rains came. Heavy rains. Three days without stopping, day and night, and no axe went into the forest, nor an ox to haul out a splinter of wood. Nothing. When the first drops started falling, Dunn scampered for the village. On the second day, his workers came to me complaining that their tents were standing in water. I told them not to bother me, I had nothing to do with them. I pointed out that the same rain was

263

falling on the Italians, but they weren't being flooded out of their tents. When I had heard the marsh lourie calling, and had felt the wind changing to the west, I'd told Miriam that she and the women had to go and cut bedding-bush and see that the earth bank behind the tents was strengthened where the children had broken it in their play. The men and I had cut enough firewood and had got it under the wood-shelter in time. When it started raining that night, I lay down to sleep without a worry. Except about Miriam who remained withdrawn and still had the saddest sadness about her.

When it stopped raining, we were three days' wages behind, but the drought was broken. Dunn, back from the village, called me to come and look at the water in the dam. When I stood up there on the dam wall, it was as though I looked down on one of my own dreams. For so many years I had longed for a dam on the highland, it's just that I never thought I would gain it from a sawmill.

When I got home the following night, Miriam said Chief Constable Ralph had been there that afternoon. Christie and three of the Italians were being charged with killing an ox and had to appear in court the coming Thursday. The three accomplices were Mangiagalli and Tomé and Cuicatti. I pushed away my plate of food and got up from the table. One problem was hardly over before the next one arrived. And every time the axes had to be laid down and wages lost.

'What is this I hear about an ox?' I went and asked Christie.

'They want to get rid of me, Miggel.' He was sitting in his office tent, a candle flickering beside him. 'If they can get me out of the way, it means they are absolved of all further responsibility towards the Italians. As long as I am here to make representations and demand justice, the failed silk industry remains an embarrassment to them.'

'What ox?'

'Now that they've come to realise that I will not be intimidated by threats, a fabricated case of ox-killing has been pointed at me.'

'What ox?'

'According to Constable Ralph, it's the ox one of the forest warders came across the day before Christmas, down in the first gorge to the east.'

'Why don't I know about it?'

'Because it has nothing to do with either you or me or any of the Italians. You were at Portland that day, I was coming back from the village and found Mangiagalli, Cuicatti and Tomé down in the gorge. They had been to the village as well and were resting at the water's edge. That is where I found them, and we walked on from there together. We hadn't gone far when the warder suddenly appeared on the path in front of us saying there was an ox lying slaughtered in the underbush, and did we have any knowledge of it? I assured him that none of us knew anything about it.'

I wasn't so sure. I didn't think Christie had actually had anything to do with the killing of the ox, but I did remember that things were very bad at the tents just before Christmas and that the last of the government oxen that were sent to haul the ploughs disappeared at the same time.

'Are you sure this isn't about the ox they slaughtered right at the beginning?' I asked.

'I don't know anything about any ox ever having been slaughtered!' he denied vehemently. 'You're the one that suggested that they slaughter an ox. I think you had better come along to court with us in case we need another witness.'

'Listen, Mr Christie, I might go and testify before Magistrate Jackson in a matter of life or death but not for an ox. Go and tell him about the half-dead oxen the government sent out here shortly after the Italians arrived, tell him you didn't see what happened to them. I'm not telling you to go and make up stories, just go and play stupid.'

'You don't understand, Miggel, this isn't so much about the ox, it's a made-up case against me in an effort to get rid of me! You must come and testify for me.'

'I'm not going anywhere near Jackson. If you did not slaughter the ox, you did not slaughter the ox. Maybe the Italians did. Maybe it's your imagination telling you they want to be rid of you. Maybe you should write fewer letters reporting everyone. Go and tell Jackson that all this going to court must end, the Italians can't keep on losing wages for his blooming pleasure. Go and tell him that.'

It was a close-run thing, Christie nearly landed in jail for that ox. Jeary the woodbuyer and De Klerk, one of the village's legal agents, stood bail for him which kept him from being locked up.

But in reality it was the three Italians that saved him. And themselves perhaps. Whether they did it knowingly or unknowingly is difficult to say, although I think it was knowingly. Christie said that when they stood in court that morning, they became so dim-witted that they seemed not to understand a single word. He interpreted himself hoarse, Jackson got angry and threatened them, but they just shook their heads, clearly they weren't prepared to understand a thing. And nobody could get them anywhere near the Bible to be sworn in, they just hunched their shoulders, and stared at the ground.

'Instead of me then being questioned,' Christie said, 'I was placed in the dock and roundly accused of having killed an ox. When I asked who my accuser was, Jackson answered that it was the Crown and that he represented the Crown. The man is a tyrant, Miggel! He was at the one time my accuser, prosecutor, judge and jury. When there was not enough evidence against me, I was asked to find bail till the case was referred to the Attorney General in Cape Town.'

'And now?' I asked.

'Now we have to wait and see if the Attorney General can manufacture a better case against me.'

I understood little of the affair, but somewhere something was wrong. Christie didn't slaughter that ox, of that I was sure; he was too soft to kill a fly, let alone cut an ox's throat. I began to wonder if he wasn't right after all, that they wanted to be rid of him. Why didn't they tell him so then? He was no friend of mine, but without him things could still go very wrong.

Two days later, one of the warders came up to where we were cutting and said that Walker had sent him to tell me that the Italians had to be in the village on Saturday to be vaccinated.

'Warder,' I said, 'I'm beginning to get very tired of this smallpox business.'

'It can't be helped, uncle.'

'Why don't you go and give the message to Christie? Why bring it to me?'

'Mr Walker told me to come and tell you, uncle.'

'Well then, you go and tell him that they'll be cutting wood on Saturday. He can have himself vaccinated as far as I care, for they don't have smallpox.'

'You know I can't tell him that. You better see that they're there on Saturday, uncle.'

I threw down my axe. 'Listen here, warder, Christie assured me that they were vaccinated in Italy before they got on the ship.'

'That was not confirmed in England, uncle. Nor in Cape Town. The papers confirming it got lost somewhere. You must see that they get to the village on Saturday so that Dr Gorman can look them over.'

'They can't lose Saturday's wages. March is three-quarters over and almost a week's wages have been lost. I'm not complaining about the days that it rained, I'm complaining about the days they have had to put down the axes through other people's stupidity. The Italians are working for food, and for money to buy themselves tickets home on a ship, mister.'

'Mr Walker's not going to like it. You're asking for trouble, uncle.'

I didn't answer him. And little did I know then that I would be the one to lay down the axe on that Saturday. As I walked through my gate to collect the men from the tents, I saw a horse coming at full gallop across the highland and then I saw that the rider was Hal. I put down the axes and took off my hat, for I knew.

'Good morning, Uncle Silas.'

'Good morning, Hal.'

'I've just come to say that my father passed away last night, uncle.'

'May God be with your good mother and with all of you.'

'Thank you, uncle.'

'Did he have a struggle to give up this life?'

'Yes, uncle. He was in great pain.'

'Come to the house, have some coffee.'

'I don't have the time, uncle. I've got to take the news further. My mother says you promised my father to see to the oxen and that you will drive the wagon.'

'That is what I promised to your departed father and that's how it shall be.'

'The funeral is on Monday afternoon at two, uncle.'

'Has the wagon been greased?'

'I don't think so.'

267

'I'll see to it and get the oxen together.'

'Thank you, uncle.'

'Is John back from Cape Town?' John had been away for three months, selling the wood.

'He came back last week, we were already anxious then.'

When Hal rode off, I remained standing there, a strange kind of sadness coming over me. Barrington was Barrington, he was high and I was low, but our hands had often touched. When I looked up, I saw a crowned eagle slowly drifting on the wind above the gorge that lay between the highland and Portland and that was strange too. I hadn't seen a crowned eagle over the highland for years.

I went back to the house to tell Miriam. I took the mourning-band I had last worn for Magriet from the cupboard and put it round my arm. Then I went to the tents to say that I wouldn't be able to go to the forest again before Tuesday. God willing. I went and told Dunn as well.

'I believe you were employed at Portland for many years, Miggel,' he asked, prying. 'Is it true that the old man kept his four beautiful daughters almost living like hermits?'

'In the first place,' I corrected him, 'I was never employed at Portland, I went and helped out the late Mr Barrington when he sent for me, just as I am helping you out with the Italians. Silas Miggel belongs to himself, he is in no one's service but his own, as is the way of us forest people. Concerning Mr Barrington's daughters, I can only say that I never saw them restricted to the house.' I didn't tell him that they were seldom allowed further than Portland and Karawater. It was none of Dunn's business anyway. Barrington had declined on their behalf every invitation they received to a dance or a party and I had seen them cry many a tear because of it. 'I'll be back at work on Tuesday,' I told him.

'Don't worry, Miggel, I'll send one of my other foremen to cut with them.'

I said nothing.

Miriam was still crying when I got back to the house. 'He was a good man, Pa.'

'Yes. One mustn't reproach the dead.' Whenever I had seen the mess on the highland, I had become angry and blamed Barrington for everything all over again. 'Yes,' I said, 'in his own way he was a good man. It's just that he's now up in heaven and I'm still down below here with his Italians.'

'You should be ashamed of yourself speaking like that of the dead, Pa.'

'One must never be ashamed of the truth. And you must stop crying now. Before I can load him on the wagon, my two feet must take me to many a place and my hands must do many a task. Pack me some extra food, I've got to go many miles to round up the oxen. If I'm not back by dark, bolt the door and load the gun, and reckon I'll be sleeping wherever I am.'

'You'll never manage the oxen alone, Pa.'

'I know. I'm on my way to call on Koos Matroos, he will have to help me and on Monday he will have to lead the oxen for me as well. Tomorrow is Sunday, God forgive me, but I will have to use the day to get everything done. If Barrington had died earlier in the week, it would have been better.'

'Pa!'

'Pack the food, Miriam, I must be on my way.'

By midday on Sunday, Koos and I had the last of the oxen at Portland, twelve black ones, but I was worried. 'I'll have to get hold of a bush-pig,' I said to Koos, 'this lot is going to make trouble.'

'I've been thinking the same thing since yesterday, Master Silas. These oxen are likely to break out and stampede.'

'You'll have to stay here with them so that I can get back to the highland. Keep the rest of my food and don't take your eyes off them.'

I had to go and set a bush-pig snare. Pull a whip through the melted fat of a bush-pig, and the most unruly ox will have respect for that whip. Not that I had much faith in the twelve I had found to take Barrington to his grave; lion fat would have been the thing for them. And that day, for the first time in my life, I laid a snare on a Sunday; four snares, and it didn't feel right. From the snares, I walked north to my sister Hannie at Creek Bush Island to borrow her late husband's black breeches and coat. Barrington had said I must be dressed in black.

When Hannie opened the door and saw me standing there with the mourning-band round my arm, she had such a fright that she almost fainted right there at the door.

269

'I always knew she wouldn't live to see the day of her twentieth,' Hannie said and started crying. 'I always knew.'

'What's wrong now, Hannie?'

'Is it Miriam?'

'Don't be so blooming silly, woman! Don't stand there tempting fate. My Miriam is in good health, it's Barrington that's gone.'

'Oh.'

'I've come to borrow Hans's black for the funeral.'

'Come in and sit down, I want to talk to you.'

Whenever Hannie invited you to sit down for a talk, you were trapped. 'Hannie, I don't have time for your preachings today. I would be grateful if you'll let me borrow Hans's black, but that's all.'

'Hans's black is at Big Island with Wiljam who borrowed it for Cornelius van Huyssteen's funeral – may his soul be with the angelings. Your own blood kin, but you didn't even take the trouble to come and help us bury him. You're too busy digging your own grave down on the highland amongst strangers and a sawmill. Then you have the nerve to come and tell me your Miriam is in good health. If you think your Miriam is in good health, you're blind. The child was here yesterday, she is so unhappy that she can hardly put one foot in front of the other.'

'Leave Miriam alone, she'll be all right soon.'

'Be all right from what?'

'Don't put your nose into my cupboards, Hannie!'

'If I'm putting my nose into your cupboards, it's because I'm worried sick about Miriam. Why don't you move back here with her where I can keep a mother's eye on her as it should be? What is it that bothers the child so much? Has she taken a fancy to one of those Italians?'

I had to restrain myself. 'Hannie,' I said, 'as long as I'm alive, it will be my eye that's on her, not yours. It's bad enough that you had to put the story of the blooming curse into her head.'

'I asked you if she has taken a fancy to one of the Italians?'

'No.'

'Have you taken a fancy to one of them?'

'What?'

'I'm asking if you have taken a fancy to one of those hot-eyed women I've seen with Miriam in the village.'

'Hannie, if I lose my temper with you on this holy day, I'll get up and walk out, and never put a foot in your house again.'

'What difference would it make? You hardly ever come here in any case. I've understood why you've lived alone with the child on the highland all these years because I knew why you wanted to keep her apart, but I no longer understand you. The highland has been invaded by all kinds of strangers, but you haven't made any urgent plans to move away from there with her. Have you turned your back on your paternal responsibility? Why are you still there?'

'The highland is my place. It's my home. It's my right. It's Miriam's right and no one will come and take that away from her or me. At the most we'll have to hold out for five years. After that, there'll be no trace left of either Italian or sawmill. It's a matter of holding out. You'll see. And Miriam will raise her head again, you'll see that too. I had hoped to borrow Hans's black so I could keep my word to Barrington, but now you say it's still with Wiljam.'

'Yes. You can fetch it from him if you want to. I'm lending it to you, not to Barrington. He never had a penny's worth of time for us forest people, I don't know why you're in mourning for him.'

'His house was good to my Miriam.'

So I then had to walk to Big Island to get Hans's black with the result that it was almost dark by the time I got back home.

'Did the Italians go to the forest to cut yesterday?' I asked Miriam.

'No, Pa. Mr Dunn sent a man to go with them, but he couldn't get them into the forest, not even with Mr Christie's help.'

'What were you doing at your Aunt Hannie's yesterday?'

'I went to the forest, Pa. I just wanted to be alone for a while and in the end I walked as far as Creek Bush.'

'Did you take the gun?' Since the sawmill workers had arrived, I didn't even want her to go without the gun on a Sunday any more.

'I did.'

'What did you want to be alone for?' I asked her. 'You were alone at home, weren't you?'

'One can no longer be alone on the highland, Pa. When it was

271

only the Italians here, it was rather nice. Now it's not so nice any more. There are too many strangers, too many oxen, too many tents, it's making me scared, Pa. And the house feels like a prison with this terrible fence round it.'

'It can't be helped. We've just got to hold out and keep our eyes in front of us. The sawmill means deliverance for the Italians and money in my tin. I know it's a bitter kind of outcome and a long haul, but we have to hold out.'

'Borolini says the minute he has enough ship money, he's off, but Fardini says they've all got to leave together.'

'Fardini is a sensible man. Hand me the Bible, girl, I must find strength for tomorrow and for the week ahead. I don't trust those oxen.' She fetched me the Bible and went to her room. I thanked God that the Italians had refused to go with the other man; as long as Dunn couldn't do without me, I was sure of my wages and as long as I was sure of my wages there was a chance of getting one of the lots. I asked God to keep His hand over the oxen for me so that I could take Barrington to his resting place with dignity. When I looked up Miriam was standing at the door.

'Pa?'

'What is it, Miriam?'

'Pontiggia is back.'

'What?'

'He came back this afternoon. He says they worked in Port Elizabeth for two weeks and then they got on a ship going back to Cape Town. He did all kinds of work there in order to get enough money to come back here.'

I didn't like it. 'What did he come back for?' I did not like it at all.

'I don't know, Pa.'

'And the others?'

'They're working in Cape Town. America sent word with Pontiggia that you must please send him the money to return here.'

This was bad news indeed. 'They can't start coming back here one after the other! Gone is gone,' I said.

'Pontiggia says he's joining the cutters tomorrow to earn his ship money back to Italy.'

'If I was a rich man, I would go and give it to him right now.'

'Don't be nasty to him, Pa.'

When she turned and went back to her room, I went on my knees and I told God I would manage the oxen so long as He just kept a hand over Miriam for me. I was most uneasy about Pontiggia being back.

I set out for the snares before dawn the following day, Monday. By the time the sun was up, I had the whip well smeared with bush-pig fat and at halfday, Koos and I yoked the oxen over at Portland and made a wide circle round the house with the wagon to test them. On each side, there were a few that wanted to buck off the yokes, but when I flicked the whip over them, it was like a voice from the skies itself that urged them back into place. By the time we halted before the front door, they stood like a colossal black snake, straight in line, the white horns two magnificent rows of half moons. Splendid.

The bearers came and put the coffin on the wagon; others then placed beautiful wreaths around him – wreaths made of loquat leaves with flowers stuck in between; wreaths made of his own roses he had always tended with such care. I took the wreath Miriam had made, and laid it at his feet. When Mrs Barrington came from the house with her four daughters to take their place behind the wagon, I had to swallow the lump in my throat. But when I moved the wagon forward, it went so smoothly that Barrington cannot have moved an inch in the coffin. I drove ahead of the procession slowly and on to the Redlands road; this was the road Barrington had made for another of his dreams that never came true. Redlands road was supposed to have joined the road they were making through the gorge of the Homtini River. While they worked on the pass for all those years, Barrington believed they would name it after him: Barrington Pass. But the pass didn't get his name; they named it instead Homtini Pass, and the Redlands road was never finished.

I didn't take my eyes off those oxen for a moment. If one of them just tried to step out of line, I gave him a whiff of bush-pig and he was back in position. But all the time, the queerest shivers crept up and down my back; it was as if Barrington was sitting right up in front of the wagon, keeping his eyes on me. As we made the last turn before stopping at the grave, I said in my heart: Honourable, Honourable can go and rest in peace now,

I've brought Honourable here without a thing having gone wrong. If Honourable is dissatisfied because Hans's breeches are a bit short and tight on me, I can only say I'm sorry. I am a much taller man than he was.

it was a fine funeral. Respectful and moving as is proper for a man of high standing. When they lowered him into the grave, sixteen years between me and Portland went down with him.

My feet never touched Portland soil again.

That same night, Koos and I delivered every ox back to where it belonged. When I got home, I didn't think I would get my tired body to the door. And the whole world seemed to be whirling around me: sawmill oxen, sawmill parts, sawmill tents full of yellow candlelight and noise. Someone was playing a mouth organ at the dam diggers' tents, children were yelling at the Italians' tents. I said to myself: look in front of your feet, Silas Miggel, a tired man stumbles easily. As Koos and I had been busy unyoking the oxen after the funeral, Hal had come up to me and had asked if I thought he might find work at the sawmill. What for? A man with all of Karawater's acres to his name didn't work at a sawmill. It was then that he had told me that he had been disinherited, Karawater was no longer his. Things between him and his father had not been smoothed out. I couldn't understand it. How could you disinherit your child and leave discord behind in your house?

Not that I found contentment in my own house when I got there. The food was cooked, the bread baked, everything was in its place, but Miriam's face was swollen from crying and I was too tired to say anything.

274

FIFTEEN

THE NEXT MORNING I was back in the forest with the full team plus Pontiggia – and almost returned with one less that evening. When we got to the shelter to gather our things to go home, Ilario was missing. We called him, but he didn't answer. I saw the others immediately become anxious, but I was not alarmed. At midday he had told me that he was going to visit the snares; perhaps there was a buck we could take home, reserves of meat were low at the tents. I knew, however, that it wouldn't have taken him that long to visit the snares.

'Bigfeet got him, Signor Miggel?' one of Fardini's sons, Giuseppe, asked.

'No. Stay at the shelter, I'll take the gun and go and look for him.'

One couldn't be sure, of course, but I didn't think an elephant had trampled him although the elephants had been almost too quiet for my liking in recent weeks. Every Monday morning we found their dung, dropped on the Sunday where we had cut the week before, but that was all. For the rest of the week, I didn't hear or see a single one. I said to Miriam that one might almost think they came on Sundays to count the trees we had felled during the week. One thing was sure: *if* Ilario had landed up under an elephant, Dunn could forget about an Italian ever lifting an axe for him again. Not a day went by without the ladder being carried into the forest and leant against a tree, ready for an emergency. Not a branch cracked in the forest without them looking up to see what my reaction was.

As I walked along, I decided Ilario had either fallen ill somewhere, or he had got himself lost. Had he got lost, I would wring his neck because I had forbidden him to go anywhere outside the stretch of forest I had marked out for him for the snares.

One day I asked a foreman of one of the other teams whether the elephants ever bothered them. The stupid fool said no, they had been assured that there were no elephants in Gouna's part of the forest. I asked him who had given them that sort of assurance?

'Mr Dunn of Fox & Dunn. And we were told not to take any notice of whatever you might say, you're appointed over the Italians and that's all.'

'Is that so?' It was good to know what was being said behind my back. 'I would advise you, nevertheless, to take notice when I tell you not to call them by their names as openly as you're doing; they hear you from far off and think you're calling them. Every Italian working under me knows that.'

He took no notice.

I must have been about half a mile from the shelter when I heard Ilario calling out faintly but anxiously from somewhere in the area. I hurried closer and called out to him. He called back. I heard him but I couldn't see him, for the underbush was very thick. I called him again, and this time when he answered I knew he wasn't on the ground at all, he was somewhere up in the air.

'Where the devil are you?' It was beginning to get dark in the forest. And when I finally saw him, it was only his feet I saw, dangling through the branches of a white alder. This gave me a fright as my first thought was that he had tried to hang himself and then didn't fall properly. 'What are you doing up there?' I shouted. 'How did you get there?'

'Help, Signor Miggel! No get down.'

If it hadn't been so late in the day, I would have left him there to get himself out of the tree; for a sick man, he had climbed blooming high and now I was the one that had to climb up after him to get him down.

'What were you doing up the tree?' I asked when I had him back on the ground.

'Bigfoot, Signor Miggel. Very big. Teeth very fat.'

'Where was the bigfoot?'

'When I bent down at snare and came up again.'

'It was your imagination, man. Did you *see* him?'

276

'Bigfoot very high.'

'Come on,' I said, 'you can decide later on whether or not you've dreamt it, it's getting dark.'

We hadn't gone a hundred yards when an elephant trumpeted very close to us in the thickets, shaking the whole forest. This I knew was an elephant in anger. I shouted at Ilario to run. Who or what had angered that elephant, I didn't know; not a shot had been fired during the day, nothing, but somewhere something was wrong. Ilario couldn't keep up with me so I turned back and grabbed hold of him by his shirt collar, put the other hand under his behind and pushed him along in front of me.

At the shelter, everyone except Fardini was up in the trees.

The next morning not a single hand was prepared to pick up an axe and go into the forest. Not one in Dunn's teams, not one of the Italians. 'Danger, Signor Miggel, big danger,' Robolini said on behalf of the others. Dunn was over at the tents as well. He was hoping that if I could get the Italians into the forest, he would get the others to follow. The whole world had heard the elephant the day before; even Christie was frightened out of his wits.

'*I* am responsible for the safety of the Italians,' he said, 'I demand an enquiry into the incident and a guarantee for their future safety.'

'What guarantee?' I asked him.

'The elephants must be shot.'

'Don't talk bloody nonsense, man! Who do you think will come and shoot more than five hundred bigfoot? Who's going to round them up from everywhere? How long do you think it's going to take, how long before anyone would be able to cut again? On what will the Italians live in the meantime? How are they to earn their ship money?'

'I will not give permission for them to cut any more before the matter has been investigated.'

He made me so cross that I gave him a push between the shoulder blades with the butt of my gun. 'There is nothing to be investigated!' I said. 'And if you call them by their names once more on this highland, you'll have me to contend with.'

'I shall lay a charge of assault against you!'

'Do it and be done with it. But before you do, just tell these blooming scared arses that *I* say they aren't to come running to

277

me when they have no food to eat. Tell them they can go and rot in the tents, I'll go and find myself a team of cutters from the forest.'

I took my axes and the ropes, the gun and the knapsack of food and walked off in the direction of the sled-path. Christie didn't interpret but I knew the Italians had understood enough of what I had said.

When the forest was all around me, I knew I wasn't alone, but I didn't look round. When I came across the first elephant dung lying on the path, I prepared the gun for the tracks were Old Foot's. I felt the sweat breaking out all over my body but I still didn't look round. I just kept going. It was only when I was almost at the place where we were cutting that I looked round and counted the row of grim faces behind me: they were all there except Pontiggia. He never picked up an axe again.

The moment I put my foot through the door when I got home that night, I knew it wasn't the same place I had left that morning. The table still stood where it always stood, the chairs, the cupboard, the water buckets, but it was not the same place. And Miriam was not the same Miriam.

'Hallo, Pa.' She almost seemed to glow, everything about her seemed to shine.

'Miriam?'

'Why are you standing in the door like that, Pa?' Her voice was light and clear and laughing.

'Did you have any visitors?'

'Mr Dunn was here to complain about Mr Christie; Mr Christie was here to complain about Mr Dunn.' Playful. 'I've got a nice francolin in the pot for you and sweet potatoes baked in the ashes.' Not a sign of sadness. Just joy glowing from her.

'Who else was here?'

'Petroniglia. She brought you a sausage.'

'Who else? Has Pontiggia been in my house?'

'He's been in the village all day, looking for work. Go and wash your hands and come to the table.'

'Miriam, I don't want a bite of food before I hear what's going on here! When I left this morning, you were like a bird dragging both its wings; now you're suddenly up in the air. Have you been in the forest?'

'Yes.' Still playfully. 'And the forest is green again, the crabs are back in the creeks, the dragonflies are back and so are the frogs and the birds. One must never give up, Pa, never.' A serious note crept into her voice as she said this.

'Don't give me riddles, Miriam! I want to know what has happened here to make this change in you. I want to know the truth!' My heart was hammering in my head.

'Come and eat, Pa.' Like a tree that said: cut me, I will not fall.

'Did you see Jacob, husband of Susanna, in the forest?'

'Don't ask me, Pa. Please.'

I asked her again. And again and again. I had to get the truth from her, but she wouldn't give in, she went and hid behind an impenetrable silence.

It was a difficult time for me. At night my body was exhausted from swinging the axe all day and struggling with the Italians who just wouldn't get used to the forest; my mind was weary and confused about Miriam and many a night I fell asleep at the table. I couldn't leave my work to look after her, I couldn't lock her in and I couldn't take her with me to the forest, although there was many a day I threatened to do so.

'I don't understand you, Pa: when I was unhappy, you didn't like it; now that I'm happy again, you still don't like it. What is it that you want then?'

'I'm not stupid, Miriam, your happiness is not an ordinary happiness and you know it.'

Every time I tried to reach her, she retreated into her silence. On Sundays she stayed at home. In other words, I worked out, it was during the week that she was seeing someone. I couldn't discover if he was coming to the house, I swept outside the door in the mornings and inspected every footprint in the evenings. Dunn's were there too often for my liking and I kept an eye on him, but I still suspected that she was going into the forest to meet whomever. For the whole of March, Nols Terblans's team was cutting down in Kom's Bush and that wasn't too far for Jacob to slip away to Gouna's Bush. In the end I became so mixed up that I kicked aside my pride one April Sunday morning and set out for Creek Bush Island to see Mieta. If anyone knew what was going on, it was Mieta. She was like the bigfeet, she knew everything that went on in the forest.

279

'My Miriam is after a man,' I told her as we sat down. 'I know it is wrong of me to come to you about it, but there is no other solution. I don't want to spy on her, but I've got to know because all this worrying is getting to me now.'

'Is it one of the Italians?'

'No. I was hoping you would know.'

'Is it one of the sawmill workers?'

'No.'

'Could it be one of old Barrington's sons? May he rest with the angelings. That would seem possible, from the few times I've seen them.'

'It's not one of them.'

'Are you sure she's got a man, Silas Miggel?'

'Yes. I came here hoping you would know something.'

'Maybe I do, maybe I don't.'

'Mieta, I don't want to hear any more riddles, I've had enough of that!'

'Say I know and I tell you, you'd go and shoot the man and his blood would be on me, Silas Miggel.'

'I won't shoot him. I'll just try and do something to stop her because she's already like someone no longer of this earth.'

'Don't talk like that!'

'She should have had a mother.'

'Do you think a mother would have you stop her? She's *your* child, Silas Miggel. Where she wants to go, she'll go. She'll ask permission from no one.'

'I've got to know where she goes.'

'I've found her at the lilies, but she sits alone. I've seen her on a footpath, but she walks alone. I've seen her on a sled-path, she still walks alone. She treads softly.'

'What are you saying?'

'I'm saying that I can't help you. But from now on, I'll keep a closer watch and maybe I'll come and tell you, Silas Miggel. Maybe.'

I don't know why but I just didn't trust the old witch.

And Miriam didn't go to the forest every day either. Sometimes more than a week went by without her going. But when she did go, I could tell she'd been by the happiness in her when I got home at night. There were nights when she was as tired as I was, and when I had to take off her shoes.

'Petroniglia and I had to go and catch eels, Pa. We're getting fewer and fewer francolins in the gin. There is too much noise on the highland.'

As I watched over the men, she watched over the women and children, and often I wondered who had the hardest task, she or I. The men and I took care of the firewood and the meat; I skinned, Miriam shared out. Miriam gathered the herbs and roots and brewed the medicine; Miriam cared for the sick. Miriam kept up the school. Miriam consoled where I would have lost my temper long before. When Mariarosa got the screaming fits, Miriam was the one that ran across with the parsley-bush brew.

'If only they could get out of the tents, Pa, it's almost a year now!'

Dunn had promised that the first planks coming out of the mill would be given to the Italians. He was confident that the saws would be running by the end of March but at the end of April the sawmill's parts were still lying exactly where the wagons had off-loaded them. One setback after another hit him: if it wasn't with the building of the open shed under which the mill had to be erected, it was Robinson who hadn't turned up to put the parts together.

'Mr Dunn,' I said purposefully one day, 'this forest has a way of casting spells on sawmills.' Dunn's problem that day was an ox that one of the other teams had lost while hauling out wood. Of the hundred and twenty-one oxen, ninety-eight were left.

Dunn got angry. 'Don't give me rubbish of that sort, Miggel! Concentrate on the Italians and the wood, you brought out less last week.'

'The days are getting shorter and we can't work in the dark. And even if we are bringing out less, we are still bringing out the most and the best.' I was not prepared to let him criticise my work in any way, but there was something else I had to get off my chest. 'Mr Dunn,' I asked him, 'when last did you take the trouble of going to have a look where your other teams are cutting?' I knew very well that he never set foot north into the forest. 'The only team that cuts in a section is mine. The others are felling as if they had been ordered to clear the whole world around here.'

'I'm glad you've brought that up, Miggel. One of my foremen

says you pushed him to the ground a while ago, and I take the strongest exception to that.'

'Next time I'll break his neck for him if I find a white alder cut up for firewood again. White alder grows in this forest for climbing into when the bigfeet chase you, and the bees need the flowers for making their honey.'

'Surely you don't expect my workers to know every tree in this wilderness, do you?'

'The warders came and showed them the two kinds of yellowwood they may cut for the mill, they showed them what dead wood looks like which they can cut for the boiler and their own fires, but I've noticed that the team cutting for firewood, cuts everything they can lay an axe on! Stinkwood, yellowwood, white alder, kamassi, even the only four knobwoods that grew this side of the forest have been cut.' Dunn tried to stop me, but I would not be stopped. 'Not one of the other teams are working in a section; for every tree they fell, two, three, four stand ruined forever after. I've seen some left lying right where they've felled it because no man or beast could ever get it out from there, but worst of all are the ones from which only a few hacks have been cut and then just left like that. It's bloody well not right.'

'Miggel, you must stop interfering with the other teams!' He was angry. 'This is a government contract, we have permission to cut what we need. We work according to instructions from the government, not instructions from you! The Superintendent of Woods and Forests, Count de Regné, determines the conservation methods that must be followed, not Silas Miggel.'

Fardini once said: when your superior talks nonsense, stand still and pretend you're listening attentively; one day, when you need a favour from him, he will remember your face. I tried to hold my tongue and walk away, but my head didn't work like an Italian's. 'De Regné sits on his backside in an office in the village,' I said to Dunn. 'All he does is send out orders to the forest along with the warders and now you call it government instructions and conservation. What conservation? I have never understood what is meant by conservation, but I know plain ruin when I see it.'

'If you don't restrict your energy to your axe and the Italians, Miggel, you may take your things and go.'

It was a hard blow. He knew very well there was nowhere else

I could earn at eight shillings a day. Whilst he forgot that he was the one that needed the Italians and that they wouldn't go into the forest without me, he had the axe with which to cut, not me.

It wasn't a week later that one of the warders turned up where we were cutting, and with him was a stranger, a certain Mr Dumbleton.

'He's the newly appointed Inspector of Woods,' said the warder, 'and will be mostly concerned with the cutting that is being done for the sawmill. He does not understand Dutch, uncle.'

'That's all right so long as he understands what's going on here and does something about it. Dunn told me to keep out of it.'

'It's a disgrace, it's a goddamn disgrace!' the inspector said.

'That you can say again, mister.'

'I've already taken him to have a look where the others are cutting, uncle. He's going to write a fierce report about matters.'

'It's a disgrace, it's a goddamn disgrace.'

'Yes,' I said. But I never saw Dumbleton in the forest again. And the only team that kept cutting in a section was mine.

And one cannot swing axes together, day after day, without something rubbing off on each side. As time went by, I got to know them better, even if it was still mostly by the bark and not in the heart. We laid down the axes three times a day to go to the shelter to eat and rest, and smoke for the ones that smoked. It was then that most of the talking was done. They never seemed to grow tired of talking. They spoke Dutch quite well by now, and I almost understood everything they said. Where interpretation was still necessary, Fardini did it. He was clever in the head.

They always liked to tell me about their country and spoke of the places they came from. Of the snow in winter, the heat in summer. Of the cities with the huge churches all made of stone, just as Christie had said. They spoke of the many people in the streets one could talk to and laugh with. Important people. Beautiful women. Of the enormous halls filled with golden hangings, halls built specially for music-making, beautiful music. Of the lakes from which the mountains rose like castles; lakes far bigger than the lagoon at Knysna, far deeper, far more beautiful. Of the statues, some as tall as trees, cut from snow-white stone, some even standing along the streets; statues, it seemed, of every holy person in the Bible. Of fountains that never ran wild as they wished, the water sprouting from the mouths of lions and fishes and angelings. They told me about Fardini's home, Firenze, where all the roofs were red and the church was built of green and white stones. Of Tomé's home, where all the streets were of water and people went around in boats instead of by horse and carriage or wagon.

At first I thought they were making it up to make me laugh, but then I saw the tears shamelessly running down Tomé's face and I got cross again.

'What the devil did you come here for then?' I asked.

'Lies, Signor Miggel. Lies.'

'Promised good land.'

'Mulberry forest.'

'Sheds for our worms.'

'Many money.'

'Now we cut with axe.'

'No church.'

'No school for children.'

'Coffee no good.'

'Wine no good.'

They all had their say before Fardini spoke out: 'Signor Miggel see, old trouble always better than new trouble.' As time went by, the truth slowly emerged from Fardini. For years they had been plagued by a silkworm disease which killed off up to half their worms in a season. Half a silkworm crop was a lot for they were big silk farmers. They farmed on hired land, however, and the rent had to be paid. They were good farmers, they didn't use the cheap eggs which were sold on the markets at the end of summer, they bought only the best eggs. When the yellow worms of their own country kept dying, they got eggs from a place called Japan. But before long, the new eggs' worms contracted the disease as well. Apart from that, the Japanese worms spun less silk to a cocoon than their own yellow worms did. Silkworms were flighty in any case; if the weather suddenly turned cold, they perished. If it was too hot, the Japanese worms perished. The Japanese worms withstood the cold of the mountainous areas better, the yellow worms withstood the heat of the valleys better. The year before the Italians left, an unseasonal frosty spell not only destroyed just about the whole grape crop, but the foliage on the mulberry trees as well, with the result that they didn't have enough leaves to feed to the thousands upon thousands of silkworms. All the silk farmers in all the districts could not supply half the required cocoons to the six hundred spinning mills, so the mills had to start buying cocoons from other countries.

More information came out bit by bit, much of which I did not understand.

'Italia old, Signor Miggel. Many wars, many blood,' Robolini said one day, sitting with his back to a tree. That was the day I learned that all the people in their land were very much afraid of poverty. Just like the forest people, I said. Well, perhaps not quite, Mangiagalli said, those that didn't have money were forever afraid that they would never obtain money; those that had money were forever in fear of losing it. The poor were afraid of the rich landowners, the rich landowners were afraid of the hundreds of thousands of poor who were always rebelling and making trouble; the ordinary people in between were afraid of the rich landowners as well as of the hundreds of thousands of poor. To keep everyone in their place, laws were made, many laws. Some of the laws were hundreds of years old, some were made yesterday and the others were promised for tomorrow. If you but moved, it seemed you stepped on a law. Robolini said everyone's desire was that his children would have a better life than he had had, but there were not enough schools, thousands of children never learnt to read or write, and there wasn't enough work for everyone either.

Then one day, Cruci's uncle – a very important man in Milano – had read in a newspaper about a place called Il Capo di Buona Speranza, a place of Good Hope, where they were looking for silk farmers, and the newspaper said that they would be given good land. Robolini's sister's husband – a very rich merchant in Firenze – read the same thing in another newspaper. One told the other and passed on the address of the man they had to write to, a certain Mr Burnett in London. Hundreds wrote, those that could not write themselves found someone to write for them. Of the many hundreds who had written, about two hundred received word that they had to be in a place called Torino on a certain day where the English consul

285

would select the most suitable. Many went on foot to Torino.

'And who was the shit that told you that you were coming to a mulberry forest?'

'Shit man in Torino.'

One could no longer let anything slip in front of them. 'Forget that first word, it's a bad word. What did the man tell you?'

'Not consul, other man at consul's place told us about mulberry forest when we ask about place where we were going, place of Good Hope.'

The day they boarded the ship, most of them did not know where this place was. Fardini and Robolini and a few of the others knew. Sort of.

'When did Christie join you then?'

'Genova, where we got on first ship who take us to London.'

'And then?'

'Place of Good Hope far. Very far.'

'And now?'

'Forest no good, Italia better. Italia has church for children.'

'Nobody here to pray for our sins, Signor Miggel.'

'I have to pray for my own,' I said.

'We not want to stay in forest,' Tomé said. 'Forest for bigfeet and robbers.'

'How much money have you put aside for the ship?' I asked them that regularly.

'Three pounds.'

'Two pounds.'

'One pound ten shillings, buy shoes for child.'

'Food dear, Signor Miggel, everything dear.'

'You must try and eat less!' I told them.

If only we could plant some vegetables for each tent, but everything was buried under the sawmill. Every potato and onion and egg, every drop of milk and bit of butter and lard had to be bought out of their wages. I got sweet potatoes for them at a good price from the forest islands; often the woodcutters didn't charge at all. Only Miriam and I still kept a patch of vegetables going on the highland and the last of my pumpkin crop was stolen from my roof. I told Dunn that the thief was in one of his tents, he had to get him out of there so I could kick him off the highland. Some of the Italians' things had also disappeared.

In the middle of April, they let Christie know that the Attorney General had decided not proceed with the ox-killing case. But at the same time they didn't pay him his month's salary. And not a week went by without him reporting someone to the government. If it wasn't Dunn, it was Walker or one of the warders, or a constable, or the man at the post office who had offended him.

'They are trying to get rid of me, Miggel.'

'Why then don't you take your things and go back to England?' I asked him.

'I came here with the Italians, and I will leave with them. I have demanded free passage for each one of us and, until then, the immediate resumption of the allowance of a shilling per day per head. And I want my salary paid promptly on the last day of each month. Furthermore, I have demanded to be allowed to sell my land; this is a British colony and I am a British subject. My price for the land, Miggel, is now three hundred pounds. I cannot sell for less.'

'Mr Christie, you won't even get three hundred pounds for the whole of the highland. When do the Italians have to make the first payments for the lots?'

'On or before the twentieth of June.'

I refused to rejoice before the time, I had to be patient and cautious. I was not interested in Fardini or Cruci's allotments, I had no use for land through which the so-called *New Road to Knysna* ran. I had my heart set on Christie's lot first, then on Robolini's, then on Ilario's.

At the end of May, Robinson arrived at last and started putting together the sawmill parts. Piece by piece. More workers arrived. More tents. An extra team of cutters was sent into the forest to help cut the firewood for the boiler. Night after night, when I came past with the Italians, it was as if a monster was growing under the open shed and, at the same time, as if a stone was lodged in my stomach, growing heavier and heavier.

'They're putting up a store on the highland, Pa,' Miriam said one evening as we sat down at the table.

'You must have dreamt such a thing.'

'No, Pa. They brought four loads of planks and they're

287

already putting it up down at the foot of the highland near the workers' tents.'

I wouldn't believe it, I didn't want it to be true. 'Perhaps it's a woodshed?'

'No, Pa, it's a shop. One of the British immigrants is putting it up and the marsh lourie called all day, it's going to rain.'

'Not a penny of mine will go into that store, I'm telling you. Not a penny of the Italians', either. They must take the thing away from here, this isn't a village!'

'Don't become too blinkered, Pa. I'm the one who has to take the ox and the sled on Saturdays to fetch the Italians' provisions from the village. Do you think anyone will walk nine miles for a penny's worth of salt if he can buy it here?'

She was right. And I was too tired to put up a fight. It's just that a store on the highland was like a louse on my body. On top of everything, the boiler stood assembled and ready when we came out of the forest that afternoon.

'Pa?'

'Yes, Miriam?'

'Canovi is back. He arrived this morning.'

It was like news of another louse. 'What for?'

'I think it's because of Monica. He says the other three are still in Cape Town, they are working where the tracks for the trains are being laid. America asked him to ask you please to send him money to get back to Italy. He sent an address.'

'He can stay where he is.' Canovi was the second one of the five to return and I didn't like it. It was unsettling for the others. 'If Canovi is back,' I said, 'he should join the team as from tomorrow. No sitting around doing nothing will be allowed. Everyone must help to earn the ship money. It's bad enough that Pontiggia's doing nothing.'

'He's not doing nothing, Pa. He has already painted three horse-carts and quite a few more are waiting.'

'What horse-carts?' I didn't know anything about this.

'He paints curls and patterns and crests on carts for people. I saw the one he did for Mr Duthie, it's beautiful and very fine and they're paying him well. He says he'll be back in Italy before the year is out.'

'I hope that's the truth.' I don't know why, but I was still not at ease about Pontiggia. His clothes were too tight on his body and

288

his eyes went sort of glazed when he looked at Miriam.

'I went to Creek Bush Island today, Pa.' She didn't say it, she threw it at me.

The moment she did, I knew it was an accusation and I suddenly realised that she was sulking, that she had been sulking since I got home. 'You've been to Creek Bush Island,' I said, playing dumb in the hope of warding off a quarrel.

'Yes. Aunt Hannie says you've been to see Mieta, Pa, and she thinks it was about me.'

Old Sarel van Rensburg always said: the day a woman learned to keep her mouth shut, peace descended on your house. 'Your Aunt Hannie is a troublemaker. I've told her to stay out of my cupboards.'

'What did you go to Mieta for?'

I didn't answer her. No child was my magistrate.

'I want to know why you went to Mieta. If it was about nothing, you would have told me that you'd been there.'

'Miriam,' I said – realising at the same time that many a thing that had been bottled up in me was going to come out – 'day after day I swing an axe, night after night I lie awake over you because you cover your tracks like a thief! If I have been to see Mieta, I have been to see her. If you don't want to tell me the truth, I must go and find it somewhere else.'

'And?' she asked cautiously.

'The truth will come out.'

'Is that why Mieta has tried twice recently to steal up on me in the forest, thinking I wouldn't know? Did you appoint her to spy on me? If you did, Pa, I'm afraid you've forgotten that you yourself taught me to walk the forest softly. More softly than she does.'

'I didn't teach you to walk like a dodger!'

'I don't walk like a dodger.' She went and stood with her back to the fire and looked me straight in the face. 'For once in my life, Pa, I'm asking to be allowed one moment to live as I may and to go where no one will follow me. *No one.* I'm asking for just one moment. When it's over and it's time to turn back, I won't come crying to you, that I swear before you tonight. I won't fight against anything, I will live at peace with myself for the rest of my life – but I want that moment now. I know what you're thinking, Pa, I know what makes you lie awake at night, but this is *my* life, Pa. It is *my* fate against which I'm pleading for just a moment of my life. Give it to me, Pa.'

Tears ran down her face. My beautiful Miriam stood there, shamelessly begging me for a piece of her life as if it were in my hands to give her. If I could have laid my arms on a chopping-block at that moment and sacrificed them in return that she might be freed from her fate, I would have run at once to the block, so deep was my pity for her. God knows, you have no power over your heart once a certain desire for someone starts growing in you. There comes an aching in your body that nothing can stop. I knew. And for some people there was a way out, for others there was no way out.

'Is it Jacob, Miriam?' I asked her quietly.

'I cannot tell you, Pa. Please. You've seen what the lilies look like after they've flowered and when the bush-pigs go in to root up the bulbs.'

'Is it Jacob, Miriam?'

'Don't ask me, Pa. All I can tell you is that it won't be long before I'll have to turn back.'

It was Jacob, I had no doubt about it any more. My daughter was walking in shame. 'If Mieta finds you, your name will be branded forever!'

'She won't find me.'

'You're playing with fire!'

'I know, Pa. But I'm not stupid, I'm careful.'

'You don't know what you're saying! You must turn back now, Miriam!' I was so frightened for her that I could hardly get the words out of my mouth.

'I'll turn back in time, Pa. I promise.'

'In time?'

'Yes. Just please don't stop me now.'

'Miriam, you can't ask this of me.'

'I'll turn back in time, Pa.'

'When?'

'Do you remember that time when my cat died, what you did then?'

I remembered it well. Barrington had given her a blooming kitten from Portland's stables, after I had asked him not to give it to her. When I asked him why he had gone against my word, he said that anyone that cared for an animal was a good person.

290

Miriam was a good child, that was why he had given her the kitten. I admitted straight out that I wasn't a good person then, for I planned to drown that fleabag in the river on our way home that afternoon. When I was ready to go home, however, Miriam was nowhere to be found; she had gone ahead to cross the river with the cat before I got there. And for five long years I had had to live with that blooming tomcat under my roof; during the night he slept at her feet, and by day he slept in the sun, and for the rest of the time he ate. On the day he fell sick and died, I let Miriam have her way and I joined in the funeral, I even sang because I was glad he was under the earth at last. She wouldn't stop crying about the cat; on the third day, I put my foot down and I told her that she could cry until the Friday, but then it was enough. One more tear after that, and I threatened to dig up the cat so that she could see if she still felt like crying for it. She had until the Friday. On the Thursday night she stopped.

'How long until you turn back, Miriam?' I now asked her.

'Till the lilies bloom again, Pa. February.'

And I, Silas Miggel, a man of simple ways but a man of honour, did not stop her and with that just as well as gave her my consent. In a moment of pity, when I wanted to die for her, I gave in. I gave my consent and later I couldn't believe what I had done. Neither could I turn back and stop her because she was like a bird whose wings had been untied.

SIXTEEN

ON THE SEVENTH day of June, they put the first wood through the saws. Dunn declared the day a holiday for the teams of cutters; no one needed to lift a hand but would earn a full day's wages. That was the only day in my life I ever got something for doing nothing.

People started arriving early in the morning: Walker, Jackson the magistrate, Harison the Conservator of Forests, John Barrington on horseback – without looking down to greet me; Mr Stewart, Mr Smit. Christie pushed himself to the front, of course. What had happened to Hal Barrington, I don't know, he never came looking for work at the sawmill.

Fardini and Cuicatti, Mangiagalli and Miriam, Petroniglia and Mariarosa and I found ourselves a place to stand below the dam. It was a bit muddy underfoot but we could see well from there. Why I went, I don't know. The dam had a sluice from where a ditch took water to a smaller dam and from that the boiler was fed; and to the south of the mill, the highland lay without water.

'Pull back your shoulders, you look as though you're standing at a funeral,' Miriam came and whispered in my ear.

I didn't see it as a funeral; at a funeral everyone was gathered to lay the dead to rest. Here it was the opposite: the dead had to be brought to life. From the beginning, the sawmill had taken on the shape of a monster to me, and a monster it would stay. At the back was the boiler with the fire in its belly and thick black smoke coming from its chimney. From early that morning, the stoker had battled to keep the fire going so that the water could boil to the satisfaction of the man that had to feed the steam to the crane that had to lift the logs, and steam for the belts that had to drive the saws which had to cut the wood. Robinson made a last inspection, feeling a belt here, adjusting something there, talking to the machine men and making sure that everyone was in his place: six men at the beginning of the operation where the logs had to be split, four at the band-saw, two at the circular saw, three standing close to the boiler with a man or two in between. When he was satisfied, he gave a sign and Dunn of Fox & Dunn climbed on to a box and made a speech. When he was finished, Jackson the magistrate took his place on the box, thanked Dunn, declared the sawmill ready for the enormous task ahead, and stepped off the box.

When the man in charge of the boiler turned on the steam, a heavy gunshot rang out to the north towards Gouna's Hill and before the boom had died down properly, a second shot rang out – and a third – and then it was quiet. Somewhere, someone had pulled down bigfoot.

But all eyes were on the mill where the steam had started pushing the powerful levers, setting everything in motion. One man, one single man, lifted a yellowwood block with the steam crane, a block that had taken me and the Italians twelve oxen to get there; he laid it neatly in the path of the saws without a drop of sweat breaking out on his body. Everyone watching clapped hands and moved closer, and the machine man had to keep them away from the rushing belts that had to operate the hungry saws; as the block was pushed into the first saw, the most terrible screeching came from the wood as if coming from hell itself. I wanted to turn away and leave, but I stood there, bewitched, until the block had gone through the last of the saws and the men held aloft the first planks for all to see. Up at the front, the second block was already moving into the saws. In the forest, it would have taken two men a full day in a pit pulling a two-handed saw to do what that goddamn dead thing had done in the wink of an eye.

I turned away and walked into the forest and kept on walking until the sound of the saws no longer reached me and I could only hear the wind and the birds and my own body moving. I walked to where the Red Alder River plunges over the cliffs, foaming into the gorge below. I squatted down and said to myself: Silas Miggel, don't look up, look just in front of your feet. Five months of the five years of the sawmill lay behind me. The day would come, as sure as the sun was shining, that they would drag that mill from the highland, but not Silas Miggel.

On the following Monday, Walker sent a warder to tell me to tell the Italians that there were twelve days left before they had to make the first payments on the allotments. On the same day, extension for the tents was up as well. He wanted them handed in, clean and neatly folded. Not a tent-peg was to be missing.

I pushed the news of the payments to the back of my mind, the tents were the problem. 'Why have you come to tell me? It's Christie you should tell,' I told the warder.

'Mr Walker said I was to come and tell you, uncle. Mr Christie's time as interpreter and foreman ends on the same day; they're not going to appoint him again. I believe he can stay on as an ordinary immigrant, but that's all. Mr Walker asked if you would please take the tents to him on your sled.'

I treated this order as though it was a load of wood he was talking about. 'That shouldn't be a bother. Tell Mr Walker that I'll come and see him tomorrow, tell him I'll be there early.' I had no choice but to lose a day's wages; the Italians as well if they refused to go into the forest on their own. But I had to go and see Walker before things got worse. I could not plead for Christie's tents or for his post as interpreter for he had brought this on himself by his pen and paper. I didn't know and neither did I care how many times he had reported me but without him things could still be difficult. One should give a man his due, even Christie; at least he was a stone that kept on trying to roll under the government's wheel – even if his stones turned out to be clods most of the time. As long as he was on the highland, the government at least knew about it. I, alone in charge of the Italians, was nothing. Who knew of Silas Miggel's existence? Walker, yes, but that was all. Mangiagalli said one day: only a man of power can threaten and scare another man. That was true. Not that I was scared because I had no power; they would not shift me from the highland.

When Walker walked into his office the next morning, I walked in behind him. When he sat down at his table and picked up a nib, I planted my feet on the other side of the table as though anchoring them there. Before he could say a word, I told him that if ever there had been a handsome man in the village, it was he and it was a pleasure to stand before him. I was not lying about his looks, he was a handsome man; I wasn't so sure about the pleasure. But Robolini had said: place a few good words at an important man's feet, and you quickly soften him.

'What can I do for you, Miggel?' He did not sound very soft, only wary.

'There isn't much you can do for me, it's just that I don't know how I'm going to get the Italians in houses in eleven days' time. The sawmill only started sawing on Wednesday, as you know. According to Mr Dunn, they should have started sawing in March and the first planks were promised to the Italians. But it is now June and they've only just started work. Everything at that mill has gone wrong, one can't help wondering if the place isn't under some sort of a spell.'

'Bad management, Miggel.'

It seemed as though I was going in the right direction. 'You will know about that better than me,' I said. 'I have to concentrate on the wood and keeping the Italians working, they can't live without the wages. Nor without the tents; winter is upon us and the world lies cold around a man's body at night.' Walker appeared to want to say something, but I was too quick for him. 'If I had had the planks as promised, mister, I would not have to be standing here today. The Italians would have been in houses, and there would have been no trouble in returning the tents. The wood from which the planks are being sawn is green, of course. When summer comes, they are going to warp very badly and we'll just have to patch up the gaps by nailing other planks on top. In the meantime, we will knock together houses as fast as Fox & Dunn can saw the planks, but you must let them have the tents a little longer.'

'I've already given them six months' grace.'

'That's right, and if it wasn't for that grace, half of them would have been dead by now.'

'Why didn't they start cutting wood for themselves long ago, sawing their own planks?'

'Don't make me laugh, mister. They were too scared to go into the forest.'

'Yes, and had we not taken away the allowance and forced

295

them to work for themselves, I suppose they would have sat in the tents fo.· the rest of their lives.'

'I won't be able to let you have all the tents at once, but as they fall empty, I'll send them. Clean and folded. First, I will get roofs over the four families with children, and then over Giuditta who is about to calf. That's the first five tents to come back. But every house must have a roof, and a roof needs corrugated iron, mister, and I thought if perhaps the government could help them with that . . .'

Walker nearly threw the nib at me. 'The government, Miggel, will most definitely not buy them corrugated iron sheets! Enough has been done for them. They were granted land, work has been made available to them on the highland, and I don't want to hear another word about them after the twentieth. They are now employed by Fox & Dunn. Everything they need from now on, they must buy for themselves. An interpreter will no longer be employed for them either.'

'In other words, on the twentieth, the government is turning its back on them?' I could understand that they no longer wanted to keep Christie, I could understand that they wanted the tents back sometime, I could more or less understand everything – except why the government just wanted to drop them and forget about them. Who had arranged for the silkwormers to come in the first place?

'And what about me, mister?' I asked him. 'Where do I stand?'

'As far as I know, you are employed by Fox & Dunn as well.'

'I was appointed by Mr White to assist Mr Christie with the Italians. I was promised dwelling rights for it. What became of that?' I just wanted to know.

'After the twentieth of this month, of June, no one is appointed over the Italians any longer. Neither you, nor Christie. As for the dwelling rights promised you by Mr White, that's nothing to do with me. All employees of Fox & Dunn have dwelling rights on the highland as long as they are employed by Fox & Dunn.' He got up, took some papers out of a cupboard and handed them to me. 'Give these to Mr Christie, please. It's a list of the amounts each must pay at the magistrate's office on or before the twentieth. They may use the tents till the end of July, but not a day longer. Good day.'

One could say I was kicked out on the arse, together with Christie and the Italians. I stood outside Walker's office, looking up the street, down the street, horse-carts, divers people, a man on horseback, a herd of young oxen driven by two harrying youngsters; a smartly-dressed woman crossed the street, lifting her skirts and stepping deftly over the dung; a wagon, old Bart von Huyssteen's wagon from the forest, heavily loaded and creaking under a huge yellowwood block.

'Silas.'

'Uncle Bart.'

Three seamen with provisions tucked under their arms, including a live chicken. I looked at the world all around me yet felt as if I stood apart from it. I said to myself: Silas Miggel, go and dismantle your house, take what you possess, take Miriam and get off the highland; trek into the forest, and keep on trekking until the mountains halt you. Then never again need you see another government agent or Italian or sawmill in your life. Trek. Go and get your things.

While my body stood there in the street, my spirit flew away into the forest, cleared a piece of land for my house and my woodshed and my vegetable plots, and I felt at peace. But I knew I was dreaming. I knew that, should anything happen to me, I could never leave Miriam abandoned in the forest; the highland was her place. Mine too. I stopped dreaming and came back to my senses. The sawmill's life was five hundred thousand sleepers long. The Italians' life was ship money long. I couldn't go back and persuade the sawmill to saw faster and faster, but I could go back and keep the Italians at the axes, cutting and cutting – and this was what gave me courage to start moving my feet again. When I walked away from Walker's door that morning, I left him and the whole blooming government right there in the street to go to hell. Henceforth, I said to myself, Silas Miggel would govern alone.

Just outside the village, the devil caught up with me, asking: what if the Italians decide to make the first payments on the allotments? I couldn't answer that and felt the stone grow heavier in the pit of my stomach. I decided that it would be best to call them all together when I got back to the highland. I went to Christie's tent and told him I was having a meeting with the Italians and he was welcome to attend if he wanted to. If he felt like interpreting for me, fine, if he didn't feel like it, I would manage by myself. After all, I added, he was being paid off on the twentieth in any case. He flew from his tent, shouting that it wasn't yet the twentieth, that *he* would call the Italians together, that *he* would fight for justice until the end. Not me.

'Justice?' I said and laughed in his face. 'What justice? I'll tell you what justice is, Mr Christie. In Dutch we say *geregtigheid* and that means 'to have a right to'. It means that Barrington – may his soul be with the angelings – it means that Barrington had a right to his jam-jar of silkworms. It means that trains have a right to railways, railways have a right to sleepers, sleepers have a right to sawmills, and sawmills have a right to wood from the forest no matter how. The Italians have no right to ship money because the law says that only those the government *desires* to send back, will get their fares; the government has a right to decide who it wants to send back or who it doesn't. Therefore, mister, before you go fighting for justice, make sure your justice doesn't only mean having your own way. It seems to me that when you start fighting for justice, you must blindfold one eye and screw up the other, for if you don't, you might discover the difference between shit and the real thing. The Italians will have to work for their own justice, and I for mine. If you still feel it's your right to call them together, do so.' I handed him the papers Walker had given me. 'Tell them that Walker said that they can have the tents until the end of July. Tell them that Walker said that the first payments must be made on the twentieth of this month. There is three months' grace on the payments but not on the tents. That means we will have to set to and knock together houses for them if they don't want to sit out in the open. That means a couple of weeks without wages if we don't get help, and they will have to buy the corrugated iron for the roofs themselves.'

How much he added to that when he had them together, I couldn't tell, but he gave them a long speech. They stood stock-still, listening to every word, eyes watching him closely. When he finished with the speech, he started reading out what each one had to pay on the twentieth:

' "Robolini: allotment number ten, 21.822 acres. Payment due on 20.6.1882, £1 1s 10d plus 10/– as payment for implements, oxen and money advanced. Grassi: allotment number fourteen, 21.654 acres. Payment due, £1 1s 2d plus 10/– as payment on implements, oxen, money advanced." '

Whether they had decided on their plan of action beforehand, I could not say, but that was as far as the meeting lasted. Before Christie could turn the page to read the next one's debt, they turned around and simply walked off. All Fardini said as he passed me, was: 'Signor Miggel, no other way, we must start houses.'

By the end of July, there stood on the allotments belonging to Fardini and Robolini, Ilario, Mangiagalli and Cruci, a two-roomed wooden house. On Cuicatti's allotment, the one he had exchanged for Taiani's, stood a good sod house and the same on Tomé's for there had not been enough planks for them all. Each house was the size of four tents at least, but still the women wailed.

'Houses blow over, Signor Miggel.'

'Don't be daft! The day these houses blow over, the whole forest will be blown into the sea.'

'Bigfeet break houses, Signor Miggel.'

'Bigfeet only break down houses that stand in the paths they make for themselves. There are no bigfoot paths crossing the highland.'

'Don't want to stay here, Signor Miggel.'

'You'll just have to hold out. The wages have fallen behind, but not by too much, we'll catch up.'

Not one of them had gone to pay a penny on the allotments on the twentieth of June. Neither had Christie. I would not rejoice too soon, but the stone felt lighter in my stomach. Eleven tents had been returned, and just three remained: Christie's two and the one which Pontiggia and Canovi, Borolini and Coccia shared. Canovi didn't have an allotment, and the other three were busy putting up a one-roomed house for them all on Borolini's lot. Something was wrong with Borolini, but I couldn't fathom what. He seemed to stoop more and more each day.

'Are you sick?' I asked him.

'No good, Signor Miggel, no good.'

'What's no good?'

'No good.'

That was all I could get out of him and he wouldn't drink parsley-bush tea any more. Even a warder asked me one day if Borolini might perhaps have sores on his body.

'Rubbish, man!' I told him.

'You better watch him, uncle. They're erecting a hospital made from wood on Steenbok Island in the lagoon in case of smallpox breaking out. If you notice anything, bring him in immediately so he can be isolated.'

'Borolini doesn't have smallpox, get that into your head and keep it there!'

Down at the foot of the highland a few shacks had gone up around the so-called store: they were all bunched together and were crammed full of sawmill workers. The rest were still in tents. Fortunately these were all well away from me and Miriam, Dunn and the Italians at our top end of the highland. It was only the blessed oxen that were spread everywhere, but they were slowly dwindling in numbers.

Dunn didn't take much notice the day I told him that Walker wanted the remaining tents by the end of July. But three days later when we were carrying planks to get Mangiagalli's house finished so Giuditta should have a roof over her head, Dunn came rushing across as though his feet were on fire.

'Miggel!'

'Yes, Mr Dunn?'

'How long are you people going to be working on the houses before you can start cutting again?'

'Not soon, mister. There are still a number of families that must have roofs over their heads.'

'Mr Walker asked me to see to it that every man's house is erected on his own allotment. Whose house is this?'

'Mangiagalli's. His wife is about to have a child any day now. Another mouth to be fed.'

'Whose lot is it?'

'Legally speaking it's the government's, humanly speaking it's Mangiagalli's for the time being.'

'Fine. I'll come and see you tonight.'

The first day we had started on the houses, Walker had sent a warder to spy where we were erecting them. When Dunn said we could start taking the planks, Fardini, Robolini and Pontiggia came and spread out a large sheet of paper on my table. Dunn

300

was present and so was Christie. On the paper were twelve houses, neatly drawn. Pontiggia's work. And the twelve houses were placed round a square: three to the east, three to the south, three to the north, three to the west. Side by side. The square in the centre was laid out in stone.

'And this?' I asked and told Miriam to open the window, they were making my place stuffy.

'Piazza,' Pontiggia answered. 'Houses round piazza.'

It was like a small square, Christie said. They wanted the houses round a square, not in rows, not spread over the allotments. Christie explained that Italians liked living close together. The children played on the piazza, the grown-ups sat around the piazza, it was like one big sitting room. Dunn had no objections, I had no objections. All I said was that they would have to carry the stones up from the river themselves if they wanted to pave it and that this would have to be done without interfering with the woodcutting. They mustn't lose wages while carrying up stones. They agreed to that. But Christie stood there, blown up with his own importance, saying that permission would have to be obtained from Walker first to put up the houses round a piazza. According to the Immigration Act, every immigrant's house had to stand on his own allotted land.

It was like war. They ended up in Walker's office where it almost came to blows. Dreyer, the clerk, got a grazing blow from Cuicatti when he cut in front of him by accident, but luckily Dunn, Christie and I managed to keep the rest of the Italians away from Walker. Walker then called in a constable, but the constable was afraid of them so Walker had to take the only way out left open to him. 'Very well then,' he said, 'if you don't want to obey the law, I want you off the allotments and off the highland immediately.'

Immediately. Without tents. What could they do? Nothing. And it was urgent that Mangiagalli's house should be built, Giuditta could no longer sleep on the canvas bed in the tent, she was too heavy with child. Every day Miriam nagged at me to allow her to bring Giuditta into our house, but I wouldn't give in. She just had to hold out.

And as Dunn had promised, he came to see me that evening. Or rather, he came and spoke to me, but his eyes stayed on

301

Miriam. 'Miggel, the government is most displeased because we haven't yet started on the sleepers.'

'There are many things I am displeased about too, mister.'

'I cannot afford to have one fewer team of cutters in the forest at this stage. Least of all yours.'

It was cold, I went and stood with my back to the fire. 'What do you suggest I do, mister?' I asked. 'Should I get the tents back to Mr Walker, or should I go and cut wood for the sawmill?'

'Surely you don't need the full team to put up the houses, do you?'

'No. But they're not very good with hammer and nail. Where they come from, houses are built from stone. I have to watch every plank and nail, and, apart from that, you know they won't go into the forest without me. Seems to me that you'll have to send me through the mill and have me sawn in two.'

He didn't think this was funny. 'We have a contract for yellowwood sleepers that is more than a year behind! Yet at the moment only planks are being sawn. I thought you were on my side, I thought you were anxious for the Italians' wages so that they can pay their fares home, but half of them spend time passing the nails while the other half gets in the way of the person knocking the nail in.'

'If you can think of a better plan, I'll go back to the forest with them tomorrow morning. I'm worried sick about their wages, but what can I do? Walker wants the tents. Law is law.'

'All I can suggest is that the team putting up the woodshed in the village leaves that and comes and puts up the Italians' houses first.'

I felt like clapping my hands in relief. That was what I'd had in mind from the start, but three days had to be wasted while it filtered into his head as well. Why should a whole team put up a woodshed in the village if there wasn't a single sleeper to put in it yet?

By the end of June there were four houses up and Giuditta had a son: Giuseppe. Then Cuicatti came and told me that he also wanted a house since he and Luigia were getting married. Blooming child she was. Scarcely fourteen, but she thought she could handle him. And no sooner had I scolded Cuicatti than Canovi came and told me he also wanted a house, he had

302

filled in the necessary Immigration forms in the village so that Borolini's allotment could be made over to him, he and Monica Grassi were getting married too. I went straight to Petroniglia and reminded her that she didn't even know where the man came from, how could she and Ilario allow it?

'She wants him, Signor Miggel.'

'Since when does a girl of fourteen have a say?'

'She's fifteen now, Signor Miggel.'

On two Sundays in a row I saw Pontiggia and Coccia come out of the forest late in the afternoon, carrying the ladder. I had taught them where to find honey and how to take it out of the nests, but not on the Sabbath, not as long as they lived on the highland under Silas Miggel's eye. I called Miriam and asked her if she knew anything about it, and at first she just stood laughing.

'Why are you laughing? I want to know what they're doing with the ladder in the forest on a Sunday!'

'You know the ladder is used for getting into a tree should the bigfeet chase them. That apart, you must be getting very blind if you've only just noticed that they go into the forest on Sundays. They've been going to Creek Bush Island on Sundays for a long time.'

I refused to believe it. They didn't even know where Creek Bush was, let alone the Island. 'What are you talking about?'

'Pontiggia goes visiting Susie of Aunt Emma, and Coccia goes visiting Anna of Aunt Hannie.'

I thought I would fall off the chair I was sitting on. 'How did they ever get to know Susie and Emma?'

'We are not the only people going to the village through Gouna's Drift, Pa.'

'How can the island people allow them to visit the girls?'

'No one has driven them away yet, Pa.'

For every question I asked, she stood ready with an answer. It appeared that I was the only person in the dark and I wouldn't tolerate it. I got up and walked over to Christie, and told him to tell them that no forest girl would get on the ship with them.

'Tell them not start things around here that can have no ending!'

Christie hardly looked up. Ever since one of Fox & Dunn's

303

other foremen had hit at him with a pole, he had been sulking. I had warned him many times to stop interfering with the sawmill workers, but no; when they started putting up the shacks for them at the foot of the highland, he kept on trying to stop them because it happened to be on the so-called commonage set aside for him and the Italians. The foreman got fed up with him. I couldn't understand why Christie still kept on about the land allotted to them; not one of them had made a payment on it.

'Until the three months' grace has expired, we have every right to the land, Miggel. My price is a hundred and fifty pounds now. You'll regret it if you don't buy from me.'

'Mr Dunn says the lots won't fetch even twenty pounds a piece on a sale.'

At the end of July, the houses were finished. Most of them were made from wooden planks like mine was, the roofs were of corrugated iron like mine, but theirs were different as the people in them were different. In front of each door there was a flat stone bedded into the ground on which one had to wipe one's feet. Next to each house a pit had been dug and neatly lined with stones into which a gutter pipe led from the roof; this was for catching rain-water. Clever. Every pit was covered with a lid made of corrugated iron or wood and by each one a bucket on a rope stood ready for drawing the water.

'You better keep those lids closed, don't come running to me when the children fall in and drown.'

For every house that was finished, Pontiggia carved a wooden crucifix which stood on a little shelf in the front room. Next to some of the crucifixes, small doll-like figures were put, or little jars with twigs and flowers from Miriam's garden, or a picture in a frame. Where they got everything from, I had no idea.

'In the trunks that were on the sleds that first day, Pa.'

Table cloths of the softest material were laid over the rough wooden furniture, pillow cases without pillows were placed over the chair backs. Beautiful covers on the beds. Dunn told them to stop taking any more planks from the mill; if they wanted to make furniture, they would have to cut and saw their own planks. I kept quiet. I knew they were bartering sausages and meat with the sawmill workers for wood; from me they got bone-glue and tools in return for two lace collars for Miriam

304

and combs for her hair. All I insisted on was that they made their
furniture at night by lantern-light, not during the day when they
had to earn their wages.

Everything in and around the houses was positioned as if a
line had been drawn first. Nothing was out of place. When
everything was finished, the doors were shut and bolted and no
one was easily invited in again. The discontent about the houses
being set so far apart never left them, however.

'No good, Signor Miggel, no good.'

Shortly before the end of July, the first sleepers were sawn.

'Now your team will have to cut and bring out wood like
you've never done before, Miggel,' Dunn said, driving us on.
'Don't let the saws catch up with you.'

'The blooming mill is like a monster that just guzzles and
guzzles without ever getting enough!' I said. 'And my team
brings out double what the others bring out, but for the same
wages.'

'Don't complain, Miggel, your wages are good. Before July
next year, Fox & Dunn want to deliver a hundred thousand
sleepers. You'll have to keep those axes swinging, I'm telling
you.'

Before dawn every morning, I heard the stoker go past to start
the fire in the boiler furnace so that there would be enough
steam to set everything running when the others arrived. Every
morning I was thankful to get into the forest and away from the
screeching saws. I no longer looked up when we passed where
the other teams were cutting; I was afraid of seeing the havoc
and wanting to wring their bloody necks. If they could destroy
that much in a little more than six months, it was best not to
imagine what it would look like after five years.

My only consolation came on Saturday nights when I counted
the money in the tin. When the first sleepers lay stacked in the
Yard for Sleepers and Timber, there were forty pounds in my tin. I
would not rejoice too early, but according to the law and
according to Walker, the sale had to take place towards March
of the following year. If they had not paid by then, of course.
That possibility was always there like a rock waiting to fall on my
head and I often asked Fardini about it.

'We go back, Signor Miggel.'

'All of you?'

'All of us.'

And all the time, the sun kept shining from my Miriam. Every Sunday I went on my knees and begged the Hand to keep watch over her and to forgive me for having given my consent. I could not have wished for anyone better than Miriam to keep an eye on the women and children, nor a better daughter in my house. Every night the food was cooked, the bread baked, the bit of garden hoed and watered. She was able to report on every Italian's house, on every footprint that lay at the door. I could tell when she went into the forest by the stillness that combined with the happiness in her.

I learned to ask less and less and just to count the days to February.

The cold came early that year; by the end of July, it felt as if the sun were passing over you so far up in the sky that hardly a drop of warmth came through the forest roof. At midday the early morning moisture was still dripping from the trees. The forest floor stayed damp under your feet, the cold crept up every sinew in your body, down your arms and into your hands clasping the axe handle.

'Cold, Signor Miggel.'

'Cut!'

'Sick, Signor Miggel.'

'Cut!'

'No more cut.'

'You can go and warm your bodies at the fire when we stop at halfday.'

Coccia kept moaning that day. 'Want to go to Cape Town, Signor Miggel. No good here.'

'You can go to Cape Town so long as you don't come back again like Pontiggia and Canovi,' I told him. 'And as long you don't think Anna will run after you.' He and Pontiggia still went off to Creek Bush Island every Sunday. They wouldn't listen to me. I even went there myself to try and put a stop to it, I told them not to come running to me if things went wrong. But the girls were as pig-headed as can be.

'I take Anna with, Signor Miggel.'

I didn't answer him. It was just talk. Apart from anything, it

306

was Saturday, the week was over and they were exhausted. They seemed to hate the axes and the forest more at the end of a week.

'Bloody axe no good.'

'It's you that didn't sharpen it properly, Cuicatti!'

'Christie says he wrote to Governor, Sir Hercules Robinson, he will help us.'

'What, to come and help you cut wood?'

'He will send ship money.'

'That axe in your hand will make you ship money, swing it!'

The next day, Sunday, as I was sitting at my table with the Bible, I looked up and saw Christie standing in the door. He hadn't been in my house for weeks and hadn't spoken to me for days.

'Are you sick?' I asked him.

He just stood there. 'No, I've come to say goodbye.'

I knew he had to go away sooner or later, his time on the highland was up; he couldn't live off the wind and he would never stoop to pick up an axe. Still, when he stood there telling me he had come to say goodbye, it was a shock to me. It was as though he had come to put the last remaining weight of the Italians on my shoulders and leave me to it. Although he'd often been dumb and back to front, at least he had been there to interpret when things really went wrong. I had stopped having faith in his letters long before, but at least there had been a mite of hope that somewhere one might have fallen into the right hands, even if it might have produced only part of the ship money.

He came up to the table and Miriam came from her room, looking even more shocked than I was.

'Sit down,' I said to him, 'we must talk before you go.'

From his clothes, one could see that he had been living in a tent for too long. The same pride he had arrived with, however, still tried to cling to his face and body. It was the same pride I had so often seen in Barrington. The English were different; Fardini once said it was because their blood is not warm like other people's. You never know what they're thinking, their faces remain cold because of the cold blood in them, he said. I suggested to Fardini that Italians must then have boiling blood.

307

They never really trusted Christie. They never trusted him to fight on their behalf; they always said he did it for what *he* would get out of it.

'Where are you going?' I asked.

'At first I'm going as far as Cape Town where I shall consult with certain people at the highest level. If the discussions are successful, I shall return here. If I don't get satisfaction, however, I will continue on to London where I shall address myself to Mr Burnett in person.'

'And I am left to cope with everything.'

'Perhaps it's part of what the government saw as a solution, Miggel. Who knows? I'm going to make a full investigation of the whole matter.'

'What about your allotment?'

'My tents are to stay where they are. I am leaving a few personal belongings behind in Coccia's care. If I obtain satisfaction in Cape Town, I shall return, as I've said. If I am forced to proceed to London, I shall advise you where to send my effects.'

'I asked you about your land.' His was still the best of the allotments, and the day they put that up for sale, I would be standing in the front row to get it.

'Everything depends on what happens in Cape Town, whether I'm coming back or not.'

'How are you going to get to the village?'

'I've asked Tomé and Cuicatti to carry my trunks as far as the hotel. Weather permitting, I leave for Cape Town on the *Ambulent* tomorrow. Remember that the priest has to be met next Friday; the wedding banns for Cuicatti and Canovi have been posted, and they are getting married on Saturday.'

'What for?' I was under the impression that they had given up on this madcap idea.

'I have handed all the documents that were still in my possession to Fardini.'

I stood up and put out my hand to take leave of him. Miriam came round the table and it seemed as if she was about to cry. She stood before him shamelessly, telling him how much she would miss him. 'Give him your hand and be done with it!' I said, for I was afraid that she was about to kiss him on the mouth. Right up to the end, Christie had to provoke me for, as

308

he gave her his hand, he turned to me, saying: 'Miggel, you have a good, kind-hearted daughter, she's not like you.'

How the devil was I then?

Late that Monday afternoon, when we came out of the forest with the last haul of logs, both his tents were gone. Walker had sent a warder to fetch them, Miriam said. No one could tell me what had become of his chair, table and bed. When I lay on my own bed that night, I said to myself: Silas Miggel, now you're on your own – foreman, peacemaker, medicine brewer and all the rest, with Fox & Dunn paying your wages. The government was either far more clever than I had thought, or Providence had seen further ahead for everyone.

'Right,' I said to the Italians when we stood ready to start cutting the next morning, 'if all goes well, you'll be packing and on your way home this time next year.' They looked at me like people with very little faith left, but when they hacked into the trees, there was a strength in the blows I had not seen before.

But all day I sensed an uneasiness in the forest around us. I could tell it by the birds: when one lourie stopped hissing and gurgling in agitation, the next one started. Somewhere above us, I heard a flock of red-billed hoopoes but apparently they couldn't decide in which tree they wanted to settle, they kept hopping and cackling from tree to tree. Perhaps it's a tiger, I said to myself, but why would they take so much notice of a tiger? Perhaps I decided on a tiger to keep my mind from drifting to an elephant; perhaps it was one of those days when a rascal stood right behind your back in the thickets without your knowing it. Not before he charged. Sometimes he stood there without intending to charge at all. The trouble was, how were you to know?

It wasn't my imagination, I knew the forest, I knew its moods, in the end I had goose flesh all over my body.

'Signor Miggel see something?' Cuicatti asked when I had made a fourth inspection of the swinging axes.

'I see nothing, cut!'

'Signor Miggel hear something?' They were sharp.

'I hear nothing, cut!'

Fardini and Robolini were at the two-handed saw, cutting the wood to length. I would have been happier if I could have stopped all of them working for a bit while I listened properly. One could sometimes hear an elephant's bowels rumble from quite a distance. But if I stopped the axes and the saw, and made them suspicious, it could take me the rest of the day to get them working again.

Coccia was cutting on his own that day so that I could cut with Borolini in order to watch him a bit. He was a strong young man, but everything about him seemed to sag lower by the day. Just the week before, we had all been sitting down at the shelter for the midday break when a branch had cracked to the west of the creek; in a second, food had gone flying and the Italians had raced to the ladder. I had shouted to them that we were safe: not only had the wind been on our side, but the place where the bigfeet went through the creek had been more than a mile away from us. When the second branch had cracked, however, Fardini had even helped Ilario to get up the ladder. Only Borolini had stayed sitting as if he hadn't cared whether an elephant came and stood right in front of him. I had said to myself then that a man who sits like that is either very sick, or very down in his heart.

That's why I had decided to cut with him that morning, to watch him a bit. 'Borolini,' I said, 'you're not cutting, you're just making the movements. Have you got a pain somewhere?'

'No pain.'

'What's wrong then?'

'Want to go home, Signor Miggel, year too long.'

'How much ship money have you now got?'

'Six pounds, Signor Miggel. Fardini keep ship money.'

'That's right, because you must all go back together.'

I was about to tell him that he had to take courage, a year went by quickly when one worked hard, but I didn't say it because, as I was swinging back my axe, I saw a movement in the underbush from the corner of my eye, and dropped the axe. Not ten yards from where I was, in the underbush, stood Josafat Stander. Not his ghost. Him. Yet not quite him either. My first thought was that he had been shot and wounded. He was wearing a coat, not the buck-skin garb he always wore in winter; a good coat, but it looked as if there was blood on it and one of the sleeves was torn from its shoulder seam. He looked directly at me, stock-still, without a word. His hair was shorter, his beard too; and it was as

310

though hatred glowed from his eyes. Or it could have been anger.

'Josafat Stander?' I said.

'Yes.' Bluntly, half-rudely. As if he were wild with the world and was blaming me for it. At first I stood there shocked, but the next moment I was angry because he had come back from the grave and the first thing he did was to look for trouble.

'Did they kick you out of heaven?' I asked him.

'No, out of hell,' he hit back at me like a heathen.

'No wonder the louries have been warning us since early this morning that danger was on its way.' When he stepped out of the underbush, I saw that the dirt on his clothes was fresh, that he must have slept out in the open somewhere. 'We buried you, Josafat Stander,' I said when he put out his hand to greet me.

'I know.'

'Where have you been?'

'Somewhere you will never see, uncle, where ivory has its true price.'

'Then it must have been far away.'

'It was.'

'How long have you been back?'

'For some time. Have you got any food, uncle?'

'At the shelter, yes.'

It was no good getting angry with Josafat Stander. He was like Old Foot: everyone hated him with respect, but without either of them, the forest would not be the same. Strange that I had thought of Old Foot like that, for hardly had we sat down than he told me that Petrus Brand Island's bull had been shot the day before, and immediately I got cross again.

'What the devil did you do that for?' I asked him. Petrus Brand Island was more than half a day's walking to the east of Gouna, on the other side of the wagon-road going to the Long Kloof. Everyone knew Petrus Brand Island's bull. It was believed to be Old Foot's first calf, his eldest; not quite as big as his sire, not quite as bedevilled, but still a handsome bull. 'Why did you shoot him?'

'I didn't.'

'Who did then?'

'Thesen and Duthie and Metelerkamp and a man by the name of Harran or something.'

311

I didn't know Harran, but the other three were important men from the village and district. Barrington's peers. 'How do you know it was them?'

'I know. I was on my way to the Poort yesterday morning when I met them on the other side of Job Terblans's place. I had spent the night in the village. I could see by their guns that they weren't after bush-pigs, ten-to-the-pounders they were and the men were carrying a lot of lead. "You're Stander, aren't you?" Thesen said. "Biggest ivory thief in the forest, I'm told." I didn't reply to that. He said Job had told them there was a large herd of bigfeet in the vicinity of the Poort, and they had permission to shoot one. Actually it was more than permission, it was a special *commission* from Cape Town to shoot one for the museum there. They want it stuffed.'

'Stuffed?' I felt sure they had played the fool with him and now he was playing the fool with me.

'Yes. To have it stuffed and then displayed so that people can come and look closely at a bigfoot and touch it. That's the point of a museum.'

I refused to understand. 'You mean stuff like a blooming doll?'

'More or less.'

'It would take a hell of a lot of stuffing to stuff a bigfoot.' The Italians sat listening to every word. I had stopped them cutting, they wouldn't, in any case, have carried on without my being there. I saw them watching Josafat with suspicion and awe, and I had to tell Ilario a second time to pour the man some coffee. 'And then?' I asked.

'Thesen invited me to go with them. I told him I didn't feel quite happy about the guns they had and I didn't have my own with me. He said their guns were all right and they preferred to shoot the animal themselves as it was a rather important commission. What's more, the name of the person that pulled him down would be put on a copper plate in the museum with the bigfoot. He asked me if I would just consider joining them until they found signs or tracks of the animals. The others nagged at me too. Duthie said that he had heard from Job Terblans that the herd was in a clearing about two miles to the north of them. I knew the clearing they meant. I also knew that men like that often go into the forest with lots of courage and heavy guns to shoot bigfeet, but the moment the forest closes in

312

around them, their courage falls out at their feet. I knew that was why they kept on at me to go with them.'

'So that you could go ahead of them, naturally.'

'Quite. The wind was on our side and if it stayed that way, it wouldn't take long. So I told Thesen I'd go with them and asked him what they preferred: a cow or a bull? Duthie said a bull. We started walking. They didn't do too badly at all, it was obviously not the first time they had walked through the forest on a hunt. And not half an hour later, we walked right into a herd of at least thirty. Whether it was the same herd Job had told them about, I couldn't tell. We were still quite some distance below the clearing and when the animals got wind of us, we just saw the underbush swaying and branches breaking as they started fleeing. There was no chance to shoot, the underbush was too thick and they were gone within moments. All except one. A bull with at least three feet of ivory on either side, and I realised what he was doing. I saw his ears flap and his trunk coming up, but I knew he probably wouldn't charge, he was scaring us off in order to give the others time to get away. It was a bluff. But the men came past me and Duthie fired first. Then Thesen. Then Metelerkamp. Then Harran. At first the bull still didn't charge, but they must have hit him because he started shaking and pulling up the saplings around him and only then did he charge. Thesen and Metelerkamp were the closest and they fired together. The bull stopped in his tracks and trumpeted as if he wanted to blast them out of his way. I saw he was wounded in the front leg. The next moment, Duthie and Harran both hit him in the shoulder and that gave Thesen and Metelerkamp a chance to get a few yards up a half-fallen tree. But they couldn't fire from there as they didn't have a secure enough foothold. Duthie fired again, Harran followed. The bull disappeared out of sight into the thickets, but we knew he was there by the noise of him crashing through the underbush. When he came out, Thesen was back on the ground and fired. Harran fired. Duthie fired. Metelerkamp was out of the tree and fired as well. The bull went mad. Every time he trumpeted, blood rained into the air. I tried to grab Harran's gun, but he jumped away from me as the bull charged. I no longer knew who was shooting, I was trying to protect my own body and the bull was trying to protect his. One moment he charged to the right, then to the left and as

313

he did, he trampled everything in his way flat or pulled it up from the earth in fury. Thesen and Duthie got a stand on a tree stump, Metelerkamp and Harran on either side. Bullet after bullet had hit the bull, but he charged and ravaged without a sign of his strength giving way. Harran fired at twenty paces and hit him in the trunk; ten paces before the bull reached Harran, Duthie fired and hit him in the trunk as well. The shot kicked Duthie off the stump and he fell to the ground. The bull charged. A few paces before he reached Duthie, two shots were fired from the other side which made him swerve away again. Duthie's next shot hit him in the side and for the first time the bull staggered, and then he did a thing I've never seen before. He got himself to a kalander, some ten paces away, and leant against the tree as though resting. Thesen fired, Harran fired. The bull charged a few paces, turned back and leant against the tree again. He was full of lead, but he wouldn't give up. Metelerkamp fired. Duthie fired. The bull charged. Back to the tree. Rest. Blood poured from one ear. Harran fired. Thesen fired. I saw the bull was finished, but he charged a last time and when Metelerkamp hit him, he fell. It had taken twenty-seven bullets to get him down. I counted them.'

'Jesus,' I said, 'they'll first have to darn him before they can stuff him.'

'Yes. And it was Petrus Brand Island's bull.'

'No wonder there's unrest in the forest.'

'They started cutting at the meat and innards this morning and will get the carcass on a ship to Cape Town to the expert that will be stuffing it.'

'Stuff no good,' Mangiagalli said from over by the fire. 'Marmo. Give Pontiggia marmo, he carve out nice bigfoot. Stuff no good.'

It was all change. Christie was gone. Josafat Stander was back. Petrus Brand Island's bull was shot. And as we came out of the forest that afternoon, Mariarosa came running up to us, crying: 'Aiuto, Signor Miggel! Aiuto! Help! Snake bite Felitze!'

I threw down the axes and started running with her to Robolini's house. With every step I took, I kicked up a ghost. It was too late in the day to send for Mieta: if it was a sheep-sticker snake, I would be able to save him myself; if it was a puff-adder, we wouldn't make it to the village with him. Who had been with him? Who had seen the snake? Where was Christie to help me find out what kind of snake it was? When the Italians got excited, they hardly remembered a word of Dutch. If it was a hornsman snake, I doubted if we would reach the doctor with him. It couldn't have been a tree snake or Mariarosa would have told us of his death. August was a bit early for snakes, but Koos Matroos's eldest child – may his soul be with the angelings – was also bitten in August. As I came up to the house, I heard Miriam crying with the women. I knew that if we had to bury the child, she wouldn't get over it for a long time. It wasn't a cat this time.

They cleared a way for me to get to the child. Petroniglia stood with him in her arms and Miriam held his foot. Someone had tied a piece of rope tightly round his leg below the knee; I gave the foot one look before cutting the thong.

'Have the children been in the forest?' I asked.

'We must get him to the doctor, Pa!'

'I asked if the children were in the forest?' I had to shout because they were all talking and crying together.

'Yes, we were cutting poles, Pa, and some of the children went too. Please don't let him die, Pa!'

'This isn't a snake, it's camphor bush.' I knew the difference between snake and camphor bush: the difference was very little. Especially when it was a child.

'What are we going to do, Pa?'

The poison had flowed through his body, his head was hot already. 'Take him up to my house,' I said. There was no other way. 'Lay him on the table and start tearing cloth for the poultices and heat plenty of water. Miriam, get yourself together, there's some dogwood-brew left that Mieta gave the children when they had those sores, give him a good dose, we must get his blood cleansed.'

'Shouldn't we try and get him to the village, Pa?'

'No.' There was no time for arguments; I had to get hold of some bee-sting bush and the nearest bee-sting I knew of was growing down in the gorge to west of the highland. They grew profusely at Goukamma but that was too far, the sun was down. I ran and fetched a lantern and a hatchet from the shed and told myself: Silas Miggel, run and keep on running.

315

It was no use trying to get him to the village; a man that drinks, drinks at his best when the sun goes down, and the doctor was a man that drank. What was the use of getting the child to him only to find him incapable? It had happened to Dunn one afternoon when one of his men was hurt at the mill.

How many times had I told them that the children had to be kept out of the forest? When the women started pestering me about having fences stacked around their houses, I said they could have fences if they went and cut the poles and the branches themselves. Miriam would show them how to stack the branches. It wasn't long before I noticed that she was getting them surprisingly confident of the forest, that they were cutting more and more deeply into the thickets. I told them not to take the children with them, however; I warned them that if they ever had to come to me, saying one had got lost, I would let him stay lost. And Miriam knew about camphor bush. She knew I never put an axe near it. Years ago, Stefaans van Rooyen cut down camphor bush for a stranger; the man said he would pay him well, he wanted to take the wood to England so he could have a violin made from it. Stefaans worked carefully, but while dressing the wood, he got a splinter in the hand, deep, and for that he almost died.

I had to light the lantern before I got down into the gorge properly, and by the grace of God I went straight to the bee-sting bush and I hacked it out roots and all. One had to brew both the leaves and the roots otherwise it was no good. On my way back, I picked snake-bush leaves as well, filling every pocket I had. We would need anything that would draw out the poison. When I reached the house, Petroniglia stood waiting for me in the dark, giving me quite a fright. 'Is he dead?' I asked her.

'No. Very sick.'

'Come on!' As she walked with me, I realised that she was barefoot. 'Where are your shoes, Petroniglia? Why on earth are you walking around like this in the cold?'

'No more shoes, Signor Miggel. Ilario no buy shoes, every money go for food and ship.'

'I'll see if there's an old pair of Miriam's.' I had noticed that the families were buying less and less.

Right through the night, Petroniglia stayed on her two bare

feet, helping Miriam and me struggle with the child as if he were one of her own. When I sent the others home at midnight, she stayed. But I couldn't get the poison out of him. We made poultice after poultice and put it on the foot, we added snake-bush leaves, we brewed bee-sting, we gave him everything we had; most of it he brought up again and so we gave him more. I forced the bitter snake-bush leaves into his mouth and made him chew. Miriam grew quieter and more scared. Petroniglia placed her beads with the little crucifix attached on the motherless child's chest, and it was as though this made him sleep a little, but by dawn I knew we weren't going to pull him through.

'Run!' I said to Miriam. 'Take the gun and fetch Mieta, tell her it's camphor bush. Tell her to hurry. Watch out for the bigfeet, Petrus Brand Island's bull has been shot, the whole forest is angry and Josafat Stander is back; listen where he's shooting, don't go anywhere near where he's firing.'

'What did you say?' She was already reaching up to take down the gun when she spun round.

'Run!' I shouted. 'It's not Josafat's ghost, it's him!'

Mariarosa came and took over from Petroniglia so that she could go and rest a while. I went and asked Dunn if he could not find work for the Italians at the sawmill yard for the day since I couldn't get away from the house. He took four at full wages and the rest at half wages, but that was better than nothing. It was only Ilario who I ordered to stay at home instead.

As I waited for Miriam to turn up with Mieta, the blessed sawmill drove the last bit of patience out of me with its screeching saws. Commonsense told me she couldn't be back yet, but I went repeatedly from the child to the gate, from the gate to the child. Petroniglia came back and took over from Mariarosa again, we put on fresh snake-leaves, we gave him what was left of the bee-sting brew, but he seemed to grow weaker every moment. As we were tending him, someone knocked on the door and I shouted to whoever it was to come inside; I thought it was Dunn again, or Fardini or Robolini to see how the child was doing. But it wasn't any of them, it was one of the blessed warders who had once again chosen the worst of times to come and bedevil everything. When he stood in the doorway and saw the child, he took a fast step backwards.

'What's the matter with that child?' he asked, putting his hand over his mouth and nose.

'Camphor bush. And what's the matter with you?' I asked.

'I was sent to bring terrible news: smallpox has broken out in Cape Town, the ships are sailing past without stopping. Mr Jackson the magistrate wants every immigrant in the district to go to the village to see Dr Gorman immediately. They have started preparing the Red Store outside the village as a smallpox hospital. All cases will be isolated there and not on Steenbok Island any more.'

'It's camphor bush,' I said, restraining myself.

'How can you be sure, uncle?'

'I am. And if you dare go and say it's anything else, I'll break your neck.'

'Smallpox has broken out, uncle! Don't you realise what I'm saying? The pox is here!'

'I hear you. And I'm almost glad for your sakes, you've been inviting it for months now, you've prepared one place after the other for it and now you want to feel bad about it? I made no predictions, I didn't invite smallpox; the immigrants under my care don't have smallpox. Go and talk to Mr Dunn at the sawmill, perhaps he's got a few cases for you to gladden your heart over.'

'If Mr Jackson hears about your attitude, uncle, you'll be in serious trouble. His orders are that the Italians must be the first to see Dr Gorman. Tomorrow. All of them. You'd better see that they get there, it's a government order.'

If Mieta hadn't pushed him aside at that moment to reach the child, I would have pushed him outside and off the highland.

Mieta took over. Towards the evening, I made myself a bed in the woodshed since no man could stay under the same roof with Mieta once she'd taken over. At first I told Miriam to see that the child was wrapped up well and carried across to Robolini's house so that Mieta could look after him there, but from the looks I got, one would have thought I had told her to wrap the child up and bury him.

I was already in my makeshift bed in the woodshed when Dunn turned up to tell me that the warder had visited him as well. Smallpox was truly a dreadful thing, he said, and it would be best if I didn't make trouble and saw to it that the Italians

318

went to the doctor. He also told me that he wanted to take Coccia out of the cutting team and put him to work at the boiler as stoker.

'I can't let you have any of my men,' I told him.

'Since Canovi got back, you're thirteen in the team and that, Miggel, is an uneven number. And it so happens that my stoker isn't at all well. I want Coccia at the mill from this coming Monday.'

I couldn't tell him that we were an even number for the axes since Ilario stayed at the shelter. If he took away Coccia, it meant I had to cut for two again. Not that I was afraid to do the work of two men, I was used to it, it's just that I dared not talk openly to him about Ilario. What if he didn't understand and the Grassis ended up without wages? What then? I had to keep my wits about me or it was two steps forward and one step back; the moment I thought things were starting to look up, a blooming child got a camphor bush splinter in his foot and Mieta had to be fetched. And Mieta cost money; Robolini would have to pay. Then smallpox broke out in Cape Town and Jackson saw fit to make them all lose a full day's wages. Or the price of meal went up, or one of them had to have a new pair of breeches or an extra blanket.

And I didn't even get any peace in my own woodshed. Dunn had hardly gone when I had to light the candle again. This time it was Petroniglia who came and stood at the open end of the shed like a ghost.

'Come inside and sit there on the chopping block, Petroniglia,' I said. 'Pull yourself up, woman, you look like someone who is carrying a mountain on her back!'

'We must get to church, Signor Miggel, God forget about us and all go wrong. We don't get to church, God no see us, He forget us.'

'God sees right down on to the highland, Petroniglia,' I told her, suddenly turning into a preacher as well. 'You people must just be patient.'

'God not see to highland, God see in church. Who pray for our sins?'

'You'll have to pray for your sins yourselves.'

'Signor Miggel not understand. God only see you in church.'

I knew where she was heading. 'Petroniglia,' I said, 'if you

319

came here suggesting I should take you people to George, you can just go straight back to your house. There are two churches in the village, I'll take you there, but not to George, it's two days' walking.'

'Knysna church not right church. God sees only in right church.'

'Don't be so blooming stupid, Petroniglia! God sees everywhere!'

'Only in church.'

'Petroniglia, don't argue with me!'

'Only in right church, and I don't wear old shoes of Miriam, Signor Miggel.'

One never knew what went on in their crazy heads. Hardly had Petroniglia gone when I had to light the candle a third time; this time it was Mieta. 'Why am I not allowed to have a moment's rest?' I asked. 'How is it going with the child?'

'The poison is weakening, he'll live. You came and asked me to find out where your Miriam goes, but you never came back to find out the answer.'

'I know.'

'She doesn't visit the girls on the islands any more; she is like a cow pushed out of its herd.'

'She doesn't have the time to go gossiping on the islands any more. You can see yourself how much trouble we're having on the highland.' I didn't want to talk to her about Miriam.

'What did that black-eyed woman want with you in the woodshed just now?'

I felt like throwing a piece of wood at her. 'Don't see what isn't there to see, Mieta! I don't like it. Why don't you go back and see that the child gets well so that I can have my house back?'

'You're still a strong man, Silas Miggel. Johanna has been waiting and hoping all these years.'

'Mieta!'

'It must be your blood that's in Miriam; I see her footprints where many would like to go but few dare.'

I was on my feet in an instant. 'What are you trying to tell me?'

'She walked too softly for both of us, Silas Miggel. Her will is her will, her fate is her fate.'

320

I could hardly breathe. 'Where did you find her footprints? Tell me! I've got to know!'

'In the fire. And it *was* a snake, not camphor bush.'

I turned cold as death.

SEVENTEEN

I TOOK THEM ALL to the village the next morning, Ilario and Felitze on the sled, the others on foot. Miriam stayed at home. They did not go willingly; from early morning I had to struggle to get them together and then keep them together.

'No sick, Signor Miggel, it's all on papers,' Mangiagalli protested. 'Papers taken in London.'

'They just want to see who's been vaccinated and who not.'

'All vaccinated. On papers.'

'They've lost the papers, and it won't help you to carry on about it. Jackson wants the doctor to look all of you over. Now, hurry, we must make a start, the sun's out already!'

'Jackson no good,' Coccia said.

'He's the magistrate; if you don't get there today, he'll send the constable to fetch you and march you to the village in rows like prisoners.'

That got them on their feet. Soon after the ostrich trouble, I had noticed that they were all immensely proud. Fardini said they had arrived with good reputations and they'd leave with good reputations. 'Poverty, Signor Miggel, you can hide; bad name you can no hide.'

I got them to the doctor's place in the main street before ten o'clock. At midday, we were still waiting. The children became troublesome, Felitze was getting cold on the sled, the rest gambled. Every time I went inside to enquire about the doctor, the sourplum behind the desk said: 'He's busy, wait your turn.' After the fifth time, I told her I'd waited long enough, the weather was turning bad and I had to get them back through Gouna's Drift. 'Wait your turn.' It was then that I walked down the street to Walker's office and when I stood before him, it seemed that the man was having trouble remembering who I was.

'Yes? Is there something I can do for you?'

'I've just come to tell you that you must tell the magistrate that I had them here to be checked for the smallpox, but the doctor is too busy. We're standing about in the street; there's not even a tree the children can pee behind so every time I have to take them halfway up the hill. Tell the magistrate that I waited for hours, but now I'm taking them back.'

'Who are you talking about?'

'The Italians, of course!'

'What Italians?' He looked straight at me, but his face assumed a blank look and I knew he was doing it on purpose.

'The Italians the government off-loaded up at Gouna, in the mulberry forest,' I said. If he wanted to play the fool with me, I would play along.

He did not waver his stare, however, he just picked out a nib. 'As far as my information goes, there aren't any Italians up at Gouna,' he said. 'There *were* Italians. I even remember that land was allotted to them, but no payments have been made on it and no silk industry was established as they had undertaken to do.'

This time I knew I would not be able to hold my tongue. 'Mister,' I said, 'what actually happened is that the government made a pile of shit up there, the Italians stepped in it and Silas Miggel had to drag them out.'

He chased me from his office.

When I got back to the doctor's place, more than half of the Italians had been checked. Three of the smallest children walked around with rolled-up sleeves, vaccinated and yowling. Two village ladies in grand dresses came across the street and asked me from behind softly-gloved hands: 'Are these the silk people?'

'Yes,' I said.

'Shame.'

'Yes,' I said, 'shame.' One took out a penny and gave it to Mariarosa's child who was nearest, but before I could stop her, Mariarosa grabbed the money from the child and threw it on the ground at the woman's feet.

'La mia bambina non è una zingara!' she spat in the woman's face.

'Not a gipsy child,' Fardini's son interpreted from behind me and I, Silas Miggel, was the one who had to bend down and pick up the penny. The woman said I could keep it, maybe I would be a little more grateful, seeing it was obvious I came from the forest.

That penny burned my pocket all the way home.

And Miriam was gone into the forest.

If, up until then, there had remained in me a glimmer of hope that as little as a child's ship money would fall from the government's hand, I went to bed without that glimmer that night. There was only one way home for the Italians and that was by cutting wood and hauling it out to feed the sawmill.

And cut they did. Cut, saw, haul out. Cut, saw, haul out. On Sundays, they lay like corpses.

'You're driving them harder than oxen, Pa!'

Dunn took away Coccia as he had said and put him at the boiler. At the end of September, he took Canovi as well and put him to work at the band-saw, but I still had to see that we brought out the same amount of wood.

'I'm sorry, Miggel, but it can't be helped.'

Below the sawmill, the stacks of sleepers kept mounting and beyond that, the mountain of sawdust. I told Dunn to have it raked through regularly; sawdust was like cowdung, it lies there and lies there and before you know it, it starts smouldering from the bottom. He said I wasn't to teach him what he already knew, but that very Sunday, as I was sitting at my table reading the Bible, I heard Miriam screaming outside. I grabbed the gun and ran because I thought it was an elephant, but when I got outside, I saw smoke coming from the sawdust heap and before I had enough hands to carry water, flames were shooting into the air.

Had there been a wind that day, and had it been from the west, Fox & Dunn would have been burned to the ground and I would have been burned out of my house.

It was still dark the next morning when I was woken by somebody knocking at my window. My first thought was the sawdust, I jumped up and ran to the door, struggling into my

324

breeches. It was Coccia, stiff with shock and repeatedly crossing himself.

'What is it?' I asked.

'Thing in sky, Signor Miggel.'

'What?'

'Thing in sky. I go to start fire for boiler, I look up, I see thing. Signor Miggel must come and look.'

The man was delirious. Behind me, Miriam came out of her room, looking just as scared. 'What's this about a thing in the sky, Pa?'

'He's ailing. Give me my coat and put something on yourself.'

When I got outside, I felt like crossing myself as well: to the east of the Southern Cross, on the hump of the Water Snake, a strange bright streak lay between the stars as though someone had gone and strewn a bucketful of fireflies up there. Blink your eyes, Silas Miggel, I said, perhaps it's just a bit of dirt. I blinked my eyes, but it wasn't dirt.

'Cometa, Signor Miggel.'

'Yes. I suppose so.' What else?

'What is it, Pa?'

'Tail-star. Comet.'

'What's it doing up there? Why is Coccia so upset?' She herself sounded uneasy. 'Have you ever seen anything like it before, Pa?'

'No, I was too small. But my late mother always used to tell us that when your Aunt Hannie was born, half the sky was covered with a tail-star, I suppose that's why Hannie is so pig-headed. A stranger told them that the same tail-star would return one day when Hannie is well into her seventies. This cannot be that star since Hannie isn't yet fifty. Perhaps it came back earlier, or perhaps it's another one.'

'No good, Signor Miggel, no good. World finish.'

'Don't talk shit, Coccia!'

'Don't swear, Pa!'

'The world was finished the day White arrived with you lot up here on the highland! Now go and get your fire going.' I told Miriam to get back to the house and to calm down.

I've never been a timid man. How many times had I not crossed the drift at Oudebrand where they say the ghost of old Samuel Terblans, who hanged himself there, appeared even in

325

broad daylight? Not once did it even bother me. But an apparition on earth and an apparition in the sky are two quite different things. What's down on earth, one can deal with, but what's up in the heavens is too high for man. The sun and the moon and the stars have their places up there, you don't ever doubt they'll be there. It's only when a bright streak appears where it doesn't belong that a man becomes uneasy down below. All around me, the highland was still quiet and dark; in the forest, the sounds of the night were dying away. The air seemed rather close which didn't feel right to me for that time of the year, and neither did I feel quite right. I stood there looking at the thing and the thing looked back. Just the two of us. I said to myself: Silas Miggel, don't be so blooming silly. But with the same breath I thought: what if the thing starts coming closer and closer, and the world starts getting hotter and hotter? I'd had dreams like that, of a forest fire creeping up on me and everything getting hotter and hotter. It must be a terrible death.

I stayed outside until it got light and the thing disappeared, together with the stars. 'It can only be a tail-star,' I said when I returned to the house and opened the curtains which Miriam had pulled as close as they would come. 'It won't help you to fret about it, the thing's too high for us.'

'Why does it give one such an eerie feeling then, Pa?'

'It's not the star that gives you an eerie feeling, it's your imagination that doesn't know which way to run. How are the Italians off for meat?'

'They've got enough until Wednesday. We'll have to try for eels on Thursday again, we didn't even get a bite last week.'

'They're getting wiped out, like everything else.'

'Do you think the tail-star is a kind of omen, Pa?'

'Miriam, stop acting like an old woman ready to crawl under the bed! The only omen I see coming is that the sun will catch Silas Miggel in his house today.' I couldn't understand why she was so edgy; while I myself was not totally at ease about the thing, one didn't have to take such a fright. 'You must carry a little water to the pumpkin and mealie patch. The walls of Cruci and Robolini's houses must be wiped over with paraffin, I don't want trouble with lice. When was the children's hair last combed through properly with the louse-comb?'

'Their heads are clean, Pa. We combed last week.'

As far as I could gather, none of the others had seen the star. I hoped to get a chance to talk to Fardini about it later in the day, I knew he had some knowledge about stars. We had stood together outside one night and I had noticed he kept on looking up at the sky to where the crop-star was shining brighter than the others.

'That's one of the wandering stars,' I said. 'The old people call it the crop-star, when he comes out, you can start planting.'

'We call it Saturno. It's the star of my country, Saturno, father of all the gods.'

I had asked him if they had more than one god then, but he had said no, not any more, they only had one now. And His throne on earth was in Italy too. In Roma. And I had immediately got cross again, and I'd said to him: they had God's throne on earth, they had their own star in the sky, why hadn't they stayed where they were? And at first he hadn't answered me, he'd just looked at his star and, in the half-light, I'd seen a look of longing come over him like a sadness. He had said that I wouldn't understand. His land was different from my land. Italia was like a beautiful woman: she was cheerful, she was sad, she was pure, sometimes crazy, she was gentle, sometimes cruel, she sometimes brought you to your knees; it is only when you start looking for a woman's faults that she becomes what you think of her. Then she is no longer beautiful and you leave her – and almost immediately you start pining for her.

I felt sorry for him. When a certain feeling comes over you for a woman, it's there. It doesn't easily go away.

By the time we got home from the forest that afternoon, the witless Coccia had the star blown up from horizon to horizon and every woman and child in fear of it. When the first stars came out, the whole lot of them gathered at Fardini's house, eyes lifted to heaven.

'The thing came out with the Water Snake!' I told them, 'and the Water Snake only rises long after midnight. Take the children inside, otherwise they'll be walking around tomorrow sniffing and coughing and holding their aching ears, and you'll come running to Miriam and me for help!'

I had hardly sat down to eat my supper when Dunn arrived. 'One of my most important workers, Tomlinson, the one operating the crane, packed his things this afternoon and is on his way back to England. I'll have to take Tomé out of your team and train him to work the crane.'

'Mister, you take away my men one after the other, but I still have to bring out the same quantity of wood.'

'You have enough men left. I noticed the Grassi chap didn't work two days last week.'

'He wasn't feeling well.' Every time Dunn turned the conversation in Ilario's direction, I became uneasy. 'But at least he had a better reason than the two full teams that laid down axes last week.' Perhaps he thought I didn't know that the elephants had chased them, and that they had refused to go back into the forest for two days.

'Might Grassi have smallpox?'

'You're beginning to sound like the warders, mister.'

'It's a serious matter, Miggel! If you took the trouble to buy a newspaper now and again, you would know what was going on in the rest of the world and you would have known what alarming dimensions smallpox is reaching at the Cape.'

'I've got nothing to do with what goes on in the rest of the world, I've enough of a struggle on the highland. However, I would like to know what your paper says about the thing in the sky, or don't those people ever look up?'

'That's the other thing I came to talk to you about. Four of my other cutters refused to go into the forest this morning as a result of Coccia's prophecies and nonsense. I'm warning you, the first man that refuses to work for that kind of reason again will be paid off immediately. That applies to you and the Italians as well.'

'What does the paper say?'

'It's a comet, man! It's no abnormal occurrence. All around the world, people have been observing it since early in September, and they've named it September's Comet. There are places where it's even been seen in broad daylight.'

'Mister,' I said, 'if that thing comes hanging over the highland in broad daylight, I don't think you'll find a single hand to pick up an axe. I'm just warning you.'

'I'm appealing to you then to keep the Italians sensible and at their axes. You must talk to Coccia.'

'I can't make the thing go away.'

'You can at least put a stop to all this talk. We are months behind.'

'It seems to me that the government is putting pressure on you, and that's why you come and put pressure on me. How far have they got with the new jetty?'

'About halfway. We can't start taking out the sleepers and shipping them before the jetty is finished. There's nothing that goes smoothly.'

'That's a lie. What I'm responsible for goes smoothly.'

'See that it stays that way. And tell Tomé he must start at the mill tomorrow morning.'

The tail-star was back just before dawn. One after the other, the lanterns came swaying across the highland and up towards my house: Fardini, Robolini, Cuicatti, Mangiagalli, Tomé, Canovi, Cruci, Petroniglia, Mariarosa, Vittoria Robolini, Antonia and some of the older children as well.

'Cometa,' Fardini said.

'World finish. Finito,' Coccia said. The women stood saying prayers by their beads.

'Big disaster come,' Tomé said.

'Yes, Dunn said you've got to start at the mill this morning,' I told him.

'Our sins are not forgiven,' Antonia moaned. 'Who pray for our sins?'

'Plank houses no good.'

'We must no die here.'

All the old rebellion flared up in them again. Had I been a rich man at that moment, I would have bought them a ship right then to enable them to get away from the highland and out from under the tail-star. I myself was not particularly sure about the thing, but neither was I stupid enough to take it as an omen of the world coming to an end. Barrington once read in a book that the end of the world would come the day man felled the last of the God-planted trees; I had said to him that we were lucky that the forest is as big as it is.

'Signor Miggel?'

'Yes, Petroniglia?'

'Ilario no good, can't work any more.'

'Then you'd better come and do his work instead if you want to go home.' I couldn't cut myself in two and do his work as well.

He just had to hold out, even if I had to drag him there in the mornings.

It started getting light in the east. Here and there a bat made a last swoop over our heads and the birds started stirring in the trees. Before the Italians and the sawmill arrived on the highland, that was the time of day – winter or summer – that I always walked around outside to shake the night out of my body. Never did a day break without my saying to myself: Silas Miggel, you may have few earthly things, you may have plenty of worries about your Miriam, but no king has a highland such as you have.

On Thursday, the fifth of October, Miriam turned nineteen. I took ten shillings from the money tin and gave it to her. 'Remember I had nothing to give you last year? Remember I said I would make up for it this year?'

'I don't want anything, Pa.'

'Take it, buy yourself something.'

'How old was Ma when I was born?'

Strange that she asked that on this particular morning. 'As old as you are now. Buy yourself some cloth for a dress and ask Mariarosa to help you make it. A really nice dress, perhaps a green one with red sleeves.'

'I have enough dresses, Pa. But I'll take the money, thank you.'

I didn't ask her if she was going to the forest, it wasn't necessary. She already had on her best dress and her hair was swept up on her head and fastened with the combs as the women had showed her how.

Dunn had asked me one day if I didn't think it unfair to keep a girl like Miriam living in the forest. I told him to go and mind his mill. What did he know? But afterwards I thought about it, and decided that Mieta should teach Miriam all about the medicine of the forest. Everything. Mieta was the oldest person in the forest; it would be good if my Miriam could take over when she gave up. Not only would it be a good service to give back to the forest, but it would mean a little income for her as well, for emergencies. Mieta herself had told me that Miriam's hands were adept at picking herbs and brewing. Not that I would allow Miriam to adopt all Mieta's ways. Where I had to put my foot down, I would put it down, like the day I had found

330

a bunch of dogwood twigs hanging at every tent flap. It was when things were very bad at the tents and we couldn't get Cruci's child better. I went and asked Miriam about the twigs.

'I don't know what to do next, Pa,' she had said. 'Mieta told me that dogwood leaves ward off evil. In fact, she offered to make me a pouch filled with dried leaves to hang round my own neck.'

'Go and take it off those tents!' I ordered, and went with her myself to see that she did. 'This is no place for witchery or the doings of heathens!'

My eyes had to be everywhere. The day Luigia and Monica married Cuicatti and Canovi, Miriam made them posies to hold, and between the flowers were secreted more dogwood leaves. You talk, you keep watch, but somehow things still slip past.

At least the tail-star was like an extra whip which kept the Italians going. Every night it came out earlier and brighter, and it kept them in fear and in a hurry to go back to Italy. They bought less and less with their wages. And it wasn't only the Italians that were afraid of the tail-star: by November, it had moved away from the Water Snake, climbing higher into the sky, getting brighter, bigger, and three more of Dunn's men packed their things and went back to England. When two more set out on foot for Cape Town, Dunn took one of Fardini's boys, Alberto, from my team and the day after that he took Cuicatti as well.

The star gradually moved over to the west with the night sky. There were some nights when it seemed to have two tails, and then the women drew the curtains even before the sun went down and kept the children inside. Miriam was just as frightened; she thought I didn't notice, but I did. I stayed silent when I got home one night and found a whole jug full of dogwood leaves standing on the table. I kept quiet because the days were hard and there was no strength left for tussles in the evening. Every night I stood watching the comet, saying to myself: Silas Miggel, something is wrong. What it was I did not know: it was in the air, it was as if my feet and my legs and my arms and hands knew but it was not yet in my body nor in my head.

At the end of December, Dunn put up my wages by a shilling a day and the Italians by eight pennies a day. Fardini kept a book

331

detailing the saved ship money and it was getting gradually more and more. The sawmill sawed and the sleepers mounted. I no longer stopped work on the days that it rained; we hauled out the wood then, no matter how soggy the sled-path got.

'How long can you keep driving them like this, Pa?'

'You heard what Robolini said on Christmas morning: they want to be home long before next Christmas.'

'When did you last look at yourself, Pa? See what you're coming to. Look at your clothes – except they're not even clothes any more, they're rags. Why don't you take some money from the tin and at least buy yourself a coat?'

'Dunn says that, according to Walker, the first lots will be put up for sale in March. Law is law.'

I had no doubt that the worst was behind us; the only thing that remained was to hold out. But still there was something not quite right. I tried to pin it down, but couldn't. There were days when I imagined seeing it on the faces of others when they looked at me. Even on Dunn's face. It seemed as though people were looking at me differently, as if I had smallpox without knowing it.

The mountain of sleepers grew right up against my back fence, and the tail-star grew until it lay right across the sky. We somehow managed to grow a fair amount of potatoes and onions for the Italians and this saved on the wages. Potatoes were costing twelve shillings and sixpence a bag, and onions were ten shillings.

'When are you going to start taking out the sleepers to the village?' I asked Dunn.

'February. I'll need extra wagons; tell the forest people I will pay sixpence for every sleeper off-loaded at the new jetty.'

'How far have they got with the jetty?'

'Just about finished. You must say if there's anything I can help with.'

'Help with what?'

'I just want you to know.'

I didn't quite understand. 'If only I had a wagon, I would make the Italians take sleepers out at night,' I said. 'Sixpence a sleeper is good money, it can pay for a child or two on the ship.'

'How much longer do they need to work for their fares?'

'Another ten months at the most. And I'm telling you now:

332

the day I get them on the blooming ship is the day I stop work at this blooming mill.'

'They're good workers, Miggel; I know they cannot stay here, but I'm prepared to look at their wages again later if they'll stay on an extra year. If only I could catch up with the contract, Miggel.'

'Mister, I may be wrong, but I don't think they'll stay here an extra hour.'

'My brother is interested in buying part of Portland. He would very much like to employ Coccia and Pontiggia.'

'He can forget about it. When one goes, they all go.'

'If they stay on an extra six months, I'll undertake to pay two of the Grassi children's fares.'

'You won't buy them, mister.' I had in any case already decided that should anything happen to Ilario, I would help Petroniglia by giving her ship money for one or two of the children.

The very next day, when we went down to the shelter at midday, I found Mieta having coffee with Ilario. She looked at me closely and said: 'Silas Miggel, the lilies are blooming.'

'I know,' I said. 'It's February, but I don't know if I'll get there this year. I hope you've brought Ilario some of that medicine again. He's better at the moment and must stay that way.'

'I'm more worried about you than about him. If only you could see what you look like. You're too busy working to notice anything. The lilies are blooming, I said!'

She wasn't always coherent any longer. 'I know the lilies are blooming. Please tell that son of yours I need that old broken wagon of his. I'll fix it for him and in return I'll borrow it to take sleepers to the village at night.'

'The sign is above us in the sky.'

'It's getting fainter every night now.'

'That's right. When you've spoken, you've spoken. Those that had to hear, did not hear; those that had to see, did not see.'

She was certainly not right in the head any more.

From the middle of February, the wagons came and started taking the sleepers to the village. Load upon load upon load. Stefaans van Rooyen and Jeremiah Eye and Adam Barnard all came from the forest with their wagons to earn extra money.

'This mill is sawing the very bread from our mouths, Silas,' Adam said. 'We're having trouble selling yellowwood in sleeper lengths, the woodbuyers says there's too much wood coming out of the forest. Stinkwood's price is down too. Annie asked me to tell you that we'll help where we can.'

'Help with what?'

'If there's anything we can do for you and Miriam.'

'We still have enough of what we need, thank you. The battle is to keep the Italians going. The wood is killing them.'

'Yes, one can see that they're no longer the same people as when they first came here, they're ruined.'

'If things work out, I'll have them on a ship by November.'

'Just say if there's anything.'

The following Saturday, Sias van Rooyen of Creek Bush Island turned up where we were cutting. He had a message from my sister, Hannie, saying I had to go to see her on the Sunday. It was urgent. I asked him if anyone was ill, but he said he hadn't noticed anything except that Hannie had been crying quite a lot lately. I told him Hannie liked to cry, and asked him to tell her that I'd come. It was the third message she had sent me in any case.

In the morning, I asked Miriam if she wanted to come with me; she said no, she'd stay because she had a feeling that Roberto, Robolini's eldest child, was coming down with measles. I told her to change her dress, it was Sunday, and she was forever in the same one; she said she would. I told her to rest a little while I was gone, I would have something to eat with Hannie so she need not bother with food. The whole week she and Petroniglia, Mariarosa and Antonia and most of the older children had been cutting branches and stacking fences around two vegetable plots down on Cuicatti's lot, the one he had swopped with Taiani. It was the one furthest to the west and was out of the sawmill's way. Every bit of food the women could grow would save wages. Where they got the vine shoots from that were planted at the bottom corner, I did not ask. Things were better when they kept busy and Mariarosa had fewer screaming fits.

'They've started mending and stuffing the mattresses, Pa.'

'That's good. They must see that a mattress is made for Borolini, he came without one.'

334

'We'll make him one.'

'There's something we keep avoiding, Miriam. It lies in the house, it lies on your face, but we don't talk about it. It's February. The lilies are blooming.'

'I know, Pa. I promised Pa I would turn back quietly when the lilies bloom. I don't go to the forest any more. It's over.'

I would have felt better if she had been rebellious or if she had cried, but she did not. She just went about her way, being endlessly patient with the women and children, doing the chores. When she was small and a thorn went deep into her foot, she would always grit her teeth and refuse to limp in case I noticed and took the needle to the foot. She would let it fester and finally get it out herself.

When Hannie opened the door, she started crying. I asked her if anyone was ill. No, there wasn't any illness. She poured me coffee and broke open a sweet potato for me. She didn't speak to me, she just sniffed while I sat there slowly losing my temper.

'Hannie,' I said, 'I didn't drag my tired body here to come and watch you cry. The sawmill is getting us all down and if I don't get one day's rest in the week, I don't make it through the one ahead. If you're in need, tell me so I can take something from my money tin for you, even though I'm doing everything I can at the moment not to take a penny too much out of it. But just don't stand there sniffing so.'

'The Bible says that there will be signs in the last days.'

'It's too late to cry about the tail-star, Hannie. It's getting fainter every night and the world is still on its feet.'

Suddenly she wiped her face on her apron and flew at me with dry eyes: 'Your world may still be on its feet, Silas, but there are others for whom it has toppled over for good! When last did you look at your daughter?'

'I look at her every day, she's in good health. I know she works hard, but things will soon begin to get better, we must just hold out.'

'Your daughter, Silas, is with child!'

My feet knew it, my legs, my hands and my arms; my body stopped it from getting to my head because my body knew I would go out of my mind. I got up and walked straight out of

Hannie's house so that I could be alone when I collapsed. And first your eyes give in, nothing stays in place. You walk through the forest, but the trees are no longer rooted to the earth, they stand loosely on the ground, ready to fall over. No, it's you that wants to fall over. Your head grows heavier. You swallow, but there's something in your throat; your breathing rattles because you forget to cough. Your eyes don't look where you're going, you just go because you've got to get away from Hannie's words so that they are not true. You want to run, but your head is too heavy; you call out to God, but there's nobody up there, only a flock of red-billed hoopoes laughing at you from the tree tops. Twenty-seven shots for Petrus Brand Island's bull. One shot for Silas Miggel. Petrus Brand Island's bull rested his body against a kalander, Silas Miggel rested his body against an upright. Mieta. Mieta said I was to bring her, but it had to be quickly. How quickly? I had to go and see Mieta. God could forgive me later on. My feet found a short-cut through the thickets to get back to Creek Bush Island; my body did not feel a scratch as the branches struck me from all sides, I had to get there quickly. And Mieta sat outside her house as though she were waiting for me.

'It's too late, she's too far gone.'

You walk. You walk and you walk. If only I could put her with a herd of cow elephants so that she could graze with them until it was her time; cow elephants helped each other to calf. I was confused, it was like being drunk. If it had been smallpox, I could have rubbed her face with oil to keep it from scarring too much, but I would have been able to pull her through. Then the anger started rising in me; slowly at first; I walked faster and faster, I walked until I reached my own door and then I went mad.

'*Who?*' I took the first thing that came to hand and hurled it into the fire and it was the lamp. '*Who?*'

'Do you want to burn the house down on top of us, Pa?' She spoke as if there were nothing the matter with her, as if she had to appease me. Flames shot up into the chimney and the sweet smell of lamp oil hung in the room.

'*Who?* I want to know who did it to you!'

'Don't carry on so, Pa.'

'Was it Jacob?'

336

'Are you going to start naming everyone, Pa?'

'I want to know!'

'You can kill me, Pa, but I won't tell.'

'God help us.' I was finished, I had to sit down. The fear that came over me was darker than the darkest night. 'We must do something!' I shouted at her.

'There is nothing we can do, Pa. I'm sorry. Forgive me for bringing shame on this house and on you. I hate seeing you like this. I shall pray that it's a boy because if something should happen to me, you will have to bring him up.'

When Magriet had died, I went into the forest to weep alone. Now I got up and went to the woodshed and just sat down. I didn't cry, I just sat and somehow that was worse. You stoop lower and lower, your body doubles up until your head is down below your knees. America used to sit like that outside the tent at the beginning. Borolini sat like that on Sundays now. You can't help it, you just crumple up.

At daybreak Miriam brought me some coffee.

'Why? Just tell me why.'

'Drink your coffee, Pa.'

'When?'

'The end of April.' She was so calm. I couldn't understand it. 'Drink your coffee, Pa, Robolini and Mangiagalli are already at the gate.'

'I'm finished with them. I'm finished with the mill.'

'You can't leave off now, Pa! They've got more than half their ship money, you can't stop now!'

'I'm finished. You are not to touch another broom or a spade, you will go and lie in bed; not an eel will you go and catch again, you won't skin another buck. I'll do it. There's a new doctor in the village and there's money in the tin, I can pay. I'll pay to the last penny.'

'You're being silly now, Pa, but you don't realise it. Get up and go to the forest, you can't leave them now.'

'No, I'm finished with them.'

'Then I'll take the gun and go cutting with them.'

The worst thing was that I knew she would. On top of everything, she was still stubborn. So I had to force myself to my feet and take up the axe, although I felt like dying instead.

How I got through that week, I don't know. The axe grew

337

heavier in my hands by the day, and at night I could hardly get my body home.

'Signor Miggel just show him to us, we carry him to village, he marry Miriam.'

'You don't know what you're talking about.'

'We'll get him for Signor Miggel.'

I went back to the forest the next Sunday. To Lily Bush. And up there at the lilies I went on my knees in the mud and I prayed like only a man in utter destitution can pray. I said to God: take me, take Silas Miggel, wipe him out, let a bigfoot trample him, but let Miriam live. The lilies were blooming that year as I had never seen them bloom before, the little marsh was a solid bed of red. At midday, it was as though my prayers rolled over them like ripples across water, drifting away into the forest on the breeze. I prayed the very birds to silence, the wind as well. When my bottom wanted to sag down to rest on my heels, I arched my back and pulled myself up again. I wanted to torture myself before God in my despair. I asked God that if it came out that it was Pontiggia after all, that He would stay my hands from killing him. I prayed until the shadows stretched across the marsh, but when I got up from my knees I had a faith in me as strong as a mountain.

'Miriam,' I said when I got home, 'we must start preparing for the child. He will not come into the world and be wrapped in rags. I'll ask Dunn to put the team to work in the yard on Tuesday, even if it is at half wages. Then I shall go to the village and buy material, and the women will have to take up their needles and start sewing. We must have smocks and napkins and navel-bandages and swaddling flannel. Flannel bonnets for the head. I must get enough flannel. What he must have, he must have. Making the cradle will be easy, I've got the wood and I'll make it in the evenings by the lantern.' I talked and talked, but she appeared quite disinterested. 'Two mattresses must be made; if one gets wet, you will still have a dry one. Miriam, leave the dishes and listen to what I'm saying! God will help us, we must just keep faith!'

'Yes, Pa.'

'I think it would be best if I buy two large blankets to cut in half and seam. That will give us four blankets. I'll get a few

338

lengths of linen to go between the child and the blanket. I always wrapped you in a piece of linen before I put the blankets over you. Miriam, leave the dishes and say something! I'm halfway out of my mind and you just stand there as if you couldn't care less!'

'I'm sorry, Pa. I can't tell you how sorry I am for what I'm doing to you.'

'Never mind what you're doing to me. It's what you did to yourself! Why, Miriam, why?' She stood there twisting the dishcloth slowly in her hands, as though deciding whether to answer me or not. When she looked up, she looked me straight in the face and she didn't try to hide her bitterness from me. 'Why, Miriam?'

'Because I didn't think it would ever happen to me,' she said. 'I thought God would take pity on me and keep it from happening to me, for only God knows how much I love one man on this earth. God knew I didn't lie to you that day when I said I only wanted a moment of my life before turning back to accept what I had to accept. I didn't lie to you when I said I would turn back when the lilies bloomed again, it was a road that would go no further. When I discovered that I was going to have a child, I wanted to put my hands into my body, and grab and grind until it was no longer true, for suddenly the lilies were not the end of the road any more, but the child. When Giuditta was expecting her child, she was happy and Mangiagalli was happy with her. I'm not happy, Pa.'

I had to keep my body rigid to stop it from trembling all over; Miriam was talking like someone who had already given up. 'You are not to say that, Miriam! We must have faith and we must get ready for the child's arrival. You must tell me who the child's father is, I've got to know. Miriam, don't just stand there like that!'

'There is something I have to ask you. Something you must promise me before God.'

'What?'

'Promise me that you will get Petroniglia or Mariarosa to look after the child during the day, but that you won't stop helping the Italians before they've got their ship money together.'

'You're talking like someone giving final orders. Don't! God will help us!' I wanted to shout a little faith into her, and perhaps into myself as well.

'I am not without hope altogether, Pa.' She walked round the table and closed the door. 'The tail-star is almost gone now. I wonder where it's going, I wonder where one goes when one dies.'

'*Miriam, no!*'

She spun round and looked me hard in the eyes. 'Don't let us lie to one another, Pa,' she said. 'I'm scared. More scared than Pa. Every day the sky is a little bluer, a little more beautiful. I walk in the forest, I touch the trees, I feel how soft the moss is under my fingers; I walk through the underbush and it touches me, I pull my hands through the ferns and they tickle my face. I look up and see how tall and proud the yellowwoods are, what kings they are. I see how daintily the blue bucks tread, how carefree the birds are, how clean the creeks are and how full of joy. Don't let us lie to one another, Pa; if I live, I will live. When I sit with the Italians, I see under all their noisiness and under all their bitterness about what's happened to them, a zest for life, and it makes me even more afraid of dying. Don't get so impatient with them, Pa, don't drive them so hard. It's not necessary, they long to go back home to their country. Only Pontiggia may stay behind.'

The moment she said it, suspicion grabbed hold of me like a hand round my throat. '*Why?*' I asked. 'Why Pontiggia?'

'It's just a feeling I have, Pa.'

'When they go, they all go.'

'You must keep an eye on Borolini.'

'It's no use, I've tried but I don't know what's wrong with him.'

'He's homesick.'

EIGHTEEN

ON THE LAST DAY of February they loaded the first three thousand sleepers on to the *Ambulent*, anchored at the new jetty. Another two, three thousand lay ready to be shipped on the next ship.

'Wood, Miggel, wood! You're bringing out a good amount, but it's not enough. From now on, I want to ship a couple of thousand every week!'

We hacked and sawed and hauled out. My eyes were everywhere, my mind without a moment's rest from worries and cares. I wanted to drive a wedge in front of the sun's passage to slow down the days until Miriam reached her time. There were times when I panicked and I broke out in a sweat as though I were in a fever. I made the cradle, a beautiful cradle made of stinkwood. Petroniglia and Mariarosa made the child's garments and Miriam hardly looked at them.

I went to the village twice and each time waited the whole day before I could see the new doctor and tell him about Miriam. About her mother and her grandmother. I liked the man, a Dr Brown, who listened to me attentively. I told him I had money to pay him with, but he said that wasn't important, Miriam was. I told him I would mend the road going up the hill on the other side of Gouna's Drift so that he could get out to the highland with his horse and cart without too much trouble. I would see to the horse's fodder. He said it would be better if I lodged her with people in the village before her time. With whom? I asked him if he possibly had room for her; unfortunately not, he said, he was sorry. Petroniglia said she herself and Mariarosa had

341

helped Giuditta. When Miriam's time came, they would help her too. I told her Miriam was not Giuditta.

I went back to the village and found a room with Smit at the back of his house. I told him it would only be for about fourteen days and just for Miriam and me, and that I would bring our own beds, a table and a chair, everything. I told Dunn he would have to let me off when it was time; I decided to ask Josafat Stander to take over the Italians for me, they would trust him. I knew. Dunn said he was happy with the arrangement.

'Where's the bastard, Miggel?' he asked me. 'Why doesn't he marry Miriam?'

I said nothing. One quickly learned just to look away. I went to the village yet again, paid Smit for the room and told him I would come during the first week of April and clean the place out a bit and bring the furniture. Joram Barnard had offered to bring his wagon and help me.

'Is it one of the Italians who got your daughter in trouble, Miggel?' Smit asked me. I said nothing. I just looked away.

The road out to the highland was badly pitted from the wagons carting out the sleepers. I decided that it would be best if I put a mattress on the sled and under Miriam the day I took her in.

In the third week of March I started a new section in the forest about two miles north of the old one and we moved the shelter as well. One afternoon we were about finished for the day when Mieta came past with her bag of pickings.

'Don't you pick at night any more, Mieta?'

'Only sometimes. I hear you're taking her to the village?'

'Yes.'

'That's the best thing. I'm too old, my heart wouldn't last out if I had to watch her dying as well. It's right that you're taking her to the village.'

The day after that we hauled out the last of the logs from where we had been cutting since the start, and as we came out of the forest, I looked up and saw Vittoria Robolini and Antonia and Luigia and Monica standing at my gate, and from the way they stood, I knew there was something wrong at my house. I shouted to Robolini to take over leading the oxen and started running.

Mariarosa was in the kitchen by the fire, boiling water.

342

Petroniglia was with Miriam in her room. She was already lying down. I stood in the door, and could not breathe for fear.

'Fetch Mieta,' Petroniglia said, very loudly.

'No, I must get Miriam on the sled.'

'Fetch Mieta, Signor Miggel!'

'No, I must get the doctor.'

'Fetch Mieta!' Petroniglia repeated. 'Run fast, she start this morning. Go fetch Mieta, please.'

I could not move. My daughter's eyes were closed, her arms were spread limply above her head but when the next pain came, she grabbed hold of the bedpost so fiercely that I cried out to heaven and ran. I didn't even pause to fetch the lantern, I just ran. I ran until I stood at Mieta's door and only then did I realise that I had gone through a herd of bigfeet somewhere on my way, but they had let me past. Mieta took the knapsacks that contained her medicines, I took the lantern she held out to me and God alone knew where that old woman got the strength from to keep up with me going back.

When we reached the highland the Southern Cross sat at ten o'clock in the night sky and Miriam battled to deliver the child. Just as Magriet had done. I crouched down in a corner of the room; three candles were burning at the foot of the bed. One moment it was Magriet lying there, the next it was Miriam. I knew I was in a daze, I knew, but I couldn't get out of it, I was dreaming a dream I had dreamed before. Someone had carried in the cradle. Dark figures moved in and out of the room; Petroniglia was murmuring in her own tongue, maybe she was praying. I couldn't pray. I just kept on saying: please, God. Please, God. Mieta wiped Miriam's forehead. She tied a rope to the bottom post of the bed and put the other end in Miriam's hands. Outside, below the window, the rest of the Italians gathered and softly sang. When I tasted the tears in my mouth, I realised I was crying.

Hour after hour she struggled to get the child out of her tortured body. I heard her pant, I heard her tossing her head, but it was only at the end that she opened her mouth to scream as only a woman in childbirth can scream. Take the child, God! Take the child! Petroniglia laid her beads on Miriam's stomach and again wiped her forehead. She was no longer covered, her breathing was coming faster and faster and Mieta took over at

343

the foot of the bed. When it had been Magriet, I was the one that had helped her that night.

'Take hold of the rope, Miriam, pull when I tell you to start pushing.'

I closed my eyes and felt my body slump until my head was between my knees. Take the child, God. Take the child. But God did not take the child, the child was born because I heard a baby cry. I didn't want to see him. Magriet had lived another hour. I would sit waiting for the hour to go by.

'Silas Miggel?'

'Mieta?'

'Look up, it's a boy. It was difficult, but she's not like her mother, she pulled through. I never believed the curse, anyway.'

I lifted my head and opened my eyes. Next to Miriam, a man was kneeling with his back to me and he was stroking her sweat-drenched hair. Someone had fetched the doctor. No, it wasn't the doctor – it was Josafat Stander.

The warder brought the news at midday; the first three thousand sleepers that had arrived in Cape Town had been rejected. A special committee had been appointed to carry out an investigation and until they came to a decision, the mill had to close down and no more sleepers were to be shipped.

The warder had tracked me down to the woodshed where I was lying. I heard every word of what he said, but I put the implication aside because I had no room in my body for it. I was like someone who had collapsed under too heavy a load. I couldn't keep a morsel of food in my stomach, everything came out.

On the morning of the third day, Josafat Stander had the gall to come and look me in the face. 'Are you feeling better, uncle?'

'If you are a man, you'll fetch my gun and bring it to me!' I was definitely feeling better, yes. 'I won't shoot you dead, but I'll wound you in such a way that you'll remember it for the rest of your life. Adder!'

'You must get up, uncle, Miriam is worried about you and she wants to show you our child.'

'Rogue! You led my daughter astray right under my nose!'

'We're getting married as soon as she's out of bed.'

'In that case, I won't just wound you, I'll shoot you dead

properly.' I started pulling on my breeches. 'My daughter will not marry an ivory thief and a rogue. You need not worry about her child, I'll help her to bring him up.'

'It's my child. And for the past three days, I've looked after the Italians for you, uncle. I went and cut them firewood, I went and caught them eels, I went and shot them three bucks, but there's nothing else I can do for them. They're in a state of complete panic and I think it's time you went to them. They're without work, uncle. The men are stomping around, the women keep on crying. Dunn has left for Cape Town to find out what's happening; the latest word is that yellowwood won't last on the ground under the railway tracks. The government may well cancel the whole contract.'

'Get out of my way so that I can get to my shoes. You're old enough to be Miriam's father!'

'I'm not. I'm sixteen years older than her and that is how I want it. We will marry as soon as she's out of bed.'

'Forget it.' I kicked aside the rumour of the sleepers; I wasn't stupid, there was nothing wrong with the sleepers. I was back on my feet and I wanted to get to Miriam, the rest could wait. I told Josafat Stander to get off the highland and get off fast. I wanted to be alone with my daughter.

She was sitting up, propped against the pillows, lovelier than ever. The baby lay next to her in the cradle I had made.

'I'm alive, Pa.'

'You're alive, Miriam.'

'I have a child, Pa.'

'You have a child, Miriam. God be praised. I'll have to put in a bigger window here, there's not enough sun coming in for him.'

'Josafat says the child won't grow up on the highland, he's going to buy us a house in the village.'

'We'll talk about things like that later, Miriam.' She had to rest. The highland was her home, it was my home, it would be the child's home, but we would get to that later on. Discord was not good for her, it would seep into her milk and into the child.

'I was worried sick about you. I knew you couldn't carry on like that.'

'Sometimes one has to lie down to regain strength, Miriam. You must also get back your strength. Mieta must stay until

345

you're strong again; I'll ask Petroniglia to come and help as well.'

'Fardini was here. He says you kept on chasing them away from the woodshed. You must go and find out what's happening. Fardini says there's a possibility that the sleepers might be able to be dipped in some sort of mixture and then the government won't cancel the contract, and that would mean they would get their work back. But they're frightened, Pa.'

'There's nothing to be frightened of. There's nothing wrong with the sleepers.'

'I've loved Josafat ever since I can remember, Pa.'

'The child's head is lying awkwardly. Petroniglia has stuffed the pillow too full, she must come and take out some of the stuffing right away.'

He was a beautiful child. I would never allow him to be an ivory thief.

I set out for the village to see Walker. I told Fardini to keep the others calm until I got back. It was no good believing every rumour they were fed, we had to get to the bottom of the truth and work from there. In the meantime, no one was to touch a penny of the ship money, and I told him to see that the women used the meal sparingly.

'I've come to find out the truth about the sleepers,' I said when I stood in Walker's office.

'We are waiting for the appointed committee to come to a decision.'

'What committee? What do they know about yellowwood?'

'This is a matter that doesn't concern you at all, Miggel. Mr Laing rejected the sleepers and an unbiased investigation has been ordered.'

'What are the Italians supposed to live on in the meantime? When you took away their daily shillings, you knew that the sawmill was on its way, you knew you could starve them with a clear conscience. What have you got in mind for them this time?'

'Miggel, please. This is a matter that doesn't concern you.'

'Oh yes? Who the hell has seen to everything right from the beginning? Who stands foreman over them day and night? Where do they run when things go wrong as it's going now?'

'As far as I know, you shouldn't be running to me either because you are all employed by Fox & Dunn.'

'It all seems to be all up with Fox & Dunn, man!'

'Who said that? We are waiting for the outcome of the investigation. You must wait, the Italians must wait.'

We waited all right. Mariarosa started getting the screaming fits again, and twice I had to go and fetch Borolini from deep in the forest where he went cutting all by himself.

'I cut, Signor Miggel, I get wages, we go home.'

'You can't go cutting on your own! We must wait and see what they're going to decide in Cape Town. Come on!'

The sawmill stood like a creature that had breathed its last. The highland grew almost quiet again. The English woodcutters and sawmill workers moved themselves to the village to wait there. The shop no longer opened, it wasn't worth the storekeeper's trouble any more.

And Miriam was as stubborn and pig-headed as could be. I told her she shouldn't put the child in the tin bath every morning to wash him down, his skin was still thin, but she wouldn't listen. She even soaped him. I drove Josafat Stander away from my house every day, but he wouldn't leave completely. He moved into one of the sawmill workers' empty shacks down at the foot of the highland and there he stayed.

'Stop fighting against yourself!' Miriam said. 'You should look after the Italians, and Josafat will take care of me and the child. Borolini has gone off with the axe again.'

We waited. I told Fardini they should slaughter one of the oxen since the snares were lying empty. They were not to touch a penny of the ship money. Every second day, I walked to the village to ask Walker if the results of the investigation had come through yet, or whether Dunn had returned.

'You are wasting my time, Miggel! When I hear something, I'll send one of the warders to tell you people.'

'The Italians are more than halfway home, mister, as true as God, so you must do something for them. Tell the government to give them the rest, do anything, mister. Things are bad again up there on the highland; everything's going backwards. I'm telling you, mister, they are not going to touch the money they've saved; before that happens, I'll be bringing them in every day for pauper rations at the jail.'

'You can't just do that. Application for pauper's rations must be made at the magistrate's office. He will then get the necessary permission from Cape Town.'

I knew I had to remain patient. 'Mister,' I said, 'could you not put me on a ship to Cape Town so I can speak up for the sleepers myself? Who says those people know anything about wood anyway?'

'There is a rumour that the wood cut for the sleepers is of inferior quality.'

'That's a bloody lie!'

'That's what I've heard.'

'All the trains in the world could run over those sleepers and the wood would still hold. I'm telling you, mister, before this whole affair turns into another mulberry forest, you'd better get me to Cape Town.'

'Go away, Miggel, you're wasting my time.'

The following Friday, I met Robolini, Tomé and Mangiagalli halfway back from the village with meal and sugar, coffee and other provisions from the store, and I knew they had started using the ship money.

'No other way, Signor Miggel, sorry. No other way.'

Hell.

Every time I got to Walker's office I had to wait longer outside before he would see me. One Wednesday, he didn't even appear. It was Dreyer, his clerk, who brought me the latest news: the sleepers had been cut and sawed and stockpiled too long before they were shipped, the wood was showing signs of serious weathering.

'You go and tell Mr Walker to write and say that Silas Miggel says they're talking shit. It's their blooming heads that are weathered; all wood changes colour after being cut. They must come and ask me, I'll tell them what's what.'

'The committee should conclude their investigation by next week.'

'I'll be here to hear the outcome.'

'We'll send a warder, Miggel. You must stop bothering Mr Walker, he's going to lose his temper with you and I don't think you can afford that.'

'Mr Dreyer,' I said, 'I'm telling you, and I'm telling Walker, and I'm telling the whole government, that if they condemn those sleepers, it would be an underhand thing to do and they'll need more than their tempers to deal with Silas Miggel. My advice is that they must send Dunn back to start that blooming mill working again so that things can get going.'

I went back to the village the following Tuesday. At Gouna's Drift I came across one of the warders and when I asked him where he was going, he mumbled something about having work to do, he didn't look me in the face properly, he just walked on. At Walker's office the door was opened almost immediately after I knocked which I found rather strange. It was as though they had been waiting for me. Walker was sitting behind his table, already playing with the nib, and he wouldn't look me in the face either.

'The sleepers, Miggel, were deemed totally unsuitable.' Just like that, as though it were nothing. 'The contract has been cancelled.'

One of my ears started ringing, but I stayed calm. 'And now? What about the Italians now?' I asked.

'Fox & Dunn will receive compensation – according to first reports it will hardly be enough to meet their expenses.'

'What about the Italians, mister?' I asked him a second time, politely.

'There is a possibility that the government may eventually take over the mill and move it to the village. I'm sure anyone interested would be able to apply for work at the mill again, but that's not for me to decide about at this stage.'

'What about the Italians?'

'Everybody who was employed at Fox & Dunn is naturally dismissed. You too. I've sent a warder out to the highland to tell the Italians.'

I clasped my hands behind my back and said to myself: Silas Miggel, if you hit him, you'll kill him. Stay calm. 'I've asked you again and again; what about the Italians, mister?'

He flicked the nib across his desk and laughed, mockingly. 'Come now, Miggel,' he said, 'what do *you* care about them? Don't try and bluff me. If I look at the list of complaints lodged against you, I can't believe that you care a damn about what happens to them. You're much more concerned about your own interests, not the Italians'. So don't come wasting my time, the matter is closed and so is the mill.'

'What complaints? What are you talking about now?'

'Complaints lodged against you, Miggel. Here they are, on my table, I shall read them to you if that's what you want.'

My other ear started ringing. He began cleaning his glasses and then opened some papers lying right in front of him. In other words, I said to myself, he had those papers lying ready before I arrived? 'What are you trying to throw at me now?' I asked him.

'I'll read them to you, Miggel: "June 12th, 1881: Silas van Huyssteen, also known as Silas Miggel, refuses to lend Italians an axe for cutting firewood. Wood consequently has to be broken up by hand. June 14th, 1881: Drives Petroniglia Grassi, wife of Ilario Grassi, to the village with stick when she was on her way to enquire about her child that had been stolen; in the presence of Constable Ralph he threatened to beat her." Still in June: "Denies silk farmers freedom of religion and suggests they adopt another religion which does not prescribe fish on Fridays." '

I stood there, not knowing whether to laugh or to turn the blooming table over on top of him. 'Those are Christie's complaints you've got there, mister. Tear them up, he was an old woman.'

' "Suggests that they wash themselves with leaves from the forest instead of soap. Denies them the right to get water from the furrow to the west and forces them to use inferior water place to the east which is where he also waters his two oxen." '

'The bastard!' I said. 'What about the firewood? What about all those buck I skinned for them? What about moving the tents and putting in bedding-bush floors for them and all the other things I did?' I stood listing all I'd done, but it was like throwing a stone that had no force behind it. It was nothing. And Walker kept on reading.

' "Deliberately withholds information about wild mulberry in forest. Refuses initially to point out said tree to silk farmers." '

'Am I now being judged before a magistrate?' I asked.

'No. These complaints were lodged at this office. "During the months of August and September, he forced the Italians to cut branches for fences while standing over them with a gun." '

'That's a bloody lie! If I hadn't stood there with the gun, they wouldn't have cut because they kept on looking out for whatever

350

danger they were expecting to jump on them from the forest. You're trying to rile me with Christie's nonsense in order to get away from the Italians, mister.'

'Are you denying these allegations, Miggel? Do you deny that you even tied the children to the tent-poles with ropes, using a bit of fog as an excuse? Do you deny that you refused to testify for one of them in an extremely unfair case about an ostrich? Do you deny that it was you that suggested they slaughter an ox and that in the end an innocent man had to be insulted in court for it?'

'It wasn't the same ox,' I tried another stone.

'Do you deny making death threats to Mr Christie on more than one occasion? Do you deny that you wanted to ship the Italians to Cape Town illegally for elephant tusks? How many of these complaints do you want to hear? You, Miggel, *never* had any time for these people; all this time, you were looking to your own interests on the highland. There was even a time when you encouraged Mr Christie to *walk* them to Cape Town, more than three hundred miles away, knowing that at least one of them would not have made it there on foot. So don't come telling me that you are now concerned for their future; you are only concerned for your own and nothing else. You never cared for them, you never will care for them and therefore I ask you not to come and waste my time any longer. The matter is closed.'

I had nothing to say. What can you say to a man without ears? All I did say, however, was if he thought Silas Miggel was that easily run over by a bloody government wheel, he was dumb. And if he thought he had heard the last of me and the Italians, he was even more dumb.

When I got back to the highland, they stood gathered by my gate, confused, angry; Mariarosa stood pulling her hair, some crossed themselves, some kissed their beads, others stamped about but, above all, fear lay on every face.

'Mill closed, no work, Signor Miggel!'

'No wages!'

'No ship money!'

'Planks pull apart in house walls!'

'No work!'

'How we get home?'

I let them clamour for a while before I spoke. 'Go to your

351

houses,' I said, 'go and rest. Tomorrow morning we shall all start work again, because tomorrow we are going to stoke that mill's boiler as it has never been stoked before. Those saws are going to run like they've never run before. There are enough of you who know how to work the mill, and can teach the others. We are going to saw every piece of wood lying over there in the yards into planks and beams and sell it in George for the rest of your ship money. I'll get hold of some wagons. We'll start at dawn and when the sun goes down, we'll light the lanterns and continue to work. By the time the government comes to move the mill to the village or whatever, you will have gone home long before.'

I could tell by their eyes that they liked what they heard, I could see it by the movement in their bodies and their hands, and by the way they started talking amongst themselves. And it gave me a chance to get past into my house.

Miriam was suckling the child. Her face was drawn with concern which worried me.

'They've closed down the mill, Pa!'

'Don't get upset, girl, it gets to your milk! The saws will be running tomorrow morning, we're opening the mill. Unfortunately I'll be needing that ivory thief to get things going.'

'Who told you the mill's opening? The warder came to say that it's closed down.'

'Forget about what the warder said, I'm telling you it's opening tomorrow morning. Where's Josafat Stander?'

'The baboons are in the mealie camp on Cuicatti's allotment. He's gone to fire a few shots to drive them off.'

'You can't shoot sense into a baboon's head, it's a waste of gunpowder. That child must be christened, we're taking him to the village on Sunday.' I was about to add that I wanted him to have my late father's names as well as my own, but I didn't get that far. Somewhere outside a woman had started screaming and screaming and I knew it wasn't Mariarosa so I ran. It was Antonia. She was up on the dam wall and Borolini was floating in the water, face down, drowned in waist-deep water.

It was Josafat Stander who waded in to get him out. It was Josafat Stander that walked to the village to tell the constable and to send word to the priest. A cloud of despondency had enveloped the highland which nothing could lift. I tried talking

352

to them, I skinned them a buck, I left a measure of sweet potatoes at every door, I told them that we would re-start the mill on Thursday, a day later than planned, but the cloud would not lift. I let the blame lie at my own door: I should have realised that he was giving up, I should have taken more notice of him, I could have sent him home ahead of the others. When the sun went down, I went from house to house, handing out parsley-bush brew and silently I said: yes, Mr Barrington, you're up in heaven and I'm down here below with the mess.

Early the next morning I sent Josafat to Creek Bush Island to borrow a coffin. There was a hot wind blowing from the mountains and the weather was close; if the priest didn't turn up, we would have to bury Borolini ourselves. I set Cruci and Cuicatti to digging the grave, I went and opened a furrow from the dam to get water to the vegetable patches. There was enough for the boiler as well.

When Josafat came back with the coffin, I pulled him aside. 'Selling only wood may not get them on a ship soon enough,' I said. 'That is why I want to know how much you'll charge to shoot them a few bigfeet. I want to hear your price – and don't think you can have my daughter in return because you're not going to get her.'

'I've bought a house in the village.'

'I can't wait for you to move there. How much?'

'I have four good tusks already that you can have and sell with the wood, uncle. I know a fair buyer in George.'

'How much do you want for the tusks?'

'I'm giving them to you, uncle.'

'So that you can then come and say I owe you?'

'No. So that these people can get away from the highland and you can rest.'

'I'll take them.'

In the middle of the afternoon, I called them together. We couldn't wait any longer for the priest, he would have to hold the service afterwards as he did for Catarina. When we stood by the grave, I talked to them myself, I told them I knew they were standing there heartsore and angry, that I knew Borolini was laid to rest far away from his home, but there was nothing we could do about it – except guard against any more of them staying behind six feet under the ground. When I was finished, Fardini

353

took over in their own tongue and Hailed Mary while fingering the beads: some words he said alone, others they all said together. I stood aside until it was time to fill in the grave.

'The mill will work tomorrow, Signor Miggel?' Fardini came and asked me while the women were laying flowers on the grave.

'Yes. Coccia must start stoking as early as possible. We're going to keep those saws running while we can. You're going home.'

When I saw the man on horseback coming across the highland, I thought at first it was the priest, but then I saw that it was Chief Constable Ralph and I started walking to meet him. It would be about the corpse, I said to myself, perhaps we shouldn't have buried him without the death certificate. One thing was for sure, however, we would not dig him up again.

'Good afternoon, uncle,' the constable greeted me as he got off his horse. He took a paper from his pocket and handed it to me, saying: 'I'm sorry, uncle.'

'Yes, I'm afraid we buried him without it, but the weather being what it is, we couldn't wait too long. It's a sad thing to have happened almost at the end. Did you happen to see the priest along the way, constable?'

'No, uncle. And that is a summons I've handed you. As a messenger of the Court, I'm delivering it to you in person, uncle. It's for you.'

I wasn't alarmed. 'What for?' I asked. 'I don't owe anybody anything. If it's in English, I won't be able to read it in any case.'

'Then it is my duty to read it out to you and explain what it says, uncle.'

'Are you sure it's for me, constable?' I wanted to save him any trouble.

'It is.' He took back the paper, opened it and started reading: ' "Court of the Resident Magistrate for Knysna. To John Ralph, messenger of the Court." That's me, uncle.'

'I told you it wasn't for me.'

'It is, uncle. "You" – that's still me – "are hereby required in Her Majesty's name to summon Silas van Huyssteen" – that's you, uncle – "to appear personally before this Court at Knysna on the eighteenth day of April 1883 at ten o'clock in the forenoon upon a charge of squatting unlawfully on Crown land. Serve on the said Silas van Huyssteen a copy of this summons."

354

You must be in court tomorrow morning at ten o'clock.'

Pieter Kapp. Chased off the clearing at Kras Bush for squatting on Crown land. My heart went wild. 'Listen here, constable, you're not standing in front of Pieter Kapp now, you're standing in front of Silas Miggel and Silas Miggel has dwelling rights on this highland until the day he becomes owner of one of these lots. Get on to your horse and get going.'

'I'm afraid I must warn you then that if you are not in court tomorrow morning, you will have to be arrested, uncle.'

'I'm not that stupid. Go and tell Jackson I'll be there.'

When I turned around, Josafat was standing behind me, a head taller than me and as handsome as only a rogue could be. At that moment, I knew why Mieta had said Miriam's footprints were lying where few would have dared. He stood there looking at me without a word, but his eyes said: you're in trouble, Silas Miggel. Beyond him, I saw Tomé and Alberto Fardini and Cuicatti go towards the mill, and I saw Petroniglia standing outside her house and I knew that she was watching the man riding away on his horse. Everything around me was suddenly in sharp focus: the forest, the gorges, the flock of redwing starlings fluttering up from behind the woodshed, the mill, the dam wall, the clouds against the very blue sky. Deep in the forest I heard a lourie call and behind me a butcher-bird screeched.

I wasn't Pieter Kapp.

At ten o'clock the next morning, I stood in the court room, me and a youngish constable I didn't know. He watched me as though he thought I might turn round and walk out again. I had no such intention. I would stand where I stood. I had told Fardini I would be back shortly after midday, and then we'd start sawing. I had told Miriam to stop crying, the child was being affected. On Sunday, I planned to wrap him up and take him into the forest so that he could breathe in the air and know where his home was. I had told Josafat Stander I wanted the tusks to be in the woodshed when I got home. I had also told him that I wasn't stupid, that I knew he wasn't going to leave Miriam alone so he should buy himself a couple of the allotments and build her a house on one of them so that I could still keep an eye on her. He didn't answer me.

'Where's the magistrate, constable? I haven't got all day.'

'He'll be here soon. You should keep quiet and keep your hat on.'

'What for?'

'Magistrate's orders. All accused must keep their hats on so that he can distinguish them from the others in court.'

'I'm not an accused, I'm Silas Miggel.'

'Silence in court!'

I don't know why he had to shout so, nor why he had to order everyone to rise, I was the only one there and already on my feet in the box when Jackson entered like a king. He walked to his throne, slowly, like a king; he had quite a big head and a square face. When he looked up and spotted me, his eyes stayed on me for a while as though I were standing there without any breeches on.

'Are you Silas van Huyssteen, also known as Silas Miggel?'

'Yes, your worship.' I would stand where I stood.

'Are you resident at Gouna?'

'For more than seventeen years, your worship.'

'Please answer yes or no. I repeat the question: Are you resident at Gouna?'

'Yes, your worship.' Yes or no might prove to be a problem.

'Were you warned on many occasions that it's Crown land that you're living on?'

'Yes, your worship. But I got dwelling rights from Mr White later on.'

'Answer yes or no. I repeat the question: were you warned on many occasions that it's Crown land that you're living on?'

'Yes, your honour.' Yes or no could certainly turn out to be bad for me.

'Are you still living unlawfully up at Gouna on Crown land?'

'I have dwelling rights.'

'Answer yes or no!' He shouted so loudly that even the constable jumped. 'Are you still living unlawfully on Crown land?'

'Yes!'

'Address the Bench with respect!'

'Yes, your honour.' I was in trouble and badly placed. I had to get on to safer ground, but I didn't know which way to go. Everywhere I turned, I ran up against a yes or a no and before I could think of a solution, he was sentencing me.

356

'You are hereby found guilty of unlawful squatting on Crown land and you are instructed to vacate the Crown land at Gouna within a week from today. You will be permitted to remove only private effects such as clothing and furnishings; no existing building or buildings may be demolished or removed.'

'I beg your worship's pardon? How can I be sentenced without having had a chance to say a word except yes and no?' I asked him and he seemed to rise up out of his throne. They say he had knocked a man clean off his horse-cart one day. 'I just want a chance to explain things. I can't be sentenced off the highland like this.'

'Another word from you and I will have you arrested for contempt of court!'

Fardini was correct: he had warned me that a man never went to court when he was in the right since the chances were that he'd be proved wrong; a man only went to court when he was in the wrong in the hope that he'd be proved right.

'I'm sorry, your worship, but you can't sentence me off that highland on a yes or a no today.' That was as far as I got before he called the constable. I didn't think he'd do it. As true as God is my witness, I didn't think he would really do it.

The constable wasn't a match for me, however: it took three of them to get me handcuffed and across the street to the cells at the police station. I didn't have a chance to go back to plead with Jackson. Not that I would have gone back to plead but what went on inside me when they led me across that street, I'll never forget, because it's a downfall from which a man never again recovers. Worst of all were the eyes in the street that witnessed my fall. When they locked me up, the blooming constable still had the gall to say, 'I'm sorry, uncle.'

Could you not have seen the wheel coming? I said to myself. God in heaven, could You not have seen the wheel coming?

I refused to sit down, I stayed on my feet. They brought me food, I did not eat it. I waited. I waited until it was dark and then I broke out and at midnight I knocked on my own door which Josafat Stander came to open. Miriam stood behind him with the candle. I told them there was no time to be alarmed, I had to pack. The first place they would come looking for me when it got light was my home. I had to get away, the wheel had knocked me into hell. Miriam cried, she helped me get my things

357

together and packed me food and candles and my Bible. Josafat
fetched me an axe and a saw and rope; I couldn't take the sled
and the ox since they'd follow the tracks. Miriam cried; when
she asked me where I would go, I said I would let her know. My
head was clear, my body calm. I gave my last instructions and,
although it was against my will, I gave Josafat Stander my
daughter. I told them I'd come and tell them where I had made
myself a shelter. Miriam cried; she said that she and Josafat
were moving to the village with the child, what was to become of
me? I told her that I would look after myself, that she wasn't to
worry about me, but she took hold of my arm.

'What about the Italians, Pa? What about the Italians?' she
cried.

'What Italians?' I asked. 'I don't know of any Italians.'

*For fifteen years I've kept watch over the lilies. At all times I have to
keep my eyes open for strangers that might get too close to the little
marsh, and for the blooming warders who are still trying to find me.
The old ones have learned to be careful of me, some say I'm dead. It's
the young ones that think they can lie in wait for me and capture me
for their own good fortune. I had to shoot one the other day, wounded
him in the leg. I look after the lilies. Perhaps I am dead. No, I don't
remember the Italians – except I remember that I had wanted to show
Petroniglia the lilies, that's all. I hear they buried Ilario on the
highland too.*

POSTSCRIPT

WHAT BECAME OF THE ITALIANS?

Only one of them finally returned to Italy and that was Pietro Fardini who had arrived on the highland as an eight-year-old boy with his parents, Pietro and Anna Fardini.

About a year after the sleepers were rejected, the government reopened the sawmill and re-employed some of the Italians. The younger Pietro Fardini lost an arm in a freak accident at the mill, and then qualified as a teacher and later taught at Gouna. After he returned to Italy, no one heard of him again.

Many of the Italians moved away to Cape Town: Petroniglia Grassi arrived in Cape Town in about 1897. Her daughter, Monica, followed after her husband, Canovi, died and married a second time. This man, however, left her after a year. It is said that she was renowned for being strict and rather outspoken and for the beautiful carnations she grew.

The Crucis left for Cape Town and so did most of the bachelors. Pontiggia and Coccia worked for Dunn of Fox & Dunn at Portland for some years; Coccia died on the highland and was buried there.

The name Cuicatti is spelled Sciocatti today and like most of the descendants of the silk farmers, the Sciocattis are Afrikaans ('Dutch') speaking today. Domenico Cuicatti and his wife, Luigia (née Fardini) had thirteen children. Domenico became a registered forest worker, Luigia lived on the highland at Gouna until her ninety-fifth year. Of her and Domenico's children, some were landowners at Gouna for many years. One son, Henri, prospered as a timber buyer and shopkeeper and in

1930 he bought the entire commonage for one thousand and six pounds. In 1963 he was shot dead in front of his house at Gouna by another landowner during an altercation about a road. The youngest of Luigia's sons, John, trained as a teacher.

Angelo and Giuditta Mangiagalli (née Fardini) also moved to Cape Town and later bought land in one of the suburbs. They had eight children and Giuditta (Nonna) was the area's beloved midwife for many years and made all her rounds on horseback. Most of the Mangiagalli descendants have to this day married Italians.

Domenico Tomé and his wife, Antonia (née Fardini), kept a small farm on the highland. Domenico sometimes worked on the roads and later became a foreman forester. Their daughter, Angelina, married Felitze (Felix) Radulfini. Angelina and her lover, Edman Prinsloo, were sentenced to death in George in 1914 for the murder of Felitze. One of their sons became a Catholic priest.

The name Robolini is spelled Rabbolini today.

Due to the reduced circumstances of the Italians, no payments were ever made on the original allotments. The government regularly confiscated their oxen, selling them in lieu of their debts being paid. In the end, however, their debts were written off. The allotments were sold for eleven pounds and fifteen shillings at public auction.

THE LILIES

At the beginning of this century the Forestry Department put an impenetrable barbed wire fence around the marsh to protect the lilies (*Valotta speciosa/Valotta purpurea*) against possible damage by stray oxen. What they didn't know was that the bush-pigs were part of the delicate ecology of the lilies and had to root up the lilies at certain times of the year to limit the growth of the bulbs. After the fence was erected, the bush-pigs couldn't get to the lilies and consequently all the lilies died.